Detective Molly &
the Old Man

Detective Molly & the Old Man

Two Detective Story Collections

Lady Molly of Scotland Yard

and

The Case of Miss Elliott

Baroness Orczy

LEONAUR

Detective Molly & the Old Man
Two Detective Story Collections
Lady Molly of Scotland Yard
and
The Case of Miss Elliott
by Baroness Orczy

FIRST EDITION

First published under the titles
Lady Molly of Scotland Yard
and
The Case of Miss Elliott

Leonaur is an imprint of Oakpast Ltd

Copyright in this form © 2022 Oakpast Ltd

ISBN: 978-1-915234-22-3 (hardcover)
ISBN: 978-1-915234-23-0 (softcover)

http://www.leonaur.com

Publisher's Notes

The views expressed in this book are not necessarily
those of the publisher.

Contents

Lady Molly of Scotland Yard

Contents

The Ninescore Mystery

1

Well, you know, some say she is the daughter of a duke, others that she was born in the gutter, and that the handle has been soldered on to her name in order to give her style and influence.

I could say a lot, of course, but "my lips are sealed," as the poets say. All through her successful career at the Yard she honoured me with her friendship and confidence, but when she took me in partnership, as it were, she made me promise that I would never breathe a word of her private life, and this I swore on my Bible oath—"wish I may die," and all the rest of it.

Yes, we always called her "my lady," from the moment that she was put at the head of our section; and the chief called her "Lady Molly" in our presence. We of the Female Department are dreadfully snubbed by the men, though don't tell me that women have not ten times as much intuition as the blundering and sterner sex; my firm belief is that we shouldn't have half so many undetected crimes if some of the so-called mysteries were put to the test of feminine investigation.

Do you suppose for a moment, for instance, that the truth about that extraordinary case at Ninescore would ever have come to light if the men alone had had the handling of it? Would any man have taken so bold a risk as Lady Molly did when—But I am anticipating.

Let me go back to that memorable morning when she came into my room in a wild state of agitation.

"The chief says I may go down to Ninescore if I like, Mary," she said in a voice all a-quiver with excitement.

"You!" I ejaculated. "What for?"

"What for—what for?" she repeated eagerly. "Mary, don't you understand? It is the chance I have been waiting for—the chance of a lifetime? They are all desperate about the case up at the Yard; the public is furious, and columns of sarcastic letters appear in the daily press. None of our men know what to do; they are at their wits' end, and so this morning I went to the chief——"

"Yes?" I queried eagerly, for she had suddenly ceased speaking.

"Well, never mind now how I did it—I will tell you all about it on the way, for we have just got time to catch the 11 a.m. down to Canterbury. The chief says I may go, and that I may take whom I like with me. He suggested one of the men, but somehow, I feel that this is woman's work, and I'd rather have you, Mary, than anyone. We will go over the preliminaries of the case together in the train, as I don't suppose that you have got them at your fingers' ends yet, and you have only just got time to put a few things together and meet me at Charing Cross booking-office in time for that 11.0 sharp."

She was off before I could ask her any more questions, and anyhow I was too flabbergasted to say much. A murder case in the hands of the Female Department! Such a thing had been unheard of until now. But I was all excitement, too, and you may be sure I was at the station in good time.

Fortunately, Lady Molly and I had a carriage to ourselves. It was a non-stop run to Canterbury, so we had plenty of time before us, and I was longing to know all about this case, you bet, since I was to have the honour of helping Lady Molly in it.

The murder of Mary Nicholls had actually been committed at Ash Court, a fine old mansion which stands in the village of Ninescore. The Court is surrounded by magnificently timbered grounds, the most fascinating portion of which is an island in the midst of a small pond, which is spanned by a tiny rustic bridge. The island is called "The Wilderness," and is at the furthermost end of the grounds, out of sight and earshot of the mansion itself. It was in this charming spot, on the edge of the pond, that the body of a girl was found on the 5th of February last.

I will spare you the horrible details of this gruesome discovery. Suffice it to say for the present that the unfortunate woman was lying on her face, with the lower portion of her body on the small grass-covered embankment, and her head, arms, and shoulders sunk in the slime of the stagnant water just below.

It was Timothy Coleman, one of the under-gardeners at Ash Court, who first made this appalling discovery. He had crossed the rustic bridge and traversed the little island in its entirety, when he noticed something blue lying half in and half out of the water beyond. Timothy is a stolid, unemotional kind of yokel, and, once having ascertained that the object was a woman's body in a blue dress with white facings, he quietly stooped and tried to lift it out of the mud.

But here even his stolidity gave way at the terrible sight which was revealed before him. That the woman—whoever she might be—had been brutally murdered was obvious, her dress in front being stained with blood; but what was so awful that it even turned old Timothy sick with horror, was that, owing to the head, arms and shoulders having apparently been in the slime for some time, they were in an advanced state of decomposition.

Well, whatever was necessary was immediately done, of course. Coleman went to get assistance from the lodge, and soon the police were on the scene and had removed the unfortunate victim's remains to the small local police-station.

Ninescore is a sleepy, out-of-the-way village, situated some seven miles from Canterbury and four from Sandwich. Soon everyone in the place had heard that a terrible murder had been committed in the village, and all the details were already freely discussed at the Green Man.

To begin with, everyone said that though the body itself might be practically unrecognisable, the bright blue serge dress with the white facings was unmistakable, as were the pearl and ruby ring and the red leather purse found by Inspector Meisures close to the murdered woman's hand.

Within two hours of Timothy Coleman's gruesome find the identity of the unfortunate victim was firmly established as that of Mary Nicholls, who lived with her sister Susan at 2, Elm Cottages, in Nine-score Lane, almost opposite Ash Court. It was also known that when the police called at that address, they found the place locked and apparently uninhabited.

Mrs. Hooker, who lived at No. 1 next door, explained to Inspector Meisures that Susan and Mary Nicholls had left home about a fortnight ago, and that she had not seen them since.

"It'll be a fortnight tomorrow," she said. "I was just inside my own front door a-calling to the cat to come in. It was past seven o'clock, and as dark a night as ever you did see. You could hardly see your 'and afore your eyes, and there was a nasty damp drizzle comin' from everywhere. Susan and Mary come out of their cottage; I couldn't rightly see Susan, but I 'eard Mary's voice quite distinck. She says: 'We'll have to 'urry,' says she. I, thinkin' they might be goin' to do some shoppin' in the village, calls out to them that I'd just 'eard the church clock strike seven, and that bein' Thursday, and early closin', they'd find all the shops shut at Ninescore. But they took no notice, and walked off towards the village, and that's the last I ever seed o' them two."

Further questioning among the village folk brought forth many curious details. It seems that Mary Nicholls was a very flighty young woman, about whom there had already been quite a good deal of scandal, whilst Susan, on the other hand—who was very sober and steady in her conduct—had chafed considerably under her younger sister's questionable reputation, and, according to Mrs. Hooker, many were the bitter quarrels which occurred between the two girls. These quarrels, it seems, had been especially violent within the last year whenever Mr. Lionel Lydgate called at the cottage. He was a London gentleman, it appears—a young man about town, it afterwards transpired—but he frequently stayed at Canterbury, where he had some friends, and on those occasions, he would come over to Ninescore in his smart dogcart and take Mary out for drives.

Mr. Lydgate is brother to Lord Edbrooke, the multi-millionaire, who was the recipient of birthday honours last year. His lordship resides at Edbrooke Castle, but he and his brother Lionel had rented Ash Court once or twice, as both were keen golfers and Sandwich Links are very close by. Lord Edbrooke, I may add, is a married man. Mr. Lionel Lydgate, on the other hand, is just engaged to Miss Marbury, daughter of one of the canons of Canterbury.

No wonder, therefore, that Susan Nicholls strongly objected to her sister's name being still coupled with that of a young man far above her in station, who, moreover, was about to marry a young lady in his own rank of life.

But Mary seemed not to care. She was a young woman who only liked fun and pleasure, and she shrugged her shoulders at public opinion, even though there were ugly rumours anent the parentage of a little baby girl whom she herself had placed under the care of Mrs. Williams, a widow who lived in a somewhat isolated cottage on the Canterbury road. Mary had told Mrs. Williams that the father of the child, who was her own brother, had died very suddenly, leaving the little one on her and Susan's hands; and, as they couldn't look after it properly, they wished Mrs. Williams to have charge of it. To this the latter readily agreed.

The sum for the keep of the infant was decided upon, and thereafter Mary Nicholls had come every week to see the little girl, and always brought the money with her.

Inspector Meisures called on Mrs. Williams, and certainly the worthy widow had a very startling sequel to relate to the above story.

"A fortnight tomorrow," explained Mrs. Williams to the inspector, "a little after seven o'clock, Mary Nicholls come runnin' into my cottage. It was an awful night, pitch dark and a nasty drizzle. Mary says to me she's in a great hurry; she is goin' up to London by a train from Canterbury and wants to say goodbye to the child. She seemed terribly excited, and her clothes were very wet. I brings baby to her, and she kisses it rather wild-like and says to me: 'You'll take great care of her, Mrs. Williams,' she says; 'I may be gone some time.' Then she puts baby down and gives me £2, the child's keep for eight weeks."

After which, it appears, Mary once more said "goodbye" and ran out of the cottage, Mrs. Williams going as far as the front door with her. The night was very dark, and she couldn't see if Mary was alone or not, until presently she heard her voice saying tearfully: "I had to kiss baby——" then the voice died out in the distance "on the way to Canterbury," Mrs. Williams said most emphatically.

So far, you see, Inspector Meisures was able to fix the departure of the two sisters Nicholls from Ninescore on the night of January 23rd. Obviously they left their cottage about seven, went to Mrs. Williams, where Susan remained outside while Mary went in to say goodbye to the child.

After that all traces of them seem to have vanished. Whether they did go to Canterbury, and caught the last up train, at what station they alighted, or when poor Mary came back, could not at present be discovered.

According to the medical officer, the unfortunate girl must have been dead twelve or thirteen days at the very least, as, though the stagnant water may have accelerated decomposition, the head could not have got into such an advanced state much under a fortnight.

At Canterbury station neither the booking-clerk nor the porters could throw any light upon the subject. Canterbury West is a busy station, and scores of passengers buy tickets and go through the barriers every day. It was impossible, therefore, to give any positive information about two young women who may or may not have travelled by the last up train on Saturday, January 23rd—that is, a fortnight before.

One thing only was certain—whether Susan went to Canterbury and travelled by that up train or not, alone or with her sister—Mary had undoubtedly come back to Ninescore either the same night or the following day, since Timothy Coleman found her half-decomposed remains in the grounds of Ash Court a fortnight later.

Had she come back to meet her lover, or what? And where was Susan now?

From the first, therefore, you see, there was a great element of mystery about the whole case, and it was only natural that the local police should feel that, unless something more definite came out at the inquest, they would like to have the assistance of some of the fellows at the Yard.

So, the preliminary notes were sent up to London, and some of them drifted into our hands. Lady Molly was deeply interested in it from the first, and my firm belief is that she simply worried the chief into allowing her to go down to Ninescore and see what she could do.

2

At first it was understood that Lady Molly should only go down to Canterbury after the inquest, if the local police still felt that they were in want of assistance from London. But nothing was further from my lady's intentions than to wait until then.

"I was not going to miss the first act of a romantic drama," she said to me just as our train steamed into Canterbury station. "Pick up your bag, Mary. We're going to tramp it to Ninescore—two lady artists on a sketching tour, remember—and we'll find lodgings in the village, I dare say."

We had some lunch in Canterbury, and then we started to walk the six and a half miles to Ninescore, carrying our bags. We put up at one of the cottages, where the legend "Apartments for single respectable lady or gentleman" had hospitably invited us to enter, and at eight o'clock the next morning we found our way to the local police-station, where the inquest was to take place. Such a funny little place, you know—just a cottage converted for official use—and the small room packed to its utmost holding capacity. The entire able-bodied population of the neighbourhood had, I verily believe, congregated in these ten cubic yards of stuffy atmosphere.

Inspector Meisures, apprised by the chief of our arrival, had reserved two good places for us well in sight of witnesses, coroner and jury. The room was insupportably close, but I assure you that neither Lady Molly nor I thought much about our comfort then. We were terribly interested.

From the outset the case seemed, as it were, to wrap itself more and more in its mantle of impenetrable mystery. There was precious little in the way of clues, only that awful intuition, that dark unspoken

16

suspicion with regard to one particular man's guilt, which one could feel hovering in the minds of all those present.

Neither the police nor Timothy Coleman had anything to add to what was already known. The ring and purse were produced, also the dress worn by the murdered woman. All were sworn to by several witnesses as having been the property of Mary Nicholls.

Timothy, on being closely questioned, said that, in his opinion, the girl's body had been pushed into the mud, as the head was absolutely embedded in it, and he didn't see how she could have fallen like that Medical evidence was repeated; it was as uncertain—as vague—as before. Owing to the state of the head and neck it was impossible to ascertain by what means the death blow had been dealt. The doctor repeated his statement that the unfortunate girl must have been dead quite a fortnight. The body was discovered on February 5th—a fortnight before that would have been on or about January 23rd.

The caretaker who lived at the lodge at Ash Court could also throw but little light on the mysterious event. Neither he nor any member of his family had seen or heard anything to arouse their suspicions. Against that he explained that "The Wilderness," where the murder was committed, is situated some 200 yards from the lodge, with the mansion and flower garden lying between. Replying to a question put to him by a juryman, he said that that portion of the grounds is only divided off from Ninescore Lane by a low, brick wall, which has a door in it, opening into the lane almost opposite Elm Cottages. He added that the mansion had been empty for over a year, and that he succeeded the last man, who died, about twelve months ago. Mr. Lydgate had not been down for golf since witness had been in charge.

It would be useless to recapitulate all that the various witnesses had already told the police, and were now prepared to swear to. The private life of the two sisters Nicholls was gone into at full length, as much, at least, as was publicly known. But you know what village folk are; except when there is a bit of scandal and gossip, they know precious little of one another's inner lives.

The two girls appeared to be very comfortably off. Mary was always smartly dressed; and the baby girl, whom she had placed in Mrs. Williams's charge, had plenty of good and expensive clothes, whilst her keep, 5s. a week, was paid with unfailing regularity. What seemed certain, however, was that they did not get on well together, that Susan violently objected to Mary's association with Mr. Lydgate, and that recently she had spoken to the vicar asking him to try to persuade her sister to go away from Ninescore altogether, so as to break entirely with the past. The Reverend Octavius Ludlow, Vicar of Ninescore, seems thereupon to have had a little talk with Mary on the subject, suggesting that she should accept a good situation in London.

"But," continued the reverend gentleman, "I didn't make much impression on her. All she replied to me was that she certainly need never go into service, as she had a good income of her own, and could obtain £5,000 or more quite easily at any time if she chose."

"Did you mention Mr. Lydgate's name to her at all?" asked the coroner.

"Yes, I did," said the vicar, after a slight hesitation.

"Well, what was her attitude then?"

"I am afraid she laughed," replied the Reverend Octavius, primly, "and said very picturesquely, if somewhat ungrammatically, that 'some folks didn't know what they was talkin' about.'"

All very indefinite, you see. Nothing to get hold of, no motive suggested—beyond a very vague suspicion, perhaps, of blackmail—to account for a brutal crime. I must not, however, forget to tell you the two other facts which came to light in the course of this extraordinary inquest. Though, at the time, these facts seemed of wonderful moment for the elucidation of the mystery, they only helped ultimately to plunge the whole case into darkness still more impenetrable than before.

I am alluding, firstly, to the deposition of James Franklin, a carter in the employ of one of the local farmers. He stated that about half-past six on that same Saturday night, January 23rd, he was walking along Ninescore Lane leading his horse and cart, as the night was indeed pitch dark. Just as he came somewhere near Elm Cottages, he heard a man's voice saying in a kind of hoarse whisper:

"Open the door, can't you? It's as dark as blazes!"

Then a pause, after which the same voice added:

"Mary, where the dickens are you?" Whereupon a girl's voice replied: "All right, I'm coming."

James Franklin heard nothing more after that, nor did he see anyone in the gloom.

With the stolidity peculiar to the Kentish peasantry, he thought no more of this until the day when he heard that Mary Nicholls had been murdered; then he voluntarily came forward and told his story to the police. Now, when he was closely questioned, he was quite unable to say whether these voices proceeded from that side of the lane where stand Elm Cottages or from the other side, which is edged by the low, brick wall.

Finally, Inspector Meisures, who really showed an extraordinary sense of what was dramatic, here produced a document which he had reserved for the last. This was a piece of paper which he had found in the red leather purse already mentioned, and which at first had not been thought very important, as the writing was identified by several people as that of the deceased, and consisted merely of a series of dates and hours scribbled in pencil on a scrap of notepaper. But suddenly these dates had assumed a weird and terrible significance: two of them, at least—December 26th and January 1st followed by "10 a.m."—were days on which Mr. Lydgate came over to Ninescore and took Mary for drives. One or two witnesses swore to this positively. Both dates had been local meets of the harriers, to which other folk from the village had gone, and Mary had openly said afterwards how much she had enjoyed these.

The other dates (there were six altogether) were more or less vague. One Mrs. Hooker remembered as being coincident with a day Mary Nicholls had spent away from home; but the last date, scribbled in the same handwriting, was January 23rd, and below it the hour—6 p.m.

The coroner now adjourned the inquest. An explanation from Mr. Lionel Lydgate had become imperative.

3

Public excitement had by now reached a very high pitch; it was no longer a case of mere local interest. The country inns all round the immediate neighbourhood were packed with visitors from London, artists, journalists, dramatists, and actor-managers, whilst the hotels and fly-proprietors of Canterbury were doing a roaring trade.

Certain facts and one vivid picture stood out clearly before the thoughtful mind in the midst of a chaos of conflicting and irrelevant evidence: the picture was that of the two women tramping in the wet and pitch dark night towards Canterbury. Beyond that everything was a blur.

When did Mary Nicholls come back to Ninescore, and why?

To keep an appointment made with Lionel Lydgate, it was openly whispered; but that appointment—if the rough notes were interpreted rightly—was for the very day on which she and her sister went away from home. A man's voice called to her at half-past six certainly, and she replied to it. Franklin, the carter, heard her; but half an hour afterwards Mrs. Hooker heard her voice when she left home with her sister, and she visited Mrs. Williams after that.

The only theory compatible with all this was, of course, that Mary merely accompanied Susan part of the way to Canterbury, then went back to meet her lover, who enticed her into the deserted grounds of Ash Court, and there murdered her.

The motive was not far to seek. Mr. Lionel Lydgate, about to marry, wished to silence for ever a voice that threatened to be unpleasantly persistent in its demands for money and in its threats of scandal.

But there was one great argument against that theory—the disappearance of Susan Nicholls. She had been extensively advertised for. The murder of her sister was published broadcast in every newspaper in the United Kingdom—she could not be ignorant of it. And, above all, she hated Mr. Lydgate. Why did she not come and add the weight of her testimony against him if, indeed, he was guilty?

And if Mr. Lydgate was innocent, then where was the criminal? And why had Susan Nicholls disappeared?

Why? why? why?

Well, the next day would show. Mr. Lionel Lydgate had been cited by the police to give evidence at the adjourned inquest.

Good-looking, very athletic, and obviously frightfully upset and nervous, he entered the little courtroom, accompanied by his solicitor, just before the coroner and jury took their seats.

He looked keenly at Lady Molly as he sat down, and from the expression of his face I guessed that he was much puzzled to know who she was.

He was the first witness called. Manfully and clearly, he gave a concise account of his association with the deceased.

"She was pretty and amusing," he said. "I liked to take her out when I was in the neighbourhood; it was no trouble to me. There was no harm in her, whatever the village gossips might say. I know she had been in trouble, as they say, but that had nothing to do with me. It wasn't for me to be hard on a girl, and I fancy that she has been very badly treated by some scoundrel."

Here he was hard pressed by the coroner, who wished him to explain what he meant. But Mr. Lydgate turned obstinate, and to every leading question he replied stolidly and very emphatically:

"I don't know who it was. It had nothing to do with me, but I was sorry for the girl because of everyone turning against her, including her sister, and I tried to give her a little pleasure when I could."

That was all right. Very sympathetically told. The public quite liked this pleasing specimen of English cricket-, golf- and football-loving manhood. Subsequently Mr. Lydgate admitted meeting Mary on December 26th and January 1st, but he swore most emphatically that that was the last he ever saw of her.

"But the 23rd of January," here insinuated the coroner; "you made an appointment with the deceased then?"

"Certainly not," he replied.

"But you met her on that day?"

"Most emphatically no," he replied quietly. "I went down to Edbrooke Castle, my brother's place in Lincolnshire, on the 20th of last month, and only got back to town about three days ago."

"You swear to that, Mr. Lydgate?" asked the coroner.

"I do, indeed, and there are a score of witnesses to bear me out. The family, the house-party, the servants."

He tried to dominate his own excitement. I suppose, poor man, he had only just realised that certain horrible suspicions had been resting upon him. His solicitor pacified him, and presently he sat down, whilst I must say that everyone there present was relieved at the thought that the handsome young athlete was not a murderer, after all. To look at him it certainly seemed preposterous.

But then, of course, there was the deadlock, and as there were no more witnesses to be heard, no new facts to elucidate, the jury returned the usual verdict against some person or persons unknown; and we, the keenly interested spectators, were left to face the problem—Who murdered Mary Nicholls, and where was her sister Susan?

4

After the verdict we found our way back to our lodgings. Lady Molly tramped along silently, with that deep furrow between her brows which I knew meant that she was deep in thought.

"Now we'll have some tea," I said, with a sigh of relief, as soon as we entered the cottage door.

"No, you won't," replied my lady, dryly. "I am going to write out a telegram, and we'll go straight on to Canterbury and send it from there."

"To Canterbury!" I gasped. "Two hours' walk at least, for I don't suppose we can get a trap, and it is past three o'clock. Why not send your telegram from Ninescore?"

"Mary, you are stupid," was all the reply I got.

" ' You swear to that, Mr. Lydgate? ' asked the coroner "

She wrote out two telegrams—one of which was at least three dozen words long—and, once more calling to me to come along, we set out for Canterbury.

I was tea-less, cross, and puzzled. Lady Molly was alert, cheerful, and irritatingly active.

We reached the first telegraph office a little before five. My lady sent the telegram without condescending to tell me anything of its destination or contents; then she took me to the Castle Hotel and graciously offered me tea.

"May I be allowed to inquire whether you propose tramping back to Ninescore tonight?" I asked with a slight touch of sarcasm, as I really felt put out.

"No, Mary," she replied, quietly munching a bit of Sally Lunn; "I have engaged a couple of rooms at this hotel and wired the chief that any message will find us here tomorrow morning."

After that there was nothing for it but quietude, patience, and finally supper and bed.

The next morning my lady walked into my room before I had finished dressing. She had a newspaper in her hand, and threw it down on the bed as she said calmly:

"It was in the evening paper all right last night. I think we shall be in time."

No use asking her what "it" meant. It was easier to pick up the paper, which I did. It was a late edition of one of the leading London evening shockers, and at once the front page, with its startling headline, attracted my attention:

THE NINESCORE MYSTERY
MARY NICHOLLS'S BABY DYING

Then, below that, a short paragraph:—

We regret to learn that the little baby daughter of the unfortunate girl who was murdered recently at Ash Court, Ninescore, Kent, under such terrible and mysterious circumstances, is very seriously ill at the cottage of Mrs. Williams, in whose charge she is. The local doctor who visited her today declares that she cannot last more than a few hours. At the time of going to press the nature of the child's complaint was not known to our special representative at Ninescore.

"What does this mean?" I gasped.

23

But before she could reply there was a knock at the door.

"A telegram for Miss Granard," said the voice of the hall-porter.

"Quick, Mary," said Lady Molly, eagerly. "I told the chief and also Meisures to wire here and to you."

The telegram turned out to have come from Ninescore, and was signed "Meisures." Lady Molly read it out aloud:

Mary Nicholls arrived here this morning. Detained her at station. Come at once.

"Mary Nicholls! I don't understand," was all I could contrive to say. But she only replied:

"I knew it! I knew it! Oh, Mary, what a wonderful thing is human nature, and how I thank Heaven that gave me a knowledge of it!"

She made me get dressed all in a hurry, and then we swallowed some breakfast hastily whilst a fly was being got for us. I had, perforce, to satisfy my curiosity from my own inner consciousness. Lady Molly was too absorbed to take any notice of me. Evidently the chief knew what she had done and approved of it: the telegram from Meisures pointed to that.

My lady had suddenly become a personality. Dressed very quietly, and in a smart close-fitting hat, she looked years older than her age, owing also to the seriousness of her mien.

The fly took us to Ninescore fairly quickly. At the little police-station we found Meisures awaiting us. He had Elliott and Pegram from the Yard with him. They had obviously got their orders, for all three of them were mighty deferential.

"The woman is Mary Nicholls, right enough," said Meisures, as Lady Molly brushed quickly past him, "the woman who was supposed to have been murdered. It's that silly bogus paragraph about the infant brought her out of her hiding-place. I wonder how it got in," he added blandly; "the child is well enough."

"I wonder," said Lady Molly, whilst a smile—the first I had seen that morning—lit up her pretty face.

"I suppose the other sister will turn up too, presently," rejoined Elliott. "Pretty lot of trouble we shall have now. If Mary Nicholls is alive and kickin', who was murdered at Ash Court, say I?"

"I wonder," said Lady Molly, with the same charming smile.

Then she went in to see Mary Nicholls.

The Reverend Octavius Ludlow was sitting beside the girl, who seemed in great distress, for she was crying bitterly.

Lady Molly asked Elliott and the others to remain in the passage whilst she herself went into the room, I following behind her.

When the door was shut, she went up to Mary Nicholls, and assuming a hard and severe manner, she said:

"Well, you have at last made up your mind, have you, Nicholls? I suppose you know that we have applied for a warrant for your arrest?"

The woman gave a shriek which unmistakably was one of fear.

"My arrest?" she gasped. "What for?"

"The murder of your sister Susan."

"'Twasn't me!" she said quickly.

"Then Susan *is* dead?" retorted Lady Molly, quietly.

Mary saw that she had betrayed herself. She gave Lady Molly a look of agonised horror, then turned as white as a sheet and would have fallen had not the Reverend Octavius Ludlow gently led her to a chair.

"It wasn't me," she repeated, with a heart-broken sob.

"That will be for you to prove," said Lady Molly dryly. "The child cannot now, of course, remain with Mrs. Williams; she will be removed to the workhouse, and—"

"No, that she shan't be," said the mother excitedly. "She shan't be, I tell you. The workhouse, indeed," she added in a paroxysm of hysterical tears, "and her father a lord!"

The reverend gentleman and I gasped in astonishment; but Lady Molly had worked up to this climax so ingeniously that it was obvious she had guessed it all along, and had merely led Mary Nicholls on in order to get this admission from her.

How well she had known human nature in pitting the child against the sweetheart! Mary Nicholls was ready enough to hide herself, to part from her child even for a while, in order to save the man, she had once loved from the consequences of his crime; but when she heard that her child was dying, she no longer could bear to leave it among strangers, and when Lady Molly taunted her with the workhouse, she exclaimed in her maternal pride:

"The workhouse! And her father a lord!"

Driven into a corner, she confessed the whole truth.

Lord Edbrooke, then Mr. Lydgate, was the father of her child. Knowing this, her sister Susan had, for over a year now, systematically blackmailed the unfortunate man—not altogether, it seems, without Mary's connivance. In January last she got him to come down to Ninescore under the distinct promise that Mary would meet him and

" The woman gave a shriek which unmistakably was
one of fear "

hand over to him the letters she had received from him, as well as the ring he had given her, in exchange for the sum of £5,000.

The meeting-place was arranged, but at the last moment Mary was afraid to go in the dark. Susan, nothing daunted, but anxious about her own reputation in case she should be seen talking to a man so late at night, put on Mary's dress, took the ring and the letters, also her sister's purse, and went to meet Lord Edbrooke.

What happened at that interview no one will ever know. It ended with the murder of the blackmailer. I suppose the fact that Susan had, in a measure, begun by impersonating her sister, gave the murderer the first thought of confusing the identity of his victim by the horrible device of burying the body in the slimy mud. Anyway, he almost did succeed in hoodwinking the police, and would have done so entirely but for Lady Molly's strange intuition in the matter.

After his crime he ran instinctively to Mary's cottage. He had to make a clean breast of it to her, as, without her help, he was a doomed man.

So, he persuaded her to go away from home and to leave no clue or trace of herself or her sister in Ninescore. With the help of money which he would give her, she could begin life anew somewhere else, and no doubt he deluded the unfortunate girl with promises that her child should be restored to her very soon.

Thus, he enticed Mary Nicholls away, who would have been the great and all-important witness against him the moment his crime was discovered. A girl of Mary's type and class instinctively obeys the man she has once loved, the man who is the father of her child. She consented to disappear and to allow all the world to believe that she had been murdered by some unknown miscreant.

Then the murderer quietly returned to his luxurious home at Edbrooke Castle, unsuspected. No one had thought of mentioning his name in connection with that of Mary Nicholls. In the days when he used to come down to Ash Court, he was Mr. Lydgate, and, when he became a peer, sleepy, out-of-the-way Ninescore ceased to think of him.

Perhaps Mr. Lionel Lydgate knew all about his brother's association with the village girl. From his attitude at the inquest, I should say he did, but of course he would not betray his own brother unless forced to do so.

Now, of course, the whole aspect of the case was changed: the veil of mystery had been torn asunder owing to the insight, the marvellous intuition, of a woman who, in my opinion, is the most wonderful psychologist of her time.

You know the sequel. Our fellows at the Yard, aided by the local police, took their lead from Lady Molly, and began their investigations of Lord Edbrooke's movements on or about the 23rd of January.

Even their preliminary inquiries revealed the fact that his lordship had left Edbrooke Castle on the 21st. He went up to town, saying to his wife and household that he was called away on business, and not even taking his valet with him. He put up at the Langham Hotel.

But here police investigations came to an abrupt ending. Lord Edbrooke evidently got wind of them. Anyway, the day after Lady Molly so cleverly enticed Mary Nicholls out of her hiding-place, and surprised her into an admission of the truth, the unfortunate man threw himself in front of the express train at Grantham railway station, and was instantly killed. Human justice cannot reach him now!

But don't tell me that a man would have thought of that bogus paragraph, or of the taunt which stung the motherly pride of the village girl to the quick, and thus wrung from her an admission which no amount of male ingenuity would ever have obtained.

The Frewin Miniatures

1

Although, mind you, Lady Molly's methods in connection with the Ninescore mystery were not altogether approved of at the Yard, nevertheless, her shrewdness and ingenuity in the matter were so undoubted that they earned for her a reputation, then and there, which placed her in the foremost rank of the force. And presently, when everyone—public and police alike—were set by the ears over the Frewin miniatures, and a reward of 1,000 guineas was offered for information that would lead to the apprehension of the thief, the chief, of his own accord and without any hesitation, offered the job to her.

I don't know much about so-called works of art myself, but you can't be in the detective force, female or otherwise, without knowing something of the value of most things, and I don't think that Mr. Frewin put an excessive value on his Engleheats when he stated that they were worth £10,000. There were eight of them, all on ivory, about three to four inches high, and they were said to be the most perfect specimens of their kind. Mr. Frewin himself had had an offer for them, less than two years ago, of 200,000 *francs* from the trustees of the Louvre, which offer, mind you, he had refused.

I dare say you know that he was an immensely wealthy man, a great collector himself, as well as dealer, and that several of the most unique and most highly priced works of art found their way into his private collection. Among them, of course, the Engleheart miniatures were the most noteworthy.

For some time before his death Mr. Frewin had been a great invalid, and for over two years he had not been able to go beyond the boundary of his charming property, Blatchley House, near Brighton.

There is a sad story in connection with the serious illness of Mr. Frewin—an illness which, if you remember, has since resulted in the poor old gentleman's death. He had an only son, a young man on whom the old art-dealer had lavished all the education and, subsequently, all the social advantages which money could give. The boy was exceptionally good-looking, and had inherited from his mother a great charm of manner which made him very popular. The Honourable Mrs. Frewin is the daughter of an English peer, more endowed with physical attributes than with worldly goods. Besides that, she is an exceptionally beautiful woman, has a glorious voice, is a fine violinist, and is no mean water-colour artist, having more than once exhibited at the Royal Academy.

Unfortunately, at one time, young Frewin had got into very bad company, made many debts, some of which were quite unavowable, and there were rumours current at the time to the effect that had the police got wind of certain transactions in connection with a brother officer's cheque, a very unpleasant prosecution would have followed. Be that as it may, young Lionel Frewin had to quit his regiment, and presently he went off to Canada, where he is supposed to have gone in for farming. According to the story related by some of the servants at Blatchley House, there were violent scenes between father and son before the former consented to pay some of the young spendthrift's most pressing debts, and then find the further sum of money which was to enable young Frewin to commence a new life in the colonies.

Mrs. Frewin, of course, took the matter very much to heart. She was a dainty, refined, artistic creature, who idolised her only son, but she had evidently no influence whatever over her husband, who, in common with certain English families of Jewish extraction, had an extraordinary hardness of character where the integrity of his own business fame was concerned. He absolutely never forgave his son what he considered a slur cast upon his name by the young spendthrift; he packed him off to Canada, and openly told him that he was to expect nothing further from him. All the Frewin money and the priceless art collection would be left by will to a nephew, James Hyam, whose honour and general conduct had always been beyond reproach.

That Mr. Frewin really took his hitherto idolised son's defalcations very much to heart was shown by the fact that the poor old man's health completely broke down after that. He had an apoplectic fit, and, although he somewhat recovered, he always remained an invalid.

His eyesight and brain power were distinctly enfeebled, and about nine months ago he had a renewed seizure, which resulted in paralysis first, and subsequently in his death. The greatest, if not the only, joy the poor old man had during the two years which he spent pinned to an invalid chair was his art collection.

Blatchley House was a perfect art museum, and the invalid would have his chair wheeled up and down the great hall and along the rooms where his pictures and china and, above all, where his priceless miniatures were stored. He took an enormous pride in these, and it was, I think, with a view to brightening him up a little that Mrs. Frewin invited Monsieur de Colinville—who had always been a great friend of her husband—to come and stay at Blatchley. Of course, there is no greater connoisseur of art anywhere than that distinguished Frenchman, and it was through him that the celebrated offer of £8,000 was made by the Louvre for the Engleheart miniatures.

Though, of course, the invalid declined the offer, he took a great pleasure and pride in the fact that it had been made, as, in addition to Monsieur de Colinville himself, several members of the committee of art advisers to the Louvre came over from Paris in order to try and persuade Mr. Frewin to sell his unique treasures.

However, the invalid was obdurate about that. He was not in want of money, and the celebrated Frewin art collection would go intact to his widow for her life, and then to his heir, Mr. James Hyam, a great connoisseur himself and art dealer of St. Petersburg and London.

It was really a merciful dispensation of Providence that the old man never knew of the disappearance of his valued miniatures. By the time that extraordinary mystery had come to light he was dead.

On the evening of January, the 14th, at half-past eight, Mr. Frewin had a third paralytic seizure, from which he never recovered. His valet, Kennet, and his two nurses were with him at the time, and Mrs. Frewin, quickly apprised of the terrible event, flew to his bedside, whilst the motor was at once despatched for the doctor. About an hour or two later the dying man seemed to rally somewhat, but he appeared very restless and agitated, and his eyes were roaming anxiously about the room.

"I expect it is his precious miniatures he wants," said Nurse Dawson. "He is always quiet when he can play with them."

She reached for the large, leather case which contained the priceless art treasures, and, opening it, placed it on the bed beside the patient. Mr. Frewin, however, was obviously too near death to care even for his favourite toy. He fingered the miniatures with trembling hands for a few moments, and then sank back exhausted on the pillows.

"He is dying," said the doctor quietly, turning to Mrs. Frewin.

"I have something to say to him," she then said. "Can I remain alone with him for a few minutes?"

"Certainly," said the doctor, as he himself discreetly retired; "but I think one of the nurses had better remain within earshot."

Nurse Dawson, it appeared, remained within earshot to some purpose, for she overheard what Mrs. Frewin was saying to her dying husband.

"It is about Lionel—your only son," she said. "Can you understand what I say?"

The sick man nodded.

"You remember that he is in Brighton, staying with Alicia. I can go and fetch him in the motor if you will consent to see him."

Again, the dying man nodded. I suppose Mrs. Frewin took this to mean acquiescence, for the next moment she rang for John Chipps, the butler, and gave him instructions to order her motor at once. She then kissed the patient on the forehead and prepared to leave the room; but just before she did so, her eyes lighted on the case of miniatures, and she said to Kennet, the valet:

"Give these to Chipps, and tell him to put them in the library."

She then went to put on her furs preparatory to going out. When she was quite ready, she met Chipps on the landing, who had just come up to tell her that the motor was at the door. He had in his hand the case of miniatures which Kennet had given him.

"Put the case on the library table, Chipps, when you go down," she said.

"Yes, madam," he replied.

He followed her downstairs, then slipped into the library, put the case on the table as he had been directed, after which he saw his mistress into the motor, and finally closed the front door.

About an hour later Mrs. Frewin came back, but without her son. It transpired afterwards that the young man was more vindictive than his father; he refused to go to the latter's bedside in order to be reconciled at the eleventh hour to a man who then had no longer either his wits or his physical senses about him. However, the dying man was spared the knowledge of his son's irreconcilable conduct, for, after a long and wearisome night passed in a state of coma, he died at about 6.0 a.m.

It was quite late the following afternoon when Mrs. Frewin suddenly recollected the case of miniatures, which should have been locked in their accustomed cabinet. She strolled leisurely into the library—she was very fatigued and worn out with the long vigil and the sorrow and anxiety she had just gone through. A quarter of an hour later John Chipps found her in the same room, sitting dazed and almost fainting in an armchair. In response to the old butler's anxious query, she murmured:

"The miniatures—where are they?"

Scared at the abruptness of the query and at his mistress's changed tone of voice, Chipps gazed quickly around him.

"You told me to put them on the table, ma'am," he murmured, "and I did so. They certainly don't seem to be in the room now—" he added, with a sudden feeling of terror.

"Run and ask one of the nurses at once if the case was taken up to Mr. Frewin's room during the night?"

Chipps, needless to say, did not wait to be told twice. He was beginning to feel very anxious. He spoke to Kennet and also to the two nurses, and asked them if, by any chance, the miniatures were in the late master's room. To this Kennet and the nurses replied in the negative. The last they had seen of the miniatures was when Chipps took them from the valet and followed his mistress downstairs with the case in his hands.

The poor old butler was in despair; the cook was in hysterics, and consternation reigned throughout the house. The disappearance of the miniatures caused almost a greater excitement than the death of the master, who had been a dying man so long that he was almost a stranger to the servants at Blatchley.

Mrs. Frewin was the first to recover her presence of mind.

"Send a motor at once to the police-station at Brighton," she said very calmly, as soon as she completely realised that the miniatures were nowhere to be found. "It is my duty to see that this matter is thoroughly gone into at once."

Within half an hour of the discovery of the theft, Detective Inspector Hankin and Police Constable McLeod had both arrived from Brighton, having availed themselves of Mrs. Frewin's motor. They are shrewd men, both of them, and it did not take them many minutes before they had made up their minds how the robbery had taken place. By whom it was done was quite another matter, and would take some time and some ingenuity to find out.

What Detective Inspector Hankin had gathered was this: While John Chipps saw his mistress into the motor, the front door of the house had, of necessity, been left wide open. The motor then made a start, but after a few paces it stopped, and Mrs. Frewin put her head out of the window and shouted to Chipps some instructions with regard to the nurses' evening collation, which, in view of Mr. Frewin's state, she feared might be forgotten.

Chipps, being an elderly man and a little deaf, did not hear her voice distinctly, so he ran up to the motor, and she repeated her instructions to him. In Inspector Hankin's mind there was no doubt that the thief, who must have been hanging about the shrubbery that evening, took that opportunity to sneak into the house, then to hide himself in a convenient spot until he could find an opportunity for the robbery which he had in view.

The butler declared that, when he returned, he saw nothing unusual. He had only been gone a little over a minute; he then fastened and bolted the front door, and, according to his usual custom, he put up all the shutters of the ground-floor windows, including, of course, those in the library. He had no light with him when he did this accustomed round, for, of course, he knew his way well enough in the dark, and the electric chandelier in the hall gave him what light he wanted.

While he was putting up the shutters, Chipps was giving no particular thought to the miniatures, but, strangely enough, he seems to have thought of them about an hour later, when most of the servants had gone to bed and he was waiting up for his mistress. He then, quite casually and almost absentmindedly, when crossing the hall, turned the key of the library door, thus locking it from the outside.

Of course, throughout all this we must remember that Blatchley House was not in its normal state that night, since its master was actually dying in a room on the floor above the library. The two nurses and Kennet, the valet, were all awake, and with him during the whole of that night. Kennet certainly was in and out of the room several times, having to run down and fetch various things required by the doctor or the nurses.

In order to do this, he did not use the principal staircase, nor did he have to cross the hall, but, as far as the upper landing and the secondary stairs were concerned, he certainly had not noticed anything unusual or suspicious; whilst when Mrs. Frewin came home, she went straight up to the first floor, and certainly noticed nothing in any way to arouse her suspicions. But, of course, this meant very little, as she certainly must have been too upset and agitated to see anything.

The servants were not apprised of the death of their master until after their breakfast. In the meanwhile, Emily, the housemaid, had been in, as usual, to "do" the library. She distinctly noticed, when she first went in, that none of the shutters were up and that one of the windows was open. She thought at the time that someone must have been in the room before her, and meant to ask Chipps about it, when the news of the master's death drove all thoughts of open windows from her mind. Strangely enough, when Hankin questioned her more closely about it, and she had had time to recollect everything more clearly, she made the extraordinary statement that she certainly had noticed that the door of the library was locked on the outside when she first went into the room, the key being in the lock.

"Then, didn't it strike you as very funny," asked Hankin, "that the door was locked on the outside, and yet that the shutters were unbarred and one of the windows was open?"

"Yes, I did seem to think of that," replied Emily, with that pleasant vagueness peculiar to her class; "but then, the room did not look like burglars—it was quite tidy, just as it had been left last night, and burglars always seem to leave a great mess behind, else I should have noticed," she added, with offended dignity.

"But did you not see that the miniatures were not in their usual place?"

"Oh, they often wasn't in the cabinet, as the master used to ask for them sometimes to be brought to his room."

That was, of course, indisputable. It was clearly evident that the burglar had had plenty of chances to make good his escape. You see, the actual time when the miscreant must have sneaked into the room had now been narrowed down to about an hour and a half, between the time when Mrs. Frewin finally left in her motor to about an hour later, when Chipps turned the key in the door of the library and thus undoubtedly locked the thief in. At what precise time of the night he effected his escape could not anyhow be ascertained.

It must have been after Mrs. Frewin came back again, as Hankin held that she or her chauffeur would have noticed that one of the library windows was open. This opinion was not shared by Elliott from the Yard, who helped in the investigation of this mysterious crime, as Mrs. Frewin was certainly very agitated and upset that evening, and her powers of perception would necessarily be blunted. As for the chauffeur: we all know that the strong headlights on a motor are so dazzling that nothing can be seen outside their blinding circle of light.

Be that as it may, it remained doubtful when the thief made good his escape. It was easy enough to effect, and, as there is a square of flagstones in front of the main door and just below the library windows, the thief left not the slightest trace of footprints, whilst the drop from the window is less than eight feet.

What was strange in the whole case, and struck Detective Hankin immediately, was the fact that the burglar, whoever he was, must have known a great deal about the house and its ways. He also must have had a definite purpose in his mind not usually to be found in the brain of a common housebreaker. He must have meant to steal the miniatures and nothing else, since he made his way straight to the library, and, having secured the booty, at once made good his escape without trying to get any other article which could more easily be disposed of than works of art.

You may imagine, therefore, how delicate a task now confronted Inspector Hankin. You see, he had questioned everyone in the house, including Mr. Frewin's valet and nurses, and from them he casually heard of Mrs. Frewin's parting words to her dying husband and of her mention of the scapegrace son, who was evidently in the immediate neighbourhood, and whom she wished to come and see his father. Mrs. Frewin, closely questioned by the detective, admitted that her son was staying in Brighton, and that she saw him that very evening.

"Mr. Lionel Frewin is staying at the Metropole Hotel," she said coldly, "and he was dining with my sister, Lady Steyne, last night. He was in the house at Sussex Square when I arrived in my motor," she added hastily, guessing, perhaps, the unavowed suspicion which had arisen in Hankin's mind, "and he was still there when I left. I drove home very fast, naturally, as my husband's condition was known to me to be quite hopeless, and that he was not expected to live more than perhaps a few hours. We covered the seven miles between this house and that of my sister in less than a quarter of an hour."

This statement of Mrs. Frewin's was, if you remember, fully confirmed both by her sister and her brother-in-law, Lady Steyne and Sir Michael. There was no doubt that young Lionel Frewin was staying at the Hotel Metropole in Brighton, that he was that evening dining with the Steynes at Sussex Square when his mother arrived in her motor. Mrs. Frewin stayed about an hour, during which time she, presumably, tried to influence her son to go back to Blatchley with her in order to see his dying father. Of course, what exactly happened at that family interview none of the four people present was inclined to reveal. Against that both Sir Michael and Lady Steyne were prepared to swear that Mr. Lionel Frewin was in the house when his mother arrived, and that he did not leave them until long after she had driven away.

There lay the hitch, you see, for already the public jumped to conclusions, and, terribly prejudiced as it is in a case of this sort, it had made up its mind that Mr. Lionel Frewin, once more pressed for money, had stolen his father's precious miniatures in order to sell them in America for a high sum. Everyone's sympathy was dead against the young son who refused to be reconciled to his father, although the latter was dying.

According to one of the footmen in Lady Steyne's employ, who had taken whiskies and sodas in while the interview between Mrs. Frewin and her son was taking place, Mr. Lionel had said very testily:

"It's all very well, mother, but that is sheer sentimentality. The guv'nor threw me on my beam ends when a little kindness and help would have meant a different future to me; he chose to break my life because of some early *peccadilloes*—and I am not going to fawn round him and play the hypocrite when he has no intention of altering his will and has cut me off with a shilling. He must be half imbecile by now, and won't know me anyway."

But with all this, and with public opinion so dead against him, it was quite impossible to bring the crime home to the young man. The burglar, whoever he was, must have sneaked into the library some time before Chipps closed the door on the outside, since it was still so found by Emily the following morning. Thereupon the public, determined that Lionel Frewin should in some way be implicated in the theft, made up its mind that the doting mother, hearing of her son's woeful want of money, stole the miniatures herself that night and gave them to him.

When Lady Molly heard this theory she laughed, and shrugged her pretty shoulders.

"Old Mr. Frewin was dying, was he not, at the time of the burglary?" she said. "Why should his wife, soon to become his widow, take the trouble to go through a laboured and daring comedy of a burglary in order to possess herself of things which would become hers within the next few hours?

"Even if, after Mr. Frewin's death, she could not actually dispose of the miniatures, the old man left her a large sum of money and a big income by his will, with which she could help her spendthrift son as much as she pleased."

This was, of course, why the mystery in this strange case was so deep. At the Yard they did all that they could. Within forty-eight hours they had notices printed in almost every European language, which contained rough sketches of the stolen miniatures hastily supplied by Mrs. Frewin herself. These were sent to as many of the great museums and art collectors abroad as possible, and of course to the principal American cities and to American millionaires.

There is no doubt that the thief would find it very difficult to dispose of the miniatures, and until he could sell them his booty would, of course, not benefit him in any way. Works of art cannot be tampered with, or melted down or taken to pieces, like silver or jewellery, and, so far as could be ascertained, the thief did not appear to make the slightest attempt to dispose of the booty, and the mystery became more dark, more impenetrable than ever.

"Will you undertake the job?" said the chief one day to Lady Molly.

"Yes," she replied, "on two distinct conditions."

"What are they?"

"That you will not bother me with useless questions, and that you will send out fresh notices to all the museums and art collectors you can think of, and request them to let you know of any art purchases they may have made within the last two years."

"The last two years!" ejaculated the chief, "why, the miniatures were only stolen three months ago."

"Did I not say that you were not to ask me useless questions?"

This to the chief, mind you; and he only smiled, whilst I nearly fell backwards at her daring. But he did send out the notices, and it was generally understood that Lady Molly now had charge of the case.

It was about seven weeks later when, one morning, I found her at breakfast looking wonderfully bright and excited.

"The Yard has had sheaves of replies, Mary," she said gaily, "and the chief still thinks I am a complete fool."

"Why, what has happened?"

"Only this, that the art museum at Budapest has now in its possession a set of eight miniatures by Engleheart; but the authorities did not think that the first notices from Scotland Yard could possibly refer to these, as they had been purchased from a private source a little over two years ago."

"But two years ago, the Frewin miniatures were still at Blatchley House, and Mr. Frewin was fingering them daily," I said, not understanding, and wondering what she was driving at.

"I know that," she said gaily, "so does the chief. That is why he thinks that I am a first-class idiot."

"But what do you wish to do now?"

"Go to Brighton, Mary, take you with me and try to elucidate the mystery of the Frewin miniatures."

"I don't understand," I gasped, bewildered.

"No, and you won't until we get there," she replied, running up to me and kissing me in her pretty, engaging way.

That same afternoon we went to Brighton and took up our abode at the Hotel Metropole. Now you know I always believed from the very first that she was a born lady and all the rest of it, but even I was taken aback at the number of acquaintances and smart friends she had all over the place. It was "Hello, Lady Molly! whoever would have thought of meeting you here?" and "Upon my word! this is good luck," all the time.

She smiled and chatted gaily with all the folk as if she had known them all her life, but I could easily see that none of these people knew that she had anything to do with the Yard.

Brighton is not such a very big place as one would suppose, and most of the fashionable residents of the gay city find their way sooner or later to the luxurious dining-room of the Hotel Metropole, if only for a quiet little dinner given when the cook is out. Therefore, I was not a little surprised when, one evening, about a week after our arrival and just as we were sitting down to the *table d'hôte* dinner, Lady Molly suddenly placed one of her delicate hands on my arm.

"Look behind you, a little to your left, Mary, but not just this minute. When you do you will see two ladies and two gentlemen sitting at a small table quite close to us. They are Sir Michael and Lady Steyne, the Honourable Mrs. Frewin in deep black, and her son, Mr. Lionel Frewin."

I looked round as soon as I could, and gazed with some interest at the hero and heroine of the Blatchley House drama. We had a quiet little dinner, and Lady Molly having all of a sudden become very silent and self-possessed, altogether different from her gay, excited self of the past few days, I scented that something important was in the air, and tried to look as unconcerned as my lady herself. After dinner we ordered coffee, and as Lady Molly strolled through into the lounge, I noticed that she ordered our tray to be placed at a table which was in very close proximity to one already occupied by Lady Steyne and her party.

Lady Steyne, I noticed, gave Lady Molly a pleasant nod when we first came in, and Sir Michael got up and bowed, saying "How d'ye do?" We sat down and began a desultory conversation together. Soon, as usual, we were joined by various friends and acquaintances who all congregated round our table and set themselves to entertaining us right pleasantly. Presently the conversation drifted to art matters, Sir Anthony Truscott being there, who is, as you know, one of the keepers of the Art Department at South Kensington Museum.

"I am crazy about miniatures just now," said Lady Molly in response to a remark from Sir Anthony.

I tried not to look astonished.

"And Miss Granard and I," continued my lady, quite unblushingly, "have been travelling all over the Continent in order to try and secure some rare specimens."

"Indeed," said Sir Anthony. "Have you found anything very wonderful?"

"We certainly have discovered some rare works of art," replied Lady Molly, "have we not, Mary? Now the two Englehearts we bought at Budapest are undoubtedly quite unique."

"Engleheart—and at Budapest!" remarked Sir Anthony. "I thought I knew the collections at most of the great Continental cities, but I certainly have no recollection of such treasures in the Hungarian capital."

"Oh, they were only purchased two years ago, and have only been shown to the public recently," remarked Lady Molly. "There was originally a set of eight, so the comptroller, Mr. Pulszky, informed me. He bought them from an English collector whose name I have now forgotten, and he is very proud of them, but they cost the country a great deal more money than it could afford, and in order somewhat to recoup himself Mr. Pulszky sold two out of the eight at, I must say, a very stiff price."

While she was talking, I could not help noticing the strange glitter in her eyes. Then a curious smothered sound broke upon my ear. I turned and saw Mrs. Frewin looking with glowing and dilated eyes at the charming picture presented by Lady Molly.

"I should like to show you my purchases," said the latter to Sir Anthony. "One or two foreign connoisseurs have seen the two miniatures and declare them to be the finest in existence. Mary," she added, turning to me, "would you be so kind as to run up to my room and get me the small sealed packet which is at the bottom of my dressing-case? Here are the keys."

A little bewildered, yet guessing by her manner that I had a part to play, I took the keys from her and went up to her room. In her dressing-case I certainly found a small, square, flat packet, and with that in my hand I prepared to go downstairs again. I had just locked the bedroom door when I was suddenly confronted by a tall, graceful woman dressed in deep black, whom I at once recognised as the Honourable Mrs. Frewin.

"You are Miss Granard?" she said quickly and excitedly; her voice was tremulous and she seemed a prey to the greatest possible excitement. Without waiting for my reply, she continued eagerly:

"Miss Granard, there is no time to be more explicit, but I give you my word, the word of a very wretched, heart-broken woman, that my very life depends upon my catching a glimpse of the contents of the parcel that you now have in your hand."

"But—" I murmured, hopelessly bewildered.

"There is no 'but,'" she replied. "It is a matter of life and death. Here are £200, Miss Granard, if you will let me handle that packet," and with trembling hands she drew a bundle of banknotes from her reticule.

I hesitated, not because I had any notion of acceding to Mrs. Frewin's request, but because I did not quite know how I ought to act at this strange juncture, when a pleasant, mellow voice broke in suddenly:

"You may take the money, Mary, if you wish. You have my permission to hand the packet over to this lady," and Lady Molly, charming, graceful and elegant in her beautiful *directoire* gown, stood smiling some few feet away, with Hankin just visible in the gloom of the corridor.

She advanced towards us, took the small packet from my hands, and held it out towards Mrs. Frewin. "Will you open it?" she said, "or shall I?" Mrs. Frewin did not move. She stood as if turned to stone. Then with dexterous fingers my lady broke the seals of the packet and drew from it a few sheets of plain white cardboard and a thin piece of match-boarding.

"There!" said Lady Molly, fingering the bits of cardboard while she kept her fine large eyes fixed on Mrs. Frewin; "£200 is a big price to pay for a sight of these worthless things."

"Then this was a vulgar trick," said Mrs. Frewin, drawing herself up with an air which did not affect Lady Molly in the least.

"A trick, certainly," she replied with her winning smile, "vulgar, if you will call it so—pleasant to us all, Mrs. Frewin, since you so readily fell into it."

"Well, and what are you going to do next?"

"Report the matter to my chief," said Lady Molly, quietly. "We have all been very severely blamed for not discovering sooner the truth about the disappearance of the Frewin miniatures."

"You don't know the truth now," retorted Mrs. Frewin.

"Oh, yes, I do," replied Lady Molly, still smiling. "I know that two years ago your son, Mr. Lionel Frewin, was in terrible monetary difficulties. There was something unavowable, which he dared not tell his father. You had to set to work to find money somehow. You had no capital at your own disposal, and you wished to save your son from the terrible consequences of his own folly. It was soon after M. de Colinville's visit. Your husband had had his first apoplectic seizure; his mind and eyesight were somewhat impaired. You are a clever artist yourself, and you schemed out a plan whereby you carefully copied the priceless miniatures and then entrusted them to your son for sale to the Art Museum at Budapest, where there was but little likelihood of their being seen by anyone who knew they had belonged to your husband.

"English people do not stay more than one night there, at the Hotel Hungaria. Your copies were works of art in themselves, and you had no difficulty in deceiving your husband in the state of mind he then was, but when he lay dying you realised that his will would inevitably be proved, wherein he bequeathed the miniatures to Mr. James Hyam, and that these would have to be valued for probate. Frightened now that the substitution would be discovered, you devised the clever comedy of the burglary at Blatchley, which, in the circumstances, could never be brought home to you or your son. I don't know where you subsequently concealed the spurious Engleheart miniatures which you calmly took out of the library and hid away during the night of your husband's death, but no doubt our men will find that out," she added quietly, "now that they are on the track."

With a frightened shriek Mrs. Frewin turned as if she would fly, but Lady Molly was too quick for her, and barred the way. Then, with that wonderful charm of manner and that innate kindliness which always characterised her, she took hold of the unfortunate woman's wrist.

"Let me give you a word of advice," she said gently. "We at the Yard will be quite content with a confession from you, which will clear us of negligence and satisfy us that the crime has been brought home to its perpetrator. After that try and enter into an arrangement with your husband's legatee, Mr. James Hyam. Make a clean breast of the whole thing to him and offer him full monetary compensation. For the sake of the family, he won't refuse. He would have nothing to gain by bruiting the whole thing abroad; and for his own sake and that of his late uncle, who was so good to him, I don't think you would find him hard to deal with."

Mrs. Frewin paused awhile, undecided and still defiant. Then her attitude softened; she turned and looked full at the beautiful, kind eyes turned eagerly up to hers, and pressing Lady Molly's tiny hand in both her own she whispered:

"I will take your advice. God bless you."

She was gone, and Lady Molly called Hankin to her side.

"Until we have that confession, Hankin," she said, with the quiet manner she always adopted where matters connected with her work were concerned, "Mum's the word."

"Ay, and after that, too, my lady," replied Hankin, earnestly.

You see, she could do anything she liked with the men, and I, of course, was her slave.

Now we have got the confession, Mrs. Frewin is on the best of terms with Mr. James Hyam, who has behaved very well about the whole thing, and the public has forgotten all about the mystery of the Frewin miniatures.

The Irish-Tweed Coat

1

It all began with the murder of Mr. Andrew Carrthwaite, at Palermo.

He had been found dead in the garden of his villa just outside the town, with a stiletto between his shoulder blades and a piece of rough Irish tweed, obviously torn from his assailant's coat, clutched tightly in his hand.

All that was known of Mr. Carrthwaite over here was that he was a Yorkshireman, owner of some marble works in Sicily, a man who employed a great many hands; and that, unlike most employers of labour over there, he had a perfect horror of the many secret societies and Socialist clubs which abound in that part of the world. He would not become a slave to the ever-growing tyranny of the Mafia and its kindred associations, and therefore he made it a hard and fast rule that no workman employed by him, from the foremost to the meanest hand, should belong to any society, club, or trade union of any sort or kind.

At first, robbery was thought to have been the sole object of the crime, for Mr. Carrthwaite's gold watch, marked with his initials "A. C.," and his chain were missing, but the Sicilian police were soon inclined to the belief that this was merely a blind, and that personal spite and revenge were at the bottom of that dastardly outrage.

One clue, remember, had remained in the possession of the authorities. This was the piece of rough Irish tweed, found in the murdered man's hand.

Within twenty-four hours a dozen witnesses were prepared to swear that that fragment of cloth was part of a coat habitually worn by Mr. Carrthwaite's English overseer, Mr. Cecil Shuttleworth. It appears that this young man had lately, in defiance of the rigid rules prescribed by his employer, joined a local society—semi-social, semi-religious—which came under the ban of the old Yorkshireman's prejudices.

Apparently, there had been several bitter quarrels between Mr. Carrthwaite and young Shuttleworth, culminating in one tempestuous scene, witnessed by the former's servants at his villa; and although these people did not understand the actual words that passed between the two Englishmen, it was pretty clear that they amounted to an ultimatum on the one side and defiance on the other. The dismissal of the overseer followed immediately, and that same evening Mr. Carrthwaite was found murdered in his garden.

Mind you—according to English ideas—the preliminary investigations in that mysterious crime were hurried through in a manner which we should think unfair to the accused. It seemed from the first as if the Sicilian police had wilfully made up their minds that

" He had been found dead in the garden of his villa "

Shuttleworth was guilty. For instance, although so many people were prepared to swear that the young English overseer had often worn a coat of which the piece found in the murdered man's hand was undoubtedly a torn fragment, yet the coat itself was not found among his effects, neither were his late master's watch and chain.

Nevertheless, the young man was arrested within a few hours of the murder, and—after the formalities of the preliminary "instruction"—was duly committed to stand his trial on the capital charge.

It was about this time that I severed my official connection with the Yard. Lady Molly now employed me as her private secretary, and I was working with her one day in the study of our snug little flat in Maida Vale, when our trim servant came in to us with a card and a letter on a salver.

Lady Molly glanced at the card, then handed it across to me. It bore the name: Mr. Jeremiah Shuttleworth.

The letter was from the chief.

"Not much in it," she commented, glancing rapidly at its contents. "The chief only says, 'This is the father of the man who is charged with the Palermo murder. As obstinate as a mule, but you have my permission to do what he wants.' Emily, show the gentleman in," she added.

The next moment a short, thick-set man entered our little study. He had sandy hair and a freckled skin; there was a great look of determination in the square face and a fund of dogged obstinacy in the broad, somewhat heavy jaw. In response to Lady Molly's invitation, he sat down and began with extraordinary abruptness:

"I suppose you know what I have come about—er—miss?" he suggested.

"Well!" she replied, holding up his own card, "I can guess."

"My son, miss—I mean ma'am," he said in a husky voice. "He is innocent. I swear it by the living——"

He checked himself, obviously ashamed of this outburst; then he resumed more calmly.

"Of course, there's the business about the coat, and that coat did belong to my son, but——"

"Well, yes?" asked Lady Molly, for he had paused again, as if waiting to be encouraged in his narrative, "what about that coat?"

"It has been found in London, miss," he replied quietly. "The fiendish brutes who committed the crime thought out this monstrous way of diverting attention from themselves by getting hold of my son's coat and making the actual assassin wear it, in case he was espied in the gloom."

There was silence in the little study for a while. I was amazed, aghast at the suggestion put forward by that rough north-countryman, that sorely stricken father who spoke with curious intensity of language and of feeling. Lady Molly was the first to break the solemn silence.

"What makes you think, Mr. Shuttleworth, that the assassination of Mr. Carrthwaite was the work of a gang of murderers?" she asked.

"I know Sicily," he replied simply. "My boy's mother was a native of Messina. The place is riddled with secret societies, murdering, anarchical clubs: organisations against which Mr. Carrthwaite waged deadly warfare. It is one of these—the Mafia, probably—that decreed that Mr. Carrthwaite should be done away with. They could not do with such a powerful and hard-headed enemy."

"You may be right, Mr. Shuttleworth, but tell me more about the coat."

"Well, that'll be damning proof against the blackguards, anyway. I am on the eve of a second marriage, miss—ma'am," continued the man with seeming irrelevance. "The lady is a widow. Mrs. Tadworth is her name—but her father was an Italian named Badeni, a connection of my first wife's, and that's how I came to know him and his daughter. You know Leather Lane, don't you? It might be in Italy, for Italian's the only language one hears about there. Badeni owned a house in Bread Street, Leather Lane, and let lodgings to his fellow-countrymen there; this business my future wife still carries on. About a week ago two men arrived at the house, father and son, so they said, who wanted a cheap bedroom; all their meals, including breakfast, they would take outside, and would be out, moreover, most of the day.

"It seems that they had often lodged at Badeni's before—the old reprobate no doubt was one of their gang—and when they understood that Mrs. Tadworth was their former friend's daughter they were quite satisfied.

"They gave their name as Piatti, and told Mrs. Tadworth that they came from Turin. But I happened to hear them talking on the stairs, and I knew that they were Sicilians, both of them.

"You may well imagine that just now everything hailing from Sicily is of vital importance to me, and somehow I suspected those two men from the very first. Mrs. Tadworth is quite at one with me in wanting to move heaven and earth to prove the innocence of my boy.

She watched those people for me as a cat would watch a mouse. The older man professed to be very fond of gardening, and presently he obtained Mrs. Tadworth's permission to busy himself in the little strip of barren ground at the back of the house.

"This she told me last night whilst we were having supper together in her little parlour. Somehow, I seemed to get an inspiration like. The Piattis had gone out together as usual for their evening meal. I got a spade and went out into the strip of garden. I worked for about an hour, and then my heart gave one big leap—my spade had met a certain curious, soft resistance—the next moment I was working away with hands and nails, and soon unearthed a coat—*the* coat, miss," he continued, unable now to control his excitement, "with the bit torn out of the back, and in the pocket the watch and chain belonging to the murdered man, for they bear the initials 'A. C.'The fiendish brutes! I knew it—I knew it, and now I can prove the innocence of my boy!"

Again, there was a pause. I was too much absorbed in the palpitating narrative to attempt to breathe a word, and I knew that Lady Molly was placidly waiting until the man had somewhat recovered from his vehement outburst.

"Of course, you can prove your boy's innocence now," she said, smiling encouragingly into his flushed face. "But what have you done with the coat?"

"Left it buried where I found it," he replied more calmly. "They must not suspect that I am on their track."

She nodded approvingly.

"No doubt, then, my chief has told you that the best course to pursue now will be to place the whole matter in the hands of the English police. Our people at Scotland Yard will then immediately communicate with the Sicilian authorities, and in the meanwhile, we can keep the two men in Leather Lane well under surveillance."

"Yes, he told me all that," said Mr. Shuttleworth, quietly.

"Well?"

"And I told him that his 'communicating with the Sicilian police authorities' would result in my boy's trial being summarily concluded, in his being sent to the gallows, whilst every proof of his innocence would be destroyed, or, at any rate, kept back until too late."

"You are mad, Mr. Shuttleworth!" she ejaculated.

"Maybe I am," he "rejoined quietly. "You see, you do not know Sicily, and I do.You do not know its many clubs and bands of assassins, beside whom the so-called Russian Nihilists are simple, blundering children. The Mafia, which is the parent of all such murderous organisations, has members and agents in every town, village, and hamlet in Italy, in every post-office and barracks, in every trade and profession from the highest to the lowest in the land. The Sicilian police force is infested with it, so are the Italian customs. I would not trust either with what means my boy's life and more to me."

"But——"

"The police would suppress the evidence connected with the proofs which I hold. At the frontier the coat, the watch and chain would disappear; of that I am as convinced as that I am a living man "

Lady Molly made no comment. She was meditating. That there was truth in what the man said, no one could deny.

The few details which we had gleaned over here of the hurried investigations, the summary commitment for trial of the accused, the hasty dismissal of all evidence in his favour, proved that, at any rate, the father's anxiety was well founded.

"But, then, what in the world do you propose to do?" said Lady Molly after a while. "Do you want to take the proofs over yourself to your boy's advocate? Is that it?"

"No, that would be no good," he replied simply. "I am known in Sicily. I should be watched, probably murdered, too, and my death would not benefit my boy."

"But what then?"

"My boy's uncle is chief officer of police at Cividale, on the Austro-Italian frontier. I know that I can rely on his devotion. Mrs. Tadworth, whose interest in my boy is almost equal to my own, and whose connection with me cannot possibly be known out there, will take the proofs of my boy's innocence to him. He will know what to do and how to reach my son's advocate safely, which no one else could guarantee to do."

"Well," said Lady Molly, "that being so, what is it that you want us to do in the matter?"

"I want a lady's help, miss—er—ma'am," he replied, "someone who is able, willing, strong, and, if possible, enthusiastic, to accompany Mrs. Tadworth—perhaps in the capacity of a maid—just to avert the usual suspicious glances thrown at a lady travelling alone. Also, the question of foreign languages comes in. The gentleman I saw at Scotland Yard said that if you cared to go, he would give you a fortnight's leave of absence."

"Yes, I'll go!" rejoined Lady Molly, simply.

" ' Well,' said Lady Molly, ' . . . what is it that you
    want us to do in the matter ? ' "

We sat in the study a long while after that—Mr. Shuttleworth, Lady Molly and I—discussing the plans of the exciting journey; for I, too, as you will see, was destined to play my small part in this drama which had the life or death of an innocent man for its *dénouement*.

I don't think I need bore you with an account of our discussion; all, I think, that will interest you is the plan of campaign we finally decided upon.

There seemed to be no doubt that Mr. Shuttleworth had succeeded so far in not arousing the suspicions of the Piattis. Therefore, that night, when they were safely out of the way, Mr. Shuttleworth would once more unearth the coat, and watch and chain, and then bury a coat quite similar in colour and texture in that same hole in the ground; this might perhaps serve to put the miscreants off their guard, if by any chance one of them should busy himself again in the garden.

After that Mrs. Tadworth would hide about her the proofs of young Shuttleworth's innocence and join Lady Molly at our flat in Maida Vale, where she would spend the night preparatory to the two ladies leaving London for abroad, the following morning, by the 9.0 a.m. train from Charing Cross *en route* for Vienna, Budapest, and finally Cividale.

But our scheme was even more comprehensive than that, and herein lay my own little share in it, of which I will tell you presently.

The same evening at half-past nine Mrs. Tadworth arrived at the flat with the coat, and watch and chain, which were to be placed in the hands of Colonel Grassi, the chief police officer at Cividale.

I took a keen look at the lady; you may be sure of that. It was a pretty little face enough, and she herself could not have been much more than seven or eight and twenty, but to me the whole appearance and manner of the woman suggested weakness of character, rather than that devotion on which poor Mr. Shuttleworth so implicitly relied.

I suppose that it was on that account that I felt unaccountably down-hearted and anxious when I bade farewell to my own dear lady—a feeling in which she obviously did not share. Then I began to enact the role which had been assigned to me.

I dressed up in Mrs. Tadworth's clothes—we were about the same height—and putting on her hat and closely fitting veil, I set out for Leather Lane. For as many hours as I could possibly contrive to keep up the deception, I was to impersonate Mrs. Tadworth in her own house.

As I dare say you have guessed by now, that lady was not in affluent circumstances, and the house in a small by-street off Leather Lane
did not boast of a staff of servants. In fact, Mrs. Tadworth did all the
domestic work herself, with the help of a charwoman for a couple of
hours in the mornings.

That charwoman had, in accordance with Lady Molly's plan, been
given a week's wages in lieu of notice. I—as Mrs. Tadworth—would
be supposed the next day to be confined to my room with a cold, and
Emily—our own little maid, a bright girl, who would go through fire
and water for Lady Molly or for me—would represent a new charwoman.

As soon as anything occurred to arouse my suspicions that our
secret had been discovered, I was to wire to Lady Molly at the various
points which she gave me.

Thus, provided with an important and comprehensive part, I duly
installed myself at Bread Street, Leather Lane. Emily—who had been
told just enough of the story, and no more, to make her eager, excited
and satisfied—entered into the spirit of her role as eagerly as I did
myself.

That first night was quite uneventful. The Piattis came home
sometime after eleven and went straight up to their room.

Emily, looking as like a bedraggled charwoman as her trim figure
would allow, was in the hall the next morning when the two men
started off for breakfast. She told me afterwards that the younger one
looked at her very keenly, and asked her why the other servant had
gone. Emily replied with due and proper vagueness, whereupon the
Sicilians said no more and went out together.

That was a long and wearisome day which I spent cooped up in
the tiny, stuffy parlour, ceaselessly watching the tiny patch of ground at
the back, devoured with anxiety, following the travellers in my mind
on their way across Europe.

Towards midday one of the Piattis came home and presently
strolled out into the garden. Evidently the change of servants had
aroused his suspicions, for I could see him feeling about the earth with
his spade and looking up now and again towards the window of the
parlour, whereat I contrived to show him the form of a *pseudo* Mrs.
Tadworth moving about the room.

Mr. Shuttleworth and I were having supper in that same back parlour at about nine o'clock on that memorable evening, when we sud-

denly heard the front door being opened with a latchkey, and then very cautiously shut again.

One of the two men had returned at an hour most unusual for their otherwise very regular habits. The way, too, in which the door had been opened and shut suggested a desire for secrecy and silence. Instinctively I turned off the gas in the parlour, and with a quick gesture pointed to the front room, the door of which stood open, and I whispered hurriedly to Mr. Shuttleworth.

"Speak to him!"

Fortunately, the great aim which he had in view had rendered his perceptions very keen.

He went into the front room, in which the gas, fortunately, was alight at the time, and opening the door which gave thence on to the passage, he said pleasantly:

"Oh, Mr. Piatti! is that you? Can I do anything for you?"

"Ah, yes! zank you," replied the Sicilian, whose voice I could hear was husky and unsteady, "if you would be so kind—I—I feel so fainting and queer tonight—ze warm weazer, I zink. Would you—would you be so kind to fetch me a little—er—ammoniac—er—*sal volatile* you call it, I zink—from ze apothecary? I would go lie on my bed—if you would be so kind——"

"Why, of course I will, Mr. Piatti," said Mr. Shuttleworth, who somehow got an intuition of what I wanted to do, and literally played into my hands. "I'll go at once,"

He went to get his hat from the rack in the hall whilst the Sicilian murmured profuse "Zank you's," and then I heard the front door bang to.

From where I was, I could not see Piatti, but I imagined him standing in the dimly-lighted passage listening to Mr. Shuttleworth's retreating footsteps.

Presently I heard him walking along towards the back door, and soon I perceived something moving about in the little bit of ground beyond. He had gone to get his spade. He meant to unearth the coat and the watch and chain which, for some reason or another, he must have thought were no longer safe in their original hiding-place. Had the gang of murderers heard that the man who frequently visited their landlady was the father of Cecil Shuttleworth over at Palermo?

At that moment I paused neither to speculate nor yet to plan. I ran down to the kitchen, for I no longer wanted to watch Piatti. I knew what he was doing.

I didn't want to frighten Emily, and she had been made to understand all along that she might have to leave the house with me again at any time, at a moment's notice; she and I had kept our small handbag ready packed in the kitchen, whence we could reach the area steps quickly and easily.

Now I quietly beckoned to her that the time had come. She took the bag and followed me. Just as we shut the area gate behind us, we heard the garden door violently slammed. Piatti had got the coat, and by now was examining the pockets in order to find the watch and chain. Within the next ten seconds he would realise that the coat which he held was not the one which he had buried in the garden, and that the real proofs of his guilt—or his complicity in the guilt of another—had disappeared.

We did not wait for those ten seconds, but flew down Bread Street, in the direction of Leather Lane, where I knew Mr. Shuttleworth would be on the lookout for me.

"Yes," I said hurriedly, directly I spied him at the angle of the street; "it's all up. I am off to Budapest by the early Continental tomorrow morning. I shall catch them at the Hungaria. See Emily safely to the flat."

Obviously, there was no time to lose, and before either Mr. Shuttleworth or Emily could make a remark I had left them standing, and had quickly mixed my insignificant personality with the passers-by.

I strolled down Leather Lane quite leisurely; you see, my face was unknown to the Piattis. They had only seen dim outlines of me behind very dirty window-panes.

I did not go to the flat. I knew Mr. Shuttleworth would take care of Emily, so that night I slept at the Grand Hotel, Charing Cross, leaving the next morning by the 9.0 a.m., having booked my berth on the Orient Express as far as Budapest.

3

Well, you know the saying: It is easy to be wise after the event.

Of course, when I saw the older Piatti standing in the hall of the Hotel Hungaria at Budapest I realised that I had been followed from the moment that Emily and I ran out of the house at Bread Street. The son had obviously kept me in view whilst I was still in London, and the father had travelled across Europe, unperceived by me, in the same train as myself, had seen me step into the *fiacre* at Budapest, and heard me tell the smart coachman to drive to the Hungaria.

I made hasty arrangements for my room, and then asked if "Mrs. Carey," from London, was still at the hotel with her maid—for that was the name under which Mrs. Tadworth was to travel—and was answered in the affirmative. "Mrs. Carey" was even then supping in the dining-room, whence the strains of beautiful Hungarian melodies played by Berkes' inimitable band seemed to mock my anxiety.

"Mrs. Carey's maid," they told me, was having her meal in the steward's room.

I tried to prosecute my hasty inquiries as quietly as I could, but Piatti's eyes and sarcastic smile seemed to follow me everywhere, whilst he went about calmly ordering his room and seeing to the disposal of his luggage.

Almost every official at the Hungaria speaks English, and I had no difficulty in finding my way to the steward's room. To my chagrin Lady Molly was not there. Someone told me that no doubt "Mrs. Carey's maid" had gone back to her mistress's room, which they told me was No. 118 on the first floor.

A few precious moments were thus wasted whilst I ran back towards the hall; you know the long, seemingly interminable, corridors and passages of the Hungaria! Fortunately, in one of these I presently beheld my dear lady walking towards me. At sight of her all my anxieties seemed to fall from me like a discarded mantle.

She looked quite serene and placid, but with her own quick perception she at once guessed what had brought me to Budapest.

"They have found out about the coat," she said, quickly drawing me aside into one of the smaller passages, which fortunately at the moment was dark and deserted, "and, of course, he has followed you——"

I nodded affirmatively.

"That Mrs. Tadworth is a vapid, weak-kneed little fool," she said, with angry vehemence. "We ought to be at Cividale by now—and she declared herself too ill and too fatigued to continue the journey. How that poor Shuttleworth could be so blind as to trust her passes belief."

"Mary," she added more calmly, "go down into the hall at once. Watch that idiot of a woman for all you're worth. She is terrified of the Sicilians, and I firmly believe that Piatti can force her to give up the proofs of the crime to him."

"Where are they—the proofs, I mean?" I asked anxiously.

"Locked up in her trunk—she won't entrust them to me. Obstinate little fool."

I had never seen my dear lady so angry; however, she said nothing more then, and presently I took leave of her and worked my way back towards the hall. One glance round the brilliantly-lighted place assured me that neither Piatti nor Mrs. Tadworth was there. I could not tell you what it was that suddenly filled my heart with foreboding.

I ran up to the first floor and reached room No. 118. The outer door was open, and without a moment's hesitation I applied my eye to the keyhole of the inner one.

The room was brilliantly lighted from within, and exactly opposite, but with his back to me, stood Piatti, whilst squatting on a low stool beside him was Mrs. Tadworth.

A trunk stood open close to her hand, and she was obviously busy turning over its contents. My very heart stood still with horror. Was I about to witness—thus powerless to interfere—one of the most hideous acts of cowardly treachery it was possible to conceive?

Something, however, must at that moment have attracted Piatti's attention, for he suddenly turned and strode towards the door. Needless to say, that I beat a hasty retreat.

My one idea was, of course, to find Lady Molly and tell her what I had seen. Unfortunately, the Hungaria is a veritable maze of corridors, stairs and passages, and I did not know the number of her room. At first I did not wish to attract further attention by again asking about "Mrs. Carey's maid" at the office, and my stupid ignorance of foreign languages precluded my talking to the female servants.

I had been up and down the stairs half a dozen times, tired, miserable, and anxious, when at last, in the far distance, I espied my dear lady's graceful silhouette. Eagerly I ran to her, and was promptly admonished for my careless impetuosity.

"Mrs. Tadworth is genuinely frightened," added Lady Molly in response to my look of painful suspense, "but so far she has been able to hoodwink Piatti by opening my trunk before him instead of hers, and telling him that the proofs were not in her own keeping. But she is too stupid to keep that deception up, and, of course, he won't allow himself to be put off a second time. We must start for Cividale as soon as possible. Unfortunately, the earliest train is not till 9.15 tomorrow morning. The danger to that unfortunate young man over at Palermo, brought about by this woman's cowardly idiocy and the father's misguided trust, is already incalculable."

It was, of course, useless for me to express fear now for my dear lady's safety. I smothered my anxiety as best I could, and, full of deadly forebodings, I bade her *anon* a fond goodnight.

Needless to say, that I scarcely slept, and at eight o'clock the next morning I was fully dressed and out of my room.

The first glance down the corridor on which gave No. 118 at once confirmed my worst fears. Unusual bustle reigned there at this early hour. Officials came and went, maids stood about gossiping, and the next moment, to my literally agonised horror, I beheld two *gendarmes*, with an officer, being escorted by the hotel manager to the rooms occupied by Mrs. Tadworth and Lady Molly.

Oh, how I cursed then our British ignorance of foreign tongues. The officials were too busy to bother about me, and the maids only knew that portion of the English language which refers to baths and to hot water. Finally, to my intense relief, I discovered a willing porter, ready and able to give me information in my own tongue of the events which had disturbed the serene quietude of the Hotel Hungaria.

Great heavens! Shall I ever forget what I endured when I grasped the full meaning of what he told me with a placid smile and a shrug of the shoulders!

"The affair is most mysterious," he explained, "not robbery—oh, no! no!—for it is Mrs. Carey who has gone—disappeared! And it is Mrs. Carey's maid who was found, stunned, gagged and unconscious, tied to one of the bedposts in room No. 118."

4

Well, why should I bore you by recounting the agonised suspense, the mortal anxiety, which I endured for all those subsequent weary days which at the time seemed like so many centuries?

My own dear lady, the woman for whom I would have gone through fire and water with a cheerful smile, had been brutally assaulted, almost murdered, so the smiling porter assured me, and my very existence was ignored by the stolid officials, who looked down upon me with a frown of impassive disapproval whilst I entreated, raged and stormed alternately, begging to be allowed to go and nurse the sick lady, who was my own dearest friend, dearer than any child could be to its mother.

Oh, that awful red tapeism that besets one at every turn, paralyses and disheartens one! What I suffered I really could not describe.

But if I was not allowed to see Lady Molly, at least I was able to wreak vengeance upon her cowardly assailants. Mrs. Tadworth, by her disappearance, had tacitly confessed her participation in the outrage, of that I had no doubt, but I was equally certain that she was both too stupid and too weak to commit such a crime unaided.

Piatti was at the bottom of it all. Without a moment's hesitation I laid information against him through the medium of an interpreter. I accused him boldly of being an accessory to the assault for purposes of robbery. Unswervingly I repeated my story of how I had seen him in close conversation the day before with Mrs. Carey, whose real name I declared to be Mrs. Tadworth.

The chief object of the robbery I suggested to be a valuable gold watch and chain, with initials "A. C.," belonging to my friend, who had travelled with Mrs. Carey to Budapest as her companion, not her maid. This was a bold move on my part, and I felt reckless, I can tell you. Fortunately, my story was corroborated by the fact that the floor valet had seen Piatti hanging about the corridor outside No. 118 at an extraordinarily early hour of the morning.

My firm belief was that the wretch had been admitted into the room by that horrid Mrs. Tadworth. He had terrorised her, probably had threatened her life. She had then agreed out of sheer cowardice to deliver to him the proofs of his own guilt in the Palermo murder case, and when Lady Molly, hearing the voices, came out of her own room, Piatti knocked her down lest she should intervene. Mrs. Tadworth thereupon—weak and silly little fool!—was seized with panic, and succeeded, no doubt with his help, in leaving the hotel, and probably Budapest, before the outrage was discovered.

Why Piatti had not done likewise, I could not conjecture. He seems to have gone back quietly to his own room after that; and it was not till an hour later that the chambermaid, surprised at seeing the door of No. 118 slightly ajar, had peeped in, and there was greeted by the awful sight of "the maid," gagged, bound and unconscious.

Well, I gained my wish, and had the satisfaction presently of knowing that Piatti—although, mind you, he emphatically denied my story from beginning to end—had been placed under arrest pending further inquiries.

The British Consul was very kind to me; though I was not allowed to see my dear lady, who had been removed to the hospital. I heard that the Hungarian police were moving heaven and earth to find "Mrs. Carey" and bring her to justice.

Her disappearance told severely against her, and after three days of such intense anxiety as I never wish to live through again, I received a message from the Consulate informing me that "Mrs. Carey" had been arrested at Alsorév, on the Austro-Hungarian frontier, and was even now on her way to Budapest under escort.

You may imagine how I quivered with anxiety and with rage when, on the morning after that welcome news, I was told that "Mrs. Carey" was detained at the *gendarmerie*, and had asked to see Miss Mary Granard from London, at present residing at the Hotel Hungaria.

The impudent wretch! Wanting to see me, indeed! Well, I, too, wanted to see her; the woman whom I despised as a coward and a traitor; who had betrayed the fond and foolish trust of a stricken father; who had dashed the last hopes of an innocent man in danger of his life; and who, finally, had been the cause of an assault that had all but killed, perhaps, the woman I loved best in the world.

I felt like the embodiment of hate and contempt. I loathed the woman, and I hied me in a *fiacre* to the *gendarmerie*, escorted by one of the clerks from the Consulate, simply thirsting with the desire to tell an ignoble female exactly what I thought of her.

I had to wait some two or three minutes in the bare, barrack-like room of the *gendarmerie*; then the door opened, there was a rustle of silk, followed by the sound of measured footsteps of soldiery, and the next moment Lady Molly, serene and placid and, as usual, exquisitely dressed, stood smiling before me.

"You have got me into this plight, Mary," she said, with her merry laugh; "you'll have to get me out of it again."

"But—I don't understand," was all that I could gasp.

"It is very simple, and I'll explain it all fully when we are on our way home to Maida Vale," she said. "For the moment you and Mrs. Tadworth will have to make sundry affidavits that I did not assault my maid nor rob her of a watch and chain. The British Consul will help you, and it is only a question of days, and in the meanwhile, I may tell you that Budapest prison life is quite interesting, and not so uncomfortable as one would imagine."

Of course, the moment she spoke I got an intuition of what had really occurred, and I can assure you that I was heartily ashamed that I should ever have doubted Lady Molly's cleverness in carrying through successfully so important, so vital a business as the righting of an innocent man.

Mrs. Tadworth was pusillanimous and stupid. At Budapest she cried a halt, for she really felt unstrung and ill after the hurried journey, the change of air and food, and what not. Lady Molly, however, had no difficulty in persuading her that during the enforced stay of twenty-four hours at the Hungaria their two roles should be reversed. Lady Molly would be "Mrs. Carey," coming from England, whilst Mrs. Tadworth would be the maid.

My dear lady—not thinking at the time that my knowledge of this fact would be of any importance to her own plans—had not mentioned it to me during the brief interview which I had with her. Then, when Piatti arrived upon the scene, Mrs. Tadworth got into a real panic. Fortunately, she had the good sense, or the cowardice, then and there to entrust the coat and watch and chain to Lady Molly, and when Piatti followed her into her room she was able to show him that the proofs were not then in her possession. This was the scene which I had witnessed through the keyhole.

But, of course, the Sicilian would return to the charge, and equally, of course, Mrs. Tadworth would sacrifice the Shuttleworths, father and son, to save her own skin. Lady Molly knew that. She is strong, active and determined; she had a brief hand-to-hand struggle with Mrs. Tadworth that night, and finally succeeded in tying her, half unconscious, to the bedpost, thus assuring herself that for at least twenty-four hours that vapid little fool would be unable to either act for herself or to betray my dear, intrepid lady's plans.

When, the following morning, Piatti opened the door of No. 118, which had purposely been left on the latch, he was greeted with the sight of Mrs. Tadworth pinioned and half dead with fear, whilst the valuable proofs of his own guilt and young Shuttleworth's innocence had completely disappeared.

For remember that Lady Molly's face was not known to him or to his gang, and she had caught the first train to Cividale even whilst Piatti still believed that he held that silly Mrs. Tadworth in the hollow of his hand. I may as well tell you here that she reached the frontier safely, and was quite sharp enough to seek out Colonel Grassi and, with the necessary words of explanation, to hand over to him the proofs of young Shuttleworth's innocence.

My action in the matter helped her. At the hotel she was supposed to be the mistress and Mrs. Tadworth the maid, and everyone was told that "Mrs. Carey's maid" had been assaulted, and removed to the hospital. But I denounced Piatti then and there, thinking he had attacked my dear lady, and I got him put under lock and key so quickly that he had not the time to communicate with his associates.

Thanks to Colonel Grassi's exertions, young Shuttleworth was acquitted of the charge of murder; but I may as well tell you here that neither Piatti nor his son, nor any of that gang, were arrested for the crime. The proofs of their guilt—the Irish-tweed coat and the murdered man's watch and chain—were most mysteriously suppressed, after young Shuttleworth's advocate had obtained the verdict of "not guilty" for him.

Such is the Sicilian police. Mr. Shuttleworth, senior, evidently knew what he was talking about.

Of course, we had no difficulty in obtaining Lady Molly's release. The British Consul saw to that. But in Budapest they still call the assault on "Mrs. Carey" at the Hotel Hungaria a mystery, for she exonerated Lady Molly fully, but she refused to accuse Piatti. She was afraid of him, of course, and so they had to set him free.

I wonder where he is now, the wicked old wretch!

The Fordwych Castle Mystery

1

Can you wonder that, when some of the ablest of our fellows at the Yard were at their wits' ends to know what to do, the chief instinctively turned to Lady Molly?

Surely the Fordwych Castle Mystery, as it was universally called, was a case which more than any other required feminine tact, intuition, and all those qualities of which my dear lady possessed more than her usual share.

With the exception of Mr. McKinley, the lawyer, and young Jack d'Alboukirk, there were only women connected with the case.

If you have studied Debrett at all, you know as well as I do that the peerage is one of those old English ones which date back some six hundred years, and that the present Lady d'Alboukirk is a baroness in her own right, the title and estates descending to heirs-general.

If you have perused that same interesting volume carefully, you will also have discovered that the late Lord d'Alboukirk had two daughters, the eldest, Clementina Cecilia—the present Baroness, who succeeded him—the other, Margaret Florence, who married in 1884 Jean Laurent Duplessis, a Frenchman whom Debrett vaguely describes as "of Pondicherry, India," and of whom she had issue two daughters, Henriette Marie, heir now to the ancient barony of d'Alboukirk of Fordwych, and Joan, born two years later.

There seems to have been some mystery or romance attached to this marriage of the Honourable Margaret Florence d'Alboukirk to the dashing young officer of the Foreign Legion. Old Lord d'Alboukirk at the time was British Ambassador in Paris, and he seems to have had grave objections to the union, but Miss Margaret, openly flouting her father's displeasure, and throwing prudence to the winds, ran away from home one fine day with Captain Duplessis, and from Pondicherry wrote a curt letter to her relatives telling them of her marriage with the man she loved best in all the world.

Old Lord d'Alboukirk never got over his daughter's wilfulness. She had been his favourite, it appears, and her secret marriage and deceit practically broke his heart. He was kind to her, however, to the end, and when the first baby girl was born and the young pair seemed to be in straitened circumstances, he made them an allowance until the day of his daughter's death, which occurred three years after her elopement, on the birth of her second child.

When, on the death of her father, the Honourable Clementina Cecilia came into the title and fortune, she seemed to have thought it her duty to take some interest in her late sister's eldest child, who, failing her own marriage, and issue, was heir to the barony of d'Alboukirk. Thus, it was that Miss Henriette Marie Duplessis came, with her father's consent, to live with her aunt at Fordwych Castle. Debrett will tell you, moreover, that in 1901 she assumed the name of d'Alboukirk, in lieu of her own, by royal licence. Failing her, the title and estate would devolve firstly on her sister Joan, and subsequently on a fairly distant cousin, Captain John d'Alboukirk, at present a young officer in the Guards.

According to her servants, the present Baroness d'Alboukirk is very self-willed, but otherwise neither more nor less eccentric than any north-country old maid would be who had such an exceptional position to keep up in the social world. The one soft trait in her otherwise not very lovable character is her great affection for her late sister's child. Miss Henriette Duplessis d'Alboukirk has inherited from her French father dark eyes and hair and a somewhat swarthy complexion, but no doubt it is from her English ancestry that she has derived a somewhat masculine frame and a very great fondness for all outdoor pursuits. She is very athletic, knows how to fence and to box, rides to hounds, and is a remarkably good shot.

From all accounts, the first hint of trouble in that gorgeous home was coincident with the arrival at Fordwych of a young, very pretty girl visitor, who was attended by her maid, a half-caste woman, dark-complexioned and surly of temper, but obviously of dog-like devotion towards her young mistress. This visit seems to have come as a surprise to the entire household at Fordwych Castle, her ladyship having said nothing about it until the very morning that the guests were expected.

She then briefly ordered one of the housemaids to get a bedroom ready for a young lady, and to put up a small camp-bedstead in an adjoining dressing-room. Even Miss Henriette seems to have been taken by surprise at the announcement of this visit, for, according to Jane Taylor, the housemaid in question, there was a violent word-passage between the old lady and her niece, the latter winding up an excited speech with the words:

"At any rate, aunt, there won't be room for both of us in this house!" After which she flounced out of the room, banging the door behind her.

Very soon the household was made to understand that the newcomer was none other than Miss Joan Duplessis, Miss Henriette's younger sister. It appears that Captain Duplessis had recently died in Pondicherry, and that the young girl then wrote to her aunt, Lady d'Alboukirk, claiming her help and protection, which the old lady naturally considered it her duty to extend to her.

It appears that Miss Joan was very unlike her sister, as she was *petite* and fair, more English-looking than foreign, and had pretty, dainty ways which soon endeared her to the household. The devotion existing between her and the half-caste woman she had brought from India was, moreover, unique.

It seems, however, that from the moment these newcomers came into the house, dissensions, often degenerating into violent quarrels, became the order of the day. Henriette seemed to have taken a strong dislike to her younger sister, and most particularly to the latter's dark attendant, who was vaguely known in the house as Roonah.

That some events of serious import were looming ahead, the servants at Fordwych were pretty sure. The butler and footmen at dinner heard scraps of conversation which sounded very ominous. There was talk of "lawyers," of "proofs," of "marriage and birth certificates," quickly suppressed when the servants happened to be about. Her ladyship looked terribly anxious and worried, and she and Miss Henriette spent long hours closeted together in a small *boudoir*, whence proceeded ominous sounds of heartrending weeping on her ladyship's part, and angry and violent words from Miss Henriette.

Mr. McKinley, the eminent lawyer from London, came down two or three times to Fordwych, and held long conversations with her ladyship, after which the latter's eyes were very swollen and red. The household thought it more than strange that Roonah, the Indian servant, was almost invariably present at these interviews between Mr. McKinley, her ladyship, and Miss Joan. Otherwise, the woman kept herself very much aloof; she spoke very little, hardly took any notice of anyone save of her ladyship and of her young mistress, and the outbursts of Miss Henriette's temper seemed to leave her quite unmoved.

A strange fact was that she had taken a sudden and great fancy for frequenting a small Roman Catholic convent chapel which was distant about half a mile from the Castle, and presently it was understood that Roonah, who had been a Parsee, had been converted by the attendant priest to the Roman Catholic faith.

All this happened, mind you, within the last two or three months; in fact, Miss Joan had been in the Castle exactly twelve weeks when Captain Jack d'Alboukirk came to pay his cousin one of his periodical visits. From the first he seems to have taken a great fancy to his cousin Joan, and soon everyone noticed that this fancy was rapidly ripening into love. It was equally certain that from that moment dissensions between the two sisters became more frequent and more violent; the generally accepted opinion being that Miss Henriette was jealous of Joan, whilst Lady d'Alboukirk herself, for some unexplainable reason, seems to have regarded this love-making with marked disfavour.

Then came the tragedy.

One morning Joan ran downstairs, pale, and trembling from head to foot, moaning and sobbing as she ran:

"Roonah!—my poor old Roonah!—I knew it—I knew it!"

Captain Jack happened to meet her at the foot of the stairs. He pressed her with questions, but the girl was unable to speak. She merely pointed mutely to the floor above. The young man, genuinely alarmed, ran quickly upstairs; he threw open the door leading to Roonah's room, and there, to his horror, he saw the unfortunate woman lying across the small camp-bedstead, with a handkerchief over her nose and mouth, and her throat cut.

The sight was horrible.

Poor Roonah was obviously dead.

Without losing his presence of mind, Captain Jack quietly shut the door again, after urgently begging Joan to compose herself, and to try to keep up, at any rate until the local doctor could be sent for and the terrible news gently broken to Lady d'Alboukirk.

The doctor, hastily summoned, arrived some twenty minutes later. He could but confirm Joan's and Captain Jack's fears. Roonah was indeed dead—in fact, she had been dead some hours.

2

From the very first, mind you, the public took a more than usually keen interest in this mysterious occurrence. The evening papers on the very day of the murder were ablaze with flaming headlines such as:

THE TRAGEDY AT FORDWYCH CASTLE
MYSTERIOUS MURDER OF AN IMPORTANT WITNESS
GRAVE CHARGES AGAINST PERSONS IN HIGH LIFE

. . .and so forth.

As time went on, the mystery deepened more and more, and I suppose Lady Molly must have had an inkling that sooner or later the chief would have to rely on her help and advice, for she sent me down to attend the inquest, and gave me strict orders to keep eyes and ears open for every detail in connection with the crime—however trivial it might seem. She herself remained in town, awaiting a summons from the chief.

The inquest was held in the dining-room of Fordwych Castle, and the noble hall was crowded to its utmost when the coroner and jury finally took their seats, after having viewed the body of the poor murdered woman upstairs.

The scene was dramatic enough to please any novelist, and an awed hush descended over the crowd when, just before the proceedings began, a door was thrown open, and in walked—stiff and erect—the Baroness d'Alboukirk, escorted by her niece, Miss Henriette, and closely followed by her cousin, Captain Jack, of the Guards.

The old lady's face was as indifferent and haughty as usual, and so was that of her athletic niece. Captain Jack, on the other hand, looked troubled and flushed. Everyone noted that, directly he entered the room, his eyes sought a small, dark figure that sat silent and immovable beside the portly figure of the great lawyer, Mr. Hubert McKinley. This was Miss Joan Duplessis, in a plain black stuff gown, her young face pale and tear-stained.

Dr. Walker, the local practitioner, was, of course, the first witness called. His evidence was purely medical. He deposed to having made an examination of the body, and stated that he found that a handkerchief saturated with chloroform had been pressed to the woman's nostrils, probably while she was asleep, her throat having subsequently been cut with a sharp knife; death must have been instantaneous, as the poor thing did not appear to have struggled at all.

In answer to a question from the coroner, the doctor said that no great force or violence would be required for the gruesome deed, since the victim was undeniably unconscious when it was done. At the same time, it argued unusual coolness and determination.

The handkerchief was produced, also the knife. The former was a bright-coloured one, stated to be the property of the deceased. The latter was a foreign, old-fashioned hunting-knife, one of a panoply of small arms and other weapons which adorned a corner of the hall. It had been found by Detective Elliott in a clump of gorse on the adjoining golf links. There could be no question that it had been used by the murderer for his fell purpose, since at the time it was found it still bore traces of blood.

Captain Jack was the next witness called. He had very little to say, as he merely saw the body from across the room, and immediately closed the door again and, having begged his cousin to compose herself, called his own valet and sent him off for the doctor.

Some of the staff of Fordwych Castle were called, all of whom testified to the Indian woman's curious taciturnity, which left her quite isolated among her fellow-servants. Miss Henriette's maid, however, Jane Partlett, had one or two more interesting facts to record. She seems to have been more intimate with the deceased woman than anyone else, and on one occasion, at least, had quite a confidential talk with her.

"She talked chiefly about her mistress," said Jane, in answer to a question from the coroner, "to whom she was most devoted. She told me that she loved her so, she would readily die for her. Of course, I thought that silly like, and just mad, foreign talk, but Roonah was very angry when I laughed at her, and then she undid her dress in front, and showed me some papers which were sown in the lining of her dress. 'All these papers my little missee's fortune,' she said to me. 'Roonah guard these with her life. Someone must kill Roonah before taking them from her!'

"This was about six weeks ago," continued Jane, whilst a strange feeling of awe seemed to descend upon all those present whilst the girl spoke. "Lately she became much more silent, and, on my once referring to the papers, she turned on me savage like and told me to hold my tongue."

Asked if she had mentioned the incident of the papers to anyone, Jane replied in the negative.

"Except to Miss Henriette, of course," she added, after a slight moment of hesitation.

Throughout all these preliminary examinations Lady d'Alboukirk, sitting between her cousin Captain Jack and her niece Henriette, had remained quite silent in an erect attitude expressive of haughty indifference. Henriette, on the other hand, looked distinctly bored. Once or twice, she had yawned audibly, which caused quite a feeling of anger against her among the spectators. Such callousness in the midst of so mysterious a tragedy, and when her own sister was obviously in such deep sorrow, impressed everyone very unfavourably. It was well known that the young lady had had a fencing lesson just before the inquest in the room immediately below that where Roonah lay dead, and that within an hour of the discovery of the tragedy she was calmly playing golf.

Then Miss Joan Duplessis was called.

When the young girl stepped forward there was that awed hush in the room which usually falls upon an attentive audience when the curtain is about to rise on the crucial act of a dramatic play. But she was calm and self-possessed, and wonderfully pathetic-looking in her deep black and with the obvious lines of sorrow which the sad death of a faithful friend had traced on her young face.

In answer to the coroner, she gave her name as Joan Clarissa Duplessis, and briefly stated that until the day of her servant's death she had been a resident at Fordwych Castle, but that since then she had left that temporary home, and had taken up her abode at the d'Alboukirk Arms, a quiet little hostelry on the outskirts of the town.

There was a distinct feeling of astonishment on the part of those who were not aware of this fact, and then the coroner said kindly:

"You were born, I think, in Pondicherry, in India, and are the younger daughter of Captain and Mrs. Duplessis, who was own sister to her ladyship?"

"I was born in Pondicherry," replied the young girl, quietly, "and I am the only legitimate child of the late Captain and Mrs. Duplessis, own sister to her ladyship."

A wave of sensation, quickly suppressed by the coroner, went through the crowd at these words. The emphasis which the witness had put on the word "legitimate" could not be mistaken, and everyone felt that here must lie the clue to the, so far impenetrable, mystery of the Indian woman's death.

All eyes were now turned on old Lady d'Alboukirk and on her

niece Henriette, but the two ladies were carrying on a whispered conversation together, and had apparently ceased to take any further interest in the proceedings.

"The deceased was your confidential maid, was she not?" asked the coroner, after a slight pause.

"Yes."

"She came over to England with you recently?"

"Yes; she had to accompany me in order to help me to make good my claim to being my late mother's only legitimate child, and therefore the heir to the barony of d'Alboukirk."

Her voice had trembled a little as she said this, but now, as breathless silence reigned in the room, she seemed to make a visible effort to control herself, and, replying to the coroner's question, she gave a clear and satisfactory account of her terrible discovery of her faithful servant's death. Her evidence had lasted about a quarter of an hour or so, when suddenly the coroner put the momentous question to her: "Do you know anything about the papers which the deceased woman carried about her person, and reference to which has already been made?"

"Yes," she replied quietly; "they were the proofs relating to my claim. My father, Captain Duplessis, had in early youth, and before he met my mother, contracted a secret union with a half-caste woman, who was Roonah's own sister. Being tired of her, he chose to repudiate her—she had no children—but the legality of the marriage was never for a moment in question. After that, he married my mother, and his first wife subsequently died, chiefly of a broken heart; but her death only occurred two months *after* the birth of my sister Henriette.

"My father, I think, had been led to believe that his first wife had died some two years previously, and he was no doubt very much shocked when he realised what a grievous wrong he had done our mother. In order to mend matters somewhat, he and she went through a new form of marriage—a legal one this time—and my father paid a lot of money to Roonah's relatives to have the matter hushed up. Less than a year after this second—and only legal—marriage, I was born and my mother died."

"Then these papers of which so much has been said—what did they consist of?"

"There were the marriage certificates of my father's first wife— and two sworn statements as to her death, two months *after* the birth of my sister Henriette; one by Dr. Rénaud, who was at the time a well-known medical man in Pondicherry, and the other by Roonah herself, who had held her dying sister in her arms. Dr. Rénaud is dead, and now Roonah has been murdered, and all the proofs have gone with her——"

Her voice broke in a passion of sobs, which, with manifest self-control, she quickly suppressed. In that crowded court you could have heard a pin drop, so great was the tension of intense excitement and attention.

"Then those papers remained in your maid's possession? Why was that?" asked the coroner.

"I did not dare to carry the papers about with me," said the witness, while a curious look of terror crept into her young face as she looked across at her aunt and sister. "Roonah would not part with them. She carried them in the lining of her dress, and at night they were all under her pillow. After her—her death, and when Dr. Walker had left, I thought it my duty to take possession of the papers which meant my whole future to me, and which I desired then to place in Mr. McKinley's charge. But though I carefully searched the bed and all the clothing by my poor Roonah's side, I did not find the papers. They were gone."

I won't attempt to describe to you the sensation caused by the deposition of this witness. All eyes wandered from her pale young face to that of her sister, who sat almost opposite to her, shrugging her athletic shoulders and gazing at the pathetic young figure before her with callous and haughty indifference.

"Now, putting aside the question of the papers for the moment," said the coroner, after a pause, "do you happen to know anything of your late servant's private life? Had she an enemy, or perhaps a lover?"

"No," replied the girl; "Roonah's whole life was centred in me and in my claim. I had often begged her to place our papers in Mr. McKinley's charge, but she would trust no one. I wish she had obeyed me," here moaned the poor girl involuntarily, "and I should not have lost what means my whole future to me, and the being who loved me best in all the world would not have been so foully murdered."

Of course, it was terrible to see this young girl thus instinctively, and surely unintentionally, proffering so awful an accusation against those who stood so near to her. That the whole case had become hopelessly involved and mysterious, nobody could deny. Can you imagine the mental picture formed in the mind of all present by the story, so pathetically told, of this girl who had come over to England in order to make good her claim which she felt to be just, and who, in one fell swoop, saw that claim rendered very difficult to prove through the dastardly murder of her principal witness?

That the claim was seriously jeopardised by the death of Roonah and the disappearance of the papers, was made very clear, mind you, through the statements of Mr. McKinley, the lawyer. He could not say very much, of course, and his statements could never have been taken as actual proof, because Roonah and Joan had never fully trusted him and had never actually placed the proofs of the claim in his hands.

He certainly had seen the marriage certificate of Captain Duplessis's first wife, and a copy of this, as he very properly stated, could easily be obtained. The woman seems to have died during the great cholera epidemic of 1881, when, owing to the great number of deaths which occurred, the deceit and concealment practised by the natives at Pondicherry, and the supineness of the French Government, death certificates were very casually and often incorrectly made out.

Roonah had come over to England ready to swear that her sister had died in her arms two months after the birth of Captain Duplessis's eldest child, and there was the sworn testimony of Dr. Rénaud, since dead. These affidavits Mr. McKinley had seen and read.

Against that, the only proof which now remained of the justice of Joan Duplessis's claim was the fact that her mother and father went through a second form of marriage sometime *after* the birth of their first child, Henriette. This fact was not denied, and, of course, it could be easily proved, if necessary, but even then, it would in no way be conclusive. It implied the presence of a doubt in Captain Duplessis's mind, a doubt which the second marriage ceremony may have served to set at rest; but it in no way established the illegitimacy of his eldest daughter.

In fact, the more Mr. McKinley spoke, the more convinced did everyone become that the theft of the papers had everything to do with the murder of the unfortunate Roonah. She would not part with the proofs which meant her mistress's fortune, and she paid for her devotion with her life.

Several more witnesses were called after that. The servants were closely questioned, the doctor was recalled, but, in spite of long and arduous efforts, the coroner and jury could not bring a single real fact to light beyond those already stated.

The Indian woman had been murdered!

The papers which she always carried about her body had disappeared.

Beyond that, nothing! An impenetrable wall of silence and mystery!

The butler at Fordwych Castle had certainly missed the knife with which Roonah had been killed from its accustomed place on the morning after the murder had been committed, but not before, and the mystery further gained in intensity from the fact that the only purchase of chloroform in the district had been traced to the murdered woman herself.

She had gone down to the local chemist one day some two or three weeks previously, and shown him a prescription for cleansing the hair which required some chloroform in it. He gave her a very small quantity in a tiny bottle, which was subsequently found empty on her own dressing-table. No one at Fordwych Castle could swear to having heard any unaccustomed noise during that memorable night. Even Joan, who slept in the room adjoining that where the unfortunate Roonah lay, said she had heard nothing unusual. But then, the door of communication between the two rooms was shut, and the murderer had been quick and silent.

Thus, this extraordinary inquest drew to a close, leaving in its train an air of dark suspicion and of unexplainable horror.

The jury returned a verdict of "Wilful murder against some person or persons unknown," and the next moment Lady d'Alboukirk rose, and, leaning on her niece's arm, quietly walked out of the room.

3

Two of our best men from the Yard, Pegram and Elliott, were left in charge of the case. They remained at Fordwych (the little town close by), as did Miss Joan, who had taken up her permanent abode at the d'Alboukirk Arms, whilst I returned to town immediately after the inquest. Captain Jack had rejoined his regiment, and apparently the ladies of the Castle had resumed their quiet, luxurious life just the same as heretofore. The old lady led her own somewhat isolated, semi-regal life; Miss Henriette fenced and boxed, played hockey and golf, and over the fine castle and its haughty inmates there hovered like an ugly bird of prey the threatening presence of a nameless suspicion.

The two ladies might choose to flout public opinion, but public opinion was dead against them. No one dared formulate a charge, but everyone remembered that Miss Henriette had, on the very morning of the murder, been playing golf in the field where the knife was discovered, and that if Miss Joan Duplessis ever failed to make good her claim to the Barony of d'Alboukirk, Miss Henriette would remain in undisputed possession. So now, when the ladies drove past in the village street, no one doffed a cap to salute them, and when at church the parson read out the sixth commandment, "Thou shalt do no murder," all eyes gazed with fearsome awe at the old Baroness and her niece.

Splendid isolation reigned at Fordwych Castle. The daily papers grew more and more sarcastic at the expense of the Scotland Yard authorities, and the public more and more impatient.

Then it was that the chief grew desperate and sent for Lady Molly, the result of the interview being that I once more made the journey down to Fordwych, but this time in the company of my dear lady, who had received *carte blanche* from headquarters to do whatever she thought right in the investigation of the mysterious crime.

She and I arrived at Fordwych at 8.0 p.m., after the usual long wait at Newcastle. We put up at the d'Alboukirk Arms, and, over a hasty and very bad supper, Lady Molly allowed me a brief insight into her plans.

"I can see every detail of that murder, Mary," she said earnestly, "just as if I had lived at the castle all the time. I know exactly where our fellows are wrong, and why they cannot get on. But, although the chief has given me a free hand, what I am going to do is so irregular that if I fail, I shall probably get my immediate *congé*, whilst some of the disgrace is bound to stick to you. It is not too late—you may yet draw back, and leave me to act alone."

I looked her straight in the face. Her dark eyes were gleaming; there was the power of second sight in them, or of marvellous intuition of "men and things."

"I'll follow your lead, my Lady Molly," I said quietly.

"Then go to bed now," she replied, with that strange transition of manner which to me was so attractive and to everyone else so unaccountable.

In spite of my protest, she refused to listen to any more talk or to answer any more questions, and, perforce, I had to go to my room. The next morning, I saw her graceful figure, immaculately dressed in a perfect tailor-made gown, standing beside my bed at a very early hour.

"Why, what is the time?" I ejaculated, suddenly wide awake.

"Too early for you to get up," she replied quietly. "I am going to early Mass at the Roman Catholic convent close by."

"To Mass at the Roman Catholic convent?"

"Yes. Don't repeat all my words, Mary; it is silly, and wastes time. I have introduced myself in the neighbourhood as the American, Mrs. Silas A. Ogden, whose motor has broken down and is being repaired at Newcastle, while I, its owner, amuse myself by viewing the beauties of the neighbourhood. Being a Roman Catholic, I go to Mass first, and, having met Lady d'Alboukirk once in London, I go to pay her a respectful visit afterwards. When I come back, we will have breakfast together. You might try in the meantime to scrape up an acquaintance with Miss Joan Duplessis, who is still staying here, and ask her to join us at breakfast."

She was gone before I could make another remark, and I could but obey her instantly to the letter.

An hour later I saw Miss Joan Duplessis strolling in the hotel garden. It was not difficult to pass the time of day with the young girl, who seemed quite to brighten up at having someone to talk to. We spoke of the weather and so forth, and I steadily avoided the topic of the Fordwych Castle tragedy until the return of Lady Molly at about ten o'clock. She came back looking just as smart, just as self-possessed, as when she had started three hours earlier. Only I, who knew her so well, noted the glitter of triumph in her eyes, and knew that she had not failed. She was accompanied by Pegram, who, however, immediately left her side and went straight into the hotel, whilst she joined us in the garden, and, after a few graceful words, introduced herself to Miss Joan Duplessis and asked her to join us in the coffee-room upstairs.

The room was empty and we sat down to table, I quivering with excitement and awaiting events. Through the open window I saw Elliott walking rapidly down the village street. Presently the waitress went off, and I being too excited to eat or to speak, Lady Molly carried on a running conversation with Miss Joan, asking her about her life in India and her father, Captain Duplessis. Joan admitted that she had always been her father's favourite.

"He never liked Henriette, somehow," she explained.

Lady Molly asked her when she had first known Roonah.

"She came to the house when my mother died," replied Joan, "and she had charge of me as a baby." At Pondicherry no one had thought it strange that she came as a servant into an officer's house where her own sister had reigned as mistress. Pondicherry is a French Settlement, and manners and customs there are often very peculiar.

I ventured to ask her what were her future plans.

"Well," she said, with a great touch of sadness, "I can, of course, do nothing whilst my aunt is alive. I cannot force her to let me live at Fordwych or to acknowledge me as her heir. After her death, if my sister does assume the title and fortune of d'Alboukirk," she added, whilst suddenly a strange look of vengefulness—almost of hatred and cruelty—marred the child-like expression of her face, "then I shall revive the story of the tragedy of Roonah's death, and I hope that public opinion—"

She paused here in her speech, and I, who had been gazing out of the window, turned my eyes on her. She was ashy-pale, staring straight before her; her hands dropped the knife and fork which she had held. Then I saw that Pegram had come into the room, that he had come up to the table and placed a packet of papers in Lady Molly's hand.

I saw it all as in a flash!

There was a loud cry of despair like an animal at bay, a shrill cry, followed by a deep one from Pegram of "No, you don't," and before anyone could prevent her, Joan's graceful young figure stood outlined for a short moment at the open window.

The next moment she had disappeared into the depth below, and we heard a dull thud which nearly froze the blood in my veins.

Pegram ran out of the room, but Lady Molly sat quite still.

"I have succeeded in clearing the innocent," she said quietly; "but the guilty has meted out to herself her own punishment."

"Then it was she?" I murmured, horror-struck.

"Yes. I suspected it from the first," replied Lady Molly calmly. "It was this conversion of Roonah to Roman Catholicism and her consequent change of manner which gave me the first clue."

"But why—why?" I muttered.

"A simple reason, Mary," she rejoined, tapping the packet of papers with her delicate hand; and, breaking open the string that held the letters, she laid them out upon the table. "The whole thing was a fraud from beginning to end. The woman's marriage certificate was all right, of course, but I mistrusted the genuineness of the other papers from the moment that I heard that Roonah would not part with them and would not allow Mr. McKinley to have charge of them. I am sure that the idea at first was merely one of blackmail. The papers were only to be the means of extorting money from the old lady, and there was no thought of taking them into court.

"Roonah's part was, of course, the important thing in the whole case, since she was here prepared to swear to the actual date of the first Madame Duplessis's death. The initiative, of course, may have come

" She was ashy-pale, staring straight before her "

either from Joan or from Captain Duplessis himself, out of hatred for the family who would have nothing to do with him and his favourite younger daughter. That, of course, we shall never know. At first Roonah was a Parsee, with a doglike devotion to the girl whom she had nursed as a baby, and who no doubt had drilled her well into the part she was to play. But presently she became a Roman Catholic—an ardent convert, remember, with all a Roman Catholic's fear of hell-fire.

"I went to the convent this morning. I heard the priest's sermon there, and I realised what an influence his eloquence must have had over poor, ignorant, superstitious Roonah. She was still ready to die for her young mistress, but she was no longer prepared to swear to a lie for her sake. After Mass I called at Fordwych Castle. I explained my position to old Lady d'Alboukirk, who took me into the room where Roonah had slept and died. There I found two things," continued Lady Molly, as she opened the elegant reticule which still hung upon her arm, and placed a big key and a prayerbook before me.

"The key I found in a drawer of an old cupboard in the dressing-room where Roonah slept, with all sorts of odds and ends belonging to the unfortunate woman, and going to the door which led into what had been Joan's bedroom, I found that it was locked, and that this key fitted into the lock. Roonah had locked that door herself on her own side—*she was afraid of her mistress.* I knew now that I was right in my surmise. The prayer-book is a Roman Catholic one. It is heavily thumb-marked there, where false oaths and lying are denounced as being deadly sins for which hell-fire would be the punishment. Roonah, terrorised by fear of the supernatural, a new convert to the faith, was afraid of committing a deadly sin.

"Who knows what passed between the two women, both of whom have come to so violent and terrible an end? Who can tell what prayers, tears, persuasions Joan Duplessis employed from the time she realised that Roonah did not mean to swear to the lie which would have brought her mistress wealth and glamour until the awful day when she finally understood that Roonah would no longer even hold her tongue, and devised a terrible means of silencing her for ever?

"With this certainty before me, I ventured on my big *coup*. I was so sure, you see. I kept Joan talking in here whilst I sent Pegram to her room with orders to break open the locks of her handbag and dressing-case. There!—I told you that if I was wrong I would probably be dismissed the force for irregularity, as of course I had no right to do that; but if Pegram found the papers there where I felt sure they would

75

be, we could bring the murderer to justice. I know my own sex pretty well, don't I, Mary? I knew that Joan Duplessis had not destroyed— never would destroy—those papers."

Even as Lady Molly spoke, we could hear heavy tramping outside the passage. I ran to the door, and there was met by Pegram.

"She is quite dead, miss," he said. "It was a drop of forty feet, and a stone pavement down below."

The guilty had indeed meted out her own punishment to herself!

Lady d'Alboukirk sent Lady Molly a cheque for £5,000 the day the whole affair was made known to the public.

I think you will say that it had been well earned. With her own dainty hands my dear lady had lifted the veil which hung over the tragedy of Fordwych Castle, and with the finding of the papers in Joan Duplessis's dressing-bag, and the unfortunate girl's suicide, the murder of the Indian woman was no longer a mystery.

A Day's Folly

1

I don't think that anyone ever knew that the real elucidation of the extraordinary mystery known to the newspaper-reading public as the "Somersetshire Outrage" was evolved in my own dear lady's quick, intuitive brain.

As a matter of fact, to this day—as far as the public is concerned— the Somersetshire outrage never was properly explained; and it is a very usual thing for those busybodies who are so fond of criticising the police to point to that case as an instance of remarkable incompetence on the part of our detective department.

A young woman named Jane Turner, a visitor at Weston-Super-Mare, had been discovered one afternoon in a helpless condition, bound and gagged, and suffering from terror and inanition, in the bedroom which she occupied in a well-known apartment-house of that town. The police had been immediately sent for, and as soon as Miss Turner had recovered, she gave what explanation she could of the mysterious occurrence.

She was employed in one of the large drapery shops in Bristol, and was spending her annual holiday at Weston-Super-Mare. Her father was the local butcher at Banwell—a village distant about four miles from Weston—and it appears that somewhere near one o'clock in the afternoon of Friday, the 3rd of September, she was busy in her bedroom putting a few things together in a handbag, preparatory to

" ' I sent Pegram to her room with orders to break open the
locks of her hand-bag and dressing-case ' "

driving out to Banwell, meaning to pay her parents a week-end visit.

There was a knock at her door, and a voice said, "It's me, Jane— may I come in?"

She did not recognise the voice, but somehow thought that it must be that of a friend, so she shouted, "Come in!"

This was all that the poor thing recollected definitely, for the next moment the door was thrown open, someone rushed at her with amazing violence, she heard the crash of a falling table and felt a blow on the side of her head, whilst a damp handkerchief was pressed to her nose and mouth.

Then she remembered nothing more.

When she gradually came to her senses, she found herself in the terrible plight in which Mrs. Skeward—her landlady— discovered her twenty-four hours later.

When pressed to try and describe her assailant, she said that when the door was thrown open, she thought that she saw an elderly woman in a wide mantle and wearing bonnet and veil, but that, at the same time, she was quite sure, from the strength and brutality of the onslaught, that she was attacked by a man. She had no enemies, and no possessions worth stealing; but her handbag, which, however, only contained a few worthless trifles, had certainly disappeared.

The people of the house, on the other hand, could throw but little light on the mystery which surrounded this very extraordinary and seemingly purposeless assault.

Mrs. Skeward only remembered that on Friday Miss Turner told her that she was just off to Banwell, and would be away for the week-end; but that she wished to keep her room on, against her return on the Monday following.

That was somewhere about half-past twelve o'clock, at the hour when luncheons were being got ready for the various lodgers; small wonder, therefore, that no one in the busy apartment-house took much count of the fact that Miss Turner was not seen to leave the house after that, and no doubt the wretched girl would have been left for several days in the pitiable condition in which she was ultimately found but for the fact that Mrs. Skeward happened to be of the usual grasping type common to those of her kind.

Weston-Super-Mare was over-full that weekend, and Mrs. Skeward, beset by applicants for accommodation, did not see why she should not let her absent lodger's room for the night or two that the latter happened to be away, and thus get money twice over for it.

She conducted a visitor up to Miss Turner's room on the Saturday afternoon, and, throwing open the door—which, by the way, was not locked—was horrified to see the poor girl half-sitting, half-slipping off the chair to which she had been tied with a rope, whilst a woollen shawl was wound round the lower part of her face.

As soon as she had released the unfortunate victim, Mrs. Skeward sent for the police, and it was through the intelligent efforts of Detective Parsons—a local man—that a few scraps of very hazy evidence were then and there collected.

First, there was the question of the elderly female in the wide mantle, spoken of by Jane Turner as her assailant. It seems that someone answering to that description had called on the Friday at about one o'clock, and asked to see Miss Turner. The maid who answered the door replied that she thought Miss Turner had gone to Banwell.

"Oh!" said the old dame, "she won't have started yet. I am Miss Turner's mother, and I was to call for her so that we might drive out together."

"Then p'r'aps Miss Turner is still in her room," suggested the maid. "Shall I go and see?"

"Don't trouble," replied the woman; "I know my way. I'll go myself."

Whereupon the old dame walked past the servant, crossed the hall, and went upstairs. No one saw her come down again, but one of the lodgers seems to have heard a knock at Jane Turner's door, and the female voice saying, "It's me, Jane—may I come in?"

What happened subsequently, who the mysterious old female was, and how and for what purpose she assaulted Jane Turner and robbed her of a few valueless articles, was the puzzle which faced the police then, and which—so far as the public is concerned—has never been solved. Jane Turner's mother was in bed at the time suffering from a broken ankle and unable to move. The elderly woman was, therefore, an impostor, and the search after her—though keen and hot enough at the time, I assure you—has remained, in the eyes of the public, absolutely fruitless. But of this more *anon*.

On the actual scene of the crime there was but little to guide subsequent investigation. The rope with which Jane Turner had been pinioned supplied no clue; the wool shawl was Miss Turner's own, snatched up by the miscreant to smother the girl's screams; on the floor was a handkerchief, without initial or laundry mark, which obviously had been saturated with chloroform; and close by a bottle which had contained the anaesthetic. A small table was overturned, and the articles which had been resting upon it were lying all around—such as a vase which had held a few flowers, a box of biscuits, and several issues of the *West of England Times.*

And nothing more. The miscreant, having accomplished his fell purpose, succeeded evidently in walking straight out of the house unobserved; his exit being undoubtedly easily managed owing to it being the busy luncheon hour.

Various theories were, of course, put forward by some of our ablest fellows at the Yard; the most likely solution being the guilt or, at least, the complicity of the girl's sweetheart, Arthur Cutbush—a ne'er-do-well, who spent the greater part of his time on race-courses. Inspector Danvers, whom the chief had sent down to assist the local police, declared that Jane Turner herself suspected her sweetheart, and was trying to shield him by stating that she possessed nothing of any value; whereas, no doubt, the young blackguard knew that she had some money, and had planned this amazing *coup* in order to rob her of it.

Danvers was quite chagrined when, on investigation, it was proved that Arthur Cutbush had gone to the York races three days before the assault, and never left that city until the Saturday evening, when a telegram from Miss Turner summoned him to Weston.

Moreover, the girl did not break off her engagement with young Cutbush, and thus the total absence of motive was a serious bar to the likelihood of the theory.

Then it was that the Chief sent for Lady Molly. No doubt he began to feel that here, too, was a case where feminine tact and my lady's own marvellous intuition might prove more useful than the more approved methods of the sterner sex.

2

"Of course, there is a woman in the case, Mary," said Lady Molly to me, when she came home from the interview with the chief, "although they all poohpooh that theory at the Yard, and declare that the female voice—to which the only two witnesses we have are prepared to swear—was a disguised one."

"You think, then, that a woman assaulted Jane Turner?"

"Well," she replied somewhat evasively, "if a man assumes a feminine voice, the result is a high-pitched, unnatural treble; and that, I feel convinced, would have struck either the maid or the lodger, or both, as peculiar."

This was the train of thought which my dear lady and I were following up, when, with that sudden transition of manner so characteristic of her, she said abruptly to me:

"Mary, look out a train for Weston-Super-Mare. We must try and get down there tonight."

"Chief's orders?" I asked.

"No—mine," she replied laconically. "Where's the A.B.C.?"

Well, we got off that self-same afternoon, and in the evening, we were having dinner at the Grand Hotel, Weston-Super-Mare.

My dear lady had been pondering all through the journey, and even now she was singularly silent and absorbed. There was a deep frown between her eyes, and every now and then the luminous, dark orbs would suddenly narrow, and the pupils contract as if smitten with a sudden light.

I was not a little puzzled as to what was going on in that active brain of hers, but my experience was that silence on my part was the surest card to play.

Lady Molly had entered our names in the hotel book as Mrs. Walter Bell and Miss Granard from London; and the day after our arrival there came two heavy parcels for her under that name. She had them taken upstairs to our private sitting-room, and there we undid them together.

To my astonishment they contained stacks of newspapers: as far as I could see at a glance, back numbers of the *West of England Times* covering a whole year.

"Find and cut out the 'Personal' column of every number, Mary," said Lady Molly to me. "I'll look through them on my return. I am going for a walk, and will be home by lunch time."

I knew, of course, that she was intent on her business and on that only, and as soon as she had gone out, I set myself to the wearisome task which she had allotted me. My dear lady was evidently working out a problem in her mind, the solution of which she expected to find in a back number of the *West of England Times*.

By the time she returned I had the "Personal" column of some three hundred numbers of the paper neatly filed and docketed for her perusal. She thanked me for my promptitude with one of her charming looks, but said little, if anything, all through luncheon. After that meal she set to work. I could see her studying each scrap of paper minutely, comparing one with the other, arranging them in sets in front of her, and making marginal notes on them all the while.

With but a brief interval for tea, she sat at her table for close on four hours, at the end of which time she swept all the scraps of paper on one side, with the exception of a few which she kept in her hand. Then she looked up at me, and I sighed with relief.

My dear lady was positively beaming.

"You have found what you wanted?" I asked eagerly.

"What I expected," she replied.

"May I know?"

She spread out the bits of paper before me. There were six altogether, and each of these columns had one paragraph specially marked with a cross.

"Only look at the paragraphs which I have marked," she said.

I did as I was told. But if in my heart I had vaguely hoped that I should then and there be confronted with the solution of the mystery which surrounded the Somersetshire outrage, I was doomed to disappointment.

Each of the marked paragraphs in the "Personal" columns bore the initials H. S. H., and their purport was invariably an assignation at one of the small railway stations on the line between Bristol and Weston,

I suppose that my bewilderment must have been supremely comical, for my dear lady's rippling laugh went echoing through the bare, dull hotel sitting-room.

"You don't see it, Mary?" she asked gaily.

"I confess I don't," I replied. "It completely baffles me."

"And yet," she said more gravely, "those few silly paragraphs have given me the clue to the mysterious assault on Jane Turner, which has been puzzling our fellows at the Yard for over three weeks."

"But how? I don't understand."

"You will, Mary, directly we get back to town. During my morning walk I have learnt all that I want to know, and now these paragraphs have set my mind at rest."

3

The next day we were back in town.

Already, at Bristol, we had bought a London morning paper, which contained in its centre page a short notice under the following startling headlines:

THE SOMERSETSHIRE OUTRAGE
AMAZING DISCOVERY BY THE POLICE
AN UNEXPECTED CLUE

The article went on to say:

"We are officially informed that the police have recently obtained knowledge of certain facts which establish beyond a doubt the motive of the brutal assault committed on the person of Miss Jane Turner. We are not authorised to say more at present than that certain startling developments are imminent."

On the way up my dear lady had initiated me into some of her views with regard to the case itself, which at the chief's desire she had now taken entirely in hand, and also into her immediate plans, of which the above article was merely the preface.

She it was who had "officially informed" the Press Association, and, needless to say, the news duly appeared in most of the London and provincial dailies.

How unerring was her intuition, and how well thought out her scheme, was proved within the next four-and-twenty hours in our own little flat, when our Emily, looking somewhat important and awed, announced Her Serene Highness the Countess of Hohengebirg.

H. S. H.—the conspicuous initials in the "Personal" columns of the *West of England Times!* You may imagine how I stared at the exquisite apparition—all lace and chiffon and roses—which the next moment literally swept into our office, past poor, open-mouthed Emily.

Had my dear lady taken leave of her senses when she suggested that this beautiful young woman with the soft, fair hair, with the pleading blue eyes and childlike mouth, had anything to do with a brutal assault on a shop girl?

The young countess shook hands with Lady Molly and with me, and then, with a deep sigh, she sank into the comfortable chair which I was offering her.

Speaking throughout with great diffidence, but always in the gentle tones of a child that knows it has been naughty, she began by explaining that she had been to Scotland Yard, where a very charming man—the chief, I presume—had been most kind and sent her hither, where he promised her she would find help and consolation in her dreadful, dreadful trouble.

Encouraged by Lady Molly, she soon plunged into her narrative: a pathetic tale of her own frivolity and foolishness.

She was originally Lady Muriel Wolfe-Strongham, daughter of the Duke of Weston, and when scarce out of the schoolroom had met the Grand Duke of Starkburg-Nauheim, who fell in love with her and married her. The union was a morganatic one, the Grand Duke conferring on his English wife the title of Countess of Hohengebirg and the rank of Serene Highness.

It seems that, at first, the marriage was a fairly happy one, in spite of the bitter animosity of the mother and sister of the Grand Duke: the Dowager Grand Duchess holding that all English girls were loud and unwomanly, and the Princess Amalie, seeing in her brother's marriage a serious bar to the fulfilment of her own highly ambitious matrimonial hopes.

"They can't bear me, because I don't knit socks and don't know how to bake almond cakes," said her dear little Serene Highness, looking up with tender appeal at Lady Molly's grave and beautiful face; "and they will be so happy to see a real estrangement between my husband and myself."

It appears that last year, whilst the Grand Duke was doing his annual cure at Marienbad, the Countess of Hohengebirg went to Folkestone for the benefit of her little boy's health. She stayed at one of the Hotels there merely as any English lady of wealth might do—with nurses and her own maid, of course, but without the paraphernalia and nuisance of her usual German retinue.

Whilst there she met an old acquaintance of her father's, a Mr. Rumboldt, who is a rich financier, it seems, and who at one time moved in the best society, but whose reputation had greatly suffered recently, owing to a much talked of divorce case which brought his name into unenviable notoriety.

Her Serene Highness, with more mopping of her blue eyes, assured Lady Molly that over at Schloss Starkburg she did not read the English papers, and was therefore quite unaware that Mr. Rumboldt, who used to be a *persona grata* in her father's house, was no longer a fit and proper acquaintance for her.

"It was a very fine morning," she continued with gentle pathos, "and I was deadly dull at Folkestone. Mr. Rumboldt persuaded me to go with him on a short trip on his yacht. We were to cross over to Boulogne, have luncheon there, and come home in the cool of the evening."

"And, of course, something occurred to disable the yacht," concluded Lady Molly gravely, as the lady herself had paused in her narrative.

"Of course," whispered the little countess through her tears.

"And, of course, it was too late to get back by the ordinary afternoon mail boat?"

"That boat had gone an hour before, and the next did not leave until the middle of the night." "So, you had perforce to wait until then, and in the meanwhile you were seen by a girl named Jane Turner, who knew you by sight, and who has been blackmailing you ever since."

"How did you guess that?" ejaculated Her Highness, with a look of such comical bewilderment in her large, blue eyes that Lady Molly and I had perforce to laugh.

"Well," replied my dear lady after a while, resuming her gravity, "we have a way in our profession of putting two and two together, haven't we? And in this case, it was not very difficult. The assignations for secret meetings at out-of-the-way railway stations which were addressed to H. S. H. in the columns of the *West of England Times* recently, gave me one clue, shall we say? The mysterious assault on a young woman, whose home was close to those very railway stations as well as to Bristol Castle—your parents' residence—where you have frequently been staying of late, was another piece that fitted in the puzzle; whilst the number of copies of the *West of England Times* that were found in that same young woman's room helped to draw my thoughts to her. Then your visit to me today—it is very simple, you see."

"I suppose so," said H. S. H. with a sigh. "Only it is worse even than you suggest, for that horrid Jane Turner, to whom I had been ever so kind when I was a girl, took a snapshot of me and Mr. Rumboldt standing on the steps of the Hotel des Bains at Boulogne. I saw her doing it and rushed down the steps to stop her. She talked quite nicely then—hypocritical wretch!—and said that perhaps the plate would be no good when it was developed, and if it were she would destroy it. I was not to worry; she would contrive to let me know through the agony column of the *West of England Times*, which—as I was going home to Bristol Castle to stay with my parents—I could see every day, but she had no idea I should have minded, and all that sort of rigmarole. Oh! she is a wicked girl, isn't she, to worry me so?"

And once again the lace handkerchief found its way to the most beautiful pair of blue eyes, I think I have ever seen. I could not help smiling, though I was really very sorry for the silly, emotional, dear little thing.

"And instead of reassurance in the *West of England Times*, you found a demand for a secret meeting at a country railway station?"

"Yes! And when I went there—terrified lest I should be seen—Jane Turner did not meet me herself. Her mother came and at once talked of selling the photograph to my husband or to my mother-in-law. She said it was worth four thousand pounds to Jane, and that she had advised her daughter not to sell it to me for less."

"What did you reply?"

"That I hadn't got four thousand pounds," said the countess rue-fully; "so after a lot of argument it was agreed that I was to pay Jane two hundred and fifty pounds a year out of my dress allowance. She would keep the negative as security, but promised never to let anyone see it so long as she got her money regularly. It was also arranged that whenever I stayed with my parents at Bristol Castle, Jane would make appointments to meet me through the columns of the *West of England Times*, and I was to pay up the instalments then just as she directed."

I could have laughed, if the whole thing had not been so tragic, for truly the way this silly, harmless little woman had allowed herself to be bullied and blackmailed by a pair of grasping females was beyond belief.

"And this has been going on for over a year," commented Lady Molly gravely.

"Yes, but I never met Jane Turner again: it was always her mother who came."

"You knew her mother before that, I presume?"

"Oh, no. I only knew Jane because she had been sewing-maid at the castle some few years ago."

"I see," said Lady Molly slowly. "What was the woman like whom you used to meet at the railway stations, and to whom you paid over Miss Turner's annuity?"

"Oh, I couldn't tell you what she was like. I never saw her prop-erly."

"Never saw her properly?" ejaculated Lady Molly, and it seemed to my well-trained ears as if there was a ring of exultation in my dear lady's voice.

"No," replied the little countess ruefully. "She always appointed a late hour of the evening, and those little stations on that line are very badly lighted. I had such difficulties in getting away from home with-out exciting comment, and used to beg her to let me meet her at a more convenient hour. But she always refused."

Lady Molly remained thoughtful for a while; then she asked abruptly:

"Why don't you prosecute Jane Turner for blackmail?"

"Oh, I dare not—I dare not!" ejaculated the little countess, in genuine terror. "My husband would never forgive me, and his female relations would do their best afterwards to widen the breach between us. It was because of the article in the London newspaper about the assault on Jane Turner—the talk of a clue and of startling developments—that I got terrified, and went to Scotland Yard. Oh, no! no! no! Promise me that my name won't be dragged into this case. It would ruin me for ever!"

She was sobbing now; her grief and fear were very pathetic to witness, and she moaned through her sobs:

"Those wicked people know that I daren't risk an exposure, and simply prey upon me like vampires because of that. The last time I saw the old woman I told her that I would confess everything to my husband—I couldn't bear to go on like this. But she only laughed; she knew I should never dare." "When was this?" asked Lady Molly.

"About three weeks ago—just before Jane Turner was assaulted and robbed of the photographs." "How do you know she was robbed of the photographs?"

"She wrote and told me so," replied the young countess, who seemed strangely awed now by my dear lady's earnest question. And from a dainty reticule she took a piece of paper, which bore traces of many bitter tears on its crumpled surface. This she handed to Lady Molly, who took it from her. It was a typewritten letter, which bore no signature. Lady Molly perused it in silence first, then read its contents out aloud to me:—

To H.S.H. the Countess of Hohengebirg.
You think I have been worrying you the past twelve months about your adventure with Mr. Rumboldt in Boulogne. But it was not me; it was one who has power over me, and who knew about the photograph. He made me act as I did. But whilst I kept the photo you were safe. Now he has assaulted me and nearly killed me, and taken the negative away. I can, and will, get it out of him again, but it will mean a large sum down. Can you manage one thousand pounds?

"When did you get this?" asked Lady Molly. "Only a few days ago," replied the countess. "And oh! I have been enduring agonies of doubt and fear for the past three weeks, for I had heard nothing from Jane since the assault, and I wondered what had happened."

"You have not sent a reply, I hope."

"No. I was going to, when I saw the article in the London paper, and the fear that all had been discovered threw me into such a state of agony that I came straight up to town and saw the gentleman at Scotland Yard, who sent me on to you. Oh!" she entreated again and again, "you won't do anything that will cause a scandal! Promise me—promise me! I believe I should commit suicide rather than face it—and I could find a thousand pounds."

"I don't think you need do either," said Lady Molly. "Now, may I think over the whole matter quietly to myself," she added, "and talk it over with my friend here? I may be able to let you have some good news shortly."

She rose, intimating kindly that the interview was over. But it was by no means that yet, for there was still a good deal of entreaty and a great many tears on the one part, and reiterated kind assurances on the other. However, when, some ten minutes later, the dainty clouds of lace and chiffon were finally wafted out of our office, we both felt that the poor, harmless, unutterably foolish little lady felt distinctly consoled and more happy than she had been for the past twelve months.

4

"Yes! she has been an utter little goose," Lady Molly was saying to me an hour later when we were having luncheon; "but that Jane Turner is a remarkably clever girl."

"I suppose you think, as I do, that the mysterious elderly female, who seems to have impersonated the mother all through, was an accomplice of Jane Turner's, and that the assault was a put-up job between them," I said. "Inspector Danvers will be delighted—for this theory is a near approach to his own."

"H'm!" was all the comment vouchsafed on my remark.

"I am sure it was Arthur Cutbush, the girl's sweetheart, after all," I retorted hotly, "and you'll see that, put to the test of sworn evidence, his alibi at the time of the assault itself won't hold good. Moreover, now," I added triumphantly, "we have knowledge which has been lacking all along—the motive."

"Ah!" said my lady, smiling at my enthusiasm, "that's how you argue, Mary, is it?"

"Yes, and in my opinion the only question in doubt is whether Arthur Cutbush acted in collusion with Jane Turner or against her."

"Well, suppose we go and elucidate that point—and some others—at once," concluded Lady Molly as she rose from the table.

She decided to return to Bristol that same evening. We were going by the 8.50 p.m., and I was just getting ready—the cab being already at the door—when I was somewhat startled by the sudden appearance

"Ten minutes later the dainty clouds of lace and chiffon
were finally wafted out"

into my room of an old lady, very beautifully dressed, with snow-white hair dressed high above a severe, interesting face.

A merry, rippling laugh issuing from the wrinkled mouth, and a closer scrutiny on my part, soon revealed the identity of my dear lady, dressed up to look like an extremely dignified *grande dame* of the old school, whilst a pair of long, old-fashioned earrings gave a curious, foreign look to her whole appearance.

I didn't quite see why she chose to arrive at the Grand Hotel, Bristol, in that particular disguise, nor why she entered our names in the hotel book as Grand Duchess and Princess Amalie von Starkburg, from Germany; nor did she tell me anything that evening.

But by the next afternoon, when we drove out together in a fly, I was well up in the role which I had to play. My lady had made me dress in a very rich black silk dress of her own, and ordered me to do my hair in a somewhat frumpish fashion, with a parting, and a "bun" at the back. She herself looked more like Royalty travelling *incognito* than ever, and no wonder small children and tradesmen's boys stared open-mouthed when we alighted from our fly outside one of the mean-looking little houses in Bread Street.

In answer to our ring, a smutty little servant opened the door, and my lady asked her if Miss Jane Turner lived here and if she were in.

"Yes, Miss Turner lives here, and it bein' Thursday and early closin' she's home from business."

"Then please tell her," said Lady Molly in her grandest manner, "that the Dowager Grand Duchess of Starkburg-Nauheim and the Princess Amalie desire to see her."

The poor little maid nearly fell backwards with astonishment. She gasped an agitated "Lor!" and then flew down the narrow passage and up the steep staircase, closely followed by my dear lady and myself.

On the first-floor landing the girl, with nervous haste, knocked at a door, opened it and muttered half audibly:

"Ladies to see you, miss!"

Then she fled incontinently upstairs. I have never been able to decide whether that little girl thought that we were lunatics, ghosts, or criminals.

But already Lady Molly had sailed into the room, where Miss Jane Turner apparently had been sitting reading a novel. She jumped up when we entered, and stared open-eyed at the gorgeous apparitions. She was not a bad-looking girl but for the provoking, bold look in her black eyes, and the general slatternly appearance of her person.

"Pray do not disturb yourself, Miss Turner," said Lady Molly in broken English, as she sank into a chair, and beckoned me to do likewise. "Pray sit down—I vill be brief. You have a compromising photograph—is it not?—of my daughter-in-law ze Countess of Hohengebirg. I am ze Grand Duchess of Starkburg-Nauheim—zis is my daughter, ze Princess Amalie. We are here *incognito*. You understand? Not?"

And, with inimitable elegance of gesture, my dear lady raised a pair of "starers" to her eyes and fixed them on Jane Turner's quaking figure.

Never had I seen suspicion, nay terror, depicted so plainly on a young face, but I will do the girl the justice to state that she pulled herself together with marvellous strength of will.

She fought down her awed respect of this great lady; or rather shall I say that the British middle-class want of respect for social superiority, especially if it be foreign, now stood her in good stead?

"I don't know what you are talking about," she said with an arrogant toss of the head.

"Zat is a lie, is it not?" rejoined Lady Molly calmly, as she drew from her reticule the typewritten letter which Jane Turner had sent to the Countess of Hohengebirg. "Zis you wrote to my daughter-in-law; ze letter reached me instead of her. It interests me much. I vill give you two tousend pounds for ze photograph of her and Mr.—er—Rumboldt. You vill sell it to me for zat, is it not?"

The production of the letter had somewhat cowed Jane's bold spirit. But she was still defiant.

"I haven't got the photograph here," she said.

"Ah, no! but you vill get it—yes?" said my lady, quietly replacing the letter in her reticule. "In ze letter you offer to get it for tousend pound. I vill give you two tousend. Today is a holiday for you. You vill get ze photograph from ze gentleman—not? And I vill vait here till you come back."

Whereupon she rearranged her skirts round her and folded her hands placidly, like one prepared to wait.

"I haven't got the photograph," said Jane Turner, doggedly, "and I can't get it today. The—the person who has it doesn't live in Bristol."

"No? Ah! but quite close, isn't it?" rejoined my lady, placidly. "I can vait all ze day."

"No, you shan't!" retorted Jane Turner, whose voice now shook with obvious rage or fear—I knew not which. "I can't get the photograph today—so there! And I won't sell it to you—I won't. I don't want your two thousand pounds. How do I know you are not an impostor?"

"From zis, my good girl," said Lady Molly, quietly; "that if I leave zis room wizout ze photograph, I go straight to ze police with zis letter, and you shall be prosecuted by ze Grand Duke, my son, for blackmailing his wife. You see, I am not like my daughter-in-law; I am not afraid of a scandal. So, you vill fetch ze photograph—isn't it? I and ze Princess Amalie vill vait for it here. Zat is your bedroom—not?" she added, pointing to a door which obviously gave on an inner room. "Vill you put on your hat and go at once, please? Two tousend pound or two years in prison—you have ze choice—isn't it?"

Jane Turner tried to keep up her air of defiance, looking Lady Molly full in the face; but I who watched her could see the boldness in her eyes gradually giving place to fear, and then to terror and even despair; the girl's face seemed literally to grow old as I looked at it— pale, haggard, and drawn—whilst Lady Molly kept her stern, luminous eyes fixed steadily upon her.

Then, with a curious, wild gesture, which somehow filled me with a nameless fear, Jane Turner turned on her heel and ran into the inner room.

There followed a moment of silence. To me it was tense and agonising. I was straining my ears to hear what was going on in that inner room. That my dear lady was not as callous as she wished to appear was shown by the strange look of expectancy in her beautiful eyes.

The minutes sped on—how many I could not afterwards have said. I was conscious of a clock ticking monotonously over the shabby mantelpiece, of an errand boy outside shouting at the top of his voice, of the measured step of the cab horse which had brought us hither being walked up and down the street.

Then suddenly there was a violent crash, as of heavy furniture being thrown down. I could not suppress a scream, for my nerves by now were terribly on the jar.

"Quick, Mary—the inner room!" said Lady Molly. "I thought the girl might do that."

I dared not pause in order to ask what "that" meant, but flew to the door.

It was locked.

"Downstairs—quick!" commanded my lady. "I ordered Danvers to be on the watch outside."

You may imagine how I flew, and how I blessed my dear lady's forethought in the midst of her daring plan, when, having literally torn open the front door, I saw Inspector Danvers in plain clothes, calmly patrolling the street. I beckoned to him—he was keeping a sharp look-out—and together we ran back into the house.

Fortunately, the landlady and the servant were busy in the basement, and had neither heard the crash nor seen me run in search of Danvers. My dear lady was still alone in the dingy parlour, stooping against the door of the inner room, her ear glued to the keyhole.

"Not too late, I think," she whispered hurriedly. "Break it open, Danvers."

Danvers, who is a great, strong man, soon put his shoulder to the rickety door, which yielded to the first blow.

The sight which greeted us filled me with horror, for I had never seen such a tragedy before. The wretched girl, Jane Turner, had tied a rope to a ring in the ceiling, which I suppose at one time held a hanging lamp; the other end of that rope she had formed into a slip-noose, and passed round her neck.

She had apparently climbed on to a table, and then used her best efforts to end her life by kicking the table away from under her. This was the crash which we had heard, and which had caused us to come to her rescue. Fortunately, her feet had caught in the back of a chair close by; the slip-noose was strangling her, and her face was awful to behold, but she was not dead.

Danvers soon got her down. He is a first-aid man, and has done these terrible jobs before. As soon as the girl had partially recovered, Lady Molly sent him and me out of the room. In the dark and dusty parlour, where but a few moments ago I had played my small part in a grim comedy, I now waited to hear what the sequel to it would be.

Danvers had been gone some time, and the shades of evening were drawing in; outside, the mean-looking street looked particularly dreary. It was close on six o'clock when at last I heard the welcome rustle of silks, the opening of a door, and at last my dear lady—looking grave but serene—came out of the inner room, and, beckoning to me, without a word led the way out of the house and into the fly, which was still waiting at the door.

"We'll send a doctor to her," were her first words as soon as we were clear of Bread Street. "But she is quite all right now, save that she wants a sleeping draught. Well, she has been punished enough, I think. She won't try her hand at blackmailing again."

"Then the photograph never existed?" I asked amazed.

"No; the plate was a failure, but Jane Turner would not thus readily give up the idea of getting money out of the poor, pusillanimous

"' Not too late, I think,' she whispered hurriedly. ' Break it open, Danvers ' "

countess. We know how she succeeded in terrorising that silly little woman. It is wonderful how cleverly a girl like that worked out such a complicated scheme, all alone."

"All alone?"

"Yes; there was no one else. She was the elderly woman who used to meet the countess, and who rang at the front door of the Weston apartment-house. She arranged the whole of the *mise en scène* of the assault on herself, all alone, and took everybody in with it—it was so perfectly done. She planned and executed it because she was afraid that the little countess would be goaded into confessing her folly to her husband, or to her own parents, when a prosecution for blackmail would inevitably follow. So, she risked everything on a big *coup*, and almost succeeded in getting a thousand pounds from Her Serene Highness, meaning to reassure her, as soon as she had the money, by the statement that the negative and prints had been destroyed. But the appearance of the Grand Duchess of Starkburg-Nauheim this afternoon frightened her into an act of despair. Confronted with the prosecution she dreaded and with the prison she dared not face, she, in a mad moment, attempted to take her life."

"I suppose now the whole matter will be hushed up."

"Yes," replied Lady Molly with a wistful sigh. "The public will never know who assaulted Jane Turner."

She was naturally a little regretful at that. But it was a joy to see her the day when she was able to assure Her Serene Highness the Countess of Hohengebirg that she need never again fear the consequences of that fatal day's folly.

A Castle in Brittany

1

Yes! we are just back from our holiday, my dear lady and I—a well-earned holiday, I can tell you that.

We went to Porhoët, you know—a dear little village in the hinterland of Brittany, not very far from the coast; an enchanting spot, hidden away in a valley, bordered by a mountain stream, wild, romantic, picturesque—Brittany, in fact.

We had discovered the little place quite accidentally last year, in the course of our wanderings, and stayed there then about three weeks, laying the foundations of that strange adventure which reached its culminating point just a month ago.

I don't know if the story will interest you, for Lady Molly's share in the adventure was purely a private one and had nothing whatever to do with her professional work. At the same time, it illustrates in a very marked manner that extraordinary faculty which she possesses of divining her fellow-creatures' motives and intentions.

We had rooms and *pension* in the dear little convent on the outskirts of the village, close to the quaint church and the picturesque presbytery, and soon we made the acquaintance of the *curé*, a simple-minded, kindly old man, whose sorrow at the thought that two such charming English ladies as Lady Molly and myself should be heretics was more than counterbalanced by his delight in having someone of the "great outside world"—as he called it—to talk to, whilst he told us quite ingenuously something of his own simple life, of this village which he loved, and also of his parishioners.

One personality among the latter occupied his thoughts and conversation a great deal, and I must say interested us keenly. It was that of Miss Angela de Genneville, who owned the magnificent *château* of Porhoët, one of the seven wonders of architectural France. She was an Englishwoman by birth—being of a Jersey family—and was immensely wealthy, her uncle, who was also her godfather, having bequeathed to her the largest cigar factory in St. Heliers, besides three-quarters of a million sterling.

To say that Miss de Genneville was eccentric was but to put it mildly; in the village she was generally thought to be quite mad. The *curé* vaguely hinted that a tragic love story was at the bottom of all her eccentricities. Certain it is that, for no apparent reason, and when she was still a youngish woman, she had sold the Jersey business and realised the whole of her fortune. After two years of continuous travelling, she came to Brittany on a visit to her sister—the widowed Marquise de Terhoven, who owned a small property close to Porhoët, and lived there in retirement and poverty with her only son, Amédé.

Miss Angela de Genneville was agreeably taken with the beauty and quietude of this remote little village. The beautiful *château* of Porhoët being for sale at the time, she bought it, took out letters of naturalisation, became a French subject, and from that moment never went outside the precincts of her newly acquired domain.

She never returned to England, and, with the exception of the *curé* and her own sister and nephew, saw no one beyond her small retinue of servants.

But the dear old *curé* thought all the world of her, for she was supremely charitable to him and to the poor, and scarcely a day passed but he told us something either of her kindness or of her eccentric ways. One day he arrived at the convent at an unaccustomed hour; we had just finished our simple *déjeuner* of steaming coffee and rolls when we saw him coming towards us across the garden.

That he was excited and perturbed was at once apparent by his hurried gait and by the flush on his kindly face. He bade us a very hasty "Good morning, my daughters!" and plunged abruptly into his subject. He explained with great volubility, which was intended to mask his agitation, that he was the bearer of an invitation to the charming English lady—a curious invitation, ah, yes! perhaps!—Mademoiselle de Genneville—very eccentric—but she is in great trouble—in very serious trouble—and very ill too, now—poor lady—half paralysed and feeble—yes, feeble in the brain—and then her nephew, the Marquis Amédé de Terhoven—such a misguided young man—has got into bad company in that den of wickedness called Paris—since then it has been debts—always debts—his mother is so indulgent !—too indulgent! but an only son !—the charming English ladies would understand.

It was very sad—very, very sad—and no wonder Mademoiselle de Genneville was very angry. She had paid *Monsieur le Marquis'* debts once, twice, three times—but now she will not pay any more—but she is in great trouble and wants a friend—a female friend, one of her own country, she declares—for he himself, alas! was only a poor *curé de village* , and did not understand great ladies and their curious ways. It would be true Christian charity if the charming English lady would come and see *Mademoiselle*.

"But her own sister, the *Marquise?*" suggested Lady Molly, breaking in on the old man's volubility.

"Ah! her sister, of course," he replied with a sigh. "*Madame la Marquise*—but then she is *Monsieur le Marquis'* mother, and the charming English lady would understand—a mother's heart, of course—"

"But I am a complete stranger to Miss de Genneville," protested Lady Molly.

"Ah, but *Mademoiselle* has always remained an Englishwoman at heart," replied the *curé*. "She said to me today: 'I seem to long for an Englishwoman's handshake, a sober-minded, sensible Englishwoman, to help me in this difficulty. Bring your English friend to me, *Monsieur le Curé*, if she will come to the assistance of an old woman who has no one to turn to in her distress.'"

Of course, after that I knew that my dear lady would yield. Moreover, she was keenly interested in Miss de Genneville, and without further discussion she told *Monsieur le Curé* that she was quite ready to accompany him to the *château* of Porhoët.

2

Of course, I was not present at the interview, but Lady Molly has so often told me all that happened and how it happened, and with such a wealth of picturesque and minute detail, that sometimes I find it difficult to realise that I myself was not there in person.

It seems that *Monsieur le Curé* himself ushered my lady into the presence of Miss Angela de Genneville. The old lady was not alone when they entered; Madame la Marquise de Terhoven, an elderly, somewhat florid woman, whose features, though distinctly coarse, recalled those of her sister, sat on a highbacked chair close to a table, on which her fingers were nervously drumming a tattoo, whilst in the window embrasure stood a young man whose resemblance to both the ladies at once proclaimed him to Lady Molly's quick perception as the son of the one and nephew of the other—the Marquis de Terhoven, in fact.

Miss de Genneville sat erect in a huge armchair; her face was the hue of yellow wax, the flesh literally shrivelled on the bones, the eyes of a curious, unnatural brilliance; one hand clutched feverishly the arm of her chair, the other, totally paralysed, lay limp and inert on her lap.

"Ah! the Englishwoman at last, thank God!" she said in a high-pitched, strident voice as soon as Lady Molly entered the room. "Come here, my dear, for I have wanted one of your kind badly. A true-hearted Englishwoman is the finest product of God's earth, after all's said and done. *Pardieu!* but I breathe again," she added, as my dear lady advanced somewhat diffidently to greet her, and took the trembling hand which Miss Angela extended to her.

"Sit down close to me," commanded the eccentric old lady, whilst Lady Molly, confused, and not a little angered at finding herself in the very midst of what was obviously a family conclave, was vaguely wondering how soon she could slip away again. But the trembling hand of the paralytic clutched her own slender wrist so tightly, forcing her to sink into a low chair close by, and holding her there as with a grip of steel, that it would have been useless and perhaps cruel to resist.

Satisfied now that her newly found friend, as well as *Monsieur le Curé*, were prepared to remain by her and to listen to what she had to say, the sick woman turned with a look of violent wrath towards the window embrasure.

"I was just telling that fine nephew of mine that he is counting his chickens before they are hatched. I am not yet dead, as *Monsieur* my nephew can see; and I have made a will—aye, and placed it where his thievish fingers can never reach it."

The young man, who up to now had been gazing stolidly out of the window, now suddenly turned on his heel, confronting the old woman, with a look of hate gleaming in his eyes.

"We can fight the will," here interposed *Madame la Marquise*, icily.

"On what grounds?" queried the other.

"That you were paralysed and imbecile when you made it," replied the *Marquise*, dryly.

Monsieur le Curé, who up to now had been fidgeting nervously with his hat, now raised his hands and eyes up to the ceiling to emphasise the horror which he felt at this callous suggestion. Lady Molly no longer desired to go; the half-paralysed grip on her wrist had relaxed, but she sat there quietly, interested with every fibre of her quick intelligence in the moving drama which was being unfolded before her.

There was a pause now, a silence broken only by the monotonous ticking of a monumental, curious-looking clock which stood in an angle of the room. Miss de Genneville had made no reply to her sister's cruel taunt, but a look, furtive, maniacal, almost dangerous, now crept into her eyes.

Then she addressed the *curé*.

"I pray you pen, ink and paper—here, on this table," she requested. Then as he complied with alacrity, she once more turned to her nephew, and pointing to the writing materials:

"Sit down and write, Amédé," she commanded. "Write what?" he queried.

"A confession, my nephew," said the old woman, with a shrill laugh. "A confession of those little *peccadilloes* of yours, which, unless I come to your rescue now, will land you for seven years in a penal settlement, if I mistake not. Eh, my fine nephew?"

"A confession?" retorted Amédé de Terhoven savagely. "Do you take me for a fool?"

"No, my nephew, I take you for a wise man—who understands that his dear aunt will not buy those interesting forgeries, perpetrated by Monsieur le Marquis Amédé de Terhoven, and offered to her by Rubinstein the money-lender, unless that confession is written and

" Confronting the old woman, with a look of hate gleaming
in his eyes "

signed by you. Write Amédé, write that confession, my dear nephew, if you do not wish to see yourself in the dock on a charge of forging your aunt's name to a bill for one hundred thousand *francs*."

Amédé muttered a curse between his teeth. Obviously, the old woman's shaft had struck home. He knew himself to be in a hopeless plight. It appears that a money-lender had threatened to send the forged bills to *Monsieur le Procureur de la République* unless they were paid within twenty-four hours, and no one could pay them but Miss de Genneville, who had refused to do it except at the price of this humiliating confession.

A look of intelligence passed between mother and son. Intercepted by Lady Molly and interpreted by her, it seemed to suggest the idea of humouring the old aunt, for the moment, until the forgeries were safely out of the money-lender's hands, then of mollifying her later on, when perhaps she would have forgotten, or sunk deeper into helplessness and imbecility.

As if in answer to his mother's look the young man now said curtly:

"I must know what use you mean to make of the confession if I do write it."

"That will depend on yourself," replied *Mademoiselle*, dryly. "You may be sure that I will not willingly send my own nephew to penal servitude.

For another moment the young man hesitated, then he sat down, sullen and wrathful, and said:

"I'll write—you may dictate—"

The old woman laughed a short, dry, sarcastic laugh. Then, at her dictation, Amédé wrote:

"I, Amédé, Marquis de Terhoven, hereby make confession to having forged Mademoiselle Angela de Genneville's name to the annexed bills, thereby obtaining the sum of one hundred thousand *francs* from Abraham Rubinstein, of Brest."

"Now, *Monsieur le Curé*, will you kindly witness *le Marquis'* signature?" said the irascible old lady when Amédé had finished writing; "and you, too, my dear?" she added, turning to Lady Molly.

My dear lady hesitated for a moment. Naturally she did not desire to be thus mixed up in this family feud, but a strange impulse had drawn her sympathy to this eccentric old lady, who, in the midst of her semi-regal splendour seemed so forlorn, between her nephew, who was a criminal and a blackguard, and her sister, who was but little less contemptible.

101

Obeying this impulse, and also a look of entreaty from the *curé*, she affixed her own signature as witness to the document, and this despite the fact that both the *Marquise* and her son threw her a look of hate which might have made a weaker spirit tremble with foreboding.

Not so Lady Molly. Those very same threatening looks served but to decide her. Then, at *Mademoiselle's* command, she folded up the document, slipped it into an envelope, sealed it, and finally addressed it to *M. le Procureur de la République*, resident at Caen.

Amédé watched all these proceedings with eyes that were burning with impotent wrath.

"This letter," now resumed the old lady, more calmly, "will be sent under cover to my lawyer, Maître Vendôme, of Paris, who drew up my will, with orders only to post it in case of certain eventualities, which I will explain later on. In the meanwhile, my dear nephew, you may apprise your friend, Abraham Rubinstein, that I will buy back those interesting forgeries of yours the day on which I hear from Maître Vendôme that he has safely received my letter with this enclosure."

"This is infamous—" here broke in the *Marquise*, rising in full wrath, unable to control herself any longer. "I'll have you put under restraint as a dangerous lunatic. I—"

"Then, of course, I could not buy back the bills from Rubinstein," rejoined *Mademoiselle*, calmly.

Then, as the *Marquise* subsided—cowed, terrified, realising the hopelessness of her son's position—the old lady turned placidly to my dear lady, whilst her trembling fingers once more clutched the slender hand of her newly found English friend.

"I have asked you, my dear, and *Monsieur le Curé*, to come to me today," she said, "because I wish you both to be of assistance to me in the carrying out of my dying wishes. You must promise me most solemnly, both of you, that when I am dead you will carry out these wishes to the letter. Promise!" she added with passionate earnestness.

The promise was duly given by Lady Molly and the old *curé*, then *Mademoiselle* resumed more calmly:

"And now I want you to look at that clock," she said abruptly, with seeming irrelevance. "It is an old heirloom which belonged to the former owners of Porhoët, and which I bought along with the house. You will notice that it is one of the most remarkable pieces of mechanism which brain of man has ever devised, for it has this great peculiarity, that it goes for three hundred and sixty-six days consecutively, keeping most perfect time.

"When the works have all but run down, the weights—which are enormous—release a certain spring, and the great doors of the case open of themselves, thus allowing the clock to be wound up. After that is done, and the doors pushed to again, no one can open them until another three hundred and sixty-six days have gone by—that is to say, not without breaking the case to pieces."

Lady Molly examined the curious old clock with great attention. Vaguely she guessed already what the drift of the old lady's curious explanations would be.

"Two days ago," continued *Mademoiselle*, "the clock was open, and *Monsieur le Curé* wound it up, but before I pushed the doors to again, I slipped certain papers into the case—you remember, *Monsieur?*"

"Yes, *Mademoiselle*, I remember," responded the old man.

"Those papers were my last will and testament, bequeathing all I possess to the parish of Porhoët," said Miss de Genneville, dryly, "and now the doors of the massive case are closed. No one can get at my will for another three hundred and sixty-four days—no one," she added with a shrill laugh, "not even my nephew, Amédé de Terhoven."

A silence ensued, only broken by the rustle of *Madame la Marquise's* silk dress as she shrugged her shoulders and gave a short, sarcastic chuckle.

"My dear," resumed *Mademoiselle*, looking straight into Lady Molly's eager, glowing face, "you must promise me that, three hundred and sixty-four days hence, that is to say on the 20th September next year, you and *Monsieur le Curé*—or one of you if the other be incapacitated—will be present in this room at this hour when the door of the clock will open. You will then wind up the family heirloom, take out the papers which you will find buried beneath the weights, and hand them over to Maître Vendôme for probate at the earliest opportunity. *Monseigneur* the Bishop of Caen, the Mayor of this Commune, and the *Sousprefet* of this Department have all been informed of the contents of my will, and also that it is practically in the keeping of *le Curé de Porhoët*, who, no doubt, realises what the serious consequences to himself would be if he failed to produce the will at the necessary time."

The poor *curé* gasped with terror.

"But—but—but—" he stammered meekly, "I may be forcibly prevented from entering the house—I might be ill or—"

He shuddered with an unavowable fear, then added more calmly:

"I might be unjustly accused then of stealing the will—of defrauding the poor of Porhoët in favour of—*Mademoiselle's* direct heirs."

"Have no fear, my good friend," said *Mademoiselle*, dryly; "though I have one foot in the grave I am not quite so imbecile as my dear sister and nephew here would suggest, and I have provided for every eventuality. If you are ill or otherwise prevented by outside causes from being present here on the day and hour named, this charming English lady will be able to replace you. But if either of you is forcibly prevented from entering this house, or if, having entered this room, the slightest violence or even pressure is put upon you, or if you should find the clock broken, damaged and—stripped of its contents, all you need do is to apprise Maître Vendôme of the fact. He will know how to act."

"What would he do?"

"Send a certain confession we all know of to *Monsieur le Procureur de la République*," replied the old lady, fixing the young Marquis Amédé with her irascible eye. "That same confession," she continued lightly, "Maître Vendôme is instructed to destroy if you, *Monsieur*, and my English friend here, and the clock, are all undamaged on the eventful day."

There was silence in the great, dark room for a while, broken only by the sarcastic chuckle of the enfeebled invalid, tired out after this harrowing scene, wherein she had pitted her half-maniacal ingenuity against the greed and rapacity of a conscienceless *roué*.

That she had hemmed her nephew and sister in on every side could not be denied. Lady Molly herself felt somewhat awed at this weird revenge conceived by the outraged old lady against her grasping relatives.

She was far too interested in the whole drama to give up her own part in it, and, as she subsequently explained to me, she felt it her duty to remain the partner and co-worker of the poor *curé* in this dangerous task of securing to the poor of Porhoët the fortune which otherwise would be squandered away on gaming tables and racecourses.

For this, and many reasons too complicated to analyse, she decided to accept her share in the trust imposed upon her by her newly-found friend.

Neither the *Marquise* nor her son took any notice of Lady Molly as she presently took leave of Mademoiselle de Genneville, who, at the last, made her take a solemn oath that she would stand by the *curé* and fulfil the wishes of a dying and much-wronged woman.

Much perturbed, *Monsieur le Curé* went away. Lady Molly went several times after that to the *château* of Porhoët to see the invalid, who had taken a violent fancy to her. In October we had, perforce, to return to England and to work, and the following spring we had news from the *curé* that Mademoiselle de Genneville was dead.

3

Lady Molly had certainly been working too hard, and was in a feeble state of health when we reached Porhoët the following 19th of September, less than twenty-four hours before the eventful moment when the old clock would reveal the will and testament of Mademoiselle de Genneville.

We walked straight from the station to the presbytery, anxious to see the *curé* and to make all arrangements for tomorrow's business. To our terrible sorrow and distress, we were informed by the housekeeper that the *curé* was very seriously ill at the hospital at Brest, whither he had been removed by the doctor's orders.

This was the first inkling I had that things would not go as smoothly as I had anticipated. Miss de Genneville's dispositions with regard to the sensational disclosure of her will had, to my mind, been so ably taken that it had never struck me until now that the Marquise de Terhoven and her precious son would make a desperate fight before they gave up all thoughts of the coveted fortune.

I imagined the *Marquis* hemmed in on every side; any violence offered against the *curé* or Lady Molly when they entered the *château* in order to accomplish the task allotted to them being visited by the sending of the confession to *Monsieur le Procureur de la République,* when prosecution for forgery would immediately follow. Damage to the clock itself would be punished in the same way.

But I had never thought of sudden illnesses, of—heaven help us!— poison or unaccountable accidents to either the *curé* or to the woman I loved best in all the world.

No wonder Lady Molly looked pale and fragile as, having thanked the housekeeper, we found our way back in silence to the convent where we had once again engaged rooms.

Somehow the hospitality shown us last year had lost something of its cordiality. Moreover, our bedrooms this time did not communicate with one another, but opened out independently on to a stone passage.

The sister who showed us upstairs explained, somewhat shame-facedly, that as the Mother Superior had not expected us, she had let the room which was between our two bedrooms to a lady visitor, who, however, was ill in bed at the present moment.

That sixth sense, of which so much has been said and written, but which I will not attempt to explain, told me plainly enough that we were no longer amidst friends in the convent.

Had bribery been at work? Was the lady visitor a spy set upon our movements by the Terhovens? It was impossible to say. I could no longer chase away the many gloomy forebodings which assailed me the rest of that day and drove away sleep during the night. I can assure you that in my heart I wished all eccentric old ladies and their hidden wills at the bottom of the sea.

My dear lady was apparently also very deeply perturbed; any attempt on my part to broach the subject of Miss de Genneville's will was promptly and authoritatively checked by her. At the same time, I knew her well enough to guess that all these nameless dangers which seemed to have crept up round her only served to enhance her determination to carry out her old friend's dying wishes to the letter.

We went to bed quite early; for the first time without that delightful final gossip, when events, plans, surmises and work were freely discussed between us. The unseen lady visitor in the room which separated us acted as a wet blanket on our intimacy.

I stayed with Lady Molly until she was in bed. She hardly talked to me whilst she undressed, but when I kissed her "goodnight" she whispered almost inaudibly right into my ear:

"The Terhoven faction are at work. They may waylay you and offer you a bribe to keep me out of the *château* tomorrow. Pretend to fall in with their views. Accept all bribes and place yourself at their disposal. I must not say more now. We are being spied upon."

That my lady was, as usual, right in her surmises was proved within the next five minutes. I had slipped out of her room, and was just going into mine, when I heard my name spoken hardly above a whisper, whilst I felt my arm gently seized from behind.

An elderly, somewhat florid, woman stood before me attired in a dingy-coloured dressing-gown. She was pointing towards my own bedroom door, implying her desire to accompany me to my room. Remembering my dear lady's parting injunctions, I nodded in acquiescence. She followed me, after having peered cautiously up and down the passage.

Then, when the door was duly closed, and she was satisfied that we were alone, she said very abruptly:

"Miss Granard, tell me! you are poor, eh?—a paid companion to your rich friend, what?"

Still thinking of Lady Molly's commands, I replied with a pathetic sigh.

"Then," said the old lady, eagerly, "would you like to earn fifty thousand *francs?*"

The eagerness with which I responded "Rather!" apparently pleased her, for she gave a sigh of satisfaction.

"You know the story of my sister's will—of the clock?" she asked eagerly: "of your friend's role in this shameless business?"

Once more I nodded. I knew that my lady had guessed rightly. This was the Marquise de Terhoven, planted here in the convent to gain my confidence, to spy on Lady Molly, and to offer me a bribe.

Now for some clever tactics on my part.

"Can you prevent your friend from being at the *château* tomorrow before one o'clock?" asked the *marquise.*

"Easily," I replied calmly.

"How?"

"She is ill, as you know. The doctor has ordered her a sleeping draught. I administer it. I can arrange that she has a strong dose in the morning instead of her other medicine. She will sleep till the late afternoon."

I rattled this off glibly in my best French. *Madame la Marquise* heaved a deep sigh of relief.

"Ah! that is good!" she said. "Then listen to me. Do as I tell you, and tomorrow you will be richer by fifty thousand *francs.* Come to the *château* in the morning, dressed in your friend's clothes. My son will be there; together you will assist at the opening of the secret doors, and when my son has wound up the old clock himself, he will place fifty thousand *francs* in your hands."

"But *Monsieur le Curé?*" I suggested tentatively.

"He is ill," she replied curtly.

But as she spoke these three words there was such an evil sneer in her face, such a look of cruel triumph in her eyes, that all my worst suspicions were at once confirmed.

Had these people's unscrupulous rapacity indeed bribed some needy country practitioner to put the *curé* temporarily out of the way? It was too awful to think of, and I can tell you that I needed all my presence of mind, all my desire to act my part bravely and intelligently to the end, not to fly from this woman in horror.

She gave me a few more instructions with regard to the services which she and her precious son would expect of me on the morrow. It seems that, some time before her death, Miss de Genneville had laid strict injunctions on two of her most trusted menservants to remain in the *château*, and to be on the watch on the eventful 20th day of September of this year, lest any serious violence be done to the English lady or to the *curé*. It was with a view to allay any suspicion which might arise in the minds of these two men that the *marquis* desired me to impersonate Lady Molly tomorrow, and to enter with him—on seemingly friendly terms—the room where stood the monumental clock.

For these services, together with those whereby Lady Molly was to be sent into a drugged sleep whilst the theft of the will was being carried through, I—Mary Granard—was to receive from Monsieur le Marquis de Terhoven the sum of fifty thousand *francs*.

All these matters being settled to this wicked woman's apparent satisfaction, she presently took hold of both my hands, shook them warmly, and called me her dearest friend; assured me of everlasting gratitude, and finally, to my intense relief, slipped noiselessly out of my room.

4

I surmised—I think correctly—that *Madame la Marquise* would spend most of the night with her ear glued to the thin partition which separated her room from that of Lady Molly; so, I did not dare to go and report myself and the momentous conversation which I had just had, and vaguely wondered when I should have an opportunity of talking matters over with my dear lady without feeling that a spy was at my heels.

The next morning when I went into her room, to my boundless amazement—and before I had time to utter a word—she moaned audibly, as if in great pain, and said feebly, but very distinctly:

"Oh, Mary! I'm so glad you've come. I feel terribly ill. I haven't had a wink of sleep all night, and I am too weak to attempt to get up."

Fortunately, my perceptions had not been dulled by the excitement of the past few hours, and I could see that she was not so ill as she made out. Her eyes sought mine as I approached her bed, and her lips alone framed the words which I believed I interpreted correctly.

"Do as they want. I stay in bed. Will explain later."

Evidently, she had reason to think that we were being closely watched; but what I could not understand was, what did she expect would happen if she herself were not present when the opening of the clock door would disclose the will? Did she want me to snatch the document: to bear the brunt of the Terhovens' wrath and disappointment? It was not like her to be afraid of fulfilling a duty, however dangerous that fulfilment might prove; and it certainly was not like her to break a promise given to a dying person.

But, of course, my business was to obey. Assuming that our movements were being watched, I poured out a dose of medicine for my dear lady, which she took and then fell back on her pillows as if exhausted.

"I think I could sleep now, Mary," she said; "but wake me later on; I must be at the *château* by twelve o'clock, you know."

As one of Lady Molly's boxes was in my room, I had no difficulty in arraying myself in some of her clothes. Thus, equipped and closely veiled, still ignorant of my lady's plans, anxious, but determined to obey like a soldier, blindly and unquestioningly, I made my way to the *château* a little before noon.

An old butler opened the door in answer to my ring, and in the inner hall sat the Marquise de Terhoven, whilst her son was walking agitatedly up and down.

"Ah! here comes my lady," said the *marquise*, with easy unconcern. "You have come, my lady," she added, rising and taking my hand, "to perform a duty which will rob my son of a fortune which by right should have been his. We can put no hindrance in your way, under penalty of an appalling disgrace which would then fall on my son; moreover, my late sister has filled this house with guards and spies. So, believe me, you need have no fear. You can perform your duty undisturbed. Perhaps you will not object to my son keeping you company. My precious sister had the door of her room removed before her death and a curtain put in its stead," she concluded with what was intended to be the sneer of a disappointed fortune-hunter, "so the least call from you will bring her spies to your assistance."

Without a word the *marquis* and I bowed to one another, then, preceded by the old family butler, we went up the monumental staircase to what I suppose had been the eccentric old lady's room.

The butler drew the *portière* curtain aside and he remained in the corridor whilst we went within. There stood the massive clock exactly as my lady had often described it to me. It was ticking with slow and deep-toned majesty.

Monsieur le Marquis pointed to an armchair for me. He was obviously in a state of terrible nerve-tension. He could not sit still, and his fingers were incessantly clasped and unclasped with a curious, febrile movement, which betrayed his intense agitation.

I was about to make a remark when he abruptly seized my wrist, placed one finger to his lips, and pointed in the direction of the *portière*. Apparently, he thought that someone was on the watch outside, but the clock itself was so placed that it could not be seen by anyone who was not actually in the room.

After that we were both silent, whilst that old piece of mechanism ticked on relentlessly, still hiding the secret which it contained.

I would have given two years' salary to know what Lady Molly would have wished me to do. Frankly, I fully expected to see her walk in at any moment. I could not bring myself to believe that she meant to shirk her duty.

But she had said to me, "Fall in with their views," so that when, presently, the *marquis* beckoned to me across the room to come and examine the clock, I obeyed readily enough. I felt, by that time, as if my entire body was stuffed with needles and pins, which were pricking my nerves and skin until I could have yelled with the agony of the sensation.

I walked across the room as if in a dream, and looked at the curious clock which, in less than fifteen minutes, would reveal its hidden secret. I suppose cleverer people than poor Mary Granard could enter into long philosophical disquisitions as to this dumb piece of mechanism which held the fate of this ruined, unscrupulous gambler safely within its doors; but I was only conscious of that incessant tick, tick, tick, whilst my eyes literally ached with staring at the door.

I don't know now how it all happened, for, of course, I was taken unawares; but the next moment I found myself quite helpless, hardly able to breathe, for a woollen scarf was being wound round my mouth, whilst two strong arms encircled my body so that I could not move.

"This is only a protection for myself, my dear Miss Granard," a trembling voice whispered in my ear; "keep quite still; no harm will come to you. In ten minutes, you shall have your fifty thousand *francs* in your pocket, and can walk unconcernedly out of the *château*. Neither your English lady nor *Monsieur le Curé* can say that they suffered any violence, nor will the clock be damaged. What happens after that I care not. The law cannot wrest the old fool's fortune from me, once I have destroyed her accursed will."

To begin to tell you what passed in my mind then were an impossibility. Did I actually guess what would happen, and what my dear lady had planned? Or was it merely the ingrafted sympathy which exists between her and me which caused me to act blindly in accordance with her wishes?

"Fall in with their views. Take their bribes," she had said, and I—like a soldier—obeyed this command to the letter.

I remained absolutely still, scarcely moving an eyelid as I watched the face of the clock, the minutes speeding on—now three—now five—now ten

I could hear the *marquis'* stertorous breathing close beside me.

Was I dreaming, or did I really see now a dark line—the width of a hair—between the massive double doors of the clock case? Oh, how my pulses throbbed!

That dark line was widening perceptibly. The doors were slowly opening! For the moment I almost felt in sympathy with the blackguard who was on the watch with me. His agitation must have been the most exquisite torture.

Now we could distinctly see the glimmer of white paper—not pressed down by the ponderous weights, but lying loosely just inside the doors; and *anon*, as the aperture widened, the papers fell out just at my feet.

With a smothered, gurgling exclamation which I will not attempt to describe, the *marquis* literally fell on that paper, like a hungry wild beast upon its prey. He was on his knees before me, and I could see that the paper was a square envelope, which, with a trembling hand, he tore open.

It contained a short document whereon the signature "Amédé de Terhoven" was clearly visible. It was the confession of forgery made by the young *marquis* just a year ago; there were also a few banknotes: some hundred thousand *francs*, perhaps. The young man threw them furiously aside, and once more turned to the clock. The doors were wide open, but they revealed nothing save the huge and complicated mechanism of the clock.

Mademoiselle de Genneville—eccentric and far seeing to the last—had played this gigantic hoax on her scheming relatives. Whilst they directed all their unscrupulous energies towards trying to obtain possession of her will in one place, she had calmly put it securely somewhere else.

Meantime, *Monsieur le Marquis* had sufficient presence of mind,

" Now we could distinctly see the glimmer of white paper "

and, I must own, sufficient dignity, not only to release me from my bonds but also to offer me the fifty thousand *francs* which he had promised me.

"I can wind up the clock now," he said dully, "and you can walk straight out of this place. No one need know that you impersonated your friend. She, no doubt, knew of this—hoax; therefore, we found the scheme to keep her out of the way so easy of accomplishment. It was a grisly joke, wasn't it? How the old witch must be chortling in her grave!"

Needless to say, I did not take his money. He escorted me downstairs silently, subdued, no doubt, by the spirit of hatred which had followed him up from the land of shadows.

He even showed no surprise when, on reaching the hall, he was met by his late aunt's lawyer, Maître Vendome, and also by Lady Molly, who had just arrived. Madame la Marquise de Terhoven was nowhere to be seen.

My dear lady smiled at me approvingly, and when I came near her she contrived to draw me aside and to whisper hurriedly:

"You have done admirably, Mary. I came to fetch you. But now that this young blackguard is thoroughly outwitted, we may as well go, for our work here is done."

The *Marquis* did not even glance at her as she slightly bowed her head to him, took leave of Maître Vendome, and finally walked out of the *château* with me.

As soon as we were out in the open air I begged for an explanation.

"Maître Vendôme has *mademoiselle's* will," she replied. "She had enjoined him to read it in the *château* today in the presence of the three trustees appointed for the poor of Porhoët, who inherit all her wealth."

"And the Terhovens?" I asked.

"They've got his confession back," she said dryly, "and they will receive an annuity from the trustees."

"And you knew this all along?" I rejoined somewhat reproachfully.

"Yes, so did the *curé*, but *mademoiselle* made me swear a most solemn oath not to reveal her secret even to you; she was so afraid of the machinations of the Terhovens. You see," continued Lady Molly, smiling at my eagerness, "Miss de Genneville possessed the ancient key wherewith she could open the clock case at any time. Obviously, even so perfect a piece of mechanism might go wrong, when examination and re-adjustment of the works would be necessary. After the family conclave wherein she had announced that her will was hidden in the clock, I—at my next interview with her—begged her to modify this idea, to send her will to her solicitor, but to leave the Terhovens under the impression that it was still lying in its strange hiding place. At first, she refused to listen to me or to discuss the subject, but I am happy to say that I finally succeeded in persuading her, with what result you already know."

"But poor *Monsieur le Curé!*" I ejaculated.

Her bright eyes gleamed with merriment.

"Oh! that was a final little hoax. He himself, poor dear, was afraid lest he might blurt out the whole thing. His illness was partly a sham, and he is quite all right again now, but the doctor at the Brest hospital is a great friend of his, and is keeping him there until all this business has blown over."

"I was the only one who was kept in the dark," I concluded ruefully.

"Yes, Mary, dear," said my dear lady, gently; "it was a promise, remember. But I never thought that we should get so much excitement outside our own professional work."

It certainly had been a non-professional experience; but here, too, as in the detection of crime, her keen intuition had proved more than a match for an unscrupulous blackguard, and certainly on the 20th day of September last I lived through the most exciting ten minutes of my life.

A Christmas Tragedy

1

It was a fairly merry Christmas party, although the surliness of our host somewhat marred the festivities. But imagine two such beautiful young women as my own dear lady and Margaret Ceely, and a Christmas Eve Cinderella in the beautiful ballroom at Clevere Hall, and you will understand that even Major Ceely's well-known cantankerous temper could not altogether spoil the merriment of a good, old-fashioned, festive gathering. It is a far cry from a Christmas Eve party to a series of cattle-maiming outrages, yet I am forced to mention these now, for although they were ultimately proved to have no connection with the murder of the unfortunate major, yet they were undoubtedly the means whereby the miscreant was enabled to accomplish the horrible deed with surety, swiftness, and—as it turned out afterwards—a very grave chance of immunity.

Everyone in the neighbourhood had been taking the keenest possible interest in those dastardly outrages against innocent animals. They were either the work of desperate ruffians who stick at nothing in order to obtain a few shillings, or else of madmen with weird propensities for purposeless crimes.

Once or twice suspicious characters had been seen lurking about in the fields, and on more than one occasion a cart was heard in the middle of the night driving away at furious speed. Whenever this occurred the discovery of a fresh outrage was sure to follow, but, so far, the miscreants had succeeded in baffling not only the police, but also the many farm hands who had formed themselves into a band of volunteer watchmen, determined to bring the cattle maimers to justice.

We had all been talking about these mysterious events during the dinner which preceded the dance at Clevere Hall; but later on, when the young people had assembled, and when the first strains of "The Merry Widow" waltz had set us aglow with prospective enjoyment, the unpleasant topic was wholly forgotten.

The guests went away early, Major Ceely, as usual, doing nothing to detain them; and by midnight all of us who were staying in the house had gone up to bed.

My dear lady and I shared a bedroom and dressing-room together, our windows giving on the front. Clevere Hall is, as you know, not very far from York, on the other side of Bishopthorpe, and is one of the finest old mansions in the neighbourhood, its only disadvantage being that, in spite of the gardens being very extensive in the rear, the front of the house lies very near the road.

It was about two hours after I had switched off the electric light and called out "Goodnight" to my dear lady, that something roused me out of my first sleep. Suddenly I felt very wide-awake, and sat up in bed. Most unmistakably—though still from some considerable distance along the road—came the sound of a cart being driven at unusual speed.

Evidently my dear lady was also awake. She jumped out of bed and, drawing aside the curtains, looked out of the window. The same idea had, of course, flashed upon us both, at the very moment of waking: all the conversations anent the cattle-maimers and their cart, which we had heard since our arrival at Clevere, recurring to our minds simultaneously.

I had joined Lady Molly beside the window, and I don't know how many minutes we remained there in observation, not more than two probably, for *anon* the sound of the cart died away in the distance along a side road. Suddenly we were startled with a terrible cry of "Murder! Help! Help!" issuing from the other side of the house, followed by an awful, deadly silence. I stood there near the window shivering with terror, while my dear lady, having already turned on the light, was hastily slipping into some clothes.

The cry had, of course, aroused the entire household, but my dear lady was even then the first to get downstairs, and to reach the garden door at the back of the house, whence the weird and despairing cry had undoubtedly proceeded.

That door was wide open. Two steps lead from it to the terraced walk which borders the house on that side, and along these steps Major Ceely was lying, face downwards, with arms outstretched, and a terrible wound between his shoulder-blades.

A gun was lying close by—his own. It was easy to conjecture that he, too, hearing the rumble of the wheels, had run out, gun in hand, meaning, no doubt, to effect, or at least to help, in the capture of the escaping criminals. Someone had been lying in wait for him; that was obvious—someone who had perhaps waited and watched for this special opportunity for days, or even weeks, in order to catch the unfortunate man unawares.

Well, it were useless to recapitulate all the various little incidents which occurred from the moment when Lady Molly and the butler first lifted the major's lifeless body from the terrace steps until that instant when Miss Ceely, with remarkable coolness and presence of mind, gave what details she could of the terrible event to the local police inspector and to the doctor, both hastily summoned.

These little incidents, with but slight variations, occur in every instance when a crime has been committed. The broad facts alone are of weird and paramount interest.

Major Ceely was dead. He had been stabbed with amazing sureness and terrible violence in the back. The weapon used must have been some sort of heavy, clasp knife. The murdered man was now lying in his own bedroom upstairs, even as the Christmas bells on that cold, crisp morning sent cheering echoes through the stillness of the air.

We had, of course, left the house, as had all the other guests. Everyone felt the deepest possible sympathy for the beautiful young girl who had been so full of the joy of living but a few hours ago, and was now the pivot round which revolved the weird shadow of tragedy, of curious suspicions and of an ever-growing mystery. But at such times all strangers, acquaintances, and even friends in a house, are only an additional burden to an already overwhelming load of sorrow and of trouble.

We took up our quarters at the "Black Swan," in York. The local superintendent, hearing that Lady Molly had been actually a guest at Clevere on the night of the murder, had asked her to remain in the neighbourhood.

There was no doubt that she could easily obtain the chief's consent to assist the local police in the elucidation of this extraordinary crime. At this time both her reputation and her remarkable powers were at their zenith, and there was not a single member of the entire police force in the kingdom who would not have availed himself gladly of her help when confronted with a seemingly impenetrable mystery.

That the murder of Major Ceely threatened to become such no one could deny. In cases of this sort, when no robbery of any kind has accompanied the graver crime, it is the duty of the police and also of the coroner to try to find out, first and foremost, what possible motive there could be behind so cowardly an assault; and among motives, of course, deadly hatred, revenge, and animosity stand paramount.

But here the police were at once confronted with the terrible difficulty, not of discovering whether Major Ceely had an enemy at all, but rather which, of all those people who owed him a grudge, hated him sufficiently to risk hanging for the sake of getting him out of the way.

As a matter of fact, the unfortunate major was one of those miserable people who seem to live in a state of perpetual enmity with everything and everybody. Morning, noon and night he grumbled, and when he did not grumble, he quarrelled either with his own daughter or with the people of his household, or with his neighbours.

I had often heard about him and his eccentric, disagreeable ways from Lady Molly, who had known him for many years. She—like everybody in the county who otherwise would have shunned the old man—kept up a semblance of friendship with him for the sake of the daughter.

Margaret Ceely was a singularly beautiful girl, and as the major was reputed to be very wealthy, these two facts perhaps combined to prevent the irascible gentleman from living in quite so complete an isolation as he would have wished.

Mammas of marriageable young men vied with one another in their welcome to Miss Ceely at garden parties, dances and bazaars. Indeed, Margaret had been surrounded with admirers ever since she had come out of the schoolroom. Needless to say, the cantankerous major received these pretenders to his daughter's hand not only with insolent disdain, but at times even with violent opposition.

In spite of this the moths fluttered round the candle, and amongst this venturesome tribe none stood out more prominently than Mr. Laurence Smethick, son of the M.P. for the Pakethorpe division. Some folk there were who vowed that the young people were secretly engaged, in spite of the fact that Margaret was an outrageous flirt and openly encouraged more than one of her crowd of adorers.

Be that as it may, one thing was very certain—namely, that Major Ceely did not approve of Mr. Smethick any more than he did of the others, and there had been more than one quarrel between the young man and his prospective father-in-law.

On that memorable Christmas Eve at Clevere none of us could fail to notice his absence; whilst Margaret, on the other hand, had shown marked predilection for the society of Captain Glynne, who, since the sudden death of his cousin, Viscount Heslington, Lord Ullesthorpe's only son (who was killed in the hunting field last October, if you remember), had become heir to the earldom and its £40,000 a year.

Personally, I strongly disapproved of Margaret's behaviour the night of the dance; her attitude with regard to Mr. Smethick—whose constant attendance on her had justified the rumour that they were engaged—being more than callous.

On that morning of December 24th—Christmas Eve, in fact—the young man had called at Clevere. I remember seeing him just as he was being shown into the *boudoir* downstairs. A few moments later the sound of angry voices rose with appalling distinctness from that room. We all tried not to listen, yet could not fail to hear Major Ceely's overbearing words of rudeness to the visitor, who, it seems, had merely asked to see Miss Ceely, and had been most unexpectedly confronted by the irascible and extremely disagreeable major.

Of course, the young man speedily lost his temper, too, and the whole incident ended with a very unpleasant quarrel between the two men in the hall, and with the major peremptorily forbidding Mr. Smethick ever to darken his doors again.

On that night Major Ceely was murdered.

2

Of course, at first, no one attached any importance to this weird coincidence. The very thought of connecting the idea of murder with that of the personality of a bright, good-looking young Yorkshireman like Mr. Smethick seemed, indeed, preposterous, and with one accord all of us who were practically witnesses to the quarrel between the two men, tacitly agreed to say nothing at all about it at the inquest, unless we were absolutely obliged to do so on oath.

In view of the major's terrible temper, this quarrel, mind you, had not the importance which it otherwise would have had; and we all flattered ourselves that we had well succeeded in parrying the coroner's questions.

The verdict at the inquest was against some person or persons unknown; and I, for one, was very glad that young Smethick's name had not been mentioned in connection with this terrible crime.

Two days later the superintendent at Bishopthorpe sent an urgent telephonic message to Lady Molly, begging her to come to the police-station immediately. We had the use of a motor all the while that we stayed at the "Black Swan," and in less than ten minutes we were bowling along at express speed towards Bishopthorpe.

On arrival we were immediately shown into Superintendent Etty's private room behind the office. He was there talking with Danvers—who had recently come down from London. In a corner of the room, sitting very straight on a high-backed chair, was a youngish woman of the servant class, who, as we entered, cast a quick, and I thought suspicious, glance at us both.

She was dressed in a coat and skirt of shabby looking black, and although her face might have been called good-looking—for she had fine, dark eyes—her entire appearance was distinctly repellent. It suggested slatternliness in an unusual degree; there were holes in her shoes and in her stockings, the sleeve of her coat was half unsewn, and the braid on her skirt hung in loops all round the bottom. She had very red and very coarse-looking hands, and undoubtedly there was a furtive expression in her eyes, which, when she began speaking, changed to one of defiance.

Etty came forward with great alacrity when my dear lady entered. He looked perturbed, and seemed greatly relieved at sight of her.

"She is the wife of one of the outdoor men at Clevere," he explained rapidly to Lady Molly, nodding in the direction of the young woman, "and she has come here with such a queer tale that I thought you would like to hear it."

"She knows something about the murder?" asked Lady Molly.

"Noa! I didn't say that!" here interposed the woman, roughly, "doan't you go and tell no lies, Master Inspector. I thought as how you might wish to know what my husband saw on the night when the major was murdered, that's all; and I've come to tell you."

"Why didn't your husband come himself?" asked Lady Molly.

"Oh, Haggett ain't well enough—he—" she began explaining, with a careless shrug of the shoulders, "so to speak—"

"The fact of the matter is, my lady," interposed Etty, "this woman's husband is half-witted. I believe he is only kept on in the garden because he is very strong and can help with the digging. It is because his testimony is so little to be relied on that I wished to consult you as to how we should act in the matter."

"What is his testimony, then?"

"Tell this lady what you have just told us, Mrs. Haggett, will you?" said Etty, curtly.

Again, that quick, suspicious glance shot into the woman's eyes. Lady Molly took the chair which Danvers had brought forward for her, and sat down opposite Mrs. Haggett, fixing her earnest, calm gaze upon her.

"There's not much to tell," said the woman, sullenly. "Haggett is certainly queer in his head sometimes—and when he is queer, he goes wandering about the place of nights."

"Yes?" said my lady, for Mrs. Haggett had paused awhile and now seemed unwilling to proceed.

"Well!" she resumed with sudden determination, "he had got one of his queer fits on on Christmas Eve, and didn't come in till long after midnight. He told me as how he'd seen a young gentleman prowling about the garden on the terrace side. He heard the cry of 'Murder' and 'Help' soon after that, and ran in home because he was frightened."

"Home?" asked Lady Molly, quietly, "where is home?"

"The cottage where we live. Just back of the kitchen garden."

"Why didn't you tell all this to the superintendent before?"

"Because Haggett only told me last night, when he seemed less queer-like. He is mighty silent when the fits are on him."

"Did he know who the gentleman was whom he saw?"

"No, ma'am—I don't suppose he did—leastways he wouldn't say—but—"

"Yes? But?"

"He found this in the garden yesterday," said the woman, holding out a screw of paper which apparently, she had held tightly clutched up to now, "and maybe that's what brought Christmas Eve and the murder back to his mind."

Lady Molly took the thing from her, and undid the soiled bit of paper with her dainty fingers. The next moment she held up for Etty's inspection a beautiful ring composed of an exquisitely carved moonstone surrounded with diamonds of unusual brilliance.

At the moment the setting and the stones themselves were marred by scraps of sticky mud which clung to them; the ring obviously having lain on the ground, and perhaps been trampled on for some days, and then been only very partially washed,

"At any rate you can find out the ownership of the ring," commented my dear lady after a while, in answer to Etty's silent attitude of expectancy. "There would be no harm in that."

Then she turned once more to the woman.

"I'll walk with you to your cottage, if I may," she said decisively, "and have a chat with your husband. Is he at home?"

I thought Mrs. Haggett took this suggestion with marked reluctance. I could well imagine, from her own personal appearance, that her home was most unlikely to be in a fit state for a lady's visit. However, she could, of course, do nothing but obey, and, after a few muttered words of grudging acquiescence, she rose from her chair and stalked towards the door, leaving my lady to follow as she chose.

Before going, however, she turned and shot an angry glance at Etty.

"You'll give me back the ring, Master Inspector," she said with her usual tone of sullen defiance. "'Findings is keepings' you know."

"I am afraid not," replied Etty, curtly; "but there's always the reward offered by Miss Ceely for information which would lead to the apprehension of her father's murderer. You may get that, you know. It is a hundred pounds."

"Yes! I knew that," she remarked dryly, as, without further comment, she finally went out of the room.

3

My dear lady came back very disappointed from her interview with Haggett.

It seems that he was indeed half-witted—almost an imbecile, in fact, with but a few lucid intervals, of which this present day was one. But, of course, his testimony was practically valueless.

He reiterated the story already told by his wife, adding no details. He had seen a young gentleman roaming on the terraced walk on the night of the murder. He did not know who the young gentleman was. He was going homewards when he heard the cry of "Murder," and ran to his cottage because he was frightened. He picked up the ring yesterday in the perennial border below the terrace and gave it to his wife.

Two of these brief statements made by the imbecile were easily proved to be true, and my dear lady had ascertained this before she returned to me. One of the Clevere under-gardeners said he had seen Haggett running home in the small hours of that fateful Christmas morning. He himself had been on the watch for the cattle-maimers that night, and remembered the little circumstance quite plainly. He added that Haggett certainly looked to be in a panic.

Then Newby, another outdoor man at the Hall, saw Haggett pick up the ring in the perennial border and advised him to take it to the police.

Somehow, all of us who were so interested in that terrible Christmas tragedy felt strangely perturbed at all this. No names had been mentioned as yet, but whenever my dear lady and I looked at one another, or whenever we talked to Etty or Danvers, we all felt that a certain name, one particular personality, was lurking at the back of all our minds.

The two men, of course, had no sentimental scruples to worry them. Taking the Haggett story merely as a clue, they worked diligently on that, with the result that twenty-four hours later Etty appeared in our private room at the "Black Swan" and calmly informed us that he had just got a warrant out against Mr. Laurence Smethick on a charge of murder, and was on his way even now to effect the arrest.

"Mr. Smethick did not murder Major Ceely," was Lady Molly's firm and only comment when she heard the news.

"Well, my lady, that's as it may be!" rejoined Etty, speaking with that deference with which the entire force invariably addressed my dear lady; "but we have collected a sufficiency of evidence, at any rate, to justify the arrest, and, in my opinion, enough of it to hang any man. Mr. Smethick purchased the moonstone and diamond ring at Nicholson's in Coney Street about a week ago.

"He was seen abroad on Christmas Eve by several persons, loitering round the gates at Clevere Hall, somewhere about the time when the guests were leaving after the dance, and, again, some few moments after the first cry of 'Murder' had been heard. His own valet admits that his master did not get home that night until long after 2.0 a.m., whilst even Miss Granard here won't deny that there was a terrible quarrel between Mr. Smethick and Major Ceely less than twenty-four hours before the latter was murdered."

Lady Molly offered no remark to this array of facts which Etty thus pitilessly marshalled before us, but I could not refrain from exclaiming:

"Mr. Smethick is innocent, I am sure."

"I hope, for his sake, he may be," retorted Etty, gravely, "but somehow 'tis a pity that he don't seem able to give a good account of himself between midnight and two o'clock that Christmas morning."

"Oh!" I ejaculated, "what does he say about that?"

"Nothing," replied the man, dryly; "that's just the trouble."

Well, of course, as you who read the papers will doubtless remember, Mr. Laurence Smethick, son of Colonel Smethick, M.P., of Pakethorpe Hall, Yorks, was arrested on the charge of having murdered Major Ceely on the night of December 24th-25th, and, after the usual magisterial inquiry, was duly committed to stand his trial at the next York assizes.

I remember well that, throughout his preliminary ordeal, young Smethick bore himself like one who had given up all hope of refuting the terrible charges brought against him, and, I must say, the formidable number of witnesses which the police brought up against him more than explained that attitude.

Of course, Haggett was not called, but, as it happened, there were plenty of people to swear that Mr. Laurence Smethick was seen loitering round the gates of Clevere Hall after the guests had departed on Christmas Eve. The head gardener, who lives at the lodge, actually spoke to him, and Captain Glynne, leaning out of his brougham window, was heard to exclaim:

"Hello, Smethick, what are you doing here at this time of night?"

And there were others, too.

To Captain Glynne's credit, be it here recorded, he tried his best to deny having recognised his unfortunate friend in the dark. Pressed by the magistrate, he said obstinately:

"I thought at the time that it was Mr. Smethick standing by the lodge gates, but on thinking the matter over I feel sure that I was mistaken."

On the other hand, what stood dead against young Smethick was, firstly, the question of the ring, and then the fact that he was seen in the immediate neighbourhood of Clevere, both at midnight and again at about two, when some men, who had been on the watch for the cattle-maimers, saw him walking away rapidly in the direction of Pakethorpe.

What was, of course, unexplainable and very terrible to witness was Mr. Smethick's obstinate silence with regard to his own movements during those fatal hours on that night. He did not contradict those who said that they had seen him at about midnight near the gates of Clevere, nor his own valet's statements as to the hour when he returned home. All he said was that he could not account for what he did between the time when the guests left the Hall and he himself went back to Pakethorpe. He realised the danger in which he stood, and what caused him to be silent about a matter which might mean life or death to him could not easily be conjectured.

The ownership of the ring he could not and did not dispute. He had lost it in the grounds of Clevere, he said. But the jeweller in Coney Street swore that he had sold the ring to Mr. Smethick on the 18th of December, whilst it was a well-known and an admitted fact that the young man had not openly been inside the gates of Clevere for over a fortnight before that.

On this evidence Laurence Smethick was committed for trial. Though the actual weapon with which the unfortunate major had been stabbed had not been found, nor its ownership traced, there was such a vast array of circumstantial evidence against the young man that bail was refused.

He had, on the advice of his solicitor, Mr. Grayson—one of the ablest lawyers in York—reserved his defence, and on that miserable afternoon at the close of the year, we all filed out of the crowded court, feeling terribly depressed and anxious.

4

My dear lady and I walked back to our hotel in silence. Our hearts seemed to weigh heavily within us. We felt mortally sorry for that good-looking young Yorkshireman, who, we were convinced, was innocent, yet at the same time seemed involved in a tangled web of deadly circumstances from which he seemed quite unable to extricate himself.

We did not feel like discussing the matter in the open streets, neither did we make any comment when presently, in a block in the traffic in Coney Street, we saw Margaret Ceely driving her smart dogcart, whilst sitting beside her, and talking with great earnestness close to her ear, sat Captain Glynne.

She was in deep mourning, and had obviously been doing some shopping, for she was surrounded with parcels; so perhaps it was hypercritical to blame her. Yet somehow it struck me that just at the moment when there hung in the balance the life and honour of a man with whose name her own had oft been linked by popular rumour, it showed more than callous contempt for his welfare to be seen driving about with another man who, since his sudden access to fortune, had undoubtedly become a rival in her favours.

When we arrived at the "Black Swan," we were surprised to hear that Mr. Grayson had called to see my dear lady, and was upstairs waiting.

Lady Molly ran up to our sitting-room and greeted him with marked cordiality. Mr. Grayson is an elderly, dry-looking man, but he looked visibly affected, and it was some time before he seemed able to plunge into the subject which had brought him hither. He fidgeted in his chair, and started talking about the weather.

"I am not here in a strictly professional capacity, you know," said Lady Molly presently, with a kindly smile and with a view to helping him out of his embarrassment. "Our police, I fear me, have an exaggerated view of my capacities, and the men here asked me unofficially to remain in the neighbourhood and to give them my advice if they should require it. Our chief is very lenient to me, and has allowed me to stay. Therefore, if there is anything I can do—"

"Indeed, indeed there is!" ejaculated Mr. Grayson with sudden energy. "From all I hear, there is not another soul in the kingdom but you who can save this innocent man from the gallows."

My dear lady heaved a little sigh of satisfaction. She had all along wanted to have a more important finger in that Yorkshire pie.

"Mr. Smethick?" she said.

"Yes; my unfortunate young client," replied the lawyer. "I may as well tell you," he resumed after a slight pause, during which he seemed to pull himself together, "as briefly as possible what occurred on December 24th last and on the following Christmas morning. You will then understand the terrible plight in which my client finds himself, and how impossible it is for him to explain his actions on that eventful night. You will understand, also, why I have come to ask your help and your advice. Mr. Smethick considered himself engaged to Miss Ceely. The engagement had not been made public because of Major Ceely's anticipated opposition, but the young people had been very intimate, and many letters had passed between them. On the morning of the 24th Mr. Smethick called at the Hall, his intention then being merely to present his *fiancée* with the ring you know of. You remember the unfortunate contretemps that occurred: I mean the unprovoked quarrel sought by Major Ceely with my poor client, ending with the irascible old man forbidding Mr. Smethick the house.

"My client walked out of Clevere feeling, as you may well imagine, very wrathful; on the doorstep, just as he was leaving, he met Miss Margaret, and told her very briefly what had occurred. She took the matter very lightly at first, but finally became more serious, and ended the brief interview with the request that, since he could not come to the dance after what had occurred, he should come and see her afterwards, meeting her in the gardens soon after midnight. She would not take the ring from him then, but talked a good deal of sentiment about Christmas morning, asking him to bring the ring to her at night, and also the letters which she had written him. Well—you can guess the rest."

Lady Molly nodded thoughtfully.

"Miss Ceely was playing a double game," continued Mr. Grayson, earnestly. "She was determined to break off all relationship with Mr. Smethick, for she had transferred her volatile affections to Captain Glynne, who had lately become heir to an earldom and £40,000 a year. Under the guise of sentimental twaddle, she got my unfortunate client to meet her at night in the grounds of Clevere and to give up to her the letters which might have compromised her in the eyes of her new lover. At two o'clock a.m. Major Ceely was murdered by one of his numerous enemies; as to which I do not know, nor does Mr. Smethick. He had just parted from Miss Ceely at the very moment when the first cry of 'Murder' roused Clevere from its slumbers.

"This she could confirm if she only would, for the two were still in sight of each other, she inside the gates, he just a little way down the road. Mr. Smethick saw Margaret Ceely run rapidly back towards the house. He waited about a little while, half hesitating what to do; then he reflected that his presence might be embarrassing, or even compromising to her whom, in spite of all, he still loved dearly; and knowing that there were plenty of men in and about the house to render what assistance was necessary, he finally turned his steps and went home a broken-hearted man, since she had given him the go-by, taken her letters away, and flung contemptuously into the mud the ring he had bought for her."

The lawyer paused, mopping his forehead and gazing with whole-souled earnestness at my lady's beautiful, thoughtful face.

"Has Mr. Smethick spoken to Miss Ceely since?" asked Lady Molly, after a while.

"No; but I did," replied the lawyer.

"What was her attitude?"

"One of bitter and callous contempt. She denies my unfortunate client's story from beginning to end; declares that she never saw him after she bade him 'good-morning' on the doorstep of Clevere Hall, when she heard of his unfortunate quarrel with her father. Nay, more; she scornfully calls the whole tale a cowardly attempt to shield a dastardly crime behind a still more dastardly libel on a defenceless girl."

We were all silent now, buried in thought which none of us would have cared to translate into words. That the impasse seemed indeed hopeless no one could deny.

The tower of damning evidence against the unfortunate young man had indeed been built by remorseless circumstances with no faltering hand.

Margaret Ceely alone could have saved him, but with brutal indifference she preferred the sacrifice of an innocent man's life and honour to that of her own chances of a brilliant marriage. There are such women in the world; thank God I have never met any but that one!

Yet am I wrong when I say that she alone could save the unfortunate young man, who throughout was behaving with such consummate gallantry, refusing to give his own explanation of the events that occurred on that Christmas morning, unless she chose first to tell the tale. There was one present now in the dingy little room at the "Black Swan" who could disentangle that weird skein of coincidences, if any human being not gifted with miraculous powers could indeed do it at this eleventh hour.

She now said, gently:

"What would you like me to do in this matter, Mr. Grayson? And why have you come to me rather than to the police?"

"How can I go with this tale to the police?" he ejaculated in obvious despair. "Would they not also look upon it as a dastardly libel on a woman's reputation? We have no proofs, remember, and Miss Ceely denies the whole story from first to last. No, no!" he exclaimed with wonderful fervour. "I came to you because I have heard of your marvellous gifts, your extraordinary intuition. Someone murdered Major Ceely! It was not my old friend Colonel Smethick's son. Find out who it was, then! I beg of you, find out who it was!"

He fell back in his chair, broken down with grief. With inexpressible gentleness Lady Molly went up to him and placed her beautiful white hand on his shoulder.

"I will do my best, Mr. Grayson," she said simply.

We remained alone and singularly quiet the whole of that evening. That my dear lady's active brain was hard at work I could guess by the brilliance of her eyes, and that sort of absolute stillness in her person through which one could almost feel the delicate nerves vibrating.

The story told her by the lawyer had moved her singularly. Mind you, she had always been morally convinced of young Smethick's innocence, but in her the professional woman always fought hard battles against the sentimentalist, and in this instance the overwhelming circumstantial evidence and the conviction of her superiors had forced her to accept the young man's guilt as something out of her ken.

By his silence, too, the young man had tacitly confessed; and if a man is perceived on the very scene of a crime, both before it has been committed and directly afterwards; if something admittedly belonging to him is found within three yards of where the murderer must have stood; if, added to this, he has had a bitter quarrel with the victim, and can give no account of his actions or whereabouts during the fatal time, it were vain to cling to optimistic beliefs in that same man's innocence.

But now matters had assumed an altogether different aspect. The story told by Mr. Smethick's lawyer had all the appearance of truth. Margaret Ceely's character, her callousness on the very day when her late *fiancé* stood in the dock, her quick transference of her affections to the richer man, all made the account of the events on Christmas night as told by Mr. Grayson extremely plausible.

No wonder my dear lady was buried in thought.

"I shall have to take the threads up from the beginning, Mary," she said to me the following morning, when after breakfast she appeared in her neat coat and skirt, with hat and gloves, ready to go out, "so, on the whole, I think I will begin with a visit to the Haggetts."

"I may come with you, I suppose?" I suggested meekly.

"Oh, yes!" she rejoined carelessly.

Somehow, I had an inkling that the carelessness of her mood was only on the surface. It was not likely that she—my sweet, womanly, ultra-feminine, beautiful lady—should feel callously on this absorbing subject.

We motored down to Bishopthorpe. It was bitterly cold, raw, damp, and foggy. The chauffeur had some difficulty in finding the cottage, the "home" of the imbecile gardener and his wife.

There was certainly not much look of home about the place. When, after much knocking at the door, Mrs. Haggett finally opened it, we saw before us one of the most miserable, slatternly places I think I ever saw.

In reply to Lady Molly's somewhat curt inquiry, the woman said that Haggett was in bed, suffering from one of his "fits."

"That is a great pity," said my dear lady, rather unsympathetically, I thought, "for I must speak with him at once."

"What is it about?" asked the woman, sullenly. "I can take a message."

"I am afraid not," rejoined my lady. "I was asked to see Haggett personally."

"By whom, I'd like to know," she retorted, now almost insolently.

"I dare say you would. But you are wasting precious time. Hadn't you better help your husband on with his clothes? This lady and I will wait in the parlour."

After some hesitation the woman finally complied, looking very sulky the while.

We went into the miserable little room wherein not only grinding poverty but also untidiness and dirt were visible all round. We sat down on two of the cleanest-looking chairs, and waited whilst a colloquy in subdued voices went on in the room over our heads.

The colloquy, I may say, seemed to consist of agitated whispers on one part, and wailing complaints on the other. This was followed presently by some thuds and much shuffling, and presently Haggett, looking uncared-for, dirty, and unkempt, entered the parlour, followed by his wife.

He came forward, dragging his ill-shod feet and pulling nervously at his forelock.

"Ah!" said my lady, kindly; "I am glad to see you down, Haggett, though I am afraid I haven't very good news for you."

"Yes, miss!" murmured the man, obviously not quite comprehending what was said to him.

"I represent the workhouse authorities," continued Lady Molly, "and I thought we could arrange for you and your wife to come into the Union tonight, perhaps."

"The Union?" here interposed the woman, roughly. "What do you mean? We ain't going to the Union?"

"Well! but since you are not staying here," rejoined my lady, blandly, "you will find it impossible to get another situation for your husband in his present mental condition."

"Miss Ceely won't give us the go-by," she retorted defiantly.

"She might wish to carry out her late father's intentions," said Lady Molly with seeming carelessness.

"The major was a cruel, cantankerous brute," shouted the woman with unpremeditated violence. "Haggett had served him faithfully for twelve years, and—"

She checked herself abruptly, and cast one of her quick, furtive glances at Lady Molly.

Her silence now had become as significant as her outburst of rage, and it was Lady Molly who concluded the phrase for her.

"And yet he dismissed him without warning," she said calmly.

"Who told you that?" retorted the woman.

"The same people, no doubt, who declare that you and Haggett had a grudge against the major for this dismissal."

"That's a lie," asserted Mrs. Haggett, doggedly; "we gave information about Mr. Smethick having killed the major because—"

"Ah," interrupted Lady Molly, quickly, "but then Mr. Smethick did not murder Major Ceely, and your information therefore was useless!"

"Then who killed the major, I should like to know?"

Her manner was arrogant, coarse, and extremely unpleasant. I marvelled why my dear lady put up with it, and what was going on in that busy brain of hers. She looked quite urbane and smiling, whilst I wondered what in the world she meant by this story of the workhouse and the dismissal of Haggett.

"Ah, that's what none of us know!" she now said lightly; "some folks say it was your husband."

"They lie!" she retorted quickly, whilst the imbecile, evidently not understanding the drift of the conversation, was mechanically stroking his red mop of hair and looking helplessly all round him.

"He was home before the cries of 'Murder' were heard in the house," continued Mrs. Haggett.

"How do you know?" asked Lady Molly, quickly.

"How do I know?"

"Yes; you couldn't have heard the cries all the way to this cottage—why, it's over half a mile from the Hall!"

"He was home, I say," she repeated with dogged obstinacy.

"You sent him?"

"He didn't do it—"

130

"No one will believe you, especially when the knife is found."

"What knife?"

"His clasp knife, with which he killed Major Ceely," said Lady Molly, quietly; "see, he has it in his hand now."

And with a sudden, wholly unexpected gesture she pointed to the imbecile, who in an aimless way had prowled round the room whilst this rapid colloquy was going on.

The purport of it all must in some sort of way have found an echo in his enfeebled brain. He wandered up to the dresser whereon lay the remnants of that morning's breakfast, together with some crockery and utensils.

In that same half-witted and irresponsible way, he had picked up one of the knives and now was holding it out towards his wife, whilst a look of fear spread over his countenance.

"I can't do it, Annie, I can't—you'd better do it," he said.

There was dead silence in the little room. The woman Haggett stood as if turned to stone. Ignorant and superstitious as she was, I suppose that the situation had laid hold of her nerves, and that she felt that the finger of a relentless Fate was even now being pointed at her.

The imbecile was shuffling forward, closer and closer to his wife, still holding out the knife towards her and murmuring brokenly:

"I can't do it. You'd better, Annie—you'd better—"

He was close to her now, and all at once her rigidity and nerve-strain gave way; she gave a hoarse cry, and snatching the knife from the poor wretch, she rushed at him ready to strike.

Lady Molly and I were both young, active and strong; and there was nothing of the squeamish *grande dame* about my dear lady when quick action was needed. But even then, we had some difficulty in dragging Annie Haggett away from her miserable husband. Blinded with fury, she was ready to kill the man who had betrayed her. Finally, we succeeded in wresting the knife from her.

You may be sure that it required some pluck after that to sit down again quietly and to remain in the same room with this woman, who already had one crime upon her conscience, and with this weird, half-witted creature who kept on murmuring pitiably:

"You'd better do it, Annie—"

Well, you've read the account of the case, so you know what followed. Lady Molly did not move from that room until she had obtained the woman's full confession. All she did for her own protection was to order me to open the window and to blow the police whistle which she handed to me. The police-station fortunately was not very far, and sound carried in the frosty air.

She admitted to me afterwards that it had been foolish, perhaps, not to have brought Etty or Danvers with her, but she was supremely anxious not to put the woman on the alert from the very start, hence her circumlocutory speeches anent the workhouse, and Haggett's probable dismissal.

That the woman had had some connection with the crime, Lady Molly, with her keen intuition, had always felt; but as there was no witness to the murder itself, and all circumstantial evidence was dead against young Smethick, there was only one chance of successful discovery, and that was the murderer's own confession.

If you think over the interview between my dear lady and the Haggetts on that memorable morning, you will realise how admirably Lady Molly had led up to the weird finish. She would not speak to the woman unless Haggett was present, and she felt sure that as soon as the subject of the murder cropped up, the imbecile would either do or say something that would reveal the truth.

Mechanically, when Major Ceely's name was mentioned, he had taken up the knife. The whole scene recurred to his tottering mind. That the major had summarily dismissed him recently was one of those bold guesses which Lady Molly was wont to make.

That Haggett had been merely egged on by his wife, and had been too terrified at the last to do the deed himself was no surprise to her, and hardly one to me, whilst the fact that the woman ultimately wreaked her own passionate revenge upon the unfortunate major was hardly to be wondered at, in the face of her own coarse and elemental personality.

Cowed by the quickness of events, and by the appearance of Danvers and Etty on the scene, she finally made full confession.

She was maddened by the major's brutality, when with rough, cruel words he suddenly turned her husband adrift, refusing to give him further employment. She herself had great ascendency over the imbecile, and had drilled him into a part of hate and of revenge. At first, he had seemed ready and willing to obey. It was arranged that he was to watch on the terrace every night until such time as an alarm of the recurrence of the cattle-maiming outrages should lure the major out alone.

This effectually occurred on Christmas morning, but not before Haggett, frightened and pusillanimous, was ready to flee rather than to accomplish the villainous deed. But Annie Haggett, guessing perhaps that he would shrink from the crime at the last, had also kept watch every night. Picture the prospective murderer watching and being watched!

When Haggett came across his wife he deputed her to do the deed herself.

I suppose that either terror of discovery or merely desire for the promised reward had caused the woman to fasten the crime on another.

The finding of the ring by Haggett was the beginning of that cruel thought which, but for my dear lady's marvellous powers, would indeed have sent a brave young man to the gallows.

Ah, you wish to know if Margaret Ceely is married? No! Captain Glynne cried off. What suspicions crossed his mind I cannot say; but he never proposed to Margaret, and now she is in Australia—staying with an aunt, I think—and she has sold Clevere Hall.

The Bag of Sand

1

Of course, I knew at once by the expression of her face that morning that my dear lady had some important business on hand.

She had a bundle in her arms, consisting of a shabby-looking coat and skirt, and a very dowdy hat trimmed with bunches of cheap, calico roses.

"Put on these things at once, Mary," she said curtly, "for you are going to apply for the situation of 'good plain cook,' so mind you look the part."

"But where in the world—?" I gasped in astonishment.

"In the house of Mr. Nicholas Jones, in Eaton Terrace," she interrupted dryly, "the one occupied until recently by his sister, the late Mrs. Dunstan. Mrs. Jones is advertising for a cook, and you must get that place."

As you know, I have carried obedience to the level of a fine art. Nor was I altogether astonished that my dear lady had at last been asked to put one of her dainty fingers in that Dunstan pie, which was puzzling our fellows more completely than any other case I have ever known.

I don't know if you remember the many circumstances, the various contradictions which were cropping up at every turn, and which baffled our ablest detectives at the very moment when they thought themselves most near the solution of that strange mystery.

Mrs. Dunstan herself was a very uninteresting individual: self-righteous, self-conscious and fat, a perfect type of the moneyed middle-class woman whose balance at the local bank is invariably heavier than that of her neighbours. Her niece, Violet Frostwicke, lived with her: a smart, pretty girl, inordinately fond of dainty clothes and other luxuries which money can give. Being totally impecunious herself, she bore with the older woman's constantly varying caprices with almost angelic patience, a fact probably attributable to Mrs. Dunstan's testamentary intentions, which, as she often averred, were in favour of her niece.

In addition to these two ladies, the household consisted of three servants and Miss Cruikshank. The latter was a quiet, unassuming girl who was by way of being secretary and lady-help to Mrs. Dunstan, but who, in reality, was nothing but a willing drudge. Up betimes in the morning, she combined the work of a housekeeper with that of an upper servant. She interviewed the tradespeople, kept the servants in order, and ironed and smartened up Miss Violet's blouses. A Cinderella, in fact.

Mrs. Dunstan kept a cook and two maids, all of whom had been with her for years. In addition to these, a charwoman came very early in the morning to light fires, clean boots, and do the front steps.

On November 22nd, 1907—for the early history of this curious drama dates back to that year—the charwoman who had been employed at Mrs. Dunstan's house in Eaton Terrace for some considerable time, sent word in the morning that in future she would be unable to come. Her husband had been obliged to move to lodgings nearer to his work, and she herself could not undertake to come the greater distance at the early hour at which Mrs. Dunstan required her.

The woman had written a very nice letter explaining these facts, and sent it by hand, stating at the same time that the bearer of the note was a very respectable woman, a friend of her own, who would be very pleased to "oblige" Mrs. Dunstan by taking on the morning's work.

I must tell you that the message and its bearer arrived at Eaton Terrace somewhere about 6.0 a.m., when no one was down except the Cinderella of the house, Miss Cruikshank.

She saw the woman, liked her appearance, and there and then engaged her to do the work, subject to Mrs. Dunstan's approval.

The woman, who had given her name as Mrs. Thomas, seemed

very quiet and respectable. She said that she lived close by, in St. Peter's Mews, and therefore could come as early as Mrs. Dunstan wished. In fact, from that day, she came every morning at 5.30 a.m., and by seven o'clock had finished her work, and was able to go home.

If, in addition to these details, I tell you that, at that time, pretty Miss Violet Frostwicke was engaged to a young Scotsman, Mr. David Athol, of whom her aunt totally disapproved, I shall have put before you all the personages who, directly or indirectly, were connected with that drama, the final act of which has not yet been witnessed either by the police or by the public.

2

On the following New Year's Eve, Mrs. Dunstan, as was her invariable custom on that day, went to her married brother's house to dine and to see the New Year in.

During her absence the usual thing occurred at Eaton Terrace. Miss Violet Frostwicke took the opportunity of inviting Mr. David Athol to spend the evening with her.

Mrs. Dunstan's servants, mind you, all knew of the engagement between the young people, and with the characteristic sentimentality of their class, connived at these secret meetings and helped to hoodwink the irascible old aunt.

Mr. Athol was a good-looking young man, whose chief demerit lay in his total lack of money or prospects. Also, he was by way of being an actor, another deadly sin in the eyes of the puritanically-minded old lady.

Already, on more than one occasion, there had been vigorous wordy warfare 'twixt Mr. Athol and Mrs. Dunstan, and the latter had declared that if Violet chose to take up with this mountebank, she should never see a penny of her aunt's money now or in the future.

The young man did not come very often to Eaton Terrace, but on this festive New Year's Eve, when Mrs. Dunstan was not expected to be home until long after midnight, it seemed too splendid an opportunity for an ardent lover to miss.

As ill-luck would have it, Mrs. Dunstan had not felt very well after her copious dinner, and her brother, Mr. Nicholas Jones, escorted her home soon after ten o'clock.

Jane, the parlour-maid who opened the front door, was, in her own graphic language, "knocked all of a heap" when she saw her mistress, knowing full well that Mr. Athol was still in the dining-room with

135

Miss Violet, and that Miss Cruikshank was at that very moment busy getting him a whisky and soda.

Meanwhile the coat and hat in the hall had revealed the young man's presence in the house.

For a moment Mrs. Dunstan paused, whilst Jane stood by trembling with fright. Then the old lady turned to Mr. Nicholas Jones, who was still standing on the doorstep, and said quietly:

"Will you telephone over to Mr. Blenkinsop, Nick, the first thing in the morning, and tell him I'll be at his office by ten o'clock?"

Mr. Blenkinsop was Mrs. Dunstan's solicitor, and as Jane explained to the cook later on, what could such an appointment mean but a determination to cut Miss Violet out of the missis's will with the proverbial shilling?

After this Mrs. Dunstan took leave of her brother and went straight into the dining-room.

According to the subsequent testimony of all three servants, the mistress "went on dreadful." Words were not easily distinguishable from behind the closed door, but it seems that, immediately she entered, Mrs. Dunstan's voice was raised as if in terrible anger, and a few moments later Miss Violet fled crying from the dining-room, and ran quickly upstairs.

Whilst the door was thus momentarily opened and shut, the voice of the old lady was heard saying, in majestic wrath:

"That's what you have done. Get out of this house. As for her, she'll never see a penny of my money, and she may starve for aught I care!"

The quarrel seems to have continued for a short while after that, the servants being too deeply awed by those last vindictive words which they had heard to take much note of what went on subsequently.

Mrs. Dunstan and Mr. Athol were closeted together for some time; but apparently the old lady's wrath did not subside, for when she marched up to bed an hour later, she was heard to say:

"Out of this house she shall go, and the first thing in the morning, too. I'll have no goings-on with a mountebank like you."

Miss Cruikshank was terribly upset.

"It is a frightful blow for Miss Violet," she said to cook, "but perhaps Mrs. Dunstan will feel more forgiving in the morning. I'll take her up a glass of champagne now. She is very fond of that, and it will help her to get to sleep."

Miss Cruikshank went up with the champagne, and told cook to see Mr. Athol out of the house; but the young man, who seemed very anxious and agitated, would not go away immediately. He stayed in the dining-room, smoking, for a while, and when the two younger servants went up to bed, he asked cook to let him remain until he had seen Miss Violet once more, for he was sure she would come down again—he had asked Miss Cruikshank to beg her to do so.

Mrs. Kennett, the cook, was a kind-hearted old woman. She had taken the young people under her special protection, and felt very vexed that the course of true love should not be allowed to run quite smoothly. So, she told Mr. Athol to make himself happy and comfortable in the dining-room, and she would sit up by the fire in the library until he was ready to go.

The good soul thereupon made up the fire in the library, drew a chair in front of it, and—went fast to sleep.

Suddenly something awoke her. She sat up and looked round in that dazed manner peculiar to people just aroused from deep sleep.

She looked at the clock; it was past three. Surely, she thought, it must have been Mr. Athol calling to her which had caused her to wake. She went into the hall, where the gas had not yet been turned off, and there she saw Miss Violet, fully dressed and wearing a hat and coat, in the very act of going out at the front door.

In the cook's own words, before she could ask a question or even utter a sound, the young girl had opened the front door, which was still on the latch, and then banged it to again, she herself having disappeared into the darkness of the street beyond.

Mrs. Kennett ran to the door and out into the street as fast as her old legs would let her; but the night was an exceptionally foggy one. Violet, no doubt, had walked rapidly away, and there came no answer to Mrs. Kennett's repeated calls.

Thoroughly upset, and not knowing what to do, the good woman went back into the house. Mr. Athol had evidently left, for there was no sign of him in the dining-room or elsewhere. She then went upstairs and knocked at Mrs. Dunstan's door. To her astonishment the gas was still burning in her mistress's room, as she could see a thin ray of light filtering through the keyhole. At her first knock there came a quick, impatient answer:

"What is it?"

"Miss Violet, 'm," said the cook, who was too agitated to speak very coherently, "she is gone—"

"The best thing she could do," came promptly from the other side of the door. "You go to bed, Mrs. Kennett, and don't worry."

Whereupon the gas was suddenly turned off inside the room, and, in spite of Mrs. Kennett's further feeble protests, no other word issued from the room save another impatient:

"Go to bed."

The cook then did as she was bid; but before going to bed she made the round of the house, turned off all the gas, and finally bolted the front door.

3

Some three hours later the servants were called, as usual, by Miss Cruikshank, who then went down to open the area door to Mrs. Thomas, the charwoman.

At half-past six, when Mary the housemaid came down, candle in hand, she saw the charwoman a flight or two lower down, also apparently in the act of going downstairs. This astonished Mary not a little, as the woman's work lay entirely in the basement, and she was supposed never to come to the upper floors.

The woman, though walking rapidly down the stairs, seemed, moreover, to be carrying something heavy.

"Anything wrong, Mrs. Thomas?" asked Mary, in a whisper.

The woman looked up, pausing a moment immediately under the gas bracket, the by-pass of which shed a feeble light upon her and upon her burden. The latter Mary recognised as the bag containing the sand which, on frosty mornings, had to be strewn on the front steps of the house.

On the whole, though she certainly was puzzled, Mary did not think very much about the incident then. As was her custom, she went into the housemaid's closet, got the hot water for Miss Cruikshank's bath, and carried it to the latter's room, where she also pulled up the blinds and got things ready generally. For Miss Cruikshank usually ran down in her dressing-gown, and came up to tidy herself later on.

As a rule, by the time the three servants got downstairs, it was nearly seven, and Mrs. Thomas had generally gone by that time; but on this occasion Mary was earlier. Miss Cruikshank was busy in the kitchen getting Mrs. Dunstan's tea ready. Mary spoke about seeing Mrs. Thomas on the stairs with the bag of sand, and Miss Cruikshank, too, was very astonished at the occurrence.

Mrs. Kennett was not yet down, and the charwoman apparently had gone; her work had been done as usual, and the sand was strewn over the stone steps in front, as the frosty fog had rendered them very slippery.

At a quarter past seven Miss Cruikshank went up with Mrs. Dunstan's tea, and less than two minutes later a fearful scream rang through the entire house, followed by the noise of breaking crockery.

In an instant the two maids ran upstairs, straight to Mrs. Dunstan's room, the door of which stood wide open.

The first thing Mary and Jane were conscious of was a terrific smell of gas, then of Miss Cruikshank, with eyes dilated with horror, staring at the bed in front of her, whereon lay Mrs. Dunstan, with one end of a piece of india-rubber piping still resting in her mouth, her jaw having dropped in death. The other end of that piece of piping was attached to the burner of a gas-bracket on the wall close by.

Every window in the room was fastened and the curtains drawn. The whole room reeked of gas.

Mrs. Dunstan had been asphyxiated by its fumes.

4

A year went by after the discovery of the mysterious tragedy, and I can assure you that our fellows at the Yard had one of the toughest jobs in connection with the case that ever fell to their lot. Just think of all the contradictions which met them at every turn.

Firstly, the disappearance of Miss Violet.

No sooner had the women in the Dunstan household roused themselves sufficiently from their horror at the terrible discovery which they had just made, than they were confronted with another almost equally awful fact—awful, of course, because of its connection with the primary tragedy.

Miss Violet Frostwicke had gone. Her room was empty, her bed had not been slept in. She herself had been seen by the cook, Mrs. Kennett, stealing out of the house at dead of night.

To connect the pretty, dainty young girl even remotely with a crime so hideous, so callous, as the deliberate murder of an old woman, who had been as a mother to her, seemed absolutely out of the question, and by tacit consent the four women, who now remained in the desolate and gloom-laden house at Eaton Terrace, forbore to mention Miss Violet Frostwicke's name either to police or doctor.

Both these, of course, had been summoned immediately; Miss Cruikshank sending Mary to the police-station and thence to Dr. Folwell, in Eaton Square, whilst Jane went off in a cab to fetch Mr.

Nicholas Jones, who, fortunately, had not yet left for his place of business.

The doctor's and the police-inspector's first thought, on examining the *mise en scène* of the terrible tragedy, was that Mrs. Dunstan had committed suicide. It was practically impossible to imagine that a woman in full possession of health and strength would allow a piece of india-rubber piping to be fixed between her teeth, and would, without a struggle, continue to inhale the poisonous fumes which would mean certain death. Yet there were no marks of injury upon the body, nothing to show how sufficient unconsciousness had been produced in the victim to permit of the miscreant completing his awesome deed.

But the theory of suicide set up by Dr. Folwell was promptly refuted by the most cursory examination of the room.

Though the drawers were found closed, they had obviously been turned over, as if the murderer had been in search either of money or papers, or the key of the safe.

The latter, on investigation, was found to be open, whilst the key lay on the floor close by. A brief examination of the safe revealed the fact that the tin boxes must have been ransacked, for they contained neither money nor important papers now, whilst the gold and platinum settings of necklaces, bracelets, and a tiara showed that the stones—which, as Mr. Nicholas Jones subsequently averred, were of considerable value—had been carefully, if somewhat clumsily, taken out by obviously inexperienced hands.

On the whole, therefore, appearances suggested deliberate, systematic, and very leisurely robbery, which wholly contradicted the theory of suicide.

Then suddenly the name of Miss Frostwicke was mentioned. Who first brought it on the tapis no one subsequently could say; but in a moment the whole story of the young girl's engagement to Mr. Athol, in defiance of her aunt's wishes, the quarrel of the night before, and the final disappearance of both young people from the house during the small hours of the morning, was dragged from the four unwilling witnesses by the able police-inspector.

Nay, more. One very unpleasant little circumstance was detailed by one of the maids and corroborated by Miss Cruikshank.

It seems that when the latter took up the champagne to Mrs. Dunstan, the old lady desired Miss Violet to come to her room. Mary, the housemaid, was on the stairs when she saw the young girl, still dressed in her evening gown of white chiffon, her eyes still swollen with tears, knocking at her aunt's door.

The police-inspector was busy taking notes, already building up in his mind a simple, if very sensational, case against Violet Frostwicke, when Mrs. Kennett promptly upset all his calculations.

Miss Violet could have had nothing to do with the murder of her aunt, seeing that Mrs. Dunstan was alive and actually spoke to the cook when the latter knocked at her bedroom door after she had seen the young girl walk out of the house.

Then came the question of Mr. Athol. But, if you remember, it was quite impossible even to begin to build up a case against the young man. His own statement that he left the house at about midnight, having totally forgotten to rouse the cook when he did so, was amply corroborated from every side.

The cabman who took him up to the corner of Eaton Terrace at 11.50 p.m. was one witness in his favour; his landlady at his rooms in Jermyn Street, who let him in, since he had mislaid his latchkey, and who took him up some tea at seven o'clock the next morning, was another; whilst, when Mary saw Miss Violet going into her aunt's room, the clock at St. Peter's, Eaton Square, was just striking twelve.

I dare say you think I ought by now to have mentioned the charwoman, Mrs. Thomas, who represented the final, most complete, most hopeless contradiction in this remarkable case.

Mrs. Thomas was seen by Mary, the housemaid, at half-past six o'clock in the morning, coming down from the upper floors, where she had no business to be, and carrying the bag of sand used for strewing over the slippery front-door steps.

The bag of sand, of course, was always kept in the area.

The moment that bag of sand was mentioned Dr. Folwell gave a curious gasp. Here, at least, was the solution to one mystery. The victim had been stunned whilst still in bed by a blow on the head dealt with that bag of sand; and whilst she was unconscious the callous miscreant had robbed her and finally asphyxiated her with the gas fumes.

Where was the woman who, at half-past six in the morning, was seen in possession of the silent instrument of death?

Mrs. Thomas had disappeared. The last that was then or ever has been seen of her was when she passed underneath the dim light of a by-pass on the landing, as if tired out with the weight which she was carrying.

Since then, as you know, the police have been unswerving in their efforts to find Mrs. Thomas. The address which she had given in St. Peter's Mews was found to be false. No one of that name or appearance had ever been seen there.

The woman who was supposed to have sent her with a letter of recommendation to Mrs. Dunstan knew nothing of her. She swore that she had never sent anyone with a letter to Mrs. Dunstan. She gave up her work there one day because she found it too hard at such an early hour in the morning; but she never heard anything more from her late employer after that.

Strange, wasn't it, that two people should have disappeared out of that house on that same memorable night?

Of course, you will remember the tremendous sensation that was caused some twenty-four hours later, when it transpired that the young person who had thrown herself into the river from Waterloo Bridge on that same eventful morning, and whose body was subsequently recovered and conveyed to the Thames Police station, was identified as Miss Violet Frostwicke, the niece of the lady who had been murdered in her own house in Eaton Terrace.

Neither money nor diamonds were found on poor Miss Violet. She had herself given the most complete proof that she, at least, had no hand in robbing or killing Mrs. Dunstan.

The public wondered why she took her aunt's wrath and her probable disinheritance so fearfully to heart, and sympathised with Mr. David Athol for the terribly sad loss which he had sustained.

But Mrs. Thomas, the charwoman, had not yet been found.

5

I think I looked an extremely respectable, good plain cook when I presented myself at the house in Eaton Terrace in response to the advertisement in the *Daily Telegraph*.

As, in addition to my prepossessing appearance, I also asked very low wages and declared myself ready to do anything except scour the front steps and the stone area, I was immediately engaged by Mrs. Jones, and was duly installed in the house the following day under the name of Mrs. Curwen.

But few events had occurred here since the discovery of the dual tragedy, now more than a year ago, and none that had thrown any light upon the mystery which surrounded it.

The verdict at the inquest had been one of wilful murder against a person known as Mrs. Thomas, the weight of evidence, coupled with her disappearance, having been very heavy against her; and there was a warrant out for her arrest.

Mrs. Dunstan had died intestate. To the astonishment of all those in the know, she had never signed the will which Messrs. Blenkinsop and Blenkinsop had drafted for her, and wherein she bequeathed £20,000 and the lease of her house in Eaton Terrace to her beloved niece, Violet Frostwicke, £1,000 to Miss Cruikshank, and other, smaller, legacies to friends or servants.

In default of a will, Mr. Nicholas Jones, only brother of the deceased, became possessed of all her wealth.

He was a very rich man himself, and many people thought that he ought to give Miss Cruikshank the £1,000 which the poor girl had thus lost through no fault of her own.

What his ultimate intentions were with regard to this no one could know. For the present he contented himself with moving to Eaton Terrace with his family; and, as his wife was a great invalid, he asked Miss Cruikshank to continue to make her home in the house and to help in its management.

Neither the diamonds nor the money stolen from Mrs. Dunstan's safe were ever traced. It seems that Mrs. Dunstan, a day or two before her death, had sold a freehold cottage which she owned near Teddington. The money, as is customary, had been handed over to her in gold, in Mr. Blenkinsop's office, and she had been foolish enough not to bank it immediately. This money and the diamonds had been the chief spoils of her assailant. And all the while no trace of Mrs. Thomas, in spite of the most strenuous efforts on the part of the police to find her.

Strangely enough, when I had been in Eaton Terrace about three days, and was already getting very tired of early rising and hard work, the charwoman there fell ill one day and did not come to her work as usual.

I, of course, grumbled like six, for I had to be on my hands and knees the next morning scrubbing stone steps, and my thoughts of Lady Molly, for the moment, were not quite as loyal as they usually were.

Suddenly I heard a shuffling footstep close behind me. I turned and saw a rough-looking, ill-dressed woman standing at the bottom of the steps.

"What do you want?" I asked sourly, for I was in a very bad humour.

"I saw you scrubbing them steps, miss," she replied in a raucous voice; "my 'usband is out of work, and the children hain't 'ad no breakfast this morning. I'd do them steps, miss, if you'd give me a trifle."

The woman certainly did not look very prepossessing, with her shabby, broad-brimmed hat hiding the upper part of her face, and her skirt, torn and muddy, pinned up untidily round her stooping figure.

However, I did not think that I could be doing anything very wrong by letting her do this one bit of rough work, which I hated, so I agreed to give her sixpence, and left her there with kneeling mat and scrubbing-brush, and went in, leaving, however, the front door open.

In the hall I met Miss Cruikshank, who, as usual, was down before everybody else.

"What is it, Curwen?" she asked, for through the open door she had caught sight of the woman kneeling on the step.

"A woman, miss," I replied, somewhat curtly. "She offered to do the steps. I thought Mrs. Jones wouldn't mind, as Mrs. Callaghan hasn't turned up." Miss Cruikshank hesitated an instant, and then walked up to the front door.

At the same moment the woman looked up, rose from her knees, and boldly went up to accost Miss Cruikshank.

"You'll remember me, miss," she said, in her raucous voice. "I used to work for Mrs. Dunstan once. My name is Mrs. Thomas."

No wonder Miss Cruikshank uttered a quickly smothered cry of horror. Thinking that she would faint, I ran to her assistance; but she waved me aside and then said quite quietly:

"This poor woman's mind is deranged. She is no more Mrs. Thomas than I am. Perhaps we had better send for the police."

"Yes, miss; p'r'aps you'd better," said the woman with a sigh. "My secret has been weighin' heavy on me of late."

"But, my good woman," said Miss Cruikshank, very kindly, for I suppose that she thought, as I did, that this was one of those singular cases of madness which sometimes cause innocent people to accuse themselves of undiscovered crimes. "You are not Mrs. Thomas at all. I knew Mrs. Thomas well, of course—and—"

"Of course, you knew me, miss," replied the woman. "The last conversation you and I had together was in the kitchen that morning, when Mrs. Dunstan was killed. I remember your saying to me—"

"Fetch the police, Curwen," said Miss Cruikshank, peremptorily.

Whereupon the woman broke into a harsh and loud laugh of defiance.

144

To tell you the truth, I was not a little puzzled. That this scene had been foreseen by my dear lady, and that she had sent me to this house on purpose that I should witness it, I was absolutely convinced. But— here was my dilemma: ought I to warn the police at once or not?

On the whole, I decided that my best plan would undoubtedly be to communicate with Lady Molly first of all, and to await her instructions. So, I ran upstairs, scribbled a hasty note to my dear lady, and, in response to Miss Cruikshank's orders, flew out of the house through the area gate, noticing, as I did so, that Miss Cruikshank was still parleying with the woman on the doorstep.

I sent the note off to Maida Vale by taxicab; then I went back to Eaton Terrace. Miss Cruikshank met me at the front door, and told me that she had tried to detain the woman, pending my return; but that she felt very sorry for the unfortunate creature, who obviously was labouring under a delusion, and she had allowed her to go away.

About an hour later I received a curt note from Lady Molly ordering me to do nothing whatever without her special authorisation.

In the course of the day, Miss Cruikshank told me that she had been to the police-station, and had consulted with the inspector, who said there would be no harm in engaging the *pseudo* Mrs. Thomas to work at Eaton Terrace, especially as thus she would remain under observation.

Then followed a curious era in Mr. Nicholas Jones's otherwise well-ordered household. We three servants, instead of being called at six as heretofore, were allowed to sleep on until seven. When we came down, we were not scolded. On the contrary, we found our work already done.

The charwoman—whoever she was—must have been a very hardworking woman. It was marvellous what she accomplished single-handed before seven a.m., by which time she had invariably gone.

The two maids, of course, were content to let this pleasant state of things go on, but I was devoured with curiosity.

One morning I crept quietly downstairs and went into the kitchen soon after six. I found the *pseudo* Mrs. Thomas sitting at a very copious breakfast. I noticed that she had on altogether different—though equally shabby and dirty—clothes from those she had worn when she first appeared on the doorstep of 180, Eaton Terrace. Near her plate were three or four golden sovereigns over which she had thrown her grimy hand.

Miss Cruikshank the while was on her hands and knees scrubbing the floor. At sight of me she jumped up, and with obvious confusion muttered something about "hating to be idle," etc.

That day Miss Cruikshank told me that I did not suit Mrs. Jones, who wished me to leave at the end of my month. In the afternoon I received a little note from my dear lady, telling me to be downstairs by six o'clock the following morning.

I did as I was ordered, of course, and when I came into the kitchen punctually at six a.m. I found the charwoman sitting at the table with a pile of gold in front of her, which she was counting over with a very grubby finger. She had her back to me, and was saying as I entered:

"I think if you was to give me another fifty quid I'd leave you the rest now. You'd still have the diamonds and the rest of the money."

She spoke to Miss Cruikshank, who was facing me, and who, on seeing me appear, turned as white as a ghost. But she quickly recovered herself, and, standing between me and the woman, she said vehemently:

"What do you mean by prying on me like this? Go and pack your boxes and leave the house this instant."

But before I could reply the woman had interposed.

"Don't you fret yourself, miss," she said, placing her grimy hand on Miss Cruikshank's shoulder. "There's the bag of sand in that there corner; we'll knock 'er down as we did Mrs. Dunstan—eh?"

"Hold your tongue, you lying fool!" said the girl, who now looked like a maddened fury.

"Give me that other fifty quid and I'll hold my tongue," retorted the woman, boldly.

"This creature is mad," said Miss Cruikshank, who had made a vigorous and successful effort to recover herself. "She is under the delusion that not only is she Mrs. Thomas, but that she murdered Mrs. Dunstan—"

"No—no!" interrupted the woman. "I only came back that morning because I recollected that you had left the bag of sand upstairs after you so cleverly did away with Mrs. Dunstan, robbed her of all her money and jewels, and even were sharp enough to imitate her voice when Mrs. Kennett, the cook, terrified you by speaking to Mrs. Dunstan through the door."

"It is false! You are not Mrs. Thomas. The two maids who are here now, and who were in this house at the time, can swear that you are a liar."

"Let us change clothes now, Miss Cruikshank," said a voice, which

" ' Go and pack your boxes and leave the house this
instant ' "

sounded almost weirdly in my ear in spite of its familiarity, for I could not locate whence it came, "and see if in a charwoman's dress those two maids would not recognise *you*."

"Mary," continued the same familiar voice, "help me out of these filthy clothes. Perhaps Miss Cruikshank would like to resume her own part of Mrs. Thomas, the charwoman."

"Liars and impostors—both!" shouted the girl, who was rapidly losing all presence of mind. "I'll send for the police."

"Quite unnecessary," rejoined Lady Molly coolly; "Detective-Inspector Danvers is just outside that door."

The girl made a dash for the other door, but I was too quick for her, and held her back, even whilst Lady Molly gave a short, sharp call which brought Danvers on the scene.

I must say that Miss Cruikshank made a bold fight, but Danvers had two of our fellows with him, and arrested her on the warrant for the apprehension of the person known as Mrs. Thomas.

The clothes of the charwoman who had so mysteriously disappeared had been found by Lady Molly at the back of the coal cellar, and she was still dressed in them at the present moment.

No wonder I had not recognised my own dainty lady in the grimy woman who had so successfully played the part of a blackmailer on the murderess of Mrs. Dunstan. She explained to me subsequently that the first inkling that she had had of the horrible truth—namely, that it was Miss Cruikshank who had deliberately planned to murder Mrs. Dunstan by impersonating a charwoman for a while, and thus throwing dust in the eyes of the police—was when she heard of the callous words which the old lady was supposed to have uttered when she was told of Miss Violet's flight from the house in the middle of the night.

"She may have been very angry at the girl's escapade," explained Lady Molly to me, "but she would not have allowed her to starve. Such cruelty was out of all proportion to the offence. Then I looked about me for a stronger motive for the old lady's wrath; and, remembering what she said on New Year's Eve, when Violet fled crying from the room, I came to the conclusion that her anger was not directed against her niece, but against the other girl, and against the man who had transferred his affections from Violet Frostwicke to Miss Cruikshank, and had not only irritated Mrs. Dunstan by this clandestine, double-faced love-making, but had broken the heart of his trusting *fiancée*.

"No doubt Miss Cruikshank did not know that the will, whereby she was to inherit £1,000, was not signed, and no doubt she and young Athol planned out that cruel murder between them. The charwoman was also a bag of sand which was literally thrown in the eyes of the police."

"But," I objected, "I can't understand how a coldblooded creature like that Miss Cruikshank could have allowed herself to be terrorised and blackmailed. She knew that you could not be Mrs. Thomas, since Mrs. Thomas never existed."

"Yes; but one must reckon a little sometimes with that negligible quantity known as conscience. My appearance as Mrs. Thomas vaguely frightened Miss Cruikshank. She wondered who I was and what I knew. When, three days later, I found the shabby clothes in the coal-cellar and appeared dressed in them, she lost her head. She gave me money! From that moment she was done for. Confession was only a matter of time."

And Miss Cruikshank did make full confession. She was recommended to mercy on account of her sex, but she was plucky enough not to implicate David Athol in the recital of her crime.

He has since emigrated to Western Canada.

The Man in the Inverness Cape

1

I have heard many people say—people, too, mind you, who read their daily paper regularly—that it is quite impossible for anyone to "disappear" within the confines of the British Isles. At the same time these wise people invariably admit one great exception to their otherwise unimpeachable theory, and that is the case of Mr. Leonard Marvell, who, as you know, walked out one afternoon from the Scotia Hotel in Cromwell Road and has never been seen or heard of since.

Information had originally been given to the police by Mr. Marvell's sister Olive, a Scotchwoman of the usually accepted type: tall, bony, with sandy-coloured hair, and a somewhat melancholy expression in her blue-grey eyes.

Her brother, she said, had gone out on a rather foggy afternoon. I think it was the 3rd of February, just about a year ago. His intention had been to go and consult a solicitor in the City—whose address had been given him recently by a friend—about some private business of his own.

Mr. Marvell had told his sister that he would get a train at South Kensington Station to Moorgate Street, and walk thence to Finsbury

Square. She was to expect him home by dinner-time.

As he was, however, very irregular in his habits, being fond of spending his evenings at restaurants and music-halls, the sister did not feel the least anxious when he did not return home at the appointed time. She had her dinner in the *table d'hôte* room, and went to bed soon after 10.0.

She and her brother occupied two bedrooms and a sitting-room on the second floor of the little private hotel. Miss Marvell, moreover, had a maid always with her, as she was somewhat of an invalid. This girl, Rosie Campbell, a nice-looking Scotch lassie, slept on the top floor.

It was only on the following morning, when Mr. Leonard did not put in an appearance at breakfast, that Miss Marvell began to feel anxious. According to her own account, she sent Rosie in to see if anything was the matter, and the girl, wide-eyed and not a little frightened, came back with the news that Mr. Marvell was not in his room, and that his bed had not been slept in that night.

With characteristic Scottish reserve, Miss Olive said nothing about the matter at the time to anyone, nor did she give information to the police until two days later, when she herself had exhausted every means in her power to discover her brother's whereabouts.

She had seen the lawyer to whose office Leonard Marvell had intended going that afternoon, but Mr. Statham, the solicitor in question, had seen nothing of the missing man.

With great adroitness Rosie, the maid, had made inquiries at South Kensington and Moorgate Street stations. At the former, the booking clerk, who knew Mr. Marvell by sight, distinctly remembered selling him a first-class ticket to one of the City stations in the early part of the afternoon; but at Moorgate Street, which is a very busy station, no one recollected seeing a tall, red-haired Scotchman in an Inverness cape—such was the description given of the missing man. By that time the fog had become very thick in the City; traffic was disorganised, and everyone felt fussy, ill-tempered, and self-centred.

These, in substance, were the details which Miss Marvell gave to the police on the subject of her brother's strange disappearance.

At first, she did not appear very anxious; she seemed to have great faith in Mr. Marvell's power to look after himself; moreover, she declared positively that her brother had neither valuables nor money about his person when he went out that afternoon.

But as day succeeded day and no trace of the missing man had yet been found, matters became more serious, and the search instituted by our fellows at the Yard waxed more keen.

A description of Mr. Leonard Marvell was published in the leading London and provincial dailies. Unfortunately, there was no good photograph of him extant, and descriptions are apt to prove vague.

Very little was known about the man beyond his disappearance, which had rendered him famous. He and his sister had arrived at the Scotia Hotel about a month previously, and subsequently they were joined by the maid Campbell.

Scotch people are far too reserved ever to speak of themselves or their affairs to strangers. Brother and sister spoke very little to anyone at the hotel. They had their meals in their sitting-room, waited on by the maid, who messed with the staff. But, in face of the present terrible calamity, Miss Marvell's frigidity relaxed before the police inspector, to whom she gave what information she could about her brother.

"He was like a son to me," she explained with scarcely restrained tears, "for we lost our parents early in life, and as we were left very, very badly off, our relations took but little notice of us. My brother was years younger than I am—and though he was a little wild and fond of pleasure, he was as good as gold to me, and has supported us both for years by journalistic work. We came to London from Glasgow about a month ago, because Leonard got a very good appointment on the staff of the *Daily Post*."

All this, of course, was soon proved to be true; and although, on minute inquiries being instituted in Glasgow, but little seemed to be known about Mr. Leonard Marvell in that city, there seemed no doubt that he had done some reporting for the *Courier*, and that latterly, in response to an advertisement, he had applied for and obtained regular employment on the *Daily Post*.

The latter enterprising halfpenny journal, with characteristic magnanimity, made an offer of £50 reward to any of its subscribers who gave information which would lead to the discovery of the whereabouts of Mr. Leonard Marvell.

But time went by, and that £50 remained unclaimed.

2

Lady Molly had not seemed as interested as she usually was in cases of this sort. With strange flippancy—wholly unlike herself—she remarked that one Scotch journalist more or less in London did not vastly matter.

I was much amused, therefore, one morning about three weeks

after the mysterious disappearance of Mr. Leonard Marvell, when Jane, our little parlour-maid, brought in a card accompanied by a letter.

The card bore the name "Miss Olive Marvell." The letter was the usual formula from the chief, asking Lady Molly to have a talk with the lady in question, and to come and see him on the subject after the interview.

With a smothered yawn my dear lady told Jane to show in Miss Marvell.

"There are two of them, my lady," said Jane, as she prepared to obey.

"Two what?" asked Lady Molly with a laugh.

"Two ladies, I mean," explained Jane.

"Well! Show them both into the drawing-room," said Lady Molly, impatiently.

Then, as Jane went off on this errand, a very funny thing happened; funny, because during the entire course of my intimate association with my dear lady, I had never known her act with such marked indifference in the face of an obviously interesting case. She turned to me and said:

"Mary, you had better see these two women, whoever they may be; I feel that they would bore me to distraction. Take note of what they say, and let me know. Now, don't argue," she added with a laugh, which peremptorily put a stop to my rising protest, "but go and interview Miss Marvell and Co."

Needless to say, I promptly did as I was told, and the next few seconds saw me installed in our little drawing-room, saying polite preliminaries to the two ladies who sat opposite to me.

I had no need to ask which of them was Miss Marvell. Tall, ill-dressed in deep black, with a heavy crape veil over her face, and black cotton gloves, she looked the uncompromising Scotchwoman to the life. In strange contrast to her depressing appearance, there sat beside her an over-dressed, much behatted, peroxided young woman, who bore the stamp of the profession all over her pretty, painted face.

Miss Marvell, I was glad to note, was not long in plunging into the subject which had brought her here.

"I saw a gentleman at Scotland Yard," she explained, after a short preamble, "because Miss—er—Lulu Fay came to me at the hotel this very morning with a story which, in my opinion, should have been told to the police directly my brother's disappearance became known, and not three weeks later."

The emphasis which she laid on the last few words, and the stern look with which she regarded the golden-haired young woman beside her, showed the disapproval with which the rigid Scotchwoman viewed any connection which her brother might have had with the lady, whose very name seemed unpleasant to her lips.

Miss—er—Lulu Fay blushed even through her rouge, and turned a pair of large, liquid eyes imploringly upon me.

"I—I didn't know. I was frightened," she stammered.

"There's no occasion to be frightened now," retorted Miss Marvell, "and the sooner you try and be truthful about the whole matter, the better it will be for all of us."

And the stern woman's lips closed with a snap, as she deliberately turned her back on Miss Fay and began turning over the leaves of a magazine which happened to be on a table close to her hand.

I muttered a few words of encouragement, for the little actress looked ready to cry. I spoke as kindly as I could, telling her that if indeed she could throw some light on Mr. Marvell's present whereabouts it was her duty to be quite frank on the subject.

She "hem"-ed and "ha"-ed for a while, and her simpering ways were just beginning to tell on my nerves, when she suddenly started talking very fast.

"I am principal boy at the Grand," she explained with great volubility; "and I knew Mr. Leonard Marvell well—in fact—er—he paid me a good deal of attention and—"

"Yes—and?" I queried, for the girl was obviously nervous.

There was a pause. Miss Fay began to cry.

"And it seems that my brother took this young—er—lady to supper on the night of February 3rd, after which no one has ever seen or heard of him again," here interposed Miss Marvell, quietly.

"Is that so?" I asked.

Lulu Fay nodded, whilst heavy tears fell upon her clasped hands.

"But why did you not tell this to the police three weeks ago?" I ejaculated, with all the sternness at my command.

"I—I was frightened," she stammered.

"Frightened? Of what?"

"I am engaged to Lord Mountnewte and—"

"And you did not wish him to know that you were accepting the attentions of Mr. Leonard Marvell—was that it? Well," I added, with involuntary impatience, "what happened after you had supper with Mr. Marvell?"

"Oh! I hope—I hope that nothing happened," she said through

more tears; "we had supper at the Trocadero, and he saw me into my brougham. Suddenly, just as I was driving away, I saw Lord Mount-newte standing quite close to us in the crowd."

"Did the two men know one another?" I asked. "No," replied Miss Fay; "at least, I didn't think so, but when I looked back through the window of my carriage, I saw them standing on the kerb talking to each other for a moment, and then walk off together towards Picca-dilly Circus. That is the last I have seen of either of them," continued the little actress with a fresh flood of tears. "Lord Mountnewte hasn't spoken to me since, and Mr. Marvell has disappeared with my money and my diamonds."

"Your money and your diamonds?" I gasped in amazement.

"Yes; he told me he was a jeweller, and that my diamonds wanted resetting. He took them with him that evening, for he said that Lon-don jewellers were clumsy thieves, and that he would love to do the work for me himself. I also gave him two hundred pounds, which he said he would want for buying the gold and platinum required for the settings. And now he has disappeared—and my diamonds—and my money! Oh! I have been very—very foolish—and——"

Her voice broke down completely. Of course, one often hears of the idiocy of girls giving money and jewels unquestioningly to clever adventurers who know how to trade upon their inordinate vanity. There was, therefore, nothing very out of the way in the story just told me by Miss—er—Lulu Fay, until the moment when Miss Marvell's quiet voice, with its marked Scotch burr, broke in upon the short silence which had followed the actress's narrative.

"As I explained to the chief detective-inspector at Scotland Yard," she said calmly, "the story which this young—er—lady tells is only partly true. She may have had supper with Mr. Leonard Marvell on the night of February 3rd, and he may have paid her certain atten-tions; but he never deceived her by telling her that he was a jeweller, nor did he obtain possession of her diamonds and her money through false statements. My brother was the soul of honour and loyalty. If, for some reason which Miss—er—Lulu Fay chooses to keep secret, he had her jewels and money in his possession on the fatal February 3rd, then I think his disappearance is accounted for. He has been robbed and perhaps murdered."

Like a true Scotchwoman she did not give way to tears, but even her harsh voice trembled slightly when she thus bore witness to her brother's honesty, and expressed the fears which assailed her as to his fate.

Imagine my plight! I could ill forgive my dear lady for leaving me in this unpleasant position—a sort of peacemaker between two women who evidently hated one another, and each of whom was trying her best to give the other "the lie direct."

I ventured to ring for our faithful Jane and to send her with an imploring message to Lady Molly, begging her to come and disentangle the threads of this muddled skein with her clever fingers; but Jane returned with a curt note from my dear lady, telling me not to worry about such a silly case, and to bow the two women out of the flat as soon as possible and then come for a nice walk.

I wore my official manner as well as I could, trying not to betray the 'prentice hand. Of course, the interview lasted a great deal longer, and there was considerably more talk than I can tell you of in a brief narrative. But the gist of it all was just as I have said. Miss Lulu Fay stuck to every point of the story which she had originally told Miss Marvell. It was the latter uncompromising lady who had immediately marched the younger woman off to Scotland Yard in order that she might repeat her tale to the police. I did not wonder that the chief promptly referred them both to Lady Molly.

Anyway, I made excellent shorthand notes of the conflicting stories which I heard; and I finally saw, with real relief, the two women walk out of our little front door.

3

Miss—er—Lulu Fay, mind you, never contradicted in any one particular the original story which she had told me, about going out to supper with Leonard Marvell, entrusting him with £200 and the diamonds, which he said he would have reset for her, and seeing him finally in close conversation with her recognised *fiancé*, Lord Mountnewte. Miss Marvell, on the other hand, very commendably refused to admit that her brother acted dishonestly towards the girl. If he had her jewels and money in his possession at the time of his disappearance, then he had undoubtedly been robbed, or perhaps murdered, on his way back to the hotel, and if Lord Mountnewte had been the last to speak to him on that fatal night, then Lord Mountnewte must be able to throw some light on the mysterious occurrence.

Our fellows at the Yard were abnormally active. It seemed, on the face of it, impossible that a man, healthy, vigorous, and admittedly sober, should vanish in London between Piccadilly Circus and Cromwell Road without leaving the slightest trace of himself or of the valuables said to have been in his possession.

Of course, Lord Mountnewte was closely questioned. He was a young Guardsman of the usual pattern, and, after a great deal of vapid talk which irritated Detective-Inspector Saunders not a little, he made the following statement—

"I certainly am acquainted with Miss Lulu Fay. On the night in question, I was standing outside the Troc, when I saw this young lady at her own carriage window talking to a tall man in an Inverness cape. She had, earlier in the day, refused my invitation to supper, saying that she was not feeling very well, and would go home directly after the theatre; therefore I felt, naturally, a little vexed. I was just about to hail a taxi, meaning to go on to the club, when, to my intense astonishment, the man in the Inverness cape came up to me and asked me if I could tell him the best way to get back to Cromwell Road."

"And what did you do?" asked Saunders.

"I walked a few steps with him and put him on his way," replied Lord Mountnewte, blandly.

In Saunders's own expressive words, he thought that story "fishy." He could not imagine the arm of coincidence being quite so long as to cause these two men—who presumably were both in love with the same girl, and who had just met at a moment when one of them was obviously suffering pangs of jealousy—to hold merely a topographical conversation with one another. But it was equally difficult to suppose that the eldest son and heir of the Marquis of Loam should murder a successful rival and then rob him in the streets of London.

Moreover, here came the eternal and unanswerable questions: If Lord Mountnewte had murdered Leonard Marvell, where and how had he done it, and what had he done with the body?

I dare say you are wondering by this time why I have said nothing about the maid, Rosie Campbell.

Well, plenty of very clever people (I mean those who write letters to the papers and give suggestions to every official department in the kingdom) thought that the police ought to keep a very strict eye upon that pretty Scotch lassie. For she was very pretty, and had quaint, demure ways which rendered her singularly attractive, in spite of the fact that, for most masculine tastes, she would have been considered too tall. Of course, Saunders and Danvers kept an eye on her—you may be sure of that—and got a good deal of information about her from the people at the hotel.

Most of it, unfortunately, was irrelevant to the case. She was maid-attendant to Miss Marvell, who was feeble in health, and who went out but little. Rosie waited on her master and mistress upstairs, carrying their meals to their private room, and doing their bedrooms. The rest of the day she was fairly free, and was quite sociable downstairs with the hotel staff.

With regard to her movements and actions on that memorable 3rd of February, Saunders—though he worked very hard—could glean but little useful information. You see, in an hotel of that kind, with an average of thirty to forty guests at one time, it is extremely difficult to state positively what any one person did or did not do on that particular day.

Most people at the Scotia remembered that Miss Marvell dined in the *table d'hôte* room on that 3rd of February; this she did about once a fortnight, when her maid had an evening "out."

The hotel staff also recollected fairly distinctly that Miss Rosie Campbell was not in the steward's room at supper-time that evening, but no one could remember definitely when she came in.

One of the chambermaids who occupied the bedroom adjoining hers, said that she heard her moving about soon after midnight; the hall porter declared that he saw her come in just before half-past twelve when he closed the doors for the night.

But one of the ground-floor valets said that, on the morning of the 4th, he saw Miss Marvell's maid, in hat and coat, slip into the house and upstairs, very quickly and quietly, soon after the front doors were opened, namely, about 7.0 a.m.

Here, of course, was a direct contradiction between the chambermaid and hall porter on the one side, and the valet on the other, whilst Miss Marvell said that Campbell came into her room and made her some tea long before seven o'clock every morning, including that of the 4th.

I assure you our fellows at the Yard were ready to tear their hair out by the roots, from sheer aggravation at this maze of contradictions which met them at every turn.

The whole thing seemed so simple. There was nothing "to it" as it were, and but very little real suggestion of foul play, and yet Mr. Leonard Marvell had disappeared, and no trace of him could be found.

Everyone now talked freely of murder. London is a big town, and this would not have been the first instance of a stranger—for Mr. Leonard Marvell was practically a stranger in London—being enticed to a lonely part of the city on a foggy night, and there done away with and robbed, and the body hidden in an out-of-the-way cellar, where it might not be discovered for months to come.

But the newspaper-reading public is notably fickle, and Mr. Leonard Marvell was soon forgotten by everyone save the chief and the batch of our fellows who had charge of the case.

Thus, I heard through Danvers one day that Rosie Campbell had left Miss Marvell's employ, and was living in rooms in Findlater Terrace, near Walham Green.

I was alone in our Maida Vale flat at the time, my dear lady having gone to spend the weekend with the Dowager Lady Loam, who was an old friend of hers; nor, when she returned, did she seem any more interested in Rosie Campbell's movements than she had been hitherto.

Yet another month went by, and I for one had absolutely ceased to think of the man in the Inverness cape, who had so mysteriously and so completely vanished in the very midst of busy London, when, one morning early in January, Lady Molly made her appearance in my room, looking more like the landlady of a disreputable gambling-house than anything else I could imagine.

"What in the world—?" I began.

"Yes! I think I look the part," she replied, surveying with obvious complacency the extraordinary figure which confronted her in the glass.

My dear lady had on a purple cloth coat and skirt of a peculiarly vivid hue, and of a singular cut, which made her matchless figure look like a sack of potatoes. Her soft brown hair was quite hidden beneath a "transformation," of that yellow-reddish tint only to be met with in very cheap dyes.

As for her hat! I won't attempt to describe it. It towered above and around her face, which was plentifully covered with brick-red and with that kind of powder which causes the cheeks to look a deep mauve.

My dear lady looked, indeed, a perfect picture of appalling vulgarity.

"Where are you going in this elegant attire?" I asked in amazement.

"I have taken rooms in Findlater Terrace," she replied lightly. "I feel that the air of Walham Green will do us both good. Our amiable, if somewhat slatternly, landlady expects us in time for luncheon. You will have to keep rigidly in the background, Mary, all the while we are there. I said that I was bringing an invalid niece with me, and, as a preliminary, you may as well tie two or three thick veils over your face. I think I may safely promise that you won't be dull."

And we certainly were not dull during our brief stay at 34, Findlater Terrace, Walham Green. Fully equipped, and arrayed in our extraordinary garments, we duly arrived there, in a rickety four-wheeler, on the top of which were perched two seedy-looking boxes.

The landlady was a toothless old creature, who apparently thought washing a quite unnecessary proceeding. In this she was evidently at one with every one of her neighbours. Findlater Terrace looked unspeakably squalid; groups of dirty children congregated in the gutters and gave forth discordant shrieks as our cab drove up.

Through my thick veils I thought that, some distance down the road, I spied a horsy-looking man in ill-fitting riding-breeches and gaiters, who vaguely reminded me of Danvers.

Within half an hour of our installation, and whilst we were eating a tough steak over a doubtful table cloth, my dear lady told me that she had been waiting a full month, until rooms in this particular house happened to be vacant. Fortunately, the population in Findlater Terrace is always a shifting one, and Lady Molly had kept a sharp eye on No. 34, where, on the floor above, lived Miss Rosie Campbell. Directly the last set of lodgers walked out of the ground-floor rooms, we were ready to walk in.

My dear lady's manners and customs, whilst living at the above aristocratic address, were fully in keeping with her appearance. The shrill, rasping voice which she assumed echoed from attic to cellar.

One day I heard her giving vague hints to the landlady that her husband, Mr. Marcus Stein, had had a little trouble with the police about a small hotel which he had kept somewhere near Fitzroy Square, and where "young gentlemen used to come and play cards of a night." The landlady was also made to understand that the worthy Mr. Stein was now living temporarily at His Majesty's expense, whilst Mrs. Stein had to live a somewhat secluded life, away from her fashionable friends.

The misfortunes of the *pseudo* Mrs. Stein in no way marred the amiability of Mrs. Tredwen, our landlady. The inhabitants of Findlater Terrace care very little about the antecedents of their lodgers, so long as they pay their week's rent in advance, and settle their "extras" without much murmur.

This Lady Molly did, with a generosity characteristic of an ex-lady of means. She never grumbled at the quantity of jam and marmalade which we were supposed to have consumed every week, and which *anon* reached titanic proportions. She tolerated Mrs. Tredwen's cat, tipped Ermyntrude—the tousled lodging-house slavey—lavishly, and lent the upstairs lodger her spirit-lamp and curling-tongs when Miss Rosie Campbell's got out of order.

A certain degree of intimacy followed the loan of those curling-tongs. Miss Campbell, reserved and demure, greatly sympathised with the lady who was not on the best of terms with the police. I kept steadily in the background. The two ladies did not visit each other's rooms, but they held long and confidential conversations on the landings, and I gathered, presently, that the *pseudo* Mrs. Stein had succeeded in persuading Rosie Campbell that, if the police were watching No. 34, Findlater Terrace, at all, it was undoubtedly on account of the unfortunate Mr. Stein's faithful wife.

I found it a little difficult to fathom Lady Molly's intentions. We had been in the house over three weeks, and nothing whatever had happened. Once I ventured on a discreet query as to whether we were to expect the sudden re-appearance of Mr. Leonard Marvell.

"For if that's all about it," I argued, "then surely the men from the Yard could have kept the house in view, without all this inconvenience and masquerading on our part."

But to this tirade my dear lady vouchsafed no reply.

She and her newly acquired friend were, about this time, deeply interested in the case known as the "West End Shop Robberies," which no doubt you recollect, since they occurred such a very little while ago. Ladies who were shopping in the large drapers' emporiums during the crowded and busy sale time, lost reticules, purses, and valuable parcels, without any trace of the clever thief being found.

The drapers, during sale-time, invariably employ detectives in plain clothes to look after their goods, but in this case, it was the customers who were robbed, and the detectives, attentive to every attempt at "shoplifting," had had no eyes for the more subtle thief.

I had already noticed Miss Rosie Campbell's keen look of excitement whenever the *pseudo* Mrs. Stein discussed these cases with her. I was not a bit surprised, therefore, when, one afternoon at about tea-time, my dear lady came home from her habitual walk, and, at the top of her shrill voice, called out to me from the hall:

"Mary! Mary! they've got the man of the shop robberies. He's given the silly police the slip this time, but they know who he is now, and I suppose they'll get him presently. 'Tisn't anybody I know," she added, with that harsh, common laugh which she had adopted for her part.

I had come out of the room in response to her call, and was standing just outside our own sitting-room door. Mrs. Tredwen, too, bedraggled and unkempt, as usual, had sneaked up the area steps, closely followed by Ermyntrude.

But on the half-landing just above us the trembling figure of Rosie Campbell, with scared white face and dilated eyes, looked on the verge of a sudden fall.

Still talking shrilly and volubly, Lady Molly ran up to her, but Campbell met her half-way, and the *pseudo* Mrs. Stein, taking vigorous hold of her wrist, dragged her into our own sitting-room.

"Pull yourself together, now," she said with rough kindness; "that owl Tredwen is listening, and you needn't let her know too much. Shut the door, Mary. Lor' bless you, m'dear, I've gone through worse scares than these. There! you just lie down on this sofa a bit. My niece'll make you a cup o' tea; and I'll go and get an evening paper, and see what's going on. I suppose you are very interested in the shop robbery man, or you wouldn't have took on so." Without waiting for Campbell's contradiction to this statement, Lady Molly flounced out of the house.

Miss Campbell hardly spoke during the next ten minutes that she and I were left alone together. She lay on the sofa with eyes wide open, staring up at the ceiling, evidently still in a great state of fear.

I had just got tea ready when Lady Molly came back. She had an evening paper in her hand, but threw this down on the table directly she came in.

"I could only get an early edition," she said breathlessly, "and the silly thing hasn't got anything in it about the matter."

She drew near to the sofa, and, subduing the shrillness of her voice, she whispered rapidly, bending down towards Campbell:

"There's a man hanging about at the corner down there. No, no; it's not the police," she added quickly, in response to the girl's sudden start of alarm. "Trust me, my dear, for knowing a 'tec when I see one! Why, I'd smell one half a mile off. No; my opinion is that it's your man, my dear, and that he's in a devil of a hole."

"Oh! he oughtn't to come here," ejaculated Campbell in great alarm. "He'll get me into trouble and do himself no good. He's been a fool!" she added, with a fierceness wholly unlike her usual demure placidity, "getting himself caught like that. Now I suppose we shall have to hook it—if there's time."

"Can I do anything to help you?" asked the *pseudo* Mrs. Stein. "You

" Still talking shrilly . . . the pseudo Mrs. Stein dragged
  her into our own sitting-room "

know I've been through all this myself, when they was after Mr. Stein. Or perhaps Mary could do something."

"Well, yes," said the girl, after a slight pause, during which she seemed to be gathering her wits together; "I'll write a note, and you shall take it, if you will, to a friend of mine—a lady who lives in the Cromwell Road. But if you still see a man lurking about at the corner of the street, then, just as you pass him, say the word 'Campbell,' and if he replies 'Rosie,' then give *him* the note. Will you do that?"

"Of course, I will, my dear. Just you leave it all to me."

And the *pseudo* Mrs. Stein brought ink and paper and placed them on the table. Rosie Campbell wrote a brief note, and then fastened it down with a bit of sealing-wax before she handed it over to Lady Molly. The note was addressed to Miss Marvell, Scotia Hotel, Cromwell Road.

"You understand?" she said eagerly. "Don't give the note to the man unless he says 'Rosie' in reply to the word 'Campbell.'"

"All right—all right!" said Lady Molly, slipping the note into her reticule. "And you go up to your room, Miss Campbell; it's no good giving that old fool Tredwen too much to gossip about."

Rosie Campbell went upstairs, and presently my dear lady and I were walking rapidly down the badly-lighted street.

"Where is the man?" I whispered eagerly as soon as we were out of earshot of No. 34.

"There is no man," replied Lady Molly, quickly.

"But the West End shop thief?" I asked.

"He hasn't been caught yet, and won't be either, for he is far too clever a scoundrel to fall into an ordinary trap."

She did not give me time to ask further questions, for presently, when we had reached Reporton Square, my dear lady handed me the note written by Campbell, and said:

"Go straight on to the Scotia Hotel, and ask for Miss Marvell; send up the note to her, but don't let her see you, as she knows you by sight. I must see the chief first, and will be with you as soon as possible. Having delivered the note, you must hang about outside as long as you can. Use your wits; she must not leave the hotel before I see her."

There was no hansom to be got in this elegant quarter of the town, so, having parted from my dear lady, I made for the nearest Underground station, and took a train for South Kensington.

Thus, it was nearly seven o'clock before I reached the Scotia. In answer to my inquiries for Miss Marvell, I was told that she was ill in bed and could see no one. I replied that I had only brought a note for her, and would wait for a reply.

Acting on my dear lady's instructions, I was as slow in my movements as ever I could be, and was some time in finding the note and handing it to a waiter, who then took it upstairs.

Presently he returned with the message: "Miss Marvell says there is no answer."

Whereupon I asked for pen and paper at the office, and wrote the following brief note on my own responsibility, using my wits as my dear lady had bidden me to do.

"Please, madam," I wrote, "will you send just a line to Miss Rosie Campbell? She seems very upset and frightened at some news she has had."

Once more the waiter ran upstairs, and returned with a sealed envelope, which I slipped into my reticule.

Time was slipping by very slowly. I did not know how long I should have to wait about outside in the cold, when, to my horror, I heard a hard voice, with a marked Scotch accent, saying:

"I am going out, waiter, and shan't be back to dinner. Tell them to lay a little cold supper upstairs in my room."

The next moment Miss Marvell, with coat, hat, and veil, was descending the stairs.

My plight was awkward. I certainly did not think it safe to present myself before the lady; she would undoubtedly recollect my face. Yet I had orders to detain her until the appearance of Lady Molly.

Miss Marvell seemed in no hurry. She was putting on her gloves as she came downstairs. In the hall she gave a few more instructions to the porter, whilst I, in a dark corner in the background, was vaguely planning an assault or an alarm of fire.

Suddenly, at the hotel entrance, where the porter was obsequiously holding open the door for Miss Marvell to pass through, I saw the latter's figure stiffen; she took one step back as if involuntarily, then, equally quickly, attempted to dart across the threshold, on which a group—composed of my dear lady, of Saunders, and of two or three people scarcely distinguishable in the gloom beyond—had suddenly made its appearance.

Miss Marvell was forced to retreat into the hall; already I had heard Saunders's hurriedly whispered words:

"Try and not make a fuss in this place, now. Everything can go off quietly, you know."

Danvers and Cotton, whom I knew well, were already standing one each side of Miss Marvell, whilst suddenly amongst this group I recognised Fanny, the wife of Danvers, who is one of our female searchers at the Yard.

"Shall we go up to your own room?" suggested Saunders.

"I think that is quite unnecessary," interposed Lady Molly. "I feel convinced that Mr. Leonard Marvell will yield to the inevitable quietly, and follow you without giving any trouble."

Marvell, however, did make a bold dash for liberty. As Lady Molly had said previously, he was far too clever to allow himself to be captured easily. But my dear lady had been cleverer. As she told me subsequently, she had from the first suspected that the trio who lodged at the Scotia Hotel were really only a duo—namely, Leonard Marvell and his wife. The latter impersonated a maid most of the time; but among these two clever people the three characters were interchangeable. Of course, there was no Miss Marvell at all. Leonard was alternately dressed up as man or woman, according to the requirements of his villainies.

"As soon as I heard that Miss Marvell was very tall and bony," said Lady Molly, "I thought that there might be a possibility of her being merely a man in disguise. Then there was the fact—but little dwelt on by either the police or public—that no one seems ever to have seen brother and sister together, nor was the entire trio ever seen at one and the same time.

"On that 3rd of February Leonard Marvell went out. No doubt he changed his attire in a lady's waiting-room at one of the railway stations; subsequently he came home, now dressed as Miss Marvell, and had dinner in the *table d'hôte* room so as to set up a fairly plausible alibi. But ultimately it was his wife, the *pseudo* Rosie Campbell, who stayed indoors that night, whilst he, Leonard Marvell, when going out after dinner, impersonated the maid until he was clear of the hotel; then he reassumed his male clothes once more, no doubt in the deserted waiting-room of some railway station, and met Miss Lulu Fay at supper, subsequently returning to the hotel in the guise of the maid.

"You see the game of criss-cross, don't you? This interchanging of characters was bound to baffle everyone. Many clever scoundrels have assumed disguises, sometimes personating members of the opposite sex to their own, but never before have I known two people play the part of three. Thus, endless contradictions followed as to the hour when Campbell the maid went out and when she came in, for at one time it was she herself who was seen by the valet, and at another it was Leonard Marvell dressed in her clothes."

He was also clever enough to accost Lord Mountnewte in the open street, thus bringing further complications into this strange case.

After the successful robbery of Miss Fay's diamonds, Leonard Marvell and his wife parted for a while. They were waiting for an opportunity to get across the Channel and there turn their booty into solid cash. Whilst Mrs. Marvell, *alias* Rosie Campbell, led a retired life in Findlater Terrace, Leonard kept his hand in with West End shop robberies.

Then Lady Molly entered the lists. As usual, her scheme was bold and daring; she trusted her own intuition and acted accordingly.

When she brought home the false news that the author of the shop robberies had been spotted by the police, Rosie Campbell's obvious terror confirmed her suspicions. The note written by the latter to the so-called Miss Marvell, though it contained nothing in any way incriminating, was the crowning certitude that my dear lady was right, as usual, in all her surmises.

And now Mr. Leonard Marvell will be living for a couple of years at the tax-payers' expense; he has "disappeared" temporarily from the public eye.

Rosie Campbell—*i.e.*, Mrs. Marvell—has gone to Glasgow. I feel convinced that two years hence we shall hear of the worthy couple again.

The Woman in the Big Hat
1

Lady Molly always had the idea that if the finger of Fate had pointed to Mathis' in Regent Street, rather than to Lyons', as the most advisable place for us to have a cup of tea that afternoon, Mr. Culledon would be alive at the present moment.

My dear lady is quite sure—and needless to say that I share her belief in herself—that she would have anticipated the murderer's intentions, and thus prevented one of the most cruel and callous of crimes which were ever perpetrated in the heart of London.

She and I had been to a *matinée* of *Trilby*, and were having tea at Lyons', which is exactly opposite Mathis' Vienna *café* in Regent Street. From where we sat, we commanded a view of the street and of the *café*, which had been very crowded during the last hour.

We had lingered over our toasted muffin until past six, when our attention was drawn to the unusual commotion which had arisen both outside and in the brilliantly lighted place over the road.

We saw two men run out of the doorway, and return a minute or two later in company with a policeman. You know what is the inevitable result of such a proceeding in London. Within three minutes a crowd had collected outside Mathis'. Two or three more constables had already assembled, and had some difficulty in keeping the entrance clear of intruders.

But already my dear lady, keen as a pointer on the scent, had hastily paid her bill, and, without waiting to see if I followed her or not, had quickly crossed the road, and the next moment her graceful form was lost in the crowd.

I went after her, impelled by curiosity, and presently caught sight of her in close conversation with one of our own men. I have always thought that Lady Molly must have eyes at the back of her head, otherwise how could she have known that I stood behind her now? Anyway, she beckoned to me, and together we entered Mathis', much to the astonishment and anger of the less fortunate crowd.

The usually gay little place was indeed sadly transformed. In one corner the waitresses, in dainty caps and aprons, had put their heads together, and were eagerly whispering to one another whilst casting furtive looks at the small group assembled in front of one of those pretty alcoves, which, as you know, line the walls all round the big tea-room at Mathis'.

Here two of our men were busy with pencil and note-book, whilst one fair-haired waitress, dissolved in tears, was apparently giving them a great deal of irrelevant and confused information.

Chief Inspector Saunders had, I understood, been already sent for; the constables, confronted with this extraordinary tragedy, were casting anxious glances towards the main entrance, whilst putting the conventional questions to the young waitress.

And in the alcove itself, raised from the floor of the room by a couple of carpeted steps, the cause of all this commotion, all this anxiety, and all these tears, sat huddled up on a chair, with arms lying straight across the marble-topped table, on which the usual paraphernalia of afternoon tea still lay scattered about. The upper part of the body, limp, backboneless, and awry, half propped up against the wall, half falling back upon the outstretched arms, told quite plainly its weird tale of death.

Before my dear lady and I had time to ask any questions, Saunders arrived in a taxicab. He was accompanied by the medical officer, Dr. Townson, who at once busied himself with the dead man, whilst Saunders went up quickly to Lady Molly.

"The chief suggested sending for you," he said quickly; "he was 'phoning you when I left. There's a woman in this case, and we shall rely on you a good deal."

"What has happened?" asked my dear lady, whose fine eyes were glowing with excitement at the mere suggestion of work.

"I have only a few stray particulars," replied Saunders, "but the chief witness is that yellow-haired girl over there. We'll find out what we can from her directly Dr. Townson has given us his opinion."

The medical officer, who had been kneeling beside the dead man, now rose and turned to Saunders. His face was very grave.

"The whole matter is simple enough, so far as I am concerned," he said. "The man has been killed by a terrific dose of *morphia*—administered, no doubt, in this cup of chocolate," he added, pointing to a cup in which there still lingered the cold dregs of the thick beverage.

"But when did this occur?" asked Saunders, turning to the waitress.

"I can't say," she replied, speaking with obvious nervousness. "The gentleman came in very early with a lady, somewhere about four. They made straight for this alcove. The place was just beginning to fill, and the music had begun."

"And where is the lady now?"

"She went off almost directly. She had ordered tea for herself and a cup of chocolate for the gentleman, also muffins and cakes. About five minutes afterwards, as I went past their table, I heard her say to him, 'I am afraid I must go now, or Jay's will be closed, but I'll be back in less than half an hour. You'll wait for me, won't you?'"

"Did the gentleman seem all right then?" "Oh, yes," said the waitress. "He had just begun to sip his chocolate, and merely said 'S'long' as she gathered up her gloves and muff and then went out of the shop."

"And she has not returned since?"

"No."

"When did you first notice there was anything wrong with this gentleman?" asked Lady Molly.

"Well," said the girl with some hesitation, "I looked at him once or twice as I went up and down, for he certainly seemed to have fallen all of a heap. Of course, I thought that he had gone to sleep, and I spoke to the manageress about him, but she thought that I ought to leave him alone for a bit. Then we got very busy, and I paid no more attention to him, until about six o'clock, when most afternoon tea customers had gone, and we were beginning to get the tables ready for dinners. Then I certainly did think there was something wrong with the man. I called to the manageress, and we sent for the police."

"And the lady who was with him at first, what was she like? Would you know her again?" queried Saunders.

"I don't know," replied the girl; "you see, I have to attend to such crowds of people of an afternoon, I can't notice each one. And she had on one of those enormous mushroom hats; no one could have seen her face—not more than her chin—unless they looked right under the hat."

"Would you know the hat again?" asked Lady Molly.

"Yes—I think I should," said the waitress. "It was black velvet and had a lot of plumes. It was enormous," she added, with a sigh of admiration and of longing for the monumental headgear.

During the girl's narrative one of the constables had searched the dead man's pockets. Among other items, he had found several letters addressed to Mark Culledon, Esq., some with an address in Lombard Street, others with one in Fitzjohn's Avenue, Hampstead. The initials M. C., which appeared both in the hat and on the silver mount of a letter-case belonging to the unfortunate gentleman, proved his identity beyond a doubt.

A house in Fitzjohn's Avenue does not, somehow, suggest a bachelor establishment. Even whilst Saunders and the other men were looking through the belongings of the deceased, Lady Molly had already thought of his family—children, perhaps a wife, a mother—who could tell?

What awful news to bring to an unsuspecting, happy family, who might even now be expecting the return of father, husband, or son, at the very moment when he lay murdered in a public place, the victim of some hideous plot or feminine revenge!

As our amiable friends in Paris would say, it jumped to the eyes that there was a woman in the case—a woman who had worn a gargantuan hat for the obvious purpose of remaining unidentifiable when the question of the unfortunate victim's companion that afternoon came up for solution. And all these facts to put before an expectant wife or an anxious mother!

As, no doubt, you have already foreseen, Lady Molly took the difficult task on her own kind shoulders. She and I drove together to Lorbury House, Fitzjohn's Avenue, and on asking of the manservant who opened the door if his mistress were at home, we were told that Lady Irene Culledon was in the drawing-room.

Mine is not a story of sentiment, so I am not going to dwell on that interview, which was one of the most painful moments I recollect having lived through.

Lady Irene was young—not five-and-twenty, I should say—*petite* and frail-looking, but with a quiet dignity of manner which was most impressive. She was Irish, as you know, the daughter of the Earl of Athyville, and, it seems, had married Mr. Mark Culledon in the teeth of strenuous opposition on the part of her family, which was as penniless as it was aristocratic, whilst Mr. Culledon had great prospects and a splendid business, but possessed neither ancestors nor high connections. She had only been married six months, poor little soul, and from all accounts must have idolised her husband.

Lady Molly broke the news to her with infinite tact, but there it was! It was a terrific blow—wasn't it?—to deal to a young wife—now a widow; and there was so little that a stranger could say in these circumstances. Even my dear lady's gentle voice, her persuasive eloquence, her kindly words, sounded empty and conventional in the face of such appalling grief.

2

Of course, everyone expected that the inquest would reveal something of the murdered man's inner life—would, in fact, allow the over-eager public to get a peep into Mr. Mark Culledon's secret orchard, wherein walked a lady who wore abnormally large velvet hats, and who nourished in her heart one of those terrible grudges against a man which can only find satisfaction in crime.

Equally, of course, the inquest revealed nothing that the public did not already know. The young widow was extremely reticent on the subject of her late husband's life, and the servants had all been fresh arrivals when the young couple, just home from their honeymoon, organised their new household at Lorbury House.

There was an old aunt of the deceased—a Mrs. Steinberg—who lived with the Culledons, but who at the present moment was very ill. Someone in the house—one of the younger servants, probably—very foolishly had told her every detail of the awful tragedy. With positively amazing strength, the invalid thereupon insisted on making a sworn statement, which she desired should be placed before the coroner's jury. She wished to bear solemn testimony to the integrity of her late nephew, Mark Culledon, in case the personality of the mysterious woman in the big hat suggested to evilly disposed minds any thought of scandal.

"Mark Culledon was the one nephew whom I loved," she stated with solemn emphasis. "I have shown my love for him by bequeathing to him the large fortune which I inherited from the late Mr. Steinberg. Mark was the soul of honour, or I should have cut him out of my will as I did my other nephews and nieces. I was brought up in a Scotch home, and I hate all this modern fastness and smartness, which are only other words for what I call profligacy."

Needless to say, the old lady's statement, solemn though it was, was of no use whatever for the elucidation of the mystery which surrounded the death of Mr. Mark Culledon. But as Mrs. Steinberg had talked of "other nephews," whom she had cut out of her will in favour of the murdered man, the police directed inquiries in those various quarters.

Mr. Mark Culledon certainly had several brothers and sisters, also cousins, who at different times—usually for some peccadillo or other—seemed to have incurred the wrath of the strait-laced old lady. But there did not appear to have been any ill-feeling in the family owing to this. Mrs. Steinberg was sole mistress of her fortune. She might just as well have bequeathed it *in toto* to some hospital as to one particular nephew whom she favoured, and the various relations were glad, on the whole, that the money was going to remain in the family rather than be cast abroad.

The mystery surrounding the woman in the big hat deepened as the days went by. As you know, the longer the period of time which elapses between a crime and the identification of the criminal, the greater chance the latter has of remaining at large.

In spite of strenuous efforts and close questionings of every one of the employees at Mathis', no one could give a very accurate description of the lady who had tea with the deceased on that fateful afternoon.

The first glimmer of light on the mysterious occurrence was thrown, about three weeks later, by a young woman named Katherine Harris, who had been parlour-maid at Lorbury House when first Mr. and Lady Irene Culledon returned from their honeymoon.

I must tell you that Mrs. Steinberg had died a few days after the inquest. The excitement had been too much for her enfeebled heart. Just before her death she had deposited £250 with her banker, which sum was to be paid over to any person giving information which would lead to the apprehension and conviction of the murderer of Mr. Mark Culledon.

This offer had stimulated everyone's zeal, and, I presume, had aroused Katherine Harris to a realisation of what had all the while been her obvious duty.

Lady Molly saw her in the chief's private office, and had much ado to disentangle the threads of the girl's confused narrative. But the main point of Harris's story was that a foreign lady had once called at Lorbury House, about a week after the master and mistress had returned from their honeymoon. Lady Irene was out at the time, and Mr. Culledon saw the lady in his smoking-room.

"She was a very handsome lady," explained Harris, "and was beautifully dressed."

"Did she wear a large hat?" asked the chief.

"I don't remember if it was particularly large," replied the girl.

"But you remember what the lady was like?" suggested Lady Molly.

"Yes, pretty well. She was very, very tall, and very good-looking."

"Would you know her again if you saw her?" rejoined my dear lady.

"Oh, yes; I think so," was Katherine Harris's reply.

Unfortunately, beyond this assurance the girl could say nothing very definite. The foreign lady seems to have been closeted with Mr. Culledon for about an hour, at the end of which time Lady Irene came home.

The butler being out that afternoon it was Harris who let her mistress in, and as the latter asked no questions, the girl did not volunteer the information that her master had a visitor. She went back to the servants' hall, but five minutes later the smoking-room bell rang, and she had to run up again. The foreign lady was then in the hall alone, and obviously waiting to be shown out. This Harris did, after which Mr. Culledon came out of his room, and, in the girl's own graphic words, "he went on dreadful."

"I didn't know I 'ad done anything so very wrong," she explained, "but the master seemed quite furious, and said I wasn't a proper parlourmaid, or I'd have known that visitors must not be shown in straight away like that. I ought to have said that I didn't know if Mr. Culledon was in; that I would go and see. Oh, he did go on at me!" continued Katherine Harris, volubly. "And I suppose he complained to the mistress, for she give me notice the next day."

"And you have never seen the foreign lady since?" concluded Lady Molly.

"No; she never come while I was there."

"By the way, how did you know she was foreign. Did she speak like a foreigner?"

"Oh, no," replied the girl. "She did not say much—only asked for Mr. Culledon—but she looked French like."

This unanswerable bit of logic concluded Katherine's statement. She was very anxious to know whether, if the foreign lady was hanged for murder, she herself would get the £250.

On Lady Molly's assurance that she certainly would, she departed in apparent content.

3

"Well! we are no nearer than we were before," said the chief, with an impatient sigh, when the door had closed behind Katherine Harris.

"Don't you think so?" rejoined Lady Molly, blandly.

"Do you consider that what we have heard just now has helped us to discover who was the woman in the big hat?" retorted the chief, somewhat testily.

"Perhaps not," replied my dear lady, with her sweet smile; "but it may help us to discover who murdered Mr. Culledon."

With which enigmatical statement she effectually silenced the chief, and finally walked out of his office, followed by her faithful Mary.

Following Katherine Harris's indications, a description of the lady who was wanted in connection with the murder of Mr. Culledon was very widely circulated, and within two days of the interview with the ex-parlour-maid another very momentous one took place in the same office.

Lady Molly was at work with the chief over some reports, whilst I was taking shorthand notes at a side desk, when a card was brought in by one of the men, and the next moment, without waiting either for permission to enter or to be more formally announced, a magnificent apparition literally sailed into the dust-covered little back office, filling it with an atmosphere of Parma violets and russia leather.

I don't think that I had ever seen a more beautiful woman in my life. Tall, with a splendid figure and perfect carriage, she vaguely reminded me of the portraits one sees of the late Empress of Austria. This lady was, moreover, dressed to perfection, and wore a large hat adorned with a quantity of plumes.

The chief had instinctively risen to greet her, whilst Lady Molly, still and placid, was eyeing her with a quizzical smile.

"You know who I am, sir," began the visitor as soon as she had sunk gracefully into a chair; "my name is on that card. My appearance, I understand, tallies exactly with that of a woman who is supposed to have murdered Mark Culledon."

She said this so calmly, with such perfect self-possession, that I literally gasped. The chief, too, seemed to have been metaphorically lifted off his feet. He tried to mutter a reply.

"Oh, don't trouble yourself, sir!" she interrupted him, with a smile. "My landlady, my servant, my friends have all read the description of the woman who murdered Mr. Culledon. For the past twenty-four hours I have been watched by your police, therefore I have come to you of my own accord, before they came to arrest me in my flat. I am not too soon, am I?" she asked, with that same cool indifference which was so startling, considering the subject of her conversation.

She spoke English with a scarcely perceptible foreign accent, but I quite understood what Katherine Harris had meant when she said that the lady looked "French like." She certainly did not look English, and when I caught sight of her name on the card, which the chief had handed to Lady Molly, I put her down at once as Viennese. Miss Elizabeth Lowenthal had all the charm, the grace, the elegance, which one associates with Austrian women more than with those of any other nation.

No wonder the chief found it difficult to tell her that, as a matter of fact, the police were about to apply for a warrant that very morning for her arrest on a charge of wilful murder.

"I know—I know," she said, seeming to divine his thoughts; "but let me tell you at once, sir, that I did not murder Mark Culledon. He treated me shamefully, and I would willingly have made a scandal just to spite him; he had become so respectable and strait-laced. But between scandal and murder there is a wide gulf. Don't you think so, madam," she added, turning for the first time towards Lady Molly.

"Undoubtedly," replied my dear lady, with the same quizzical smile.

"A wide gulf which, no doubt, Miss Elizabeth Lowenthal will best be able to demonstrate to the magistrate tomorrow," rejoined the chief, with official sternness of manner.

I thought that, for the space of a few seconds, the lady lost her self-assurance at this obvious suggestion—the bloom on her cheeks seemed to vanish, and two hard lines appeared between her fine eyes. But, frightened or not, she quickly recovered herself, and said quietly:

"Now, my dear sir, let us understand one another. I came here for that express purpose. I take it that you don't want your police to look ridiculous any more than I want a scandal. I don't want detectives to hang about round my flat, questioning my neighbours and my servants. They would soon find out that I did not murder Mark Culledon, of course; but the atmosphere of the police would hang round me, and I—I prefer Parma violets," she added, raising a daintily perfumed handkerchief to her nose.

"Then you have come to make a statement?" asked the chief.

"Yes," she replied; "I'll tell you all I know. Mr. Culledon was engaged to marry me; then he met the daughter of an earl, and thought he would like her better as a wife than a simple Miss Lowenthal. I suppose I should be considered an undesirable match for a young man who has a highly respectable and snobbish aunt, who would leave him all her money only on the condition that he made a suitable marriage. I have a voice, and I came over to England two years ago to study English, so that I might sing in *oratorio* at the Albert Hall. I met Mark on the Calais-Dover boat, when he was returning from a holiday abroad. He fell in love with me, and presently he asked me to be his wife.

"After some demur, I accepted him; we became engaged, but he told me that our engagement must remain a secret, for he had an old aunt from whom he had great expectations, and who might not approve of his marrying a foreign girl, who was without connections and a professional singer. From that moment I mistrusted him, nor was I very astonished when gradually his affection for me seemed to cool. Soon after, he informed me, quite callously, that he had changed his mind, and was going to marry some swell English lady. I didn't care much, but I wanted to punish him by making a scandal, you understand. I went to his house just to worry him, and finally I decided to bring an action for breach of promise against him. It would have upset him, I know; no doubt his aunt would have cut him out of her will. That is all I wanted, but I did not care enough about him to murder him."

Somehow her tale carried conviction. We were all of us obviously impressed. The chief alone looked visibly disturbed, and I could read what was going on in his mind.

"As you say, Miss Lowenthal," he rejoined, "the police would have found all this out within the next few hours. Once your connection with the murdered man was known to us, the record of your past and his becomes an easy one to peruse. No doubt, too," he added insinuatingly, "our men would soon have been placed in possession of the one undisputable proof of your complete innocence with regard to that fateful afternoon spent at Mathis' *café*."

"What is that?" she queried blandly.

"An alibi."

"You mean, where I was during the time that Mark was being murdered in a tea shop?"

"Yes," said the chief.

"I was out for a walk," she replied quietly.

"Shopping, perhaps?"

"No."

"You met someone who would remember the circumstance—or your servants could say at what time you came in?"

"No," she repeated dryly; 'I met no one, for I took a brisk walk on Primrose Hill. My two servants could only say that I went out at three o'clock that afternoon and returned after five."

There was silence in the little office for a moment or two. I could hear the scraping of the pen with which the chief was idly scribbling geometrical figures on his blotting pad.

Lady Molly was quite still. Her large, luminous eyes were fixed on the beautiful woman who had just told us her strange story, with its unaccountable sequel, its mystery which had deepened with the last phrase which she had uttered. Miss Lowenthal, I felt sure, was conscious of her peril. I am not sufficiently a psychologist to know whether it was guilt or merely fear which was distorting the handsome features now, hardening the face and causing the lips to tremble.

Lady Molly scribbled a few words on a scrap of paper, which she then passed over to the chief. Miss Lowenthal was making visible efforts to steady her nerves.

"That is all I have to tell you," she said, in a voice which sounded dry and harsh. "I think I will go home now."

But she did not rise from her chair, and seemed to hesitate as if fearful lest permission to go were not granted her.

To her obvious astonishment—and, I must add, to my own—the chief immediately rose and said, quite urbanely:

"I thank you very much for the helpful information which you have given me. Of course, we may rely on your presence in town for the next few days, may we not?"

She seemed greatly relieved, and all at once resumed her former charm of manner and elegance of attitude. The beautiful face was lit up by a smile.

The chief was bowing to her in quite a foreign fashion, and in spite of her visible reassurance she eyed him very intently. Then she went up to Lady Molly and held out her hand.

My dear lady took it without an instant's hesitation. I, who knew that it was the few words hastily scribbled by Lady Molly which had dictated the chief's conduct with regard to Miss Lowenthal, was left wondering whether the woman I loved best in all the world had been shaking hands with a murderess.

4

No doubt you will remember the sensation which was caused by the arrest of Miss Lowenthal, on a charge of having murdered Mr. Mark Culledon, by administering *morphia* to him in a cup of chocolate at Mathis' *café* in Regent Street.

The beauty of the accused, her undeniable charm of manner, the hitherto blameless character of her life, all tended to make the public take violent sides either for or against her, and the usual budget of amateur correspondence, suggestions, recriminations and advice poured into the chief's office in titanic proportions.

I must say that, personally, all my sympathies went out to Miss Lowenthal. As I have said before, I am no psychologist, but I had seen her in the original interview at the office, and I could not get rid of an absolutely unreasoning certitude that the beautiful Viennese singer was innocent.

The magistrate's court was packed, as you may well imagine, on that first day of the inquiry; and, of course, sympathy with the accused went up to fever pitch when she staggered into the dock, beautiful still, despite the ravages caused by horror, anxiety, fear, in face of the deadly peril in which she stood.

The magistrate was most kind to her; her solicitor was unimpeachably assiduous; even our fellows, who had to give evidence against her, did no more than their duty, and were as lenient in their statements as possible.

Miss Lowenthal had been arrested in her flat by Danvers, accompanied by two constables. She had loudly protested her innocence all along, and did so still, pleading "Not guilty" in a firm voice.

The great points in favour of the arrest were, firstly, the undoubted motive of disappointment and revenge against a faithless sweetheart, then the total inability to prove any kind of alibi, which, under the circumstances, certainly added to the appearance of guilt.

The question of where the fatal drug was obtained was more difficult to prove. It was stated that Mr. Mark Culledon was director of several important companies, one of which carried on business as wholesale druggists.

Therefore, it was argued that the accused, at different times and under some pretext or other, had obtained drugs from Mr. Culledon himself. She had admitted to having visited the deceased at his office in the City, both before and after his marriage.

Miss Lowenthal listened to all this evidence against her with a hard, set face, as she did also to Katherine Harris's statement about her calling on Mr. Culledon at Lorbury House, but she brightened up visibly when the various attendants at Mathis' *café* were placed in the box.

A very large hat belonging to the accused was shown to the witnesses, but, though the police upheld the theory that that was the headgear worn by the mysterious lady at the *café* on that fateful afternoon, the waitresses made distinctly contradictory statements with regard to it.

Whilst one girl swore that she recognised the very hat, another was equally positive that it was distinctly smaller than the one she recollected, and when the hat was placed on the head of Miss Lowenthal, three out of the four witnesses positively refused to identify her.

Most of these young women declared that though the accused, when wearing the big hat, looked as if she might have been the lady in question, yet there was a certain something about her which was different.

With that vagueness which is a usual and highly irritating characteristic of their class, the girls finally parried every question by refusing to swear positively either for or against the identity of Miss Lowenthal.

"There's something that's different about her somehow," one of the waitresses asserted positively.

"What is it that's different?" asked the solicitor for the accused, pressing his point.

"I can't say," was the perpetual, maddening reply.

Of course, the poor young widow had to be dragged into the case, and here, I think, opinions and even expressions of sympathy were quite unanimous.

The whole tragedy had been inexpressibly painful to her, of course, and now it must have seemed doubly so. The scandal which had accumulated round her late husband's name must have added the poignancy of shame to that of grief. Mark Culledon had behaved as callously to the girl whom clearly, he had married from interested, family motives, as he had to the one whom he had heartlessly cast aside.

Lady Irene, however, was most moderate in her statements. There was no doubt that she had known of her husband's previous entanglement with Miss Lowenthal, but apparently had not thought fit to make him accountable for the past. She did not know that Miss Lowenthal had threatened a breach of promise action against her husband.

Throughout her evidence she spoke with absolute calm and dignity, and looked indeed a strange contrast, in her closely fitting tailor-made costume of black serge and tiny black toque, to the more brilliant woman who stood in the dock.

The two great points in favour of the accused were, firstly, the vagueness of the witnesses who were called to identify her, and, secondly, the fact that she had undoubtedly begun proceedings for breach of promise against the deceased. Judging by the latter's letters to her, she would have had a splendid case against him, which fact naturally dealt a severe blow to the theory as to motive for the murder.

On the whole, the magistrate felt that there was not a sufficiency of evidence against the accused to warrant his committing her for trial; he therefore discharged her, and, amid loud applause from the public, Miss Lowenthal left the court a free woman.

Now, I know that the public did loudly, and, to my mind, very justly, blame the police for that arrest, which was denounced as being as cruel as it was unjustifiable. I felt as strongly as anybody on the subject, for I knew that the prosecution had been instituted in defiance of Lady Molly's express advice, and in distinct contradiction to the evidence which she had collected. When, therefore, the chief again asked my dear lady to renew her efforts in that mysterious case, it was small wonder that her enthusiasm did not respond to his anxiety. That she would do her duty was beyond a doubt, but she had very naturally lost her more fervent interest in the case.

The mysterious woman in the big hat was still the chief subject of leading articles in the papers, coupled with that of the ineptitude of the police who could not discover her. There were caricatures and picture post-cards in all the shop windows of a gigantic hat covering the whole figure of its wearer, only the feet, and a very long and pointed chin, protruding from beneath the enormous brim. Below was the device, "Who is she? Ask the police?" One day—it was the second since the discharge of Miss Lowenthal—my dear lady came into my room beaming. It was the first time I had seen her smile for more than a week, and already I had guessed what it was that had cheered her.

"Good news, Mary," she said gaily. "At last, I've got the chief to let me have a free hand. Oh, dear! what a lot of argument it takes to extricate that man from the tangled meshes of red tape!"

"What are you going to do?" I asked.

"Prove that my theory is right as to who murdered Mark Culledon," she replied seriously; "and as a preliminary we'll go and ask his servants at Lorbury House a few questions."

It was then three o'clock in the afternoon. At Lady Molly's bidding, I dressed somewhat smartly, and together we went off in a taxi to Fitzjohn's Avenue.

Lady Molly had written a few words on one of her cards, urgently requesting an interview with Lady Irene Culledon. This she handed over to the man-servant who opened the door at Lorbury House. A few moments later we were sitting in the cosy *boudoir*. The young widow, high-bred and dignified in her tight-fitting black gown, sat opposite to us, her white hands folded demurely before her, her small head, with its very close *coiffure*, bent in closest attention towards Lady Molly.

"I most sincerely hope, Lady Irene," began my dear lady, in her most gentle and persuasive voice, "that you will look with all possible indulgence on my growing desire—shared, I may say, by all my superiors at Scotland Yard—to elucidate the mystery which still surrounds your late husband's death." Lady Molly paused, as if waiting for encouragement to proceed. The subject must have been extremely painful to the young widow; nevertheless, she responded quite gently:

"I can understand that the police wish to do their duty in the matter; as for me, I have done all, I think, that could be expected of me. I am not made of iron, and after that day in the police court—"

She checked herself, as if afraid of having betrayed more emotion than was consistent with good breeding, and concluded more calmly:

"I cannot do any more."

"I fully appreciate your feelings in the matter," said Lady Molly, "but you would not mind helping us—would you ?—in a passive way, if you could, by some simple means, further the cause of justice."

"What is it you want me to do?" asked Lady Irene.

"Only to allow me to ring for two of your maids and to ask them a few questions. I promise you that they shall not be of such a nature as to cause you the slightest pain."

For a moment I thought that the young widow hesitated, then, without a word, she rose and rang the bell.

"Which of my servants did you wish to see?" she asked, turning to my dear lady as soon as the butler entered in answer to the bell.

"Your own maid and your parlour-maid, if I may," replied Lady Molly.

Lady Irene gave the necessary orders, and we all sat expectant and silent until, a minute or two later, two girls entered the room. One wore a cap and apron, the other, in neat black dress and dainty lace collar, was obviously the lady's maid.

"This lady," said their mistress, addressing the two girls, "wishes to ask you a few questions. She is a representative of the police, so you had better do your best to satisfy her with your answers."

"Oh!" rejoined Lady Molly pleasantly—choosing not to notice the tone of acerbity with which the young widow had spoken, nor the unmistakable barrier of hostility and reserve which her words had immediately raised between the young servants and the "representative of the police"—"what I am going to ask these two young ladies is neither very difficult nor very unpleasant. I merely want their kind help in a little comedy which will have to be played this evening, in order to test the accuracy of certain statements made by one of the waitresses at Mathis' tea shop with regard to the terrible tragedy which has darkened this house. You will do that much, will you not?" she added, speaking directly to the maids.

No one can be so winning or so persuasive as my dear lady. In a moment I saw the girls' hostility melting before the sunshine of Lady Molly's smile.

"We'll do what we can, ma'am," said the maid.

"That's a brave, good girl!" replied my lady. "You must know that the chief waitress at Mathis' has, this very morning, identified the woman in the big hat who, we all believe, murdered your late master. Yes!" she continued, in response to a gasp of astonishment which seemed to go round the room like a wave, "the girl seems quite positive, both as regards the hat and the woman who wore it. But, of course, one cannot allow a human life to be sworn away without bringing every possible proof to bear on such a statement, and I am sure that everyone in this house will understand that we don't want to introduce strangers more than we can help into this sad affair, which already has been bruited abroad too much."

She paused a moment; then, as neither Lady Irene nor the maids made any comment, she continued:

"My superiors at Scotland Yard think it their duty to try and confuse the witness as much as possible in her act of identification. They desire that a certain number of ladies wearing abnormally large hats should parade before the waitress. Among them will be, of course, the one whom the girl has already identified as being the mysterious person who had tea with Mr. Culledon at Mathis' that afternoon.

"My superiors can then satisfy themselves whether the waitress is or is not so sure of her statement that she invariably picks out again and again one particular individual amongst a number of others or not."

"Surely," interrupted Lady Irene, dryly, "you and your superiors do not expect my servants to help in such a farce?"

"We don't look upon such a proceeding as a farce, Lady Irene," rejoined Lady Molly, gently. "It is often resorted to in the interests of an accused person, and we certainly would ask the co-operation of your household."

"I don't see what they can do."

But the two girls did not seem unwilling. The idea appealed to them, I felt sure; it suggested an exciting episode, and gave promise of variety in their monotonous lives.

"I am sure both these young ladies possess fine big hats," continued Lady Molly with an encouraging smile.

"I should not allow them to wear ridiculous headgear," retorted Lady Irene, sternly.

"I have the one your ladyship wouldn't wear, and threw away," interposed the young parlour-maid. "I put it together again with the scraps I found in the dust-hole."

There was just one instant of absolute silence, one of those magnetic moments when Fate seems to have dropped the spool on which she was spinning the threads of a life, and is just stooping in order to pick it up.

Lady Irene raised a black-bordered handkerchief to her lips, then said quietly:

"I don't know what you mean, Mary. I never wear big hats."

"No, my lady," here interposed the lady's maid; "but Mary means the one you ordered at Sanchia's and only wore the once—the day you went to that concert."

"Which day was that?" asked Lady Molly, blandly.

"Oh! I couldn't forget that day," ejaculated the maid; "her ladyship came home from the concert—I had undressed her, and she told me that she would never wear her big hat again—it was too heavy. That same day Mr. Culledon was murdered."

"That hat would answer our purpose very well," said Lady Molly, quite calmly. "Perhaps Mary will go and fetch it, and you had better go and help her put it on."

The two girls went out of the room without another word, and there were we three women left facing one another, with that awful secret, only half-revealed, hovering in the air like an intangible spectre.

"What are you going to do, Lady Irene?" asked Lady Molly, after a moment's pause, during which I literally could hear my own heart beating, whilst I watched the rigid figure of the widow in deep black crape, her face set and white, her eyes fixed steadily on Lady Molly.

"You can't prove it!" she said defiantly.

"I think we can," rejoined Lady Molly, simply; "at any rate, I mean to try. I have two of the waitresses from Mathis' outside in a cab, and I have already spoken to the attendant who served you at Sanchia's, an obscure milliner in a back street near Portland Road. We know that you were at great pains there to order a hat of certain dimensions and to your own minute description; it was a copy of one you had once seen Miss Lowenthal wear when you met her at your late husband's office. We can prove that meeting, too. Then we have your maid's testimony that you wore that same hat once, and once only, the day, presumably, that you went out to a concert—a statement which you will find it difficult to substantiate—and also the day on which your husband was murdered."

"Bah! the public will laugh at you!" retorted Lady Irene, still defiantly. "You would not dare to formulate so monstrous a charge!"

"It will not seem monstrous when justice has weighed in the balance the facts which we can prove. Let me tell you a few of these, the result of careful investigation. There is the fact that you knew of Mr. Culledon's entanglement with Miss Elizabeth Lowenthal, and did your best to keep it from old Mrs. Steinberg's knowledge, realising that any scandal round her favourite nephew would result in the old lady cutting him—and therefore you—out of her will. You dismissed a parlour-maid for the sole reason that she had been present when Miss

Lowenthal was shown into Mr. Culledon's study.

"There is the fact that Mrs. Steinberg had so worded her will that, in the event of her nephew dying before her, her fortune would devolve on you; the fact that, with Miss Lowenthal's action for breach of promise against your husband, your last hope of keeping the scandal from the old lady's ears had effectually vanished. You saw the fortune eluding your grasp; you feared Mrs. Steinberg would alter her will. Had you found the means, and had you dared, would you not rather have killed the old lady? But discovery would have been certain. The other crime was bolder and surer. You have inherited the old lady's millions, for she never knew of her nephew's earlier *peccadillos*.

"All this we can state and prove, and the history of the hat, bought, and worn one day only, that same memorable day, and then thrown away."

A loud laugh interrupted her—a laugh that froze my very marrow.

"There is one fact you have forgotten, my lady of Scotland Yard," came in sharp, strident accents from the black-robed figure, which seemed to have become strangely spectral in the fast gathering gloom which had been enveloping the luxurious little *boudoir*. "Don't omit to mention the fact that the accused took the law into her own hands."

And before my dear lady and I could rush to prevent her, Lady Irene Culledon had conveyed something—we dared not think what—to her mouth.

"Find Danvers quickly, Mary!" said Lady Molly, calmly. "You'll find him outside. Bring a doctor back with you."

Even as she spoke Lady Irene, with a cry of agony, fell senseless in my dear lady's arms.

The doctor, I may tell you, came too late. The unfortunate woman evidently had a good knowledge of poisons. She had been determined not to fail; in case of discovery, she was ready and able to mete out justice to herself.

I don't think the public ever knew the real truth about the woman in the big hat. Interest in her went the way of all things. Yet my dear lady had been right from beginning to end. With unerring precision, she had placed her dainty finger on the real motive and the real perpetrator of the crime—the ambitious woman who had married solely for money, and meant to have that money even at the cost of one of the most dastardly murders that have ever darkened the criminal annals of this country.

I asked Lady Molly what it was that first made her think of Lady

" Lady Irene, with a cry of agony, fell senseless in my
dear lady's arms "

Irene as the possible murderess. No one else for a moment had thought her guilty.

"The big hat," replied my dear lady with a smile. "Had the mysterious woman at Mathis' been tall, the waitresses would not, one and all, have been struck by the abnormal size of the hat. The wearer must have been *petite*, hence the reason that under a wide brim only the chin would be visible. I at once sought for a *small* woman. Our fellows did not think of that, because they are men."

You see how simple it all was!

Sir Jeremiah's Will

1

Many people have asked me whether I knew when, and in what circumstances, Lady Molly joined the detective staff at Scotland Yard, who she was, and how she managed to keep her position in Society—as she undoubtedly did—whilst exercising a profession which usually does not make for high social standing.

Well, of course, there is much that I have known all along about my dear lady—just as much, in fact, as her aristocratic friends and relations did—but I had promised her not to let the general public know anything of her private life until she gave me leave to do so.

Now things have taken a different turn, and I can tell you all I know. But I must go back some years for that, and recall to your mind that extraordinary crime known in those days as the Baddock Will Case, which sent one of the most prominent and popular young men in Society to penal servitude—a life sentence, mind you, which was considered to be remarkably lenient by a number of people who thought that Captain de Mazareen ought to have been hanged.

He was such a good-looking young soldier in those days. I specially remember him at the late queen's funeral—one of the tallest men in the British Army, and with that peculiar charm of manner which, alas! one has ceased to associate with young Englishmen nowadays. If to these two undeniable advantages you add the one that Hubert de Mazareen was the dearly loved grandson of Sir Jeremiah Baddock, the multi-millionaire shipowner of Liverpool, you will realise how easy it was for that young Guardsman to ingratiate himself with every woman in Society, and more particularly with every mamma who had a marriageable daughter.

But Fate and Love have a proverbial knack of making a muddle of things. Captain de Mazareen, with a bevy of pretty and eligible girls from whom to select a wife, chose to fall in love with the one woman in the whole of England who, in his grandfather's opinion, should have remained a stranger, even an enemy, to him.

You remember the sad story—more than a quarter of a century old now—of Sir Jeremiah's unhappy second marriage with the pretty French actress, Mlle. Adèle Desty, who was then over thirty years younger than himself. He married her abroad, and never brought her to England. She made him supremely wretched for about three years, and finally ran away with the Earl of Flintshire, whom she had met at Monte Carlo.

Well! it was with a daughter of that same Earl of Flintshire, Lady Molly Robertson-Kirk, that Captain Hubert de Mazareen fell desperately in love.

Imagine Sir Jeremiah's feelings when he heard of it.

Captain Hubert, you must know, had resigned his commission in 1902 at his grandfather's request, when the latter's health first began to fail. He had taken up his permanent abode at Appledore Castle, Sir Jeremiah's magnificent home in Cumberland, and, of course, it was generally understood that ultimately, he would become possessed of the wealthy shipowner's millions as well as of the fine property, seeing that his mother had been Sir Jeremiah's only child by the latter's first marriage.

Lord Flintshire's property was quite close to Appledore; but, needless to say, old Sir Jeremiah never forgave his noble neighbour the cruel wrong he had suffered at his hands.

The second Lady Baddock, afterwards Countess of Flintshire, has been dead twenty years. Neither the county nor the more exclusive sets of London ever received her, but her daughter Molly, who inherited all her beauty and none of her faults, was the idol of her father, and the acknowledged queen of county and town Society.

You see, it was the ancient, yet ever new, story of Cappelletti and Montecchi over again, and one day Captain Hubert de Mazareen had to tell Sir Jeremiah that he desired to marry the daughter of his grandfather's most cruel enemy.

What the immediate result of that announcement was, no one could say. Neither Sir Jeremiah nor Captain Hubert de Mazareen would have allowed servants or dependents to hear a word of disagreement that might have passed between them, much less to suspect that an unpleasant scene had occurred.

Outwardly everything went on as usual at Appledore Castle for about a fortnight or so, after which Captain Hubert went away one day, ostensibly for a brief stay in London; but he never re-entered the doors of the castle until after the dark veil of an appalling tragedy had begun to descend on the stately old Cumberland home.

Sir Jeremiah bore up pretty well for a time, then he had a slight paralytic stroke and became a confirmed invalid. The postmaster at Appledore declared that after that many letters came, addressed to Sir Jeremiah in Captain Hubert's well-known handwriting and bearing the London postmark; but presumably the old gentleman felt bitterly irreconcilable towards his grandson, for Captain de Mazareen was never seen at the castle.

Soon the invalid grew more and more eccentric and morose. He ordered all the reception rooms of his magnificent home to be closed and shuttered, and he dismissed all his indoor servants, with the exception of his own male attendant and an old married couple named Bradley, who had been in his service for years, and who now did the little work that was required in what had once been one of the most richly appointed country mansions in England.

Bitter resentment against his once dearly loved grandson, and against the man who had robbed him of his young wife twenty-five years ago, seemed to have cut off the old man from contact with the outside world.

Thus, matters stood until the spring of 1903, when Sir Jeremiah announced one morning to the three members of his household that Mr. Philip Baddock was coming to stay at the castle, and that a room must be got ready immediately.

Mr. Philip Baddock came that same evening. He was a young man of quite ordinary appearance: short, rather dark, with the somewhat uncouth manners suggestive of an upbringing in a country parsonage.

His arrival created no little excitement in the neighbourhood. Who was Mr. Philip Baddock, and where did he come from? No one had ever heard of him before, and now—after a very brief time spent at the castle—he seemed to be gradually taking up the position which originally had belonged to Captain Hubert.

He took over the command of the small household, dismissing Sir Jeremiah's personal attendant after a while and engaging another. He supervised the outdoor men, reducing the staff both in the gardens and the stables. He sold most of the horses and carriages, and presently bought a motorcar, which he at once took to driving all over the country.

But he spoke to no one in the village, and soon, in answer to inquiries by one or two of Sir Jeremiah's faithful friends and cronies, the reply came regularly from Mr. Philip Baddock that the invalid was disinclined for company. Only Doctor Thorne, the local practitioner, saw the patient. Sir Jeremiah, it was understood, was slowly sinking towards the grave; but his mind was quite clear, even if his temper was abnormal.

One day Mr. Philip Baddock made inquiries in the village for a good chauffeur. George Taylor presented himself, and was at once told off to drive the car as quickly as possible to Carlisle, to the office of Mr. Steadman, solicitor, and to bring that gentleman back to the Castle as soon as he could come.

The distance from Appledore to Carlisle is over fifty miles. It was seven o'clock in the evening before George Taylor was back, bringing Mr. Steadman with him.

The solicitor was received at the castle door by old Bradley, and at Sir Jeremiah's door by Felkin, the new attendant, who showed him in. The interview between the invalid and Mr. Steadman lasted half an hour, after which the latter was driven back to Carlisle by George Taylor.

That same evening a telegram was sent off by Mr. Philip Baddock to Captain de Mazareen in London, containing the few words:

"Sir Jeremiah very ill. Come at once."

Twenty-four hours later Captain Hubert arrived at Appledore Castle—too late, however, to see his grandfather alive.

Sir Jeremiah Baddock had died an hour before the arrival of his once so tenderly cherished grandson, and all hopes of a reconciliation had now been mercilessly annihilated by death.

The end had come much more suddenly than Doctor Thorne had anticipated. He had seen the patient in the morning and thought that he might last some days. But when Sir Jeremiah had heard that Captain de Mazareen had been sent for he had worked himself into a state of such terrible agitation that the poor, overtaxed brain and heart finally gave way.

2

The events of those memorable days—in the early spring of 1904— are so graven on my memory that I can recount them as if they happened yesterday.

I was maid to Lady Molly Robertson-Kirk at the time. Since then, she has honoured me with her friendship.

Directly after Captain Hubert's first estrangement from his grandfather, she and I came down to Cumberland and lived very quietly at Kirk Hall, which, as you know, is but a stone's throw from Appledore.

Here Captain Hubert paid my dear lady several visits. She had irrevocably made up her mind that their engagement was to be indefinitely prolonged, for she had a vague hope that, sooner or later, Sir Jeremiah would relent towards the grandson whom he had loved so dearly. At any rate, there was a chance of it whilst the marriage had not actually taken place.

Captain de Mazareen, mind you, was in no sense of the word badly off. His father had left him some £25,000, and Lady Molly had a small private fortune of her own. Therefore, I assure you that there was not a single mercenary thought behind this protracted engagement or Captain Hubert's desire for a reconciliation with his grandfather.

The evening that he arrived at Appledore in response to Mr. Philip Baddock's telegram, Lady Molly met him at the station. He sent his luggage on to Kirk Hall, and the two young people walked together as far as the Elkhorn Woods, which divide the Earl of Flintshire's property from Appledore itself.

Here they met Mr. Steadman, the solicitor, who had motored over from Carlisle in response to an urgent summons from Sir Jeremiah Baddock, but whose car had broken down about two hundred yards up the road.

It seems that the chauffeur had suggested his walking on through the woods, it being an exceptionally fine and mild spring evening, with a glorious full moon overhead, which lit up almost every turn of the path that cuts through the pretty coppice.

Lady Molly had given me rendezvous at the edge of the wood, so that I might accompany her home after she had taken leave of Captain Hubert. It seems that the latter knew Mr. Steadman slightly, and we saw the two men shake hands with one another, then, after a few words of conversation, turn off to walk together through the wood. We then made our way back silently to Kirk Hall.

My dear lady was inexpressibly sad. She appreciated very deeply the love which Captain Hubert bore for his grandfather, and was loath to see the final annihilation of all her hopes of an ultimate reconciliation between the two men.

I had dressed Lady Molly for dinner, and she was just going downstairs, when Captain de Mazareen arrived at the Hall.

He announced the sad news of his grandfather's death, and looked extremely dejected and upset.

Of course, he stayed at the Hall, for Mr. Philip Baddock seemed quite to have taken command at Appledore Castle, and Captain Hubert did not care to be beholden to him for hospitality.

My dear lady asked him what had become of Mr. Steadman.

"I don't know," he replied. "He started to walk with me through the wood, then he seemed to think that the tramp would be too much for him, and that the car could be put right very quickly. He preferred to drive round, and was quite sure that he would meet me at the castle in less than half an hour. However, he never turned up."

Lady Molly asked several more questions about Sir Jeremiah, which Captain Hubert answered in a listless way. He had been met at the door of the castle by Mr. Philip Baddock, who told him that the old gentleman had breathed his last half an hour before.

I remember that we all went to bed that night feeling quite unaccountably depressed. It seemed that something more tragic than the natural death of a septuagenarian hovered in the air of these remote Cumberland villages.

The next morning our strange premonitions were confirmed. Lord Flintshire, my dear lady, and Captain Hubert were sitting at breakfast when the news was brought to the Hall that Mr. Steadman, the Carlisle solicitor, had been found murdered in the Elkhorn Woods earlier in the morning. Evidently, he had been stunned, and then done to death by a heavily-loaded stick or some similar weapon. When he was discovered in the early hours of the morning, he had, apparently, been dead some time. The local police were at once apprised of the terrible event, which created as much excitement as the death of the eccentric old millionaire at Appledore Castle.

Everyone at Kirk Hall, of course, was keenly interested, and Captain de Mazareen went over to Appledore as soon as he could in order to place his information at the service of the police.

It is a strange fact, but nevertheless a true one, that when a deadly peril arises such as now threatened Captain de Mazareen, the person most in danger is the last to be conscious of it.

I am quite sure that Lady Molly, the moment she heard that Mr. Steadman had been murdered in the Elkhorn Woods, realised that the man she loved would be implicated in that tragedy in some sinister manner. But that is the intuition of a woman—of a woman who loves.

As for Captain Hubert, he went about during the whole of that day quite unconscious of the abyss which already was yawning at his feet. He even discussed quite equably the several valuable bits of information which the local police had already collected, and which eventually formed a portion of that damning fabric of circumstantial evidence which was to bring him within sight of the gallows.

Earlier in the day, Mr. Philip Baddock sent him a stiff little note, saying that, as Captain de Mazareen was now the owner of Appledore Castle, he (Philip Baddock) did not desire to trespass a moment longer than was necessary on his relative's hospitality, and had arranged to stay at the village inn until after the funeral, when he would leave Cumberland.

To this Captain Hubert sent an equally curt note saying that, as far as he knew, he had no say in the matter of anyone coming or going from the castle, and that Mr. Philip Baddock must, of course, please himself as to whether he stayed there or not.

So far, of course, the old gentleman's testamentary dispositions were not known. He had made a will in 1902 bequeathing Appledore and everything he possessed unconditionally to his beloved grandson, Hubert de Mazareen, whom he also appointed his sole executor. That will was lodged with Mr. Truscott, who had been solicitor to the deceased practically until the last moment, when Mr. Steadman, a new arrival at Carlisle, had been sent for.

Whether that will had been revoked or not Mr. Truscott did not know; but, in the course of the afternoon, Lord Flintshire, whilst out driving, met the local superintendent of police, who told him that Mr. Steadman's senior partner—a Mr. Fuelling—had made a statement to the effect that Sir Jeremiah had sent for Mr. Steadman the day before his death and given instructions for the drafting of a new will whereby the old gentleman bequeathed Appledore and everything he possessed to his beloved grandson, Hubert de Mazareen, but only on the condition that the latter did not marry the daughter or any other relative of the Earl of Flintshire.

In the event of Hubert de Mazareen disregarding this condition at any future time of his life, Sir Jeremiah's entire fortune was to devolve on Philip Baddock, sole issue of testator's second marriage, with Adèle Desty. The draft of this will, added Mr. Fuelling, was in Mr. Steadman's pocket ready for Sir Jeremiah's signature on that fateful night when the unfortunate young solicitor was murdered.

The draft had not been found in the murdered man's pocket. A copy of it, however, was in Mr. Fuelling's safe. But as this will had never been signed by the deceased the one of 1902 remained valid, and Captain Hubert de Mazareen remained unconditionally his grandfather's sole heir.

3

Events crowded thick and fast on that day—one of the most miserable I have ever lived through.

After an early tea, which my dear lady had alone in her little *boudoir*, she sent me down to ask Captain Hubert to come up and speak to her. He did so at once, and I went into the next room—which was Lady Molly's bedroom—there to prepare her dress for the evening.

I had, of course, discreetly closed the door of communication between the two rooms, but after the first five minutes, Lady Molly deliberately reopened it, from which I gathered that she actually wished me to know what was going on.

It was then a little after four o'clock. I could hear Captain de Mazareen's voice, low-toned and infinitely tender. He adored my dear lady, but he was a very quiet man, and it was only by the passionate tensity of his attitude when he was near her that a shrewdly observant person could guess how deeply he cared. Now, through the open door, I could see his handsome head bowed very low, so that he could better look into her upturned eyes. His arms were round her, as if he were fighting the world for the possession of her, and would never let her go again. But there were tears in her eyes.

"Hubert," she said after a while, "I want you to marry me. Will you?"

"Will I?" he whispered, with an intensity of passionate longing which seemed to me then so unutterably pathetic that I could have sat down and had a good cry.

"But," rejoined Lady Molly, earnestly, "I mean as soon as possible—tomorrow, by special licence. You can wire to Mr. Hurford tonight, and he will see about it the first thing in the morning. We can travel up to town by the night train. Father and Mary will come with me. Father has promised, you know, and we can be married tomorrow ... I think that would be the quickest way."

There was a pause. I could well imagine how astonished and perturbed Captain Hubert must be feeling. It was such a strange request for a woman to make at such a time. I could see by the expression of his eyes that he was trying to read her thoughts. But she looked up quite serenely at him, and, frankly, I do not think that he had the

193

slightest inkling of the sublime motive which lay at the back of her strange insistence.

"You prefer to be married in London rather than here?" he asked quite simply.

"Yes," she replied; "I desire to be married in London tomorrow."

A few moments later my dear lady quietly shut the door again, and I heard and saw no more; but half an hour later she called me. She was alone in her *boudoir*, bravely trying to smile through a veil of tears. Captain Hubert's footsteps could still be heard going along the hall below.

Lady Molly listened until the final echo of that tread died away in the distance; then she buried her sweet face on my shoulder and sobbed her very heart out.

"Get ready as quickly as you can, Mary," she said to me when the paroxysm had somewhat subsided. "We go up to town by the 9.10."

"Is his lordship coming with us, my lady?" I asked.

"Oh, yes!" she said, whilst a bright smile lit up her face. "Father is simply grand . . . and yet he knows."

"Knows what, my lady?" I queried instinctively, for Lady Molly had paused, and I saw a look of acute pain once more darken her soft, grey eyes.

"My father knows," she said, slowly and almost tonelessly, "that half an hour ago the police found a weighted stick in the Elkhorn Woods not far from the spot where Mr. Steadman was murdered. The stick has the appearance of having been very vigorously cleaned and scraped recently, in spite of which fact tiny traces of blood are still visible on the leaden knob. The inspector showed my father that stick. I saw it too. It is the property of Captain Hubert de Mazareen, and by tomorrow, at the latest, it will be identified as such."

There was silence in the little *boudoir* now: a silence broken only by the sound of dull sobs which rose from my dear lady's overburdened heart. Lady Molly at this moment had looked into the future, and with that unerring intuition which has since been of such immense service to her she had already perceived the grim web which Fate was weaving round the destiny of the man she loved.

I said nothing. What could I say? I waited for her to speak again.

The first words she uttered after the terrible pronouncement which she had just made were:

"I'll wear my white cloth gown tomorrow, Mary. It is the most becoming frock I have, and I want to look my best on my wedding-day."

Captain Hubert de Mazareen was married to Lady Molly Robertson-Kirk by special licence on April 22nd, 1904, at the Church of St. Margaret, Westminster. No one was present to witness the ceremony except the Earl of Flintshire and myself. No one was apprised of the event at the time, nor, until recently, did anyone know that Lady Molly of Scotland Yard was the wife of De Mazareen the convict.

As you know, he was arrested at Appledore railway station the following morning and charged with the wilful murder of Alexander Steadman, solicitor, of Carlisle.

Everything was against him from the first. The draft of the will which Mr. Steadman was taking up to Sir Jeremiah for signature supplied the motive for the alleged crime, and he was the last person seen in company with the murdered man.

The chauffeur, George Taylor, who had driven to Carlisle to fetch Mr. Steadman, and brought him back that evening, explained how two of his tyres burst almost simultaneously after going over a bit of broken road close to the coppice. He had suggested to Mr. Steadman the idea of walking through the wood, and, as he had not two fresh tyres with him, he started pushing his car along, as the village was not more than half a mile away. He never saw Mr. Steadman again.

The stick with which the terrible deed had been committed was the most damning piece of evidence against the accused. It had been identified as his property by more than one witness, and was found within twenty yards of the victim, obviously cleaned and scraped, but still bearing minute traces of blood. Moreover, it had actually been seen in Captain Hubert's hand by one or two of the porters when he arrived at Appledore Station on that fatal night, was met there by Lady Molly, and subsequently walked away with her previous to meeting Mr. Steadman on the edge of the wood.

Captain de Mazareen, late of His Majesty's Household Brigade, was indicted for the wilful murder of Alexander Steadman, tried at the next assizes, found guilty, and condemned to be hanged. The jury, however, had strongly recommended him to mercy owing to his hitherto spotless reputation, and to the many services he had rendered his country during the last Boer War. A monster petition was sent up to the Home Office, and the sentence was commuted to twenty years' penal servitude.

That same year, Lady Molly applied for, and obtained, a small post on the detective staff of the police. From that small post she has worked her way upwards, analysing and studying, exercising her powers of intuition and of deduction, until at the present moment she is considered, by chiefs and men alike, the greatest authority among them on criminal investigation.

The Earl of Flintshire died some three years ago. Kirk Hall devolved on a distant cousin, but Lady Molly has kept a small home at Kirk ready for her husband when he comes back from Dartmoor.

The task of her life is to apply her gifts, and the obvious advantages at her disposal as a prominent member of the detective force, to prove the innocence of Captain Hubert de Mazareen, which she never doubted for a moment.

But it was sublime, and at the same time deeply pathetic, to see the frantic efforts at self-sacrifice which these two noble-hearted young people made for one another's sake.

Directly Captain Hubert realised that, so far as proving his innocence was concerned, he was a lost man, he used every effort to release Lady Molly from the bonds of matrimony. The marriage had been, and was still, kept a profound secret. He determined to plead guilty to murder at his trial, and then to make a declaration that he had entrapped Lady Molly into a marriage, knowing at the time that a warrant was out for his arrest, and hoping, by his connection with the Earl of Flintshire, to obtain a certain amount of leniency. When he was sufficiently convinced that such a course was out of the question, he begged Lady Molly to bring a nullity suit against him. He would not defend it. He only wished to set her free.

But the love she bore him triumphed over all. They did keep their marriage a secret, but she remained faithful to him in every thought and feeling within her, and loyal to him with her whole soul. Only I—once her maid, now her devoted friend—knew what she suffered, even whilst she threw herself heart and mind into her work.

We lived mostly in our little flat in Maida Vale, but spent some delightful days of freedom and peace in the little house at Kirk. Hither—in spite of the terrible memories the place evoked—Lady Molly loved to spend her time in wandering over the ground where that mysterious crime had been committed which had doomed an innocent man to the life of a convict.

"That mystery has got to be cleared up, Mary," she would repeat to me with unswerving loyalty, "and cleared up soon, before Captain de Mazareen loses all joy in life and all belief in me."

5

I suspect you will be interested to hear something about Appledore Castle and about Mr. Philip Baddock, who had been so near getting an immense fortune, yet had it snatched from him before his very eyes.

As Sir Jeremiah Baddock never signed the will of 1904, Captain de Mazareen's solicitors, on his behalf, sought to obtain probate of the former one, dated 1902.

In view of the terrible circumstances connected with the proposed last testamentary dispositions of the deceased, Mr. Philip Baddock was advised to fight that suit.

It seems that he really was the son of Sir Jeremiah by the latter's second marriage with Mlle. Desty, but the old gentleman, with heartless vengefulness, had practically repudiated the boy from the first, and absolutely refused to have anything to do with him beyond paying for his maintenance and education, and afterwards making him a goodly allowance on the express condition that Philip— soon to become a young man—never set his foot on English soil.

The condition was strictly complied with. Philip Baddock was born abroad, and lived abroad until 1903, when he suddenly appeared at Appledore Castle. Whether Sir Jeremiah, in a fit of tardy repentance, had sent for him, or whether he risked coming of his own accord, no one ever knew.

Captain de Mazareen was not, until that same year 1903, aware of the existence of Philip Baddock any more than was anybody else, and he spent his last days of freedom in stating positively that he would not accept the terms of the will of 1902, but would agree to Sir Jeremiah's fortune being divided up as it would have been if the old gentleman had died intestate. Thus Philip Baddock, the son, and Hubert de Mazareen, the grandson, received an equal share of Sir Jeremiah's immense wealth, estimated at close upon £2,000,000 sterling.

Appledore was put up for sale and bought in by Mr. Philip Baddock, who took up his residence there and gradually gained for himself a position in the county as one of the most wealthy magnates in the north of England. Thus, he became acquainted with the present Lord Flintshire, and, later on, met my dear lady. She neither sought nor avoided his acquaintance, and even went once to a dinner party at Appledore Castle.

That was lately, on the occasion of our last stay at Kirk. I had gone up to the castle in the brougham so that I might accompany Lady Molly home, and had been shown into the library, whither my dear lady came in order to put on her cloak.

While she was doing so Mr. Philip Baddock came in. He had a newspaper in his hand and seemed greatly agitated.

"Such extraordinary news, Lady Molly," he said, pointing to a headline in the paper. "You know, of course, that the other day a convict succeeded in effecting his escape from Dartmoor?"

"Yes, I knew that," said my dear lady, quietly.

"Well, I have reason to—to suppose," continued Mr. Baddock, "that that convict was none other than my unfortunate nephew, De Mazareen."

"Yes?" rejoined Lady Molly, whose perfect calm and serene expression of face contrasted strangely with the obvious agitation of Philip Baddock.

"Heaven knows that he tried to do me an evil turn," rejoined the latter after a while; "but of course I bear him no grudge, now that the law has given me that which he tried to wrench from me—a just share of my father's possessions. Since he has thrown himself on my mercy—"

"Thrown himself on your mercy!" ejaculated my dear lady, whose face had become almost grey with a sudden fear. "What do you mean?"

"De Mazareen is in my house at the present moment," replied Mr. Baddock, quietly.

"Here?"

"Yes. It seems that he tramped here. I am afraid that his object was to try and see you. He wants money, of course. I happened to be out in the woods this afternoon, and saw him.

"No, no!" added Philip Baddock quickly, in response to an instinctive gasp of pain from Lady Molly; "you need not have the slightest fear. My nephew is as safe with me as he would be in your own house. I brought him here, for he was exhausted with fatigue and want of food. None of my servants know of his presence in the house except Felkin, whom I can trust. By tomorrow he will have rested. . . . We'll make a start in the very early morning in my car; we'll get to Liverpool before midday. De Mazareen shall wear Felkin's clothes—no one will know him. One of the Baddock steamers is leaving for Buenos Ayres the same afternoon, and I can arrange with the captain. You need not have the slightest fear," he repeated, with simple yet earnest emphasis; "I pledge you my word that De Mazareen will be safe."

"I should like to thank you," she murmured. "Please don't," he rejoined with a sad smile. "It is a great happiness to me to be able to do this. . . . I know that you—you cared for him at one time. . . . I wish you had known and trusted me in those days—but I am glad of this opportunity which enables me to tell you that, even had my father signed his last will and testament, I should have shared his fortune with De Mazareen. The man whom you honoured with your love need never have resorted to crime in order to gain a fortune."

Philip Baddock paused. His eyes were fixed on Lady Molly with unmistakable love and an appeal for sympathy. I had no idea that he cared for her—nor had she, I am quite sure. Her heart belonged solely to the poor, fugitive convict, but she could not fail, I thought, to be touched by the other man's obvious sincerity and earnestness.

There was silence in the room for a few moments. Only the old clock in its Sheraton case ticked on in solemn imperturbability.

Lady Molly turned her luminous eyes on the man who had just made so simple, so touching a profession of love. Was she about to tell him that she was no longer free, that she bore the name of the man whom the law had ostracised and pronounced a criminal—who had even now, by this daring attempt at escape, added a few years to his already long term of punishment and another load to his burden of shame?

"Do you think," she asked quietly, "that I might speak to Captain de Mazareen for a few moments without endangering his safety?"

Mr. Baddock did not reply immediately. He seemed to be pondering over the request. Then he said:

"I will see that everything is safe. I don't think there need be any danger."

He went out of the room, and my dear lady and I were left alone for a minute or two. She was so calm and serene that I marvelled at her self-control, and wondered what was going on in her mind.

"Mary," she said to me, speaking very quickly, for already we could hear two men's footsteps approaching the library door, "you must station yourself just outside the front door; you understand? If you see or hear anything suspicious come and warn me at once."

I made ready to obey, and the next moment the door opened and Mr. Philip Baddock entered, accompanied by Captain Hubert.

I smothered the involuntary sob which rose to my throat at sight of the man who had once been the most gallant, the handsomest soldier I had ever seen. I had only just time to notice that Mr. Baddock prepared to leave the room again immediately. At the door he turned back and said to Lady Molly:

"Felkin has gone down to the lodge. If he hears or sees anything that seems suspicious, he will ring up on the telephone;" and he pointed to the apparatus which stood on the library table in the centre of the room.

After that he closed the door, and I was left to imagine the moments of joy, mingled with acute anguish, which my dear lady would be living through.

I walked up and down restlessly on the terrace which fronts the castle. The house itself appeared silent and dark: I presume all the servants had gone to bed. Far away on my right I caught the glimmer of a light. It came from the lodge where Felkin was watching. From the church in Appledore village came the sound of the clock striking the hour of midnight.

How long I had been on the watch I cannot say, when suddenly I was aware of a man's figure running rapidly along the drive towards the house. The next moment the figure had skirted the castle, apparently making for one of the back doors.

I did not hesitate a moment. Having left the big front door on the latch, I ran straight in and made for the library door.

Already Mr. Philip Baddock had forestalled me. His hand was on the latch. Without more ado he pushed open the door and I followed him in.

Lady Molly was sitting on the sofa, with Captain Hubert beside her. They both rose at our entrance.

"The police!" said Mr. Baddock, speaking very rapidly. "Felkin has just run up from the lodge. He is getting the car ready. Pray God we may yet be able to get away."

Even as he spoke the front door bell sounded with a loud clang, which to me had the sound of a death knell.

"It is too late, you see," said my dear lady, quietly.

"No, not too late," ejaculated Philip Baddock, in a rapid whisper. "Quick! De Mazareen, follow me through the hall. Felkin is at the stables getting the car ready. It will be some time before the servants are roused."

"Mary, I am sure, has failed to fasten the front door," interrupted Lady Molly, with the same strange calm. "I think the police are already in the hall."

There was no mistaking the muffled sound of feet treading the thick Turkey carpet in the hall. The library had but one exit. Captain Hubert was literally in a trap. But Mr. Baddock had not lost his presence of mind.

"The police would never dream of searching my house," he said; "they will take my word that De Mazareen is not here. Here!" he added, pointing to a tall Jacobean wardrobe which stood in an angle of the room. "In there, man, and leave the rest to me!"

"I am afraid that such a proceeding would bring useless trouble upon you, Mr. Baddock," once more interposed Lady Molly; "the police, if they do not at once find Captain de Mazareen, will surely search the house."

"Impossible! They would not dare!"

"Indeed, they would. The police know that Captain de Mazareen is here."

"I swear they do not," rejoined Mr. Baddock.

"Felkin is no traitor, and no one else—"

"It was I who gave information to the police," said Lady Molly, speaking loudly and clearly. "I called up the superintendent on the telephone just now, and told him that his men would find the escaped convict hiding at Appledore Castle."

"You!" ejaculated Mr. Baddock, in a tone of surprise and horror, not unmixed with a certain note of triumph. "You?"

"Yes!" she replied calmly. "I am of the police, you know. I had to do my duty. Open the door, Mary," she added, turning to me.

Captain Hubert had not spoken a word so far. Now, when the men, led by Detective-Inspector Etty, entered the room, he walked with a firm step towards them, held out his hands for the irons, and with a final look at Lady Molly, in which love, trust, and hope were clearly expressed, he passed out of the room and was soon lost to sight.

My dear lady waited until the heavy footfalls had died away; then she turned with a pleasant smile to Mr. Philip Baddock:

"I thank you for your kind thoughts of me," she said, "and for your noble efforts on behalf of your nephew. My position was a difficult one. I hope you will forgive the pain I have been obliged to bring upon you."

"I will do more than forgive, Lady Molly," he said earnestly, "I will venture to hope."

He took her hand and kissed it. Then she beckoned to me and I followed her into the hall.

Our brougham—a hired one—had been waiting in the stable-yard. We drove home in silence; but half an hour later, when my dear lady kissed me goodnight she whispered in my ear:

"And now, Mary, we'll prove him innocent."

The End

1

One or two people knew that at one time Lady Molly Robertson-Kirk had been engaged to Captain Hubert de Mazareen, who was now convict No. 97, undergoing a life sentence for the murder of Mr. Steadman, a solicitor of Carlisle, in the Elkhorn woods in April, 1904. Few, on the other hand, knew of the secret marriage solemnised on that never-to-be-forgotten afternoon, when all of us present in the church, with the exception of the bridegroom himself, were fully aware that proofs of guilt—deadly and irrefutable—were even then being heaped up against the man to whom Lady Molly was plighting her troth, for better or for worse, with her mental eyes wide open, her unerring intuition keen to the fact that nothing but a miracle could save the man she loved from an ignoble condemnation, perhaps from the gallows.

The husband of my dear lady, the man whom she loved with all the strength of her romantic and passionate nature, was duly tried and convicted of murder. Condemned to be hanged, he was reprieved, and his sentence commuted to penal servitude for life.

The question of Sir Jeremiah's estate became a complicated one, for his last will and testament was never signed, and the former one, dated 1902, bequeathed everything he possessed unconditionally to his beloved grandson Hubert.

After much legal argument, which it is useless to recapitulate here, it was agreed between the parties, and ratified in court, that the deceased gentleman's vast wealth should be disposed of as if he had died intestate. One half of it, therefore, went to Captain Hubert de Mazareen, grandson, and the other half to Philip Baddock, the son. The latter bought Appledore Castle and resided there, whilst his nephew became No. 97 in Dartmoor Prison.

Captain Hubert had served two years of his sentence when he made that daring and successful escape which caused so much sensation at the time. He managed to reach Appledore, where he was discovered by Mr. Philip Baddock, who gave him food and shelter and got everything ready for the safe conveyance of his unfortunate nephew to Liverpool and thence to a port of safety in South America.

You remember how he was thwarted in this laudable attempt by Lady Molly herself, who communicated with the police and gave up convict No. 97 into the hands of the authorities once more.

Of course, public outcry was loud against my dear lady's action. Sense of duty was all very well, so people argued, but no one could forget that at one time Captain Hubert de Mazareen and Lady Molly Robertson-Kirk had actually been engaged to be married, and it seemed positively monstrous for a woman to be so pitiless towards the man whom she must at one time have loved.

You see how little people understood my dear lady's motives. Some went so far as to say that she had only contemplated marriage with Captain Hubert de Mazareen because he was then, presumably, the heir to Sir Jeremiah's fortune; now—continued the gossips—she was equally ready to marry Mr. Philip Baddock, who at any rate was the happy possessor of one half of the deceased gentleman's wealth.

Certainly, Lady Molly's conduct at this time helped to foster this idea. Finding that even the chief was inclined to give her the cold shoulder, she shut up our flat in Maida Vale and took up her residence at the little house which she owned in Kirk, and from the windows of which she had a splendid view of stately Appledore Castle nestling among the trees on the hillside.

I was with her, of course, and Mr. Philip Baddock was a frequent visitor at the house. There could be no doubt that he admired her greatly, and that she accepted his attentions with a fair amount of graciousness. The county fought shy of her. Her former engagement to Captain de Mazareen was well known, and her treachery to him—so it was called—was severely censured.

Living almost in isolation in the village, her whole soul seemed wrapped in thoughts of how to unravel the mystery of the death of Mr. Steadman. Captain de Mazareen had sworn in his defence that the solicitor, after starting to walk through the Elkhorn woods with him, had feared that the tramp over rough ground would be too much for him, and had almost immediately turned back in order to regain the road. But the chauffeur, George Taylor, who was busy with the broken-down car some two hundred yards up the road, never saw Mr. Steadman again, whilst Captain de Mazareen arrived at the gates of Appledore Castle alone. Here he was met by Mr. Philip Baddock, who informed him that Sir Jeremiah had breathed his last an hour before.

No one at the castle recollected seeing a stick in Captain Hubert's hand when he arrived, whilst there were several witnesses who swore that he carried one at Appledore Station when he started to walk with her ladyship. The stick was found close to the body of the solicitor; and the solicitor, when he met with his terrible death, had in his pocket the draft of a will which meant disinheritance to Captain de Mazareen.

Here was the awful problem which Lady Molly had to face and to solve if she persisted in believing that the man whom she loved, and whom she had married at the moment when she knew that proofs of guilt were dead against him, was indeed innocent.

2

We had spent all the morning shopping in Carlisle, and in the afternoon, we called on Mr. Fuelling, of the firm of Fuelling, Steadman and Co., solicitors.

Lady Molly had some business to arrange in connection with the purchase of an additional bit of land to round off her little garden at Kirk.

Mr. Fuelling was courteous, but distinctly stiff, in his manner towards the lady who was "connected with the police," more especially when—her business being transacted—she seemed inclined to tarry for a little while in the busy solicitor's office, and to lead conversation round to the subject of the murder of Mr. Steadman.

"Five years have gone by since then," said Mr. Fuelling, curtly, in response to a remark from Lady Molly, "I prefer not to revive unpleasant memories."

"You, of course, believed Captain de Mazareen guilty?" retorted my dear lady, imperturbably.

"There were circumstances" rejoined the solicitor, "and—and, of course, I hardly knew the unfortunate young man. Messrs. Truscott and Truscott used to be the family solicitors."

"Yes. It seemed curious that when Sir Jeremiah wished to make his will, he should have sent for you, rather than for his accustomed lawyer," mused Lady Molly.

"Sir Jeremiah did not send for me," replied Mr. Fuelling, with some acerbity, "he sent for my junior, Mr. Steadman."

"Perhaps Mr. Steadman was a personal friend of his."

"Not at all. Not at all. Mr. Steadman was a new arrival in Carlisle, and had never seen Sir Jeremiah before the day when he was sent for and, in a brief interview, drafted the will which, alas! proved to be the primary cause of my unfortunate young partner's death."

"You cannot draft a will in a brief interview, Mr. Fuelling," remarked Lady Molly, lightly.

"Mr. Steadman did so," retorted Mr. Fuelling, curtly. "Though Sir Jeremiah's mind was as clear as crystal, he was very feeble, and the interview had to take place in a darkened room. That was the only time my young partner saw Sir Jeremiah. Twenty-four hours later they were both dead."

"Oh!" commented my dear lady with sudden indifference. "Well! I won't detain you, Mr. Fuelling. Good afternoon."

A few moments later, having parted from the worthy old solicitor, we were out in the street once more.

"The darkened room is my first ray of light," quoth Lady Molly to me, with a smile at her own paradoxical remark.

When we reached home later that afternoon, we were met at the garden gate by Mr. Felkin, Mr. Philip Baddock's friend and agent, who lived with him at Appledore Castle.

Mr. Felkin was a curious personality; very taciturn in manner but a man of considerable education. He was the son of a country parson, and at the time of his father's death he had been studying for the medical profession. Finding himself unable to pursue his studies for lack of means, and being left entirely destitute, he had been forced to earn his living by taking up the less exalted calling of male nurse. It seems that he had met Mr. Philip Baddock on the Continent some years ago, and the two young men had somehow drifted into close acquaintanceship. When the late Sir Jeremiah required a personal nurse-attendant Mr. Philip Baddock sent for his friend and installed him at Appledore Castle.

Here Mr. Felkin remained, even after the old gentleman's death. He was nominally called Mr. Baddock's agent, but really did very little work. He was very fond of shooting and of riding, and spent his life in the pursuit of these sports, and he always had plenty of money to spend.

But everyone voted him a disagreeable bear, and the only one who ever succeeded in making him smile was Lady Molly, who always showed an unaccountable liking for the uncouth creature. Even now, when he extended a somewhat grimy hand and murmured a clumsy apology at his intrusion, she greeted him with warm effusiveness and insisted on his coming into the house.

We all turned to walk along the little drive, when Mr. Baddock's car came whizzing round the corner of the road from the village. He pulled up at our gate, and the next moment had joined us in the drive.

There was a very black look in his eyes, as they wandered restlessly from my dear lady's face to that of his friend. Lady Molly's little hand was even then resting on Mr. Felkin's coat-sleeve; she had been in the act of leading him herself towards the house, and did not withdraw her hand when Mr. Baddock appeared upon the scene.

"Burton has just called about those estimates, Felkin," said the latter, somewhat roughly; "he is waiting at the castle. You had better take the car—I can walk home later on."

"Oh! how disappointing!" exclaimed Lady Molly, with what looked uncommonly like a pout. "I was going to have such a cosy chat with Mr. Felkin—all about horses and dogs. Couldn't you see that tiresome Burton, Mr. Baddock?" she added ingenuously.

I don't think that Mr. Baddock actually swore, but I am sure he was very near doing so.

"Burton can wait," said Mr. Felkin, curtly.

"No, he cannot," retorted Philip Baddock, whose face was a frowning mirror of uncontrolled jealousy; "take the car, Felkin, and go at once."

For a moment it seemed as if Felkin would refuse to obey. The two men stood looking at each other, measuring one another's power of will and strength of passion. Hate and jealousy were clearly written in each pair of glowering eyes. Philip Baddock looked defiant, and Felkin taciturn and sulky.

Close to them stood my dear lady. Her beautiful eyes literally glowed with triumph. That these two men loved her, each in his own curious, uncontrolled way, I, her friend and confidant, knew very well. I had seen, and often puzzled over, the feminine attacks which she had made on the susceptibilities of that morose lout Felkin. It had taken her nearly two years to bring him to her feet. During that time, she had alternately rendered him happy with her smiles and half mad with her coquetries, whilst Philip Baddock's love for her was perpetually fanned by his ever-growing jealousy.

I remember that I often thought her game a cruel one. She was one of those women whom few men could resist; if she really desired to conquer, she invariably succeeded, and her victory over Felkin seemed to me as purposeless as it was unkind. After all, she was the lawful wife of Captain de Mazareen, and to rouse hatred between two friends for the sake of her love, when that love was not hers to give, seemed unworthy of her. At this moment, when I could read deadly hatred in the faces of these two men, her cooing laugh grated unpleasantly on my ear.

" Philip Baddock looked defiant, and Felkin taciturn and
sulky "

"Never mind, Mr. Felkin," she said, turning her luminous eyes on him. "Since you have so hard a taskmaster, you must do your duty now. But," she added, throwing a strange, defiant look at Mr. Baddock, "I shall be at home this evening; come and have our cosy chat after dinner."

She gave him her hand, and he took it with a certain clumsy gallantry and raised it to his lips. I thought that Philip Baddock would strike his friend with his open hand. The veins on his temples were swollen like dark cords, and I don't think that I ever saw such an evil look in anyone's eyes before.

Strangely enough, the moment Mr. Felkin's back was turned my dear lady seemed to set herself the task of soothing the violent passions which she had wilfully aroused in the other man. She invited him to come into the house, and, some ten minutes later, I heard her singing to him. When, later on, I went into the *boudoir* to join them at tea, she was sitting on the music stool whilst he half bent over her, half knelt at her feet; her hands were clasped in her lap, and his fingers were closed over hers.

He did not attempt to leave her side when he saw me entering the room. In fact, he wore a triumphant air of possession, and paid her those little attentions which only an accepted lover would dare to offer.

He left soon after tea, and she accompanied him to the door. She gave him her hand to kiss, and I, who stood at some little distance in the shadow, thought that he would take her in his arms, so yielding and gracious did she seem. But some look or gesture on her part must have checked him, for he turned and walked quickly down the drive.

Lady Molly stood in the doorway gazing out towards the sunset. I, in my humble mind, wondered once again what was the purport of this cruel game.

3

Half an hour later she called to me, asked for her hat, told me to put on mine and to come out for a stroll.

As so often happened, she led the way towards the Elkhorn woods, which in spite, or perhaps because, of the painful memories they evoked, was a very favourite walk of hers.

As a rule, the wood, especially that portion of it where the unfortunate solicitor had been murdered, was deserted after sunset. The villagers declared that Mr. Steadman's ghost haunted the clearing, and that the cry of the murdered man, as he was being foully struck from behind, could be distinctly heard echoing through the trees.

Needless to say, these superstitious fancies never disturbed Lady Molly. She liked to wander over the ground where was committed that mysterious crime which had sent to ignominy worse than death the man she loved so passionately. It seemed as if she meant to wrench its secret from the silent ground, from the leafy undergrowth, from the furtive inhabitants of the glades.

The sun had gone down behind the hills; the wood was dark and still. We strolled up as far as the first clearing, where a plain, granite stone, put up by Mr. Philip Baddock, marked the spot where Mr. Steadman had been murdered.

We sat down on it to rest. My dear lady's mood was a silent one; I did not dare to disturb it, and, for a while, only the gentle "hush—sh—sh" of the leaves, stirred by the evening breeze, broke the peaceful stillness of the glade.

Then we heard a murmur of voices, deep-toned and low. We could not hear the words spoken, though we both strained our ears, and presently Lady Molly arose and cautiously made her way among the trees in the direction whence the voices came, I following as closely as I could.

We had not gone far when we recognised the voices, and heard the words that were said. I paused, distinctly frightened, whilst my dear lady whispered a warning "Hush!"

Never in all my life had I heard so much hatred, such vengeful malignity expressed in the intonation of the human voice as I did in the half-dozen words which now struck my ear.

"You will give her up, or——"

It was Mr. Felkin who spoke. I recognised his raucous delivery, but I could not distinguish either of the two men in the gloom.

"Or what?" queried the other, in a voice which trembled with either rage or fear—perhaps with both.

"You will give her up," repeated Felkin, sullenly. "I tell you that it is an impossibility—do you understand?—an impossibility for me to stand by and see her wedded to you, or to any other man for the matter of that. But that is neither here nor there," he added after a slight pause. "It is with you I have to deal now. You shan't have her—you shan't—I won't allow it, even if I have to——"

He paused again. I cannot describe the extraordinary effect this rough voice coming out of the darkness had upon my nerves. I had edged up to Lady Molly, and had succeeded in getting hold of her hand. It was like ice, and she herself was as rigid as that piece of granite on which we had been sitting.

"You seem bubbling over with covert threats," interposed Philip Baddock, with what was obviously a sneer; "what are the extreme measures to which you will resort if I do not give up the lady whom I love with my whole heart, and who has honoured me today by accepting my hand in marriage?"

"That is a lie!" ejaculated Felkin.

"What is a lie?" queried the other, quietly.

"She has not accepted you—and you know it. You are trying to keep me away from her—arrogating rights which you do not possess. Give her up, man, give her up. It will be best for you. She will listen to me—I can win her all right—but you must stand aside for me this time. Take the word of a desperate man for it, Baddock. It will be best for you to give her up."

Silence reigned in the wood for a few moments, and then we heard Philip Baddock's voice again, but he seemed to speak more calmly, almost indifferently, as I thought.

"Are you going now?" he asked. "Won't you come in to dinner?"

"No," replied Felkin, "I don't want any dinner, and I have an appointment for afterwards."

"Don't let us part ill friends, Felkin," continued Philip Baddock in conciliatory tones. "Do you know that, personally, my feeling is that no woman on earth is worth a serious quarrel between two old friends, such as we have been."

"I'm glad you think so," rejoined the other drily. "S'long."

The cracking of twigs on the moss-covered ground indicated that the two men had parted and were going their several ways.

With infinite caution, and holding my hand tightly in hers, my dear lady made her way along the narrow path which led us out of the wood.

Once in the road we walked rapidly, and soon reached our garden gate. Lady Molly had not spoken a word during all that time, and no one knew better than I did how to respect her silence.

During dinner she tried to talk of indifferent subjects, and never once alluded to the two men whom she had thus wilfully pitted one against the other. That her calm was only on the surface, however, I realised from the fact that every sound on the gravel path outside caused her to start. She was, of course, expecting the visit of Mr. Felkin.

At eight o'clock he came. It was obvious that he had spent the past hour in wandering about in the woods. He looked untidy and unkempt. My dear lady greeted him very coldly, and when he tried to kiss her hand, she withdrew it abruptly.

Our drawing-room was a double one, divided by portière curtains. Lady Molly led the way into the front room, followed by Mr. Felkin. Then she drew the curtains together, leaving me standing behind them. I concluded that she wished me to stay there and to listen, conscious of the fact that Felkin, in the agitated mood in which he was, would be quite oblivious of my presence.

I almost pitied the poor man, for to me—the listener—it was at once apparent that my dear lady had only bidden him come tonight in order to torture him. For about a year she had been playing with him as a cat does with a mouse; encouraging him at times with sweet words and smiles, repelling him at others with coldness not unmixed with coquetry. But tonight her coldness was unalloyed; her voice was trenchant, her attitude almost one of contempt.

I missed the beginning of their conversation, for the curtains were thick and I did not like to go too near, but soon Mr. Felkin's voice was raised. It was harsh and uncompromising.

"I suppose that I am only good enough for a summer's flirtation?" he said sullenly, "but not to marry, eh? The owner of Appledore Castle, the millionaire, Mr. Baddock, is more in your line—"

"It certainly would be a more suitable match for me," rejoined Lady Molly, coolly.

"He told me you had formally accepted him," said the man, with enforced calm; "is that true?"

"Partly," she replied.

"But you won't marry him!"

The exclamation seemed to come straight from a heart brimful of passion, of love, of hate, and of revenge. The voice had the same intonation in it which had rung an hour ago in the dark Elkhorn woods.

"I may do," came in quiet accents from my dear lady.

"You won't marry him," repeated Felkin, roughly.

"Who shall prevent me?" retorted Lady Molly, with a low, sarcastic laugh.

"I will."

"You?" she said contemptuously.

"I told him an hour ago that he must give you up. I tell you now that you shall not be Philip Baddock's wife."

"Oh!" she interposed. And I could almost see the disdainful shrug of her shoulders, the flash of contempt in her expressive eyes.

No doubt it maddened him to see her so cool, so indifferent, when he had thought that he could win her. I do believe that the poor wretch loved her. She was always beautiful, but never more so than tonight when she had obviously determined finally to dismiss him.

"If you marry Philip Baddock," he now said, in a voice which quivered with uncontrolled passion, "then within six months of your wedding-day you will be a widow, for your husband will have ended his life on the gallows."

"You are mad!" she retorted calmly.

"That is as it may be," he replied. "I warned him tonight, and he seems inclined to heed my warning; but he won't stand aside if you beckon to him. Therefore, if you love him, take my warning. I may not be able to get you, but I swear to you that Philip Baddock shan't either. I'll see him hanged first," he added, with gruesome significance.

"And you think that you can force me to do your bidding by such paltry threats?" she retorted.

"Paltry threats? Ask Philip Baddock if my threats are paltry. He knows full well that in my room at Appledore Castle, safe from thievish fingers, lie the proofs that he killed Alexander Steadman in the Elkhorn woods. Oh! I wouldn't help him in his nefarious deeds until he placed himself in my hands. He had to take my terms or leave the thing alone altogether, for he could not work without me. My wants are few, and he has treated and paid me well. Now we are rivals, and I'll destroy him before I'll let him gloat over me.

"Do you know how we worked it? Sir Jeremiah would not disinherit his grandson—he steadily refused to make a will in Philip Baddock's favour. But when he was practically dying, we sent for Alexander Steadman—a newcomer, who had never seen Sir Jeremiah before—and I impersonated the old gentleman for the occasion. Yes, I!" he repeated with a coarse laugh, "I was Sir Jeremiah for the space of half an hour, and I think that I played the part splendidly. I dictated the terms of a new will. Young Steadman never suspected the fraud for a single instant. We had darkened the room for the comedy, you see, and Mr. Steadman was destined by Baddock and myself never to set eyes on the real Sir Jeremiah.

"After the interview Baddock sent for Captain de Mazareen; this was all part of his plan and mine. We engineered it all, and we knew that Sir Jeremiah could only last a few hours. We sent for Steadman again, and I myself scattered a few dozen sharp nails among the loose stones in the road where the motorcar was intended to break down,

" ' Ask Philip Baddock if my threats are paltry ' "

thus forcing the solicitor to walk through the woods. Captain de Mazareen's appearance on the scene at that particular moment was an unrehearsed effect which nearly upset all our plans, for had Mr. Steadman stuck to him that night, instead of turning back, he would probably be alive now, and Baddock and I would be doing time somewhere for attempted fraud. We should have been done, at any rate.

"Well! you know what happened. Mr. Steadman was killed. Baddock killed him, and then ran straight back to the house, just in time to greet Captain de Mazareen, who evidently had loitered on his way. But it was I who thought of the stick, as an additional precaution to avert suspicion from ourselves. Captain de Mazareen was carrying one, and left it in the hall at the castle. I cut my own hand and stained the stick with it, then polished and cleaned it up, and later, during the night, deposited it in the near neighbourhood of the murdered body. Ingenious, wasn't it? I am a clever beggar, you see.

"Because I was cleverer than Baddock he could not do without me, and because he could not do without me, I made him write and sign a request to me to help him to manufacture a bogus will and then to murder the solicitor who had drawn it up. And I have hidden that precious document in the wing of Appledore Castle which I inhabit; the exact spot is known only to myself. Baddock has often tried to find out, but all he knows is that these things are in that particular wing of the house.

"I have the document, and the draft of the will taken out of Mr. Steadman's pocket, and the short bludgeon with which he was killed— it is still stained with blood— and the rags with which I cleaned the stick. I swear that I will never make use of these things against Philip Baddock unless he drives me to it, and if you make use of what I have just told you I'll swear that I have lied. No one can find the proofs which I hold. But on the day that you marry Baddock I'll place them in the hands of the police."

There was silence in the room. I could almost hear the beating of my own heart, so horrified, so appalled was I at the horrible tale which the man had just told to my dear lady.

The villainy of the whole scheme was so terrible, and at the same time so cunning, that it seemed inconceivable that human brain could have engendered it. Vaguely in my dull mind I wondered if Lady Molly would have to commit bigamy before she could wrench from this evil-doer's hands the proofs that would set her own husband free from his martyrdom.

What she said I did not hear, what he meant to retort I never knew, for at that moment my attention was attracted by the sound of running footsteps on the gravel, followed by a loud knock at our front door. Instinctively I ran to open it. Our old gardener was standing there hatless and breathless.

"Appledore Castle, miss," he stammered, "it's on fire. I thought you would like to know."

Before I had time to reply I heard a loud oath uttered close behind me, and the next moment Felkin dashed out of the drawing-room into the hall.

"Is there a bicycle here that I can take?" he shouted to the gardener.

"Yes, sir," replied the old man; "my son has one. Just in that shed, sir, on your left."

In fewer seconds than it takes to relate, Felkin had rushed to the shed, dragged out the bicycle, mounted it, and I think that within two minutes of hearing the awful news, he was bowling along the road, and was soon out of sight.

4

One wing of the stately mansion was ablaze when, a quarter of an hour later, my dear lady and I arrived upon the scene. We had come on our bicycles not long after Mr. Felkin.

At the very moment that the weird spectacle burst fully upon our gaze, a loud cry of horror had just risen from the hundred or so people who stood watching the terrible conflagration, whilst the local fire brigade, assisted by Mr. Baddock's men, were working with the hydrants. That cry found echo in our own throats as we saw a man clambering, with the rapidity of a monkey, up a long ladder which had been propped up against a second floor window of the flaming portion of the building. The red glow illumined the large, shaggy head of Felkin, throwing for a moment into bold relief his hooked nose and straggly beard. For the space of three seconds perhaps he stood thus, outlined against what looked like a glowing furnace behind him, and the next instant he had disappeared beyond the window embrasure.

"This is madness!" came in loud accents from out the crowd in the foreground, and before one fully realised whence that voice had come, Mr. Philip Baddock was in his turn seen clambering up that awful ladder. A dozen pairs of hands reached him just in time to drag him back from the perilous ascent. He fought to free himself, but the firemen were determined and soon succeeded in bringing him back to level ground, whilst two of them, helmeted and well-equipped, took his place upon the ladder.

The foremost had hardly reached the level of the first story when Felkin's figure once more appeared in the window embrasure above. He was staggering like a man drunk or fainting, his shaggy hair and beard were blown about his head by the terrible draught caused by the flames, and he waved his arms over his head, giving the impression to those below, who gazed horrified, that he was either possessed or dying. In one hand he held what looked like a great, long bundle.

We could see him now put one leg forward, obviously gathering strength to climb the somewhat high window ledge. With a shout of encouragement, the two firemen scrambled up with squirrel-like agility, and the cry of "They're coming! they're coming! Hold on, Felkin!" rose from a hundred excited throats.

The unfortunate man made another effort. We could see his face clearly now in the almost blinding glow which surrounded him. It was distorted with fear and also with agony.

He gave one raucous cry, which I do believe will echo in my ears as long as I live, and with a superhuman effort he hurled the bundle which he held out of the window.

At that same moment there was a terrific hissing, followed by a loud crash. The floor beneath the feet of the unfortunate man must have given way, for he disappeared suddenly in a sea of flames.

The bundle which he had hurled down had struck the foremost fireman on the head. He lost his hold, and as he fell, he dragged his unfortunate comrade down with him. The others ran to the rescue of their comrades. I don't think they were seriously hurt, but what happened directly after among the crowd, the firemen, or the burning building, I cannot tell you. I only know that at the moment when Felkin's figure was, for the second time, seen in the frame of the glowing window, Lady Molly seized my hand and dragged me forward through the crowd.

Her husband's life was hanging in the balance, just as much as that of the miserable wretch who was courting a horrible death for the sake of those proofs which—as it was proved afterwards—Philip Baddock tried to destroy by such drastic means.

The excitement round the ladder, the fall of the two firemen, the crashing in of the floor and the gruesome disappearance of Felkin caused so much excitement in the crowd that the bundle which the unfortunate man had thrown remained unheeded for the moment.

But Philip Baddock reached the spot where it fell thirty seconds after Lady Molly did. She had already picked it up, when he said harshly:

"Give me that. It is mine. Felkin risked his life to save it for me."

Inspector Etty, however, stood close by, and before Philip Baddock realised what Lady Molly meant to do, she had turned quickly and placed the bundle in the inspector's hands.

"You know me, Etty, don't you?" she said rapidly.

"Oh, yes, my lady!" he replied.

"Then take the utmost care of this bundle. It contains proofs of one of the most dastardly crimes ever committed in this country."

No other words could have aroused the enthusiasm and caution of Etty in the same manner.

After that Philip Baddock might protest, might rage, storm, or try to bribe, but the proofs of his guilt and Captain de Mazareen's innocence were safe in the hands of the police, and bound to come to light at last.

But, as a matter of fact, Baddock neither stormed nor pleaded. When Lady Molly turned to him once more, he had disappeared.

★★★★★★★★★★★★

You know the rest, of course. It occurred too recently to be recounted. Philip Baddock was found the next morning with a bullet through his head, lying on the granite stone which, with cruel hypocrisy, he himself had erected in memory of Mr. Steadman whom he had so foully murdered.

The unfortunate Felkin had not lied when he said that the proofs which he held of Baddock's guilt were conclusive and deadly.

Captain de Mazareen obtained His Majesty's gracious pardon after five years of martyrdom which he had borne with heroic fortitude.

I was not present when Lady Molly was once more united to the man who so ardently worshipped and trusted her, and to whose love, innocence, and cause she had remained so sublimely loyal throughout the past few years.

She has given up her connection with the police. The reason for it has gone with the return of her happiness, over which I—her ever faithful Mary Granard—will, with your permission, draw a veil.

The Case of Miss Elliott

"The old man in the corner."

Contents

The Case of Miss Elliott

The man in the corner was watching me over the top of his great bone-rimmed spectacles.

"Well?" he asked, after a little while.

"Well?" I repeated with some acerbity. I had been wondering for the last ten minutes how many more knots he would manage to make in that same bit of string, before he actually started undoing them again.

"Do I fidget you?" he asked apologetically, whilst his long bony fingers buried themselves, string, knots, and all, into the capacious pockets of his magnificent tweed ulster.

"Yes, that is another awful tragedy," he said quietly, after a while. "Lady doctors are having a pretty bad time of it just now."

This was only his usual habit of speaking in response to my thoughts. There was no doubt that at the present moment my mind was filled with that extraordinary mystery which was setting all Scotland Yard by the ears, and had completely thrown into the shade the sad story of Miss Hickman's tragic fate.

The Daily Telegraph had printed two columns headed "Murder or Suicide?" on the subject of the mysterious death of Miss Elliott, matron of the Convalescent Home, in Suffolk Avenue—and I must confess that a more profound and bewildering mystery had never been set before our able detective department.

"It has puzzled them this time, and no mistake," said the man in the corner, with one of his most gruesome chuckles, "but I dare say the public is quite satisfied that there is no solution to be found, since the police have found none."

"Can you find one?" I retorted with withering sarcasm.

"Oh, my solution would only be sneered at," he replied. "It is far too simple—and yet how logical! There was Miss Elliott, a good-looking, youngish, ladylike woman, fully qualified in the medical profession and in charge of the Convalescent Home in Suffolk Avenue, which is a private institution largely patronised by the benevolent.

"For some time, already, there had appeared vague comments and rumours in various papers, that the extensive charitable contributions did not all go towards the upkeep of the Home. But, as is usual in institutions of that sort, the public was not allowed to know anything very definite, and contributions continued to flow in, whilst the Honorary Treasurer of the great Convalescent Home kept up his beautiful house in Hamilton Terrace, in a style which would not have shamed a peer of the realm.

"That is how matters stood, when on 2nd November last the morning papers contained the brief announcement that at a quarter past midnight two workmen walking along Blomfield Road, Maida Vale, suddenly came across the body of a young lady, lying on her face, close to the wooden steps of the narrow footbridge which at this point crosses the canal.

"This part of Maida Vale is, as you know, very lonely at all times, but at night it is usually quite deserted. Blomfield Road, with its row of small houses and bits of front gardens, faces the canal, and beyond the footbridge is continued in a series of small riverside wharves, which is practically unknown ground to the average Londoner. The footbridge itself, with steps at right angles and high wooden parapet, would offer excellent shelter at all hours of the night for any nefarious deed.

"It was within its shadows that the men had found the body, and to their credit, be it said, they behaved like good and dutiful citizens—one of them went off in search of the police, whilst the other remained beside the corpse.

"From papers and books found upon her person, it was soon ascertained that the deceased was Miss Elliott, the young matron of the Suffolk Avenue Convalescent Home; and as she was very popular in her profession and had a great many friends, the terrible tragedy caused a sensation, all the more acute as very quickly the rumour gained ground that the unfortunate young woman had taken her own life in a most gruesome and mysterious manner.

"Preliminary medical and police investigation had revealed the fact that Miss Elliott had died through a deep and scientifically administered gash in the throat, whilst the surgical knife with which the deadly wound was inflicted still lay tightly grasped in her clenched hand."

2

The man in the corner, ever conscious of any effect he produced upon my excited imagination, had paused for a while, giving me time, as it were, to co-ordinate in my mind the few simple facts he had put before me. I had no wish to make a remark, knowing of old that my one chance of getting the whole of his interesting argument was to offer neither comment nor contradiction.

"When a young, good-looking woman in the heyday of her success in an interesting profession," he began at last, "is alleged to have committed suicide, the outside public immediately want to know the reason why she did such a thing, and a kind of freemasonic, amateur detective work goes on, which generally brings a few important truths to light. Thus, in the case of Miss Elliott, certain facts had begun to leak out, even before the inquest, with its many sensational developments. Rumours concerning the internal administration, or rather maladministration of the Home began to take more definite form.

"That its finances had been in a very shaky condition for some time was known to all those who were interested in its welfare. What was not so universally known was that few hospitals had had more munificent donations and subscriptions showered upon them in recent years, and yet it was openly spoken of by all the nurses that Miss Elliott had on more than one occasion petitioned for actual necessities for the patients—necessities which were denied to her on the plea of necessary economy.

"The Convalescent Home was, as sometimes happens in institutions of this sort, under the control of a committee of benevolent and fashionable people who understood nothing about business, and less still about the management of a hospital. Dr Kinnaird, president of the institution, was a young, eminently successful consultant; he had recently married the daughter of a peer, who had boundless ambitions for herself and her husband.

"Dr Kinnaird, by adding the prestige of his name to the Home, no doubt felt that he had done enough for its welfare. Against that, Dr Stapylton, honorary secretary and treasurer of the Home, threw himself heart and soul into the work connected with it, and gave a great deal of his time to it. All subscriptions and donations went, of course, through his hands, the benevolent and fashionable committee being only too willing to shift all their financial responsibilities on to his willing shoulders. He was a very popular man in society—a bachelor with a magnificent house in Hamilton Terrace, where he entertained the more eminent and fashionable clique in his own profession.

"It was the evening papers, however, which contained the most sensational development of this tragic case. It appears that on the Saturday afternoon Mary Dawson, one of the nurses in the Home, was going to the house surgeon's office with a message from the head nurse, when her attention was suddenly arrested in one of the passages by the sound of loud voices proceeding from one of the rooms. She paused to listen for a moment, and at once recognised the voices of Miss Elliott and of Dr Stapylton, the honorary treasurer and chairman of committee.

"The subject of conversation was evidently that of the eternal question of finance. Miss Elliott spoke very indignantly, and Nurse Dawson caught the words:

"'Surely you must agree with me that Dr Kinnaird ought to be informed at once.'

"Dr Stapylton's voice in reply seems to have been at first bitingly sarcastic, then threatening. Dawson heard nothing more after that, and went on to deliver her message. On her way back she stopped in the passage again, and tried to listen. This time it seemed to her as if she could hear the sound of someone crying bitterly, and Dr Stapylton's voice speaking very gently.

"'You may be right, Nellie,' he was saying. 'At any rate, wait a few days before telling Kinnaird. You know what he is—he'll make a frightful fuss and —'

"Whereupon Miss Elliott interrupted him.

"'It isn't fair to Dr Kinnaird to keep him in ignorance any longer. Whoever the thief may be it is your duty or mine to expose him, and if necessary bring him to justice.'

"There was a good deal of discussion at the time, if you remember, as to whether Nurse Dawson had overheard and repeated this speech accurately: whether, in point of fact, Miss Elliott had used the words '*or* mine' or '*and* mine'. You see the neat little point, don't you?" continued the man in the corner. "The little word 'and' would imply that she considered herself at one with Dr Stapylton in the matter, but 'or' would mean that she was resolved to act alone if he refused to join her in unmasking the thief.

"All these facts, as I remarked before, had leaked out, as such facts have a way of doing. No wonder, therefore, that on the day fixed for the inquest the coroner's court was filled to overflowing, both with the public—ever eager for new sensations—and with the many friends of the deceased lady, among whom young medical students of both sexes and nurses in uniform were most conspicuous.

"I was there early, and therefore had a good seat, from which I could comfortably watch the various actors in the drama about to be performed. People who seemed to be in the know pointed out various personages to one another, and it was a matter of note that, in spite of professional engagements, the members of the staff of the Convalescent Home were present in full force and stayed on almost the whole time. The personages who chiefly arrested my attention were, firstly, Dr Kinnaird, a good-looking Irishman of about forty, and president of the institution; also, Dr Earnshaw, a rising young consultant, with boundless belief in himself written all over his pleasant rubicund countenance.

"The expert medical evidence was once again thoroughly gone into. There was absolutely no doubt that Miss Elliott had died from having her throat cut with the surgical knife which was found grasped in her right hand. There were absolutely no signs of a personal struggle in the immediate vicinity of the body, and rigid examination proved that there was no other mark of violence upon the body; there was nothing, therefore, to prove that the poor girl had not committed suicide in a moment of mental aberration or of great personal grief.

"Of course, it was strange that she should have chosen this curious mode of taking her own life. She had access to all kinds of poisons, amongst which her medical knowledge could prompt her to choose the least painful and most efficacious ones. Therefore, to have walked out on a Sunday night to a wretched and unfrequented spot, and there committed suicide in that grim fashion seemed almost the work of a mad woman. And yet the evidence of her family and friends all tended to prove that Miss Elliott was a peculiarly sane, large-minded, and happy individual.

"However, the suicide theory was at this stage of the proceedings taken as being absolutely established, and when Police Constable Fiske came forward to give his evidence no one in the court was prepared for a statement which suddenly revealed this case to be as mysterious as it was tragic.

"Fiske's story was this: close upon midnight on that memorable Sunday night he was walking down Blomfield Road along the side of the canal and towards the footbridge, when he overtook a lady and gentleman who were walking in the same direction as himself. He turned to look at them, and noticed that the gentleman was in evening dress and wore a high hat, and that the lady was crying.

"Blomfield Road is at best very badly lighted, especially on the side next to the canal, where there are no lamps at all. Fiske, however, was prepared to swear positively that the lady was the deceased. As for the gentleman, he might know him again or he might not.

"Fiske then crossed the footbridge, and walked on towards the Harrow Road. As he did so, he heard St Mary Magdalen's church clock chime the hour of midnight. It was a quarter of an hour after that that the body of the unfortunate girl was found, and clasping in her hand the knife with which that awful deed had been done. By whom? Was it really by her own self? But if so, why did not that man in evening dress who had last seen her alive come forward and throw some light upon this fast-thickening veil of mystery?

"It was Mr James Elliott, brother of the deceased, however, who first mentioned a name then in open court, which has ever since in the minds of everyone been associated with Miss Elliott's tragic fate.

"He was speaking in answer to a question of the coroner's anent his sister's disposition and recent frame of mind.

"'She was always extremely cheerful,' he said, 'but recently had been peculiarly bright and happy. I understood from her that this was because she believed that a man for whom she had a great regard was also very much attached to her, and meant to ask her to be his wife.'

"'And do you know who this man was?' asked the coroner.

"'Oh yes,' replied Mr Elliott, 'it was Dr Stapylton.'

"Everyone had expected that name, of course, for everyone remembered Nurse Dawson's story, yet when it came, there crept over all those present an indescribable feeling that something terrible was impending.

"'Is Dr Stapylton here?'

"But Dr Stapylton had sent an excuse. A professional case of the utmost urgency had kept him at a patient's bedside. But Dr Kinnaird, the president of the institution, came forward.

"Questioned by the coroner, Dr Kinnaird, however, who evidently had a great regard for his colleague, repudiated any idea that the funds of the institution had ever been tampered with by the Treasurer.

"'The very suggestion of such a thing,' he said, 'was an outrage upon one of the most brilliant men in the profession.'

"He further added that, although he knew that Dr Stapylton thought very highly of Miss Elliott, he did not think that there was any actual engagement, and most decidedly he (Dr Kinnaird) had heard nothing of any disagreement between them.

"'Then did Dr Stapylton never tell you that Miss Elliott had often chafed under the extraordinary economy practised in the richly endowed Home?' asked the coroner again.

"'No,' replied Dr Kinnaird.

"'Was not that rather strange reticence?'

"'Certainly not. I am only the Honorary President of the institution—Stapylton has chief control of its finances.'

"'Ah!' remarked the coroner blandly.

"However, it was clearly no business of his at this moment to enter into the financial affairs of the Home. His duty at this point was to try and find out if Dr Stapylton and the man in evening dress were one and the same person.

"The men who found the body testified to the hour: a quarter past midnight. As Fiske had seen the unfortunate girl alive a little before twelve, she must have been murdered or had committed suicide between midnight and a quarter past. But there was something more to come.

"How strange and dramatic it all was!" continued the man in the corner, with a bland smile, altogether out of keeping with the poignancy of his narrative; "all these people in that crowded court trying to reconstruct the last chapter of that bright young matron's life and then—but I must not anticipate.

"One more witness was to be heard—one whom the police, with a totally unconscious sense of what is dramatic, had reserved for the last. This was Dr Earnshaw, one of the staff of the Convalescent Home. His evidence was very short, but of deeply momentous import. He explained that he had consulting rooms in Weymouth Street, but resided in Westbourne Square. On Sunday, 1st November, he had been dining out in Maida Vale, and returning home a little before midnight saw a woman standing close by the steps of the footbridge in the Blomfield Road.

"'I had been coming down Formosa Street and had not specially taken notice of her, when just as I reached the corner of Blomfield Road, she was joined by a man in evening dress and high hat. Then I crossed the road, and recognised both Miss Elliott and—'

"The young doctor paused, almost as if hesitating before the enormity of what he was about to say, whilst the excitement in court became almost painful.

"'And —?' urged the coroner.

"'And Dr Stapylton,' said Dr Earnshaw at last, almost under his breath.

"'You are quite sure?' asked the coroner.

"'Absolutely positive. I spoke to them both, and they spoke to me.'

"'What did you say?'

"'Oh, the usual, "Hello, Stapylton!" to which he replied, "Hello!" I then said "Goodnight" to them both, and Miss Elliott also said "Goodnight." I saw her face more clearly then, and thought that she looked very tearful and unhappy, and Stapylton looked ill-tempered. I wondered why they had chosen that unhallowed spot for a midnight walk.'

"'And you say the hour was—?' asked the coroner.

"'Ten minutes to twelve. I looked at my watch as I crossed the footbridge, and had heard a quarter to twelve strike five minutes before.'

"Then it was that the coroner adjourned the inquest. Dr Stapylton's attendance had become absolutely imperative. According to Dr Earnshaw's testimony, he had been with deceased certainly a quarter of an hour before she met her terrible death. Fiske had seen them together ten minutes later; she was then crying bitterly. There was as yet no actual charge against the fashionable and rich doctor, but already the ghostly bird of suspicion had touched him with its ugly wing."

3

"As for the next day," continued the man in the corner after a slight pause, "I can assure you that there was not a square foot of standing room in the coroner's court for the adjourned inquest. It was timed for eleven a.m., and at six o'clock on that cold winter's morning the pavement outside the court was already crowded. As for me, I always manage to get a front seat, and I did on that occasion, too. I fancy that I was the first among the general public to note Dr Stapylton as he entered the room accompanied by his solicitor, and by Dr Kinnaird, with whom he was chatting very cheerfully and pleasantly.

"Mind you, I am a great admirer of the medical profession, and I think a clever and successful doctor usually has a most delightful air about him—the consciousness of great and good work done with profit to himself—which is quite unique and quite admirable.

"Dr Stapylton had that air even to a greater extent than his colleague, and from the affectionate way in which Dr Kinnaird finally shook him by the hand, it was quite clear that the respected chief of the Convalescent Home, at any rate, refused to harbour any suspicion of the integrity of its Treasurer.

"Well, I must not weary you by dwelling on the unimportant details of this momentous inquest. Constable Fiske, who was asked to identify the gentleman in evening dress whom he had seen with the deceased at a few minutes before twelve, failed to recognise Dr Stapylton very positively: pressed very closely, he finally refused to swear either way. Against that, Dr Earnshaw repeated, clearly and categorically, looking his colleague straight in the face the while, the damnatory evidence he had given the day before.

"'I saw Dr Stapylton, I spoke to him, and he spoke to me,' he repeated most emphatically.

"Everyone in that court was watching Dr Stapylton's face, which wore an air of supreme nonchalance, even of contempt, but certainly neither of guilt nor of fear.

"Of course, by that time *I* had fully made up my mind as to where the hitch lay in this extraordinary mystery; but no one else had, and everyone held their breath as Dr Stapylton quietly stepped into the box, and after a few preliminary questions the coroner asked him very abruptly:

"'You were in the company of the deceased a few minutes before she died, Dr Stapylton?'

"'Pardon me,' replied the latter quietly, 'I last saw Miss Elliott alive on Saturday afternoon, just before I went home from my work.'

"This calm reply, delivered without a tremor, positively made everyone gasp. For the moment coroner and jury were alike staggered.

"'But we have two witnesses here who saw you in the company of the deceased within a few minutes of twelve o'clock on the Sunday night!' the coroner managed to gasp out at last.

"'Pardon me,' again interposed the doctor, 'these witnesses were mistaken.'

"'Mistaken!'

"I think everyone would have shouted out the word in boundless astonishment had they dared to do so.

"'Dr Earnshaw was mistaken,' reiterated Dr Stapylton quietly. 'He neither saw me nor did he speak to me.'

"'You can substantiate that, of course?' queried the coroner.

"'Pardon me,' once more said the doctor, with utmost calm, 'it is surely Dr Earnshaw who should substantiate *his* statement.'

"'There is Constable Fiske's corroborative evidence for that,' retorted the coroner, somewhat nettled.

"'Hardly, I think. You see, the constable states that he saw a gentleman in evening dress, etc., talking to the deceased at a minute or two before twelve o'clock, and that when he heard the clock of St Mary Magdalen chime the hour of midnight he was just walking away from the footbridge. Now, just as that very church clock was chiming that hour, I was stepping into a cab at the corner of Harrow Road, not a hundred yards *in front* of Constable Fiske.'

"'You swear to that?' queried the coroner in amazement.

"'I can easily prove it,' said Dr Stapylton. 'The cabman who drove me from there to my club is here and can corroborate my statement.'

"And amidst boundless excitement, John Smith, a hansom-cab driver, stated that he was hailed in the Harrow Road by the last witness, who told him to drive to the Royal Clinical Club, in Mardon Street. Just as he started off, St Mary Magdalen's Church, close by, struck the hour of midnight.

"At that very moment, if you remember, Constable Fiske had just crossed the footbridge, and was walking towards the Harrow Road, and he was quite sure (for he was closely questioned afterwards) that no one overtook him from behind. Now there would be no way of getting from one side of the canal to the other at this point except over that footbridge; the nearest bridge is fully two hundred yards further down the Blomfield Road. The girl was alive a minute *before* the constable crossed the footbridge, and it would have been absolutely impossible for anyone to have murdered a girl, placed the knife in her hand, run a couple of hundred yards to the next bridge and another three hundred to the corner of Harrow Road, all in the space of three minutes.

"This alibi, therefore, absolutely cleared Dr Stapylton from any suspicion of having murdered Miss Elliott. And yet, looking on that man as he sat there, calm, cool and contemptuous, no one could have had the slightest doubt but that he was lying—lying when he said he had not seen Miss Elliott that evening; lying when he denied Dr Earnshaw's statement; lying when he professed himself ignorant of the poor girl's fate.

"Dr Earnshaw repeated his statement with the same emphasis, but it was one man's word against another's, and as Dr Stapylton was so glaringly innocent of the actual murder, there seemed no valid reason at all why he should have denied having seen her that night, and the point was allowed to drop. As for Nurse Dawson's story of his alleged quarrel with Miss Elliott on the Saturday night, Dr Stapylton again had a simple and logical explanation.

"'People who listen at keyholes,' he said quietly, 'are apt to hear only fragments of conversation, and often mistake ordinary loud voices for quarrels. As a matter of fact, Miss Elliott and I were discussing the dismissal of certain nurses from the Home, whom she deemed incompetent. Nurse Dawson was among that number. She desired their immediate dismissal, and I tried to pacify her. That was the subject of my conversation with the deceased lady. I can swear to every word of it.'"

4

The man in the corner had long ceased speaking and was placing quietly before me a number of photographs. One by one I saw the series of faces which had been watched so eagerly in the coroner's court that memorable afternoon by an excited crowd.

"So, the fate of poor Miss Elliott has remained wrapt in mystery?" I said thoughtfully at last.

"To everyone," rejoined the funny creature, "except to me."

"Ah! What is your theory, then?"

"A simple one, dear lady; so simple that it really amazes me that no one, not even you, my faithful pupil, ever thought of it."

"It may be so simple that it becomes idiotic," I retorted with lofty disdain.

"Well, that may be. Shall I at any rate try to make it clear?"

"If you like."

"For this I think the best way would be, if you were to follow me through what transpired before the inquest. But first tell me, what do you think of Dr Earnshaw's statement?"

"Well," I replied, "a good many people thought that it was he who murdered Miss Elliott, and that his story of meeting Dr Stapylton with her was a lie from beginning to end."

"Impossible!" he retorted, making an elaborate knot in his bit of string. "Dr Earnshaw's friends, with whom he had been dining that night, swore that he was *not* in evening dress, nor wore a high hat. And on that point—the evening dress, and the hat—Constable Fiske was most positive."

"Then Dr Earnshaw was mistaken, and it was not Dr Stapylton he met."

"Impossible!" he shrieked, whilst another knot went to join its fellows. "He spoke to Dr Stapylton, and Dr Stapylton spoke to him."

"Very well, then," I argued; "why should Dr Stapylton tell a lie about it? He had such a conclusive alibi that there could be no object in his making a false statement about that."

"No object!" shrieked the excited creature. "Why, don't you *see* that he had to tell the lie in order to set police, coroner, and jury by the ears, because he did not wish it to be even remotely hinted at, that the man whom Dr Earnshaw saw with Miss Elliott, and the man whom Constable Fiske saw with her ten minutes later, were *two different persons?*"

"Two different persons!" I ejaculated.

"Ay! two confederates in this villainy. No one has ever attempted to deny the truth of the shaky finances of the Home; no one has really denied that Miss Elliott suspected certain defalcations and was trying to force the hands of the Honorary Treasurer towards a full enquiry. That the Honorary Treasurer knew where all the money went to was pretty clear all along—his magnificent house in Hamilton Terrace fully testifies to that. That the President of the institution was a party to these defalcations and largely profited by them I for one am equally convinced."

"Dr Kinnaird?" I ejaculated in amazement.

"Ay, Dr Kinnaird. Do you mean to tell me that he alone among the entire staff of that Home was ignorant of those defalcations? Impossible! And if he knew of them, and did neither enquire into them nor attempt to stop them, then he must have been a party to them. Do you admit that?"

"Yes, I admit that," I replied.

"Very well, then. The rest is quite simple; those two men, unworthy to bear the noble appellation of doctor, must for years have quietly stolen the money subscribed by the benevolent for the Home, and converted it to their own use: then, they suddenly find themselves face to face with immediate discovery in the shape of a young girl determined to unmask the systematic frauds of the past few years. That meant exposure, disgrace, ruin for them both, and they determine to be rid of her.

"Under the pretence of an evening walk, her so-called lover entices her to a lonely and suitable spot; his confederate is close by, hidden in the shadows, ready to give his assistance if the girl struggles and screams. But suddenly Dr Earnshaw appears. He recognises Stapylton and challenges him. For a moment the villains are nonplussed, then Kinnaird—the cleverer of the two—steps forward, greets the two lovers unconcernedly, and after two minutes' conversation casually reminds Stapylton of an appointment the latter is presumed to have at a club in St James's Street.

"The latter understands and takes the hint, takes a quick farewell of the girl, leaving her in his friend's charge, then, as fast as he can, goes off, presently takes a cab, leaving his friend to do the deed, whilst the alibi he can prove, coupled with Dr Earnshaw's statement, was sure to bewilder and mislead the police and the public.

"Thus it was that though Dr Earnshaw saw and recognised Dr Stapylton, Constable Fiske saw Dr Kinnaird, whom he did *not* recognise, on whom no suspicion had fallen, and whose name had never been coupled with that of Miss Elliott. When Constable Fiske had turned his back, Kinnaird murdered the girl and went off quietly, whilst Dr Stapylton, on whom all suspicions were bound to fasten sooner or later, was able to prove the most perfect alibi ever concocted.

"One day I feel certain that the frauds at the Home will be discovered, and then who knows what else may see the light?

"Think of it all quietly when I am gone, and tomorrow when we meet tell me whether if *I* am wrong what is *your* explanation of this extraordinary mystery."

Before I could reply he had gone, and I was left wondering, gazing at the photographs of two good-looking, highly respectable and respected men, whom an animated scarecrow had just boldly accused of committing one of the most dastardly crimes ever recorded in our annals.

The Hocussing of Cigarette

Quite by chance I found myself one morning sitting before a marble-topped table in the A.B.C. shop. I really wondered for the moment what had brought me there, and felt cross with myself for being there at all. Having sampled my tea and roll, I soon buried myself in the capacious folds of my *Daily Telegraph*.

"A glass of milk and a cheesecake, please," said a well-known voice.

The next moment I was staring into the corner, straight at a pair of mild, watery blue eyes, hidden behind great bone-rimmed spectacles, and at ten long bony fingers, round which a piece of string was provokingly intertwined.

There he was as usual, wearing—for it was chilly—a huge tweed ulster, of a pattern too lofty to be described. Smiling, bland, apologetic, and fidgety, he sat before me as the living embodiment of the reason why I had come to the A.B.C. shop that morning.

"How do you do?" I said, with as much dignity as I could command.

"I see that you are interested in Cigarette," he remarked, pointing to a special column in *The Daily Telegraph*.

"She is quite herself again," I said.

"Yes, but you don't know who tried to poison her and succeeded in making her very ill. You don't know whether the man Palk had anything to do with it, whether he was bribed, or whether it was Mrs Keeson or the groom Cockram who told a lie, or why—?"

"No," I admitted reluctantly; "I don't know any of these things."

He was fidgeting nervously in the corner, wriggling about like an animated scarecrow. Then suddenly a bland smile illuminated his entire face. His long bony fingers had caught the end of the bit of string, and there he was at it again, just as I had seen him a year ago, worrying and fidgeting, making knot upon knot, and untying them again, whilst his blue eyes peered at me over the top of his gigantic spectacles.

"I would like to know what your theory is about the whole thing," I was compelled to say at last; for the case had interested me deeply, and, after all, I had come to the A.B.C. shop for the sole purpose of discussing the adventures of Cigarette with him.

"Oh, my theories are not worth considering," he said meekly. "The police would not give me five shillings for any one of them. They always prefer a mystery to any logical conclusion, if it is arrived at by an outsider. But you may be more lucky. The owner of Cigarette did offer £100 reward for the elucidation of the mystery. The noble Earl must have backed Cigarette for all he was worth. Malicious tongues go even so far as to say that he is practically a ruined man now, and that the beautiful Lady Agnes is only too glad to find herself the wife of Harold Keeson, the son of the well-known trainer.

"If you ever go to Newmarket," continued the man in the corner after a slight pause, during which he had been absorbed in unravelling one of his most complicated knots, "anyone will point out the Keesons' house to you. It is called Manor House, and stands in the midst of beautiful gardens. Mr Keeson himself is a man of about fifty, and, as a matter of fact, is of very good family, the Keesons having owned property in the Midlands for the past eight hundred years. Of this fact he is, it appears, extremely proud. His father, however, was a notorious spendthrift, who squandered his property, and died in the nick of time, leaving his son absolutely penniless and proud as Lucifer.

"Fate, however, has been kind to George Keeson. His knowledge of horses and of all matters connected with the turf stood him in good stead: hard work and perseverance did the rest. Now, at fifty years of age, he is a very rich man, and practically at the head of a profession, which, if not exactly that of a gentleman, is, at any rate, highly remunerative.

"He owns Manor House, and lived there with his young wife and his only son and heir, Harold.

"It was Mr Keeson who had trained Cigarette for the Earl of Okehampton, and who, of course, had charge of her during her apprenticeship, before she was destined to win a fortune for her owner, her trainer, and those favoured few who had got wind of her capabilities. For Cigarette was to be kept a dark horse—not an easy matter in these days, when the neighbourhood of every racecourse abounds with rascals who eke out a precarious livelihood by various methods, more or less shady, of which the gleaning of early information is perhaps the least disreputable.

"Fortunately for Mr Keeson, however, he had in the groom, Cockram, a trusted and valued servant, who had been in his employ for over ten years. To say that Cockram took a special pride in Cigarette would be but to put it mildly. He positively loved the mare, and I don't think that anyone ever doubted that his interest in her welfare was every bit as keen as that of the Earl of Okehampton or of Mr Keeson.

"It was to Cockram, therefore, that Mr Keeson entrusted the care of Cigarette. She was lodged in the private stables adjoining the Manor House, and during the few days immediately preceding the Coronation Stakes the groom practically never left her side, either night or day. He slept in the loose box with her, and ate all his meals in her company; nor was anyone allowed to come within measurable distance of the living treasure, save Mr Keeson or the Earl of Okehampton himself.

"And yet, in spite of all these precautions, in spite of every care that human ingenuity could devise, on the very morning of the race Cigarette was seized with every symptom of poisoning, and although, as you say, she is quite herself again now, she was far too ill to fulfil her engagement, and, if rumour speaks correctly, completed thereby the ruin of the Earl of Okehampton."

2

The man in the corner looked at me through his bone-rimmed spectacles, and his mild blue eyes gazed pleasantly into mine.

"You may well imagine," he continued, after a while, "what a thunderbolt such a catastrophe means to those whose hopes of a fortune rested upon the fitness of the bay mare. Mr Keeson lost his temper for an instant, they say—but for one instant only. When he was hastily summoned at six o'clock in the morning to Cigarette's stables, and saw her lying on the straw, rigid and with glassy eyes, he raised his heavy riding-whip over the head of Cockram. Some assert that he actually struck him, and that the groom was too wretched and too dazed to resent either words or blows. After a good deal of hesitation, he reluctantly admitted that for the first time since Cigarette had been in his charge he had slept long and heavily.

"'I am such a light sleeper, you know, sir,' he said in a tear-choked voice. 'Usually, I could hear every noise the mare made if she stirred at all. But, there—last night I cannot say *what* happened. I remember that I felt rather drowsy after my supper, and must have dropped off to sleep very quickly. Once during the night, I woke up; the mare was all right then.'

"The man paused, and seemed to be searching for something in his mind—the recollection of a dream, perhaps. But the veterinary surgeon, who was present at the time, having also been hastily summoned to the stables, took up the glass which had contained the beer for Cockram's supper. He sniffed it, and then tasted it, and said quietly:

"'No wonder you slept heavily, my man. This beer was drugged: it contained opium.'

"'Drugged!' ejaculated Cockram, who, on hearing this fact, which in every way exonerated him from blame, seemed more hopelessly wretched than he had been before.

"It appears that every night Cockram's supper was brought out to him in the stables by one of the servants from the Manor House. On this particular night Mrs Keeson's maid, a young girl named Alice Image, had brought him a glass of beer and some bread and cheese on a tray at about eleven o'clock.

"Closely questioned by Mr Keeson, the girl emphatically denied all knowledge of any drug in the beer. She had often taken the supper tray across to Cockram, who was her sweetheart, she said. It was usually placed ready for her in the hall, and when she had finished attending upon her mistress's night toilet, she went over to the stables with it. She had certainly never touched the beer, and the tray had stood in its accustomed place on the hall table looking just the same as usual. 'As if I'd go and poison my Cockram!' she said in the midst of a deluge of tears.

"All these somewhat scanty facts crept into the evening papers that same day. That an outrage of a peculiarly daring and cunning character had been perpetrated was not for a moment in doubt. So much money had been at stake, so many people would be half-ruined by it, that even the nonracing public at once took the keenest interest in the case. All the papers admitted, of course, that for the moment the affair seemed peculiarly mysterious, yet all commented upon one fact, which they suggested should prove an important clue: this fact was Cockram's strange attitude.

"At first he had been dazed—probably owing to the after-effects of the drug; he had also seemed too wretched even to resent Mr Keeson's very natural outburst of wrath. But then, when the presence of the drug in his beer was detected, which proved *him*, at any rate, to have been guiltless in the matter, his answers, according to all accounts, became somewhat confused; and all Mr Keeson and the 'vet', who were present, got out of him after that, was a perpetual ejaculation: 'What's to be done? What's to be done?'

"Two days later the sporting papers were the first to announce, with much glee, that thanks to the untiring energy of the Scotland Yard authorities, daylight seemed at last to have been brought to bear upon the mystery which surrounded the dastardly outrage on the Earl of Okehampton's mare Cigarette, and that an important arrest in connection with it had already been effected.

"It appears that a man named Charles Palk, seemingly of no address, had all along been suspected of having at least a hand in the outrage. He was believed to be a bookmaker's tout, and was a man upon whom the police had long since kept a watchful eye. Palk had been seen loafing around the Manor House for the past week, and had been warned off the grounds once or twice by the grooms.

"It now transpired that on the day preceding the outrage he had hung about the neighbourhood of the Manor House the whole afternoon, trying to get into conversation with the stable-boys, or even with Mr Keeson's indoor servants. No one, however, would have anything to do with him, as Mr Keeson's orders in those respects were very strict: he had often threatened any one of his *employés* with instant dismissal if he found him in company with one of these touts.

"Detective Twiss, however, who was in charge of the case, obtained the information that Alice Image, the maid, had been seen on more than one occasion talking to Palk, and that on the very day before the Coronation Stakes, she had been seen in his company. Closely questioned by the detective, Alice Image at first denied her intercourse with the tout, but finally was forced to admit that she had held conversation with him once or twice.

"She was fond of putting a bit now and again upon a horse, but Cockram, she added, was such a muff that he never would give her a tip, for he did not approve of betting for young women. Palk had always been very civil and nice-spoken, she further explained. Moreover, he came from Buckinghamshire, her own part of the country, where she was born; anyway, she had never had cause to regret having entrusted a half-sovereign or so of her wages to him.

"All these explanations delivered by Alice Image, with the flow of tears peculiar to her kind, were not considered satisfactory, and the next day she and Charles Palk were both arrested on the charge of being concerned in the poisoning of the Earl of Okehampton's mare

Cigarette, with intent to do her grievous bodily harm."

3

"These sort of cases," continued the man in the corner after a slight pause, during which his nervous fingers toyed incessantly with that eternal bit of string—"these sort of cases always create a great deal of attention amongst the public, the majority of whom in this country have very strong sporting proclivities. It was small wonder, therefore, when Alice Image and Charles Palk were brought before the local magistrates, that the court was crowded to overflowing, both with pressmen and with the general public.

"I had all along been very much interested in the case, so I went down to Newmarket, and, in spite of the huge crowd, managed to get a good seat, whence I could command a full view of the chief personages concerned in this thrilling sporting drama.

"Firstly, there was the Earl of Okehampton—good-looking, but for an unmistakable air of the broken-down sporting man about his whole person; the trainer, Mr Keeson—a lean, clean-shaven man, with a fine, proud carriage, and a general air of ancient lineage and the Domesday Book about him; Mrs Keeson—a pale, nervous-looking creature, who seemed very much out of place in this sporting set; and, finally, the accused—Alice Image, dissolved in tears, and Charles Palk, overdressed, defiant, horsey, and unsympathetic.

"There was also Cockram, the groom. My short-sighted eyes had fastened on him the moment I entered the court. A more wretched, miserable, bewildered expression I have never seen on any man's face.

"Both Alice Image and Charles Palk flatly denied the charge. Alice declared, amid a renewed deluge of tears, that she was engaged to be married to Cockram, that she 'no more would have hurt him or the pretty creature he was in charge of, for anything'. How could she? As for Palk—conscious, no doubt, of his own evil reputation—he merely contented himself with shrugging his shoulders and various denials, usually accompanied with emphatic language.

"As neither of the accused attempted to deny that they had been together the day before the outrage, there was no occasion to call witnesses to further prove that fact. Both, however, asserted emphatically that their conversation was entirely confined to the subject of Alice's proposed flutters on the favourite for the next day's race.

"Thus, the only really important witness was the groom, Cockram. Once again, his attitude as a witness caused a great deal of surprise, and gradually, as he gave his evidence in a peculiarly halting and nervous manner, that surprise was changed into suspicion.

"Questioned by the magistrate, he tried his hardest to exonerate Alice from all blame; and yet when asked whether he had cause to suspect anyone else he became more confused than ever, said, 'No,' emphatically first, then, 'Yes,' and finally looked round the court appealingly, like some poor animal at bay. That the man was hiding something, that he was, in point of fact, lying, was apparent to everyone. He had drunk the beer, he said, unsuspectingly on that fatal night; he had then dropped off to sleep almost immediately, and never woke until about six a.m., when a glance at the mare at once told him that there was something very wrong.

"However, whether Cockram was lying or not—whether he suspected anyone else or was merely trying to shield his sweetheart, there was, in the opinion of the magistrate, quite sufficient evidence to prove that Alice Image, at any rate, had a hand in the hocussing of Cigarette, since it was she who had brought the drugged beer to Cockram. Beyond that there was not sufficient evidence to show either that she was a tool in the hands of Palk, or that they both were merely instruments in the hands of some third person.

"Anyway, the magistrate—it was Major Laverton, J.P., a great personal friend of the Earl of Okehampton, and a remarkably clever and acute man—tried his hardest to induce Alice to confess. He questioned the poor girl so closely and so rigorously that gradually she lost what little self-control she had, and everyone in the court blamed Major Laverton not a little, for he was gradually getting the poor girl into a state of hysterics.

"As for me, I inwardly commended the learned J.P., for already I had guessed what he was driving at, and was not the least astonished when the dramatic incident occurred which rendered this case so memorable.

"Alice Image, namely, now thoroughly unnerved, harassed with the major's questions, suddenly turned to where Cockram was sitting, and, with hysterical cry, she stretched out both her arms towards him.

"'Joe! my Joe!' she cried; 'you know I didn't do it! Can't you do anything to help me?'

"It was pathetic in the extreme: everyone in the court felt deeply moved. As for Cockram, a sudden change came over him. I am accustomed to read the faces of my fellow men, and in that rough countenance I saw then emerging, in response to the girl's appeal, a quick

242

and firm resolution.

"'Ay, and I will, Alice!' he said, jumping to his feet. 'I have tried to do my duty. If the gentlemen will hear me, I will say all I know.'

"Needless to say, 'the gentlemen' were only too ready to hear him. Like a man who, having made up his mind, is now resolved to act upon it, the groom Cockram began his story.

"'I told your worship that, having drunk the beer that night, I dropped off to sleep very fast and very heavy-like. How long I'd been asleep I couldn't say, when suddenly something seemed not exactly to wake me but to dispel my dreams, so to speak. I opened my eyes. and at first, I couldn't see anything, as the gas in the stable was turned on very low; but I put out my hand to feel the mare's fetlocks, just by way of telling her that I was there all right enough, and looking after her—bless her! At that moment, your worship, I noticed that the stable door was open, and that someone—I couldn't see who it was—was goin' out of it. "Who goes there?" says I, for I still felt very sleepy and dull, when, to my astonishment, who should reply to me but—'

"The man paused, and once more over his rough, honest face came the old look of perplexity and misery.

"'But—?' queried the magistrate, whose nerves were obviously as much on tension as those of everyone else in that court.

"'Speak, Joe—won't you?' appealed Alice Image pathetically.

"'But the mistress—Mrs Keeson, sir,' came from the groom in an almost inaudible whisper. 'You know, ma'am,' he added, while the gathering tears choked his voice, 'I wouldn't 'ave spoke. But she's my sweetheart, ma'am; and I couldn't bear that the shame should rest on her.'

"There was a moment's deadly silence in that crowded court. Everyone's eyes wandered towards the pale face of Mrs Keeson, which, however, though almost livid in colour, expressed nothing but the most boundless astonishment. As for Mr Keeson, surprise, incredulity, then furious wrath at the slander, could be seen chasing one another upon his handsome face.

"'What lie is this?' burst involuntarily from his lips, as his fingers closed more tightly upon the heavy riding whip which he was holding.

"'Silence, please!' said the major with authority. 'Now, Cockram, go on. You say Mrs Keeson spoke to you. What did she say?'

"'She seemed rather upset, sir,' continued Cockram, still looking with humble apology across at his mistress, 'for she only stammered something about: "Oh, it's nothing, Cockram. I only wanted to speak to my son—er—to Mr Harold—I—'"

"'Harold?' thundered Mr Keeson, who was fast losing his temper.

"'I must ask you, Mr Keeson, to be silent,' said the major. 'Go on, Cockram.'

"And Cockram continued his narrative:

"'"Mr Harold, ma'am?" I said. "What should 'e be doing 'ere in the stables at this time of night?" "Oh, nothing," says she to me, "I thought I saw him come in here. I must have been mistaken. Never mind, Cockram; it's all right. Goodnight."

"'I said goodnight, too, and then fell to wondering what Mr 'Arold could have wanted prowling round the stables at this hour of the night. Just then the clock of St Saviour's struck four o'clock, and while I was still wondering I fell asleep again, and never awoke until six, when the mare was as sick as she could be. And that's the whole truth, gentlemen; and I would never have spoke—for Mr and Mrs Keeson have always been good to me, and I'd have done anything to save them the disgrace—but Alice is goin' to be my wife, and I couldn't bear any shame to rest upon 'er.'

"When Cockram had finished speaking you might have heard a pin drop as Major Laverton asked Mrs Keeson to step into the witness-box. She looked fragile and pale, but otherwise quite self-possessed as she quietly kissed the book and said in a very firm tone of voice:

"'I can only say in reply to the extraordinary story which this man has just told that the drug in the beer must have given him peculiarly vivid dreams. At the hour he names I was in bed fast asleep, as my husband can testify; and the whole of Cockram's narrative is a fabrication from beginning to end. I may add that I am more than willing to forgive him. No doubt his brain was clouded by the opiate; and now he is beside himself owing to Alice Image's predicament. As for my son Harold, he was absent from home that night; he was spending it with some bachelor friends at the Stag and Mantle hotel in Newmarket.'

"'Yes! By the way,' said the magistrate, 'where is Mr Harold Keeson? I have no doubt that he will be able to give a very good account of himself on that memorable night.'

"'My son is abroad, your worship,' said Mrs Keeson, while a shade of a still more livid hue passed over her face.

"'Abroad, is he?' said the magistrate cheerfully. 'Well, that settles the point satisfactorily for him, doesn't it? When did he go?'

"'Last Thursday, your worship,' replied Mrs Keeson.

"Then there was silence again in the court, for that last Thursday was the day of the Coronation Stakes—the day immediately following the memorable night on which the mare Cigarette had been poisoned by an unknown hand."

4

"I doubt whether in all the annals of criminal procedure there ever occurred a more dramatic moment than that when so strange a ray of daylight was shed on the mysterious outrage on Cigarette. The magistrate, having dismissed Mrs Keeson, hardly dared to look across at the trainer, who was a personal friend of his, and who had just received such a cruel blow through this terrible charge against his only son—for at that moment I doubt if there were two people in that court who did not think that Mrs Keeson had just sworn a false oath, and that both she and her son had been in the stables that night—for what purpose only they and their own conscience could tell.

"Alice Image and Charles Palk were both discharged; and it is greatly to the credit of Cockram that in the midst of his joy in seeing his sweetheart safe he still remained very gloomy and upset. As for Mr Keeson, he must have suffered terribly at all this mud cast at his only son. He had been wounded in what he worshipped more than anything else in the world—his family honour. What was the use of money and the old estates if such a stain rested upon his name?

"As for Mrs Keeson, public sympathy was very much overshadowed with contempt for her stupidity. Had she only held her tongue when Cockram challenged her, suspicion would never have fastened upon Harold. The fact that she had lied in the witness-box in order to try and remedy her blunder was also very severely commented upon. The young man had gone abroad on that memorable Thursday accompanied by two of his bachelor friends. They had gone on a fishing expedition to Norway, and were not expected home for three weeks. As they meant to move from place to place, they had left no address: letters and telegrams were therefore useless.

"During those three weeks pending Harold Keeson's return certain facts leaked out which did not tend to improve his case. It appears that he had long been in love with Lady Agnes Stourcliffe, the daughter of the Earl of Okehampton. Some people asserted that the young people were actually—though secretly—engaged. The earl, however, seems all along to have objected to the marriage of his daughter with the son of a trainer, and on more than one occasion had remarked that he had not sunk quite so low yet as to allow so preposterous a *mésalliance*. Mr Keeson, whose family pride was at least equal to that of the earl, had naturally very much resented this attitude, and had often begged his son to give up his pretensions, since they were manifestly so unwelcome.

"Harold Keeson, however, was deeply in love; and Lady Agnes stuck to him with womanly constancy and devotion. Unfortunately, a climax was reached some days before the disastrous events at Newmarket. The Earl of Okehampton suddenly took up a very firm stand on the subject of Harold Keeson's courtship of his daughter. Some hot words were exchanged between the two men, ending in an open breach, the earl positively forbidding the young man ever to enter his house again.

"Harold was terribly unhappy at this turn of events. Pride forbade him to take an unfair advantage of a young girl's devotion, and, acting on the advice of his parents, he started for his tour in Norway, ostensibly in order to try and forget the fair Lady Agnes. This unhappy love affair, ending in an open and bitter quarrel between himself and the owner of Cigarette, did—as I said before—the young man's case no good. At the instance of the Earl of Okehampton, who determined to prosecute him, he was arrested on landing at Harwich.

"Well," continued the man in the corner, "the next events must be still fresh in your mind. When Harold Keeson appeared in the dock, charged with such meanness as to wreak his private grievance upon a dumb animal, public sympathy at once veered round in his favour. He looked so handsome, so frank and honest, that at once one felt convinced that *his* hand, at any rate, could never have done such a dastardly thing.

"Mr Keeson, who was a rich man, moreover had enlisted the services of Sir Arthur Inglewood, who had, in the short time at his disposal, collected all the most important evidence on behalf of his client.

"The two young men who had been travelling in Norway with Harold Keeson had been present with him on the memorable night at a bachelor party given by a mutual friend at the Stag and Mantle. Both testified that the party had played Bridge until the small hours of the morning, that between two rubbers—the rooms being very hot— they had all strolled out to smoke a cigar in the streets. Just as they were about to re-enter the hotel two church clocks—one of which was St Saviour's—chimed out the hour—four o'clock.

"Four o'clock was the hour when Cockram said that he had spoken to Mrs Keeson. Harold had not left the party at the Stag and Mantle since ten o'clock, which was an hour before Alice Image took the drugged beer to the groom. The whole edifice of the prosecution thus crumbled together like a house of cards and Harold Keeson was discharged, without the slightest suspicion clinging to him.

"Six months later he married Lady Agnes Stourcliffe. The earl, now a completely ruined man, offered no further opposition to the union of his daughter with a man who, at any rate, could keep her in comfort and luxury; for though both Mr Keeson and his son lost heavily through Cigarette's illness, yet the trainer was sufficiently rich to offer his son and his bride a very beautiful home."

The man in the corner called to the waitress, and paid for his glass of milk and cheesecake, whilst I remained absorbed in thought, gazing at *The Daily Telegraph*, which, in its 'London Day by Day', had this very morning announced that Mr and Lady Agnes Keeson had returned to town from 'The Rookery', Newmarket.

5

"But who poisoned Cigarette?" I asked after a while; "and why?"

"Ah, who did, I wonder?" he replied with exasperating mildness.

"Surely you have a theory," I suggested.

"Ah, but my theories are not worth considering. The police would take no notice of them."

"Why did Mrs Keeson go to the stables that night? Did she go?" I asked.

"Cockram swears she did."

"She swears she didn't. If she did why should she have asked for her son? Surely she did not wish to incriminate her son in order to save herself?"

"No," he replied; "women don't save themselves usually at the expense of their children, and women don't usually 'hocus' a horse. It is not a female crime at all—is it?"

The aggravating creature was getting terribly sarcastic; and I began to fear that he was not going to speak, after all. He was looking dejectedly all around him. I had one or two parcels by me. I undid a piece of string from one of them, and handed it to him with the most perfectly indifferent air I could command.

"I wonder if it was Cockram who told a lie?" I then said unconcernedly.

But already he had seized on that bit of string, and nervously now, his long fingers began fashioning a series of complicated knots.

"Let us take things from the beginning," he said at last. "The beginning of the mystery was the contradictory statements made by the groom Cockram and Mrs Keeson respectively. Let us take, first of all, the question of the groom. The matter is simple enough: either he saw Mrs Keeson or he did not. If he did not see her then he must have told a lie, either unintentionally or by design—unintentionally if he was mistaken; but this could not very well be since he asserted that Mrs Keeson spoke to him, and even mentioned her son, Mr Harold Keeson. Therefore, if Cockram did not see Mrs Keeson he told a lie by design for some purpose of his own. You follow me?"

"Yes," I replied, "I have thought all that out for myself already."

"Very well. Now, could there be some even remotely plausible motive why Cockram should have told that deliberate lie?"

"To save his sweetheart, Alice Image," I said.

"But you forget that his sweetheart was not accused at first, and that, from the very beginning, Cockram's manner, when questioned on the subject of the events of that night, was strange and contradictory in the extreme."

"He may have known from the first that Alice Image was guilty," I argued.

"In that case he would have merely asserted that he had seen and heard nothing during the night, or, if he wished to lie about it, he would have said that it was Palk, the tout, who sneaked into the stables, rather than incriminate his mistress, who had been good and kind to him for years."

"He may have wished to be revenged on Mrs Keeson for some reason which has not yet transpired."

"How? By making a statement which, if untrue, could be so easily disproved by Mr Keeson himself, who, as a matter of fact, could easily assert that his wife did not leave her bedroom that night, or by incriminating Mr Harold Keeson, who could prove an alibi? Not much of a revenge there, you must admit. No, no; the more you reflect seriously upon these possibilities the deeper will become your conviction that Cockram did not lie either accidentally or on purpose; that he did see Mrs Keeson at that hour at the stable door; that she did speak to him; and that it was she who told the lie in open court."

"But," I asked, feeling more bewildered than before, "why should Mrs Keeson have gone to the stables and asked for her son when she must have known that he was not there, but that her enquiry would make it, to say the least, extremely unpleasant for him?"

"Why?" he shrieked excitedly, jumping up like a veritable jack-in-the-box. "Ah, if you would only learn to reflect you might in time become a fairly able journalist. Why did Mrs Keeson momentarily incriminate her son?—for it was only a momentary incrimination. Think, think! A woman does not incriminate her child to save herself; but she might do it to save someone else—someone who was dearer to her than that child."

"Nonsense!" I protested.

"Nonsense, is it?" he replied. "You have only to think of the characters of the chief personages who figured in the drama—of the trainer Keeson, with his hasty temper and his inordinate family pride. Was it likely when the half-ruined Earl of Okehampton talked of *mésalliance*, and forbade the marriage of his daughter with his trainer's son, that the latter would not resent that insult with terrible bitterness? and, resenting it, not think of some means of being even with the noble earl? Can you not imagine the proud man boiling with indignation on hearing his son's tale of how Lord Okehampton had forbidden him the house? Can you not hear him saying to himself:

"'Well, by—the trainer's son *shall* marry the earl's daughter!'

"And the scheme—simple and effectual—whereby the ruin of the arrogant nobleman would be made so complete that he would be only too willing to allow his daughter to marry anyone who would give her a good home and him a helping hand?"

"But," I objected, "why should Mr Keeson take the trouble to drug the groom and sneak out to the stables at dead of night when he had access to the mare at all hours of the day?"

"Why?" shrieked the animated scarecrow. "Why? Because Keeson was just one of those clever criminals, with a sufficiency of brains to throw police and public alike off the scent. Cockram, remember, spent every moment of the day and night with the mare. Therefore, if he had been in full possession of his senses and could positively swear that no one had had access to Cigarette but his master and himself, suspicion was bound to fasten, sooner or later, on Keeson. But Keeson was a bit of a genius in the criminal line. Seemingly he could have had no motive for drugging the groom, yet he added that last artistic touch to his clever crime, and thus threw a final bucketful of sand in the eyes of the police."

"Even then," I argued, "Cockram might just have woke up—might just have caught Keeson in the act."

"Exactly. And that is, no doubt, what Mrs Keeson feared.

"She was a brave woman, if ever there was one. Can you not picture her knowing her husband's violent temper, his indomitable pride? and guessing that he would find some means of being revenged on the Earl of Okehampton? Can you not imagine her watching her husband and gradually guessing, realising what he had in his mind when, in the middle of the night, she saw him steal out of bed and out of the house? Can you not see her following him stealthily—afraid of him, perhaps—not daring to interfere—terrified above all things of the consequences of his crime, of the risks of Cockram waking up, of the exposure, the disgrace?

"Then the final tableau—Keeson having accomplished his purpose, goes back towards the house, and she—perhaps with a vague hope that she might yet save the mare by taking away the poison which Keeson had prepared—in her turn goes to the stables. But this time the groom is half awake, and challenges her. Then her instinct— that unerring instinct which always prompts a really good woman when the loved one is in danger—suggests to Mrs Keeson the clever subterfuge of pretending that she had seen her son entering the stables.

"She asks for him, *knowing well that she could do him no harm*, since he could so easily prove an alibi, but thereby throwing a veritable cloud of dust in the eyes of the keenest enquirer, and casting over the hocussing of Cigarette so thick a mantle of mystery that suspicion, groping blindly round, could never fasten tightly on anyone.

"Think of it all," he added as, gathering up his hat and umbrella, he prepared to go, "and remember at the same time that it was Mr Keeson alone who could disprove that his wife never left her room that night, that he did not do this, that he guessed what she had done and why she had done it, and I think that you will admit that not one link is missing in the chain of evidence which I have had the privilege of laying before you."

Before I could reply he had gone, and I saw his strange scarecrow-like figure disappearing through the glass door. Then I had a good think on the subject of the hocussing of Cigarette, and I was reluctantly bound to admit that once again the man in the corner had found the only possible solution to the mystery.

The Tragedy in Dartmoor Terrace

1

"It is not by any means the Law and Police Courts that form the only interesting reading in the daily papers," said the man in the corner airily, as he munched his eternal bit of cheesecake and sipped his glass of milk, like a frowsy old tom-cat.

"You don't agree with me," he added, for I had offered no comment to his obvious remark.

"No?" I answered. "I suppose you were thinking—"

"Of the tragic death of Mrs Yule, for instance," he replied eagerly. "Beyond the inquest, and its very unsatisfactory verdict, very few circumstances connected with that interesting case ever got into the papers at all."

"I forget what the verdict actually was," I said, eager, too, on my side to hear him talk about that mysterious tragedy, which, as a matter of fact, had puzzled a good many people.

"Oh, it was as vague and as wordy as the English language would allow. The jury found that 'Mrs Yule had died through falling downstairs, in consequence of a fainting attack, but *how* she came to fall is not clearly shown'.

"What had happened was this: Mrs Yule was a rich and eccentric old lady, who lived very quietly in a small house in Kensington; No. 9 Dartmoor Terrace is, I believe, the correct address.

"She had no expensive tastes, for she lived, as I said before, very simply and quietly in a small Kensington house, with two female servants—a cook and a housemaid—and a young fellow whom she had adopted as her son.

"The story of this adoption is, of course, the pivot round which all the circumstances of the mysterious tragedy revolved. Mrs Yule, namely, had an only son, William, to whom she was passionately attached; but, like many a fond mother, she had the desire of mapping out that son's future entirely according to her own ideas. William Yule, on the other hand, had his own views with regard to his own happiness, and one fine day went so far as to marry the girl of his choice, and that in direct opposition to his mother's wishes.

"Mrs Yule's chagrin and horror at what she called her son's base ingratitude knew no bounds; at first it was even thought that she would never get over it.

"'He has gone in direct opposition to my fondest wishes, and chosen a wife whom I could never accept as a daughter; he shall have none of the property which has enriched me, and which I know he covets.'

"At first her friends imagined that she meant to leave all her money to charitable institutions; but oh! dear me, no! Mrs Yule was one of those women who never did anything that other people expected her to. Within three years of her son's marriage, she had filled up the place which he had vacated, both in her house and in her heart. She had adopted a son, preferring, as she said, that her money should benefit an individual rather than an institution.

"Her choice had fallen upon the only son of a poor man—an ex-soldier—who used to come twice a week to Dartmoor Terrace to tidy up the small garden at the back: he was very respectable and very honest—was born in the same part of England as Mrs Yule, and had an only son whose name happened to be William; he rejoiced in the surname of Bloggs.

"'It suits me in every way,' explained Mrs Yule to old Mr Statham, her friend and solicitor. 'You see, I am used to the name of William, and the boy is nice-looking and has done very well at the Board School. Moreover, old Bloggs will die within a year or two, and William will be left without any encumbrances.'

"Herein Mrs Yule's prophecy proved to be correct. Old Bloggs did die very soon, and his son was duly adopted by the rich and eccentric old lady, sent to a good school, and finally given a berth in the Union Bank.

"I saw young Bloggs—it is not a euphonious name, is it?—at that memorable inquest later on. He was very young and unassuming, and used to keep very much out of the way of Mrs Yule's friends, who, mind you, strongly disapproved of his presence in the rich old widow's house, to the detriment of the only legitimate son and heir.

"What happened within the intimate and close circle of 9 Dartmoor Terrace during the next three years of course nobody can tell.

Certain it is that by the time young Bloggs was nearing his twenty-first birthday, he had become the very apple of his adopted mother's eye.

"During those three years Mr Statham and other old friends had worked hard in the interests of William Yule. Everyone felt that the latter was being very badly treated indeed. He had studied painting in his younger days, and now had set up a small studio in Hampstead, and was making perhaps a couple of hundred or so a year, and that with much difficulty, whilst the gardener's son had supplanted him in his mother's affections, and, worse still, in his mother's purse.

"The old lady was more obdurate than ever. In deference to the strong feelings of her friends she had agreed to see her son occasionally, and William Yule would call upon his mother from time to time—in the middle of the day when Bloggs was out of the way at the Bank—stay to tea, and part from her in frigid, though otherwise amicable, terms.

"'I have no ill-feeling against my son,' the old lady would say, 'but when he married against my wishes, he became a stranger to me—that is all—a stranger, however, whose pleasant acquaintanceship I am pleased to keep up.'

"That the old lady meant to carry her eccentricities in this respect to the bitter end, became all the more evident when she sent for her old friend and lawyer, Mr Statham, and explained to him that she wished to make over to young Bloggs the whole of her property by deed of gift, during her lifetime—on condition that on his twenty-first birthday he legally took up the name of Yule.

"Mr Statham subsequently made public, as you know, the whole of this interview which he had with Mrs Yule.

"'I tried to dissuade her, of course,' he said, 'for I thought it so terribly unfair on William Yule and his children. Moreover, I had always hoped that when Mrs Yule grew older and more feeble, she would surely relent towards her only son. But she was terribly obstinate.'

"'It is because I may become weak in my dotage,' she said, 'that I want to make the whole thing absolutely final—I don't want to relent. I wish that William should suffer, where I think he will suffer most, for he was always over-fond of money. If I make a will in favour of Bloggs, who knows I might repent it, and alter it at the eleventh hour? One is apt to become maudlin when one is dying, and has people weeping all round one. No!—I want the whole thing to be absolutely irrevocable; and I shall present the deed of gift to young Bloggs on his twenty-first birthday. I can always make it a condition that he keeps me in moderate comfort to the end of my days. He is too big a fool to be really ungrateful, and after all I don't think I should very much mind ending my life in the workhouse.'

"'What could I do?' added Mr Statham. 'If I had refused to draw up that iniquitous deed of gift, she only would have employed some other lawyer to do it for her. As it is, I secured an annuity of £500 a year for the old lady, in consideration of a gift worth some £30,000 made over absolutely to Mr William Bloggs.'

"The deed was drawn up," continued the man in the corner, "there is no doubt of that. Mr Statham saw to it. The old lady even insisted on having two more legal opinions upon it, lest there should be the slightest flaw that might render the deed invalid. Moreover, she caused herself to be examined by two specialists in order that they might testify that she was absolutely sound in mind, and in full possession of all her faculties.

"When the deed was all that the law could wish, Mr Statham handed it over to Mrs Yule, who wished to keep it by her until 3rd April—young Bloggs's twenty-first birthday—on which day she meant to surprise him with it.

"Mr Statham handed over the deed to Mrs Yule on 14th February, and on 28th March—that is to say, six days before Bloggs's majority—the old lady was found dead at the foot of the stairs in Dartmoor Terrace, whilst her desk was found to have been broken open, and the deed of gift had disappeared."

2

"From the very first the public took a great interest in the sad death of Mrs Yule. The old lady's eccentricities were pretty well known throughout all her neighbourhood, at any rate. Then, she had a large circle of friends, who all took sides, either for the disowned son or for the old lady's rigid and staunch principles of filial obedience.

"Directly, therefore, that the papers mentioned the sudden death of Mrs Yule, tongues began to wag, and, whilst some asserted 'Accident', others had already begun to whisper 'Murder'.

"For the moment nothing definite was known. Mr Bloggs had sent for Mr Statham, and the most persevering and most inquisitive persons of both sexes could glean no information from the cautious old lawyer.

"The inquest was to be held on the following day, and perforce curiosity had to be bridled until then. But you may imagine how that coroner's court at Kensington was packed on that day. I, of course, was at my usual place—well to the front, for I was already keenly interested in the tragedy, and knew that a palpitating mystery lurked behind the old lady's death.

"Annie, the housemaid at Dartmoor Terrace, was the first, and I may say the only really important, witness during the interesting inquest. The story she told amounted to this: Mrs Yule, it appears, was very religious, and, in spite of her advancing years and decided weakness of the heart, was in the habit of going to early morning service every day of her life at six o'clock. She would get up before anyone else in the house, and winter or summer, rain, snow, or fine, she would walk round to St Matthias' Church, coming home at about a quarter to seven, just when her servants were getting up.

"On this sad morning (28th March) Annie explained that she got up as usual and went downstairs (the servants slept at the top of the house) at seven o'clock. She noticed nothing wrong; her mistress's bedroom door was open as usual, Annie merely remarking to herself that the mistress was later than usual from church that morning. Then suddenly, in the hall at the foot of the stairs, she caught sight of Mrs Yule lying head downwards, her head on the mat, motionless.

"'I ran downstairs as quickly as I could,' continued Annie, 'and I suppose I must 'ave screamed, for cook came out of 'er room upstairs, and Mr Bloggs, too, shouted down to know what was the matter. At first, we only thought Mrs Yule was unconscious-like. Me and Mr Bloggs carried 'er to 'er room, and then Mr Bloggs ran for the doctor.'

"The rest of Annie's story," continued the man in the corner, "was drowned in a deluge of tears. As for the doctor, he could add but little to what the public had already known and guessed. Mrs Yule undoubtedly suffered from a weak heart, although she had never been known to faint. In this instance, however, she undoubtedly must have turned giddy, as she was about to go downstairs, and fallen headlong. She was of course very much injured, the doctor explained, but she actually died of heart failure, brought on by the shock of the fall.

"She must have been on her way to church, for her prayer-book was found on the floor close by her, also a candle—which she must have carried, as it was a dark morning—had rolled along and extinguished itself as it rolled. From these facts, therefore, it was gathered that the poor old lady came by this tragic death at about six o'clock, the hour at which she regularly started out for morning service. Both the servants and also Mr Bloggs slept at the top of the house, and it is a known fact that sleep in most cases is always heaviest in the early morning hours; there was, therefore, nothing strange in the fact that no one heard either the fall or a scream, if Mrs Yule uttered one, which is doubtful.

"So far, you see," continued the man in the corner, after a slight pause, "there did not appear to be anything very out of the way or mysterious about Mrs Yule's tragic death. But the public had expected interesting developments, and I must say their expectations were more than fully realised.

"Jane, the cook, was the first witness to give the public an inkling of the sensations to come.

"She deposed that on Thursday, the 27th, she was alone in the kitchen in the evening after dinner, as it was the housemaid's evening out, when, at about nine o'clock, there was a ring at the bell.

"'I went to answer the door,' said Jane, 'and there was a lady, all dressed in black, as far as I could see—as the 'all gas always did burn very badly—still, I think she was dressed dark, and she 'ad on a big 'at and a veil with spots. She says to me: "Mrs Yule lives 'ere?" I says, "She do, 'm," though I don't think she was quite the lady, so I don't know why I said 'm, but—'

"'Yes, yes!' here interrupted the coroner somewhat impatiently, 'it doesn't matter what you said. Tell us what happened.'

"'Yes, sir,' continued Jane, quite undisturbed, 'as I was saying, I asked the lady her name, and she says: "Tell Mrs Yule I would wish to speak with 'er," then as she saw me 'esitating, for I didn't like leaving 'er all alone in the 'all, she said, "Tell Mrs Yule that Mrs William Yule wishes to speak with 'er."'

"Jane paused to take breath, for she talked fast and volubly, and all eyes were turned to a corner of the room, where William Yule, dressed in the careless fashion affected by artists, sat watching and listening eagerly to everything that was going on. At the mention of his wife's name, he shrugged his shoulders, and I thought for the moment that he would jump up and say something; but he evidently thought better of it, and remained as before, silent and quietly watching.

"'You showed the lady upstairs?' asked the coroner, after an instant's most dramatic pause.

"'Yes, sir,' replied Jane; 'but I went to ask the mistress first. Mrs Yule was sitting in the drawing-room, reading. She says to me, "Show the lady up at once; and, Jane," she says, "ask Mr Bloggs to kindly come to the drawing-room." I showed the lady up, and I told Mr Bloggs, 'oo was smoking in the library, and 'e went to the drawing-room.

"'When Annie come in,' continued Jane with increased volubility, 'I told 'er 'oo 'ad come, and she and me was very astonished, because we 'ad often seen Mr William Yule come to see 'is mother, but we 'ad never seen 'is wife. "Did you see what she was like, cook?" says Annie to me. "No," I says, "the 'all gas was burnin' that badly, and she 'ad a veil on." Then Annie ups and says, "I must go up, cook," she says, "for my things is all wet. I never did see such rain in all my life. I tell you my boots and petticoats is all soaked through." Then up she runs, and I thought then that per'aps she meant to see if she couldn't 'ear anything that was goin' on upstairs. Presently she come down —'

"But at this point Jane's flow of eloquence received an unexpected check. The coroner preferred to hear from Annie herself whatever the latter may have overheard, and Jane, very wrathful and indignant, had to stand aside, while Annie, who was then recalled, completed the story.

"'I don't know what made me stop on the landing,' she explained timidly, 'and I'm sure I didn't mean to listen. I was going upstairs to change my things, and put on my cap and apron, in case the mistress wanted anything.

"'Then, I don't think I ever 'eard Mrs Yule's voice so loud and angry.'

"'You stopped to listen?' asked the coroner.

"'I couldn't 'elp it, sir. Mrs Yule was shouting at the top of 'er voice. "Out of my 'ouse," she says; "I never wish to see you or your precious husband inside my doors again."'

"'You are quite sure that you heard those very words?' asked the coroner earnestly.

"'I'll take my Bible oath on every one of them, sir,' said Annie emphatically. 'Then I could 'ear someone crying and moaning: "Oh! what 'ave I done? Oh! what 'ave I done?" I didn't like to stand on the landing then, for fear someone should come out, so I ran upstairs, and put on my cap and apron, for I was all in a tremble, what with what I'd 'eard, and the storm outside, which was coming down terrible.

"'When I went down again, I 'ardly durst stand on the landing, but the door of the drawing-room was ajar, and I 'eard Mr Bloggs say: "Surely you will not turn a human being, much less a woman, out on a night like this?" And the mistress said, still speaking very angry: "Very well, you may sleep here; but remember, I don't wish to see your face again. I go to church at six and come home again at seven; mind you are out of the house before then. There are plenty of trains after seven o'clock.'"

"After that," continued the man in the corner, "Mrs Yule rang for the housemaid and gave orders that the spare room should be got ready, and that the visitor should have some tea and toast brought to her in the morning as soon as Annie was up.

"But Annie was rather late on that eventful morning of the 28th. She did not go downstairs till seven o'clock. When she did, she found her mistress lying dead at the foot of the stairs. It was not until after the doctor had been and gone that both the servants suddenly recollected the guest in the spare room. Annie knocked at her door, and, receiving no answer, she walked in; the bed had not been slept in, and the spare room was empty.

"'There, now!' was the housemaid's decisive comment, 'me and cook did 'ear someone cross the 'all, and the front door bang about an hour after everyone else was in bed.'

"Presumably, therefore, Mrs William Yule had braved the elements and left the house at about midnight, leaving no trace behind her, save, perhaps, the broken lock of the desk that had held the deed of gift in favour of young Bloggs."

3

"Some say there's a Providence that watches over us," said the man in the corner, when he had looked at me keenly, and assured himself that I was really interested in his narrative, "others use the less poetic and more direct formula, that 'the devil takes care of his own'. The impression of the general public during this interesting coroner's inquest was that the devil was taking special care of his own—('his own' being in this instance represented by Mrs William Yule, who, by the way, was not present).

"What the Evil One had done for her was this: He caused the hall gas to burn so badly on that eventful Thursday night, 27th March, that Jane, the cook, had not been able to see Mrs William Yule at all distinctly. He, moreover, decreed that when Annie went into the drawing-room later on to take her mistress' orders with regard to the spare room, Mrs William was apparently dissolved in tears, for she only presented the back of her head to the inquisitive glances of the young housemaid.

"After that the two servants went to bed, and heard someone cross the hall and leave the house about an hour or so later; but neither of them could swear positively that they would recognise the mysterious visitor if they set eyes on her again.

"Throughout all these proceedings, however, you may be sure that Mr William Yule did not remain a passive spectator. In fact, I, who watched him, could see quite clearly that he had the greatest possible difficulty in controlling himself. Mind you, I knew by then exactly where the hitch lay, and I could, and will presently, tell you exactly all that occurred on Thursday evening, 27th March, at No. 9 Dartmoor Terrace, just as if I had spent that memorable night there myself; and I can assure you that it gave me great pleasure to watch the faces of the two men most interested in the verdict of this coroner's jury.

"Everyone's sympathy had by now entirely veered round to young Bloggs, who for years had been brought up to expect a fortune, and had then, at the last moment, been defrauded of it, through what looked already much like a crime. The deed of gift had, of course, not been what the lawyers call 'completed'. It had rested in Mrs Yule's desk, and had never been 'delivered' by the donor to the donee, or even to another person on his behalf.

"Young Bloggs, therefore, saw himself suddenly destined to live his life as penniless as he had been when he was still the old gardener's son.

"No doubt the public felt that what lurked mostly in his mind was a desire for revenge, and I think everyone forgave him when he gave his evidence with a distinct tone of animosity against the woman who had apparently succeeded in robbing him of a fortune.

"He had only met Mrs William Yule once before, he explained, but he was ready to swear that it was she who called that night. As for the original motive of the quarrel between the two ladies, young Bloggs was inclined to think that it was mostly on the question of money.

"'Mrs William,' continued the young man, 'made certain peremptory demands on Mrs Yule, which the old lady bitterly resented.'

"But here there was an awful and sudden interruption. William Yule, now quite beside himself with rage, had with one bound reached the witness-box, and struck young Bloggs a violent blow in the face.

"'Liar and cheat!' he roared, 'take that!'

"And he prepared to deal the young man another even more vigorous blow, when he was overpowered and seized by the constables. Young Bloggs had become positively livid; his face looked grey and ashen, except there, where his powerful assailant's fist had left a deep purple mark.

"'You have done your wife's cause no good,' remarked the coroner dryly, as William Yule, sullen and defiant, was forcibly dragged back to his place. 'I shall adjourn the inquest until Monday, and will expect Mrs Yule to be present and explain exactly what happened after her quarrel with the deceased, and why she left the house so suddenly and mysteriously that night.'

"William Yule tried an explanation even then. His wife had never left the studio in Sheriff Road, West Hampstead, the whole of that Thursday evening. It was a fearfully stormy night, and she never went outside the door. But the Yules kept no servant at the cheap little rooms; a charwoman used to come in every morning only for an hour or two, to do the rough work; there was no one, therefore, except the husband himself to prove Mrs William Yule's alibi.

"At the adjourned inquest, on the Monday, Mrs William Yule duly appeared; she was a young, delicate-looking woman, with a patient and suffering face, that had not an atom of determination or vice in it.

"Her evidence was very simple; she merely swore solemnly that she had spent the whole evening indoors, she had never been to 9 Dartmoor Terrace in her life, and, as a matter of fact, would never have dared to call on her irreconcilable mother-in-law. Neither she nor her husband were specially in want of money either.

"'My husband had just sold a picture at the Watercolour Institute,' she explained, 'we were not hard up; and certainly, I should never have attempted to make the slightest demand on Mrs Yule.'

"There the matter had to rest with regard to the theft of the document, for that was no business of the coroner's or of the jury. According to medical evidence the old lady's death had been due to a very natural and possible accident—a sudden feeling of giddiness—and the verdict had to be in accordance with this.

"There was no real proof against Mrs William Yule—only one man's word, that of young Bloggs; and it would no doubt always have been felt that his evidence might not be wholly unbiased. He was therefore well advised not to prosecute. The world was quite content to believe that the Yules had planned and executed the theft, but he never would have got a conviction against Mrs William Yule just on his own evidence."

4

"Then William Yule and his wife were left in full possession of their fortune?" I asked eagerly.

"Yes, they were," he replied; "but they had to go and travel abroad for a while, feeling was so high against them. The deed, of course, not having been 'delivered', could not be upheld in a court of law; that was the opinion of several eminent counsel whom Mr Statham, with a lofty sense of justice, consulted on behalf of young Bloggs."

"And young Bloggs was left penniless?"

"No," said the man in the corner, as, with a weird and satisfied smile, he pulled a piece of string out of his pocket; "the friends of the late Mrs Yule subscribed the sum of £1,000 for him, for they all thought he had been so terribly badly treated, and Mr Statham has taken him in his office as articled pupil. No! no! young Bloggs has not done so badly either—"

"What seems strange to me," I remarked, "is that, for all she knew, Mrs William Yule might have committed only a silly and purposeless theft. If Mrs Yule had not died suddenly and accidentally the next morning, she would, no doubt, have executed a fresh deed of gift, and all would have been *in statu quo.*"

"Exactly," he replied dryly, whilst his fingers fidgeted nervously with his bit of string.

"Of course," I suggested, for I felt that the funny creature wanted to be drawn out; "she may have reckoned on the old lady's weak heart, and the shock to her generally, but it was, after all, very problematical."

"Very," he said, "and surely you are not still under the impression that Mrs Yule's death was purely the result of an accident?"

"What else could it be?" I urged.

"The result of a slight push from the top of the stairs," he remarked placidly, whilst a complicated knot went to join a row of its fellows.

"But Mrs William Yule had left the house before midnight—or, at any rate, someone had. Do you think she had an accomplice?"

"I think," he said excitedly, "that the mysterious visitor who left the house that night had an instigator whose name was William Bloggs."

"I don't understand," I gasped in amazement.

"Point No. 1," he shrieked, while the row of knots followed each other in rapid succession. "Young Bloggs swore a lie when he swore that it was Mrs William Yule who called at Dartmoor Terrace that night."

"What makes you say that?" I retorted.

"One very simple fact," he replied, "so simple that it was, of course, overlooked. Do you remember that one of the things which Annie overheard was old Mrs Yule's irate words, 'Very well, you may sleep here; but, remember, I do not wish to see your face again. You can leave my house before I return from church; you can get plenty of trains after seven o'clock.' Now what do you make of that?" he added triumphantly.

"Nothing in particular," I rejoined; "it was an awfully wet night, and—"

"And High Street Kensington Station within two minutes' walk of Dartmoor Terrace, with plenty of trains to West Hampstead, and Sheriff Road within two minutes of this latter station," he shrieked, getting more and more excited, "and the hour only about ten o'clock, when there are plenty of trains from one part of London to another? Old Mrs Yule, with her irascible temper and obstinate ways, would have said: 'There's the station, not two minutes' walk; get out of my house, and don't ever let me see your face again.' Wouldn't she, now?"

"It certainly seems more likely."

"Of course, it does. She only allowed the woman to stay because the woman had either a very long way to go to get a train, or perhaps had missed her last train—a connection on a branch line presumably—and could not possibly get home at all that night."

"Yes, that sounds logical," I admitted.

"Point No. 2," he shrieked. "Young Bloggs having told a lie, had some object in telling it. That was my starting-point; from there I worked steadily until I had reconstructed the events of that Thursday night—nay, more, until I knew something more about young Bloggs's immediate future, in order that I might then imagine his past.

"And this is what I found.

"After the tragic death of Mrs Yule, young Bloggs went abroad at the expense of some kind friends, and came home with a wife, whom he is supposed to have met and married in Switzerland. From that point everything became clear to me. Young Bloggs had told a lie when he swore that it was Mrs William Yule who called that night—it was certainly not Mrs William Yule; therefore, it was somebody who either represented herself as such, or who believed herself to be Mrs William Yule.

"The first supposition," continued the funny creature, "I soon dismissed as impossible; young Bloggs knew Mrs William Yule by sight—and since he had lied, he had done so deliberately. Therefore, to my mind, the lady who called herself Mrs William Yule did so because she believed that she had a right to that name; that she had married a man, who, for purposes of his own, had chosen to call himself by that name. From this point to that of guessing who that man was was simple enough."

"Do you mean young Bloggs himself?" I asked in amazement.

"And whom else?" he replied. "Isn't that sort of thing done every day? Bloggs was a hideous name, and Yule was eventually to be his own. With William Yule's example before him, he must have known that it would be dangerous to broach the marriage question at all before the old lady, and probably only meant to wait for a favourable opportunity of doing so. But after a while the young wife would naturally become troubled and anxious, and, like most women under the same circumstances, would become jealous and inquisitive as well.

"She soon found out where he lived, and no doubt called there, thinking that old Mrs Yule was her husband's own fond mother.

"You can picture the rest. Mrs Yule, furious at having been deceived, herself destroys the deed of gift which she meant to present to her adopted son, and from that hour young Bloggs sees himself penniless.

"The false Mrs Yule left the house, and young Bloggs waited for his opportunity on the dark landing of a small London house. One push and the deed was done. With her weak heart, Mrs Yule was sure to die of the shock, if not of the fall.

"Before that, already the desk had been broken open and every appearance of a theft given to it. After the tragedy, then, young Bloggs retired quietly to his room. The whole thing looked so like an accident that, even had the servants heard the fall at once, there would still have been time enough for the young villain to sneak into his room, and then to reappear at his door, as if he, too, had been just awakened by the noise.

"The result turned out just as he expected. The William Yules have been and still are suspected of the theft; and young Bloggs is a hero of romance with whom everyone is in sympathy."

Who Stole the Black Diamonds?

1

"Do you know who that is?" said the man in the corner, as he pushed a small packet of photos across the table.

The picture on the top represented an entrancingly beautiful woman, with bare arms and neck, and a profusion of pearl and diamond ornaments about her head and throat.

"Surely this is the Queen of—"

"Hush!" he broke in abruptly, with mock dismay; "you must mention no names."

"Why not?" I asked, laughing, for he looked so droll in his distress.

"Look closely at the photo," he replied, "and at the necklace and tiara that the lady is wearing."

"Yes," I said. "Well?"

"Do you mean to say you don't recognise them?"

I looked at the picture more closely, and then there suddenly came back to my mind that mysterious story of the Black Diamonds, which had not only bewildered the police of Europe, but also some of its diplomats.

"Ah! I see you do recognise the jewels!" said the funny creature, after a while. "No wonder! for their design is unique, and photographs of that necklace and tiara were circulated practically throughout all the world.

"Of course, I am not going to mention names, for you know very well who the royal heroes of this mysterious adventure were. For the purposes of my narrative, suppose I call them the King and Queen of 'Bohemia'.

"The value of the stones was said to be fabulous, and it was only natural when the King of 'Bohemia' found himself somewhat in want of money—a want which has made itself felt before now with even the most powerful European monarchs—that he should decide to sell the precious trinkets, worth a small kingdom in themselves. In order to be in closer touch with the most likely customers, Their Majesties of 'Bohemia' came over to England during the season of 1902—a season memorable alike for its deep sorrow and its great joy.

"After the sad postponement of the Coronation festivities, they rented Eton Chase, a beautiful mansion just outside Chislehurst, for the summer months. There they entertained right royally, for the queen was very gracious and the king a real sportsman—there also the rumour first got about that His Majesty had decided to sell the world-famous *parure* of Black Diamonds.

"Needless to say, they were not long in the market: quite a host of American millionaires had already coveted them for their wives, and brisk and sensational offers were made to His Majesty's business man both by letter and telegram.

"At last, however, Mr Wilson, the multimillionaire, was understood to have made an offer, for the necklace and tiara, of £500,000, which had been accepted.

"But a very few days later, that is to say, on the Sunday and Monday, 6th and 7th July, there appeared in the papers the short, but deeply sensational announcement that a burglary had occurred at Eton Chase, Chislehurst, the mansion inhabited by Their Majesties the King and Queen of 'Bohemia', and that among the objects stolen was the famous *parure* of Black Diamonds, for which a bid of half a million sterling had just been made and accepted.

"The burglary had been one of the most daring and most mysterious ones ever brought under the notice of the police authorities. The mansion was full of guests at the time, among whom were many diplomatic notabilities, and also Mr and Mrs Wilson, the future owners of the gems; there was also a very large staff of servants. The burglary must have occurred between the hours of 10 and 11.30 p.m., though the precise moment could not be ascertained.

"The house itself stands in the midst of a large garden, and has deep French windows opening out upon a terrace at the back. There are ornamental iron balconies to the windows of the upper floors, and it was to one of these, situated immediately above the dining-room, that a rope ladder was found to be attached.

"The burglar must have chosen a moment when the guests were dispersed in the smoking-, billiard-, and drawing-rooms; the servants were having their own meal, and the dining-room was deserted. He must have slung his rope ladder, and entered Her Majesty's own bedroom by the window which—as the night was very warm—had been left open. The jewels were locked up in a small iron box, which stood upon the dressing-table, and the burglar took the box bodily away with him, and then, no doubt, returned the way he came.

"The wonderful point in this daring attempt was the fact that most of the windows on the ground floor were slightly open that night, that the rooms themselves were filled with guests, and that the dining-room was not empty for more than a few minutes at a time, as the servants were still busy clearing away after dinner.

"At nine o'clock some of the younger guests had strolled out on to the terrace, and the last of these returned to the drawing-room at ten o'clock; at half past eleven one of the servants caught sight of the rope ladder in front of one of the dining-room windows, and the alarm was given.

"All traces of the burglar, however, and of his princely booty had completely disappeared."

2

"Not only did this daring burglary cause a great deal of excitement," continued the man in the corner, "but it also roused a good deal of sympathy in the public mind for the King and Queen of 'Bohemia', who thus found their hope of raising half a million sterling suddenly dashed to the ground. The loss to them would, of course, be irreparable.

"Matters were, however, practically at a standstill, all enquiries from enterprising journalists only eliciting the vague information that the police 'held a clue'. We all know what that means. Then all at once a wonderful rumour got about.

"Goodness only knows how these rumours originate—sometimes solely in the imagination of the man in the street. In this instance, certainly, that worthy gentleman had a very sensational theory. It was, namely, rumoured all over London that the clue which the police held pointed to no less a person than Mr Wilson himself.

"What had happened was this: minute enquiries on the part of the most able detectives of Scotland Yard had brought to light the fact that the burglary at Eton Chase must have occurred precisely between ten minutes and a quarter past eleven; at every other moment of the entire evening somebody or other had observed either the terrace or the dining-room windows.

"I told you that until ten o'clock some of Their Majesties' guests were walking up and down the terrace; between ten and half past servants were clearing away in the dining-room, and here it was positively ascertained beyond any doubt that no burglar could have slung a rope ladder and climbed up it immediately outside those windows, for one or other of the six servants engaged in clearing away the dinner must of necessity have caught sight of him.

At half past ten John Lucas, the head gardener, was walking through the gardens with a dog at his heels, and did not get back to the lodge until just upon eleven. He certainly did not go as far as the terrace, and as that side of the house was in shadow, he could not say positively whether the ladder was there or not, but he certainly did assert most emphatically that there was no burglar about the *grounds* then, for the dog was a good watchdog and would have barked if any stranger was about. Lucas took the dog in with him and gave him a bit of supper, and only fastened him to his kennel outside at a quarter past eleven.

"Surmising, therefore, that at half past ten, when John Lucas started on his round, the deed was not yet done, that quarter of an hour would give the burglar the only possible opportunity of entering the premises *from the outside,* without being barked at by the dog. Now, during most of that same quarter of an hour, His Majesty the King of 'Bohemia' himself had retired into a small library with his private secretary, in order to glance through certain despatches which had arrived earlier in the evening.

"The window of this library was immediately next to the one outside which the ladder was found, and both the secretary and His Majesty himself think that they would have seen something or heard a noise if the rope ladder had been slung while they were in the room. They both, however, returned to the drawing-room at ten minutes past eleven.

"And here," continued the man in the corner, rubbing his long, bony fingers together, "arose the neatest little complication I have ever come across in a case of this kind. His Majesty had, it appears, privately made up his mind to accept Mr Wilson's bid, but the transaction had not yet been completed. Mr Wilson and his wife came down to stay at Eton Chase on 29th June, and directly they arrived many of those present noticed that Mr Wilson was obviously repenting of his bargain. This impression had deepened day by day, Mrs Wilson herself often throwing out covert hints about 'fictitious value' and 'fancy prices for merely notorious trinkets'. In fact, it became very obvious that the Wilsons were really seeking a loophole for evading the conclusion of the bargain.

"On the memorable evening of 5th July Mrs Wilson had been forced to retire to her room early in the evening, owing, she said, to a bad headache; her room was in the west wing of the Chase, and opened out on the same corridor as the apartments of Her Majesty the Queen. At half past eleven Mrs Wilson rang for her maid—Mary Pritchard, who, on entering her mistress' room, met Mr Wilson just coming out of it, and the girl heard him say: 'Oh, don't worry! I'll have the whole reset when we get back.'

"The detectives, on the other hand, had obtained information that two or three days previously Mr Wilson had sustained a very severe loss on the 'Change, and that he had subsequently remarked to two or three business friends that the Black Diamonds had become a luxury which he had no right to afford.

"Be this as it may, certain it is that within a week of the notorious burglary the rumour was current in every club in London that James S. Wilson, the reputed American millionaire, having found himself unable to complete the purchase of the Black Diamonds, had found this other very much less legitimate means of gaining possession of the gems.

"You must admit that the case looked black enough against him— all circumstantial, of course, for there was absolutely nothing to prove that he had the jewels in his possession; in fact, no trace of them whatever had been found, but the public argued that Mr Wilson would lie low with them for a while, and then have them reset when he returned to America.

"Of course, ugly rumours of that description don't become general about a man without his getting some inkling of them. Mr Wilson very soon found his position in London absolutely intolerable: his friends ignored him at the club, ladies ceased to call upon his wife, and one fine day he was openly cut by Lord Barnsdale, an M.F.H., in the hunting field.

"Then Mr Wilson thought it high time to take action. He placed the whole matter in the hands of an able, if not very scrupulous, solicitor, who promised within a given time to find him a defendant with plenty of means, against whom he could bring a sensational libel suit, with thundering damages.

"The solicitor was as good as his word. He bribed some of the waiters at the Carlton, and so laid his snares that within six months, Lord and Lady Barnsdale had been overheard to say in public what everybody now thought in private, namely, that Mr James S. Wilson, finding himself unable to purchase the celebrated Black Diamonds, had thought it more profitable to steal them.

"Two days later Mr James S. Wilson entered an action in the High Courts for slander against Lord and Lady Barnsdale, claiming damages to the tune of £50,000."

3

"Still the mystery of the lost jewels was no nearer to its solution. Their Majesties the King and Queen of 'Bohemia' had left England soon after the disastrous event which deprived them of what amounted to a small fortune.

"It was expected that the sensational slander case would come on in the autumn, or rather more than sixteen months after the mysterious disappearance of the Black Diamonds.

"This last season was not a very brilliant one, if you remember; the wet weather, I believe, had quite a good deal to do with the fact; nevertheless London, that great world centre, was, as usual, full of distinguished visitors, among whom Mrs Vanderdellen, who arrived the second week in July, was perhaps the most interesting.

"Her enormous wealth spread a positive halo round her, it being generally asserted that she was the richest woman in the world. Add to this that she was young, strikingly handsome, and a widow, and you will easily understand what a *furore* her appearance during this London season caused in all high social circles.

"Though she was still in slight mourning for her husband, she was asked everywhere, went everywhere, and was courted and admired by everybody, including some of the highest in the land; her dresses and jewellery were the talk of the ladies' papers, her style and charm the gossip of all the clubs. And no doubt that, although the July evening Court promised to be very brilliant, everyone thought that it would be doubly so, since Mrs Vanderdellen had been honoured with an invitation, and would presumably be present.

"I like to picture to myself that scene at Buckingham Palace," continued the man in the corner, as his fingers toyed lovingly with a beautiful and brand-new bit of string. "Of course, I was not present actually, but I can see it all before me: the lights, the crowds, the pretty women, the glistening diamonds; then, in the midst of the chatter, a sudden silence fell as 'Mrs Vanderdellen' was announced.

"All women turned to look at the beautiful American as she entered, because her dress—on this her first appearance at the English Court—was sure to be a vision of style and beauty. But for once nobody noticed the dress from Felix, nobody even gave a glance at the exquisitely lovely face of the wearer. Everyone's eyes had fastened on one thing only, and everyone's lips framed but one exclamation, and that an 'Oh!' half of amazement and half of awe.

"For round her neck and upon her head Mrs Vanderdellen was wearing a gorgeously magnificent *parure* composed of black diamonds."

4

"I don't know how the case of *Wilson* v. *Barnsdale* was settled, for it never came into court. There were many people in London who owed the Wilsons an apology, and it is to be hoped that these were tendered in full.

"As for Mrs Vanderdellen, she seemed quite unaware why her appearance at Their Majesties' Court had caused quite so much sensation. No one, of course, broached the subject of the diamonds to her, and she no doubt attributed those significant 'Oh's' to her own dazzling beauty.

"The next day, however, Detective Marsh, of Scotland Yard, had a very difficult task before him. He had to go and ask a beautiful, rich, and refined woman how she happened to be in possession of stolen jewellery.

"Luckily for Marsh, however, he had to deal with a woman who was also charming, and who met his polite enquiry with an equally pleasant reply:

"'My husband gave me the Black Diamonds,' she said, 'a year ago, on his return from Europe. I had them set in Vienna last spring, and wore them for the first time last night. Will you please tell me the reason of this strange enquiry?'

"'Your husband?' echoed Marsh, ignoring her question, 'Mr Vanderdellen?'

"'Oh yes,' she replied sweetly, 'I dare say you have never heard of him. His name is very well known in America, where they call him the "Petrol King". One of his hobbies was the collection of gems, which he was very fond of seeing me wear, and he gave me some magnificent jewels. The Black Diamonds certainly are very handsome. May I now request you to tell me,' she repeated, with a certain assumption of hauteur, 'the reason of all these enquiries?'

"'The reason is simple enough, madam,' replied the detective abruptly. 'Those diamonds were the property of Her Majesty the Queen of "Bohemia", and were stolen from Their Majesties' residence, Eton Chase, Chislehurst, on the 5th of July last year.'

"'Stolen!' she repeated, aghast and obviously incredulous.

"'Yes, stolen,' said old Marsh. 'I don't wish to distress you unnecessarily, madam, but you will see how imperative it is that you should place me in immediate communication with Mr Vanderdellen, as an explanation from him has become necessary.'

"'Unfortunately, that is impossible,' said Mrs Vanderdellen, who seemed under the spell of a strong emotion.

"'Impossible?'

"'Mr Vanderdellen has been dead just over a year. He died three days after his return to New York, and the Black Diamonds were the last present he ever made me.'

"There was a pause after that. Marsh—experienced detective though he was—was literally at his wits' ends what to do. He said afterwards that Mrs Vanderdellen, though very young and frivolous outwardly, seemed at the same time an exceedingly shrewd, far-seeing businesswoman. To begin with, she absolutely refused to have the matter hushed up, and to return the jewels until their rightful ownership had been properly proved.

"'It would be tantamount,' she said, 'to admitting that my husband had come by them unlawfully.'

"At the same time, she offered the princely reward of £10,000 to anyone who found the true solution of the mystery: for, mind you, the late Mr Vanderdellen sailed from Havre for New York on July the 8th, 1902, that is to say, three clear days after the theft of the diamonds from Eton Chase, and he presented his wife with the loose gems immediately on his arrival in New York. Three days after that he died.

"It was difficult to suppose that Mr Vanderdellen purchased those diamonds not knowing that they must have been stolen, since directly after the burglary the English police telegraphed to all their Continental colleagues, and within four-and-twenty hours a description of the stolen jewels was circulated throughout Europe.

"It was, to say the least of it, very strange that an experienced businessman and shrewd collector like Mr Vanderdellen should have purchased such priceless gems without making some enquiries as to their history, more especially as they must have been offered to him in a more or less 'hole-in-the-corner' way.

"Still, Mrs Vanderdellen stuck to her guns, and refused to give up the jewels pending certain enquiries she wished to make. She declared that she wished to be sued for the diamonds in open court, charged with wilfully detaining stolen goods if necessary, for the more publicity was given to the whole affair the better she would like it, so firmly did she believe in her husband's innocence.

"The matter was indeed brought to the High Courts, and the sensational action brought against Mrs Vanderdellen by the representative of His Majesty the King of 'Bohemia' for the recovery of the Black Diamonds is, no doubt, still fresh in your memory.

"No one was allowed to know what witnesses Mrs Vanderdellen would bring forward in her defence. She had engaged the services of Sir Arthur Inglewood, and of some of the most eminent counsel at the Bar. The court was packed with the most fashionable crowd ever seen inside the Law Courts; and both days that the action lasted Mrs Vanderdellen appeared in exquisite gowns and ideal hats.

"The evidence for the Royal plaintiff was simple enough. It all went to prove that the very day after the burglary not a jeweller, pawnbroker, or diamond merchant throughout the whole of Europe could have failed to know that a unique *parure* of black diamonds had been stolen, and would probably be offered for sale. The Black Diamonds in themselves, and out of their setting, were absolutely unique, and if the late Mr Vanderdellen purchased them in Paris from some private individual, he must at least have very strongly suspected that they were stolen.

"Throughout the whole of that first day Mrs Vanderdellen sat in court, absolutely calm and placid. She listened to the evidence, made little notes, and chatted with two or three American friends—elderly men—who were with her.

"Then came the turn of the defence.

"Everybody had expected something sensational, and listened more eagerly than ever as the name of Mr Albert V. B. Sedley was called. He was a tall, elderly man, the regular angular type of the American, with his nasal twang and reposeful manner.

"His story was brief and simple. He was a great friend of the late Mr Vanderdellen, and had gone on a European tour with him in the early spring of 1902. They were together in Vienna in the month of March, staying at the Hotel Imperial, when one day Vanderdellen came to his room with a remarkable story.

"'He told me,' continued Mr Albert V. B. Sedley, 'that he had just purchased some very beautiful diamonds, which he meant to present to his wife on his return to New York. He would not tell me where he bought them, nor would he show them to me, but he spoke about the beauty and rarity of the stones, which were that rarest of all things, beautiful black diamonds.

"'As the whole story sounded to me a little bit queer and mysterious, I gave him a word of caution, but he was quite confident as to the integrity of the vendor of the jewels, since the latter had made a somewhat curious bargain. Vanderdellen was to have the diamonds in his keeping for three months without paying any money, merely giving a formal receipt for them; then, if after three months he was quite satisfied with his bargain, and there had been no suspicion or rumour of any kind that the diamonds were stolen, then only was the money, £500,000, to be paid.

"'Vanderdellen thought this very fair and above-board, and so it sounded to me. The only thing I didn't like about it all was that the vendor had given what I thought was a false name and no address; the money was to be paid over to him in French notes when the three months had expired, at an hotel in Paris where Vanderdellen would be staying at the time, and where he would call for it.

"'I heard nothing more about the mysterious diamonds and their still more mysterious vendor,' continued Mr Sedley, amidst intense excitement, 'for Vanderdellen and I soon parted company after that, he going one way and I another. But at the beginning of July, I met him in Paris, and on the 4th, I dined with him at the Élysée Palace Hotel, where he was staying.

"'Mr Cornelius R. Shee was there too, and Vanderdellen related to him during dinner the history of his mysterious purchase of the Black Diamonds, adding that the vendor had called upon him that very day as arranged, and that he (Vanderdellen) had had no hesitation in handing him over the agreed price of £500,000, which he thought a very low one. Both Mr Shee and I agreed that the whole thing must have been clear and above-board, for jewels of such fabulous value could not have been stolen since last spring without the hue and cry being in every paper in Europe.

"'It is my opinion, therefore,' said Mr Albert V. B. Sedley, at the conclusion of this remarkable evidence, 'that Mr Vanderdellen bought those diamonds in perfect good faith. He would never have wittingly subjected his wife to the indignity of being seen in public with stolen jewels round her neck. If after 5th July he did happen to hear that a *pa-*

rure of black diamonds had been stolen in England at the date, he could not possibly think that there could be the slightest connection between these and those he had purchased more than three months ago.'

"And, amidst indescribable excitement, Mr Albert V. B. Sedley stepped back into his place.

"That he had spoken the truth from beginning to end no one could doubt for a single moment. His own social position, wealth, and important commercial reputation placed him above any suspicion of committing perjury, even for the sake of a dead friend. Moreover, the story told by Vanderdellen at the dinner in Paris was corroborated by Mr Cornelius R. Shee in every point.

"But there! a dead man's words are *not* evidence in a court of law. Unfortunately, Mr Vanderdellen had not shown the diamonds to his friends at the time. He had certainly drawn enormous sums of money from his bank about the end of June and beginning of July, amounting in all to just over a million sterling; and there was nothing to prove which special day he had paid away a sum of £500,000, whether *before* or *after* the burglary at Eton Chase.

"He had made extensive purchases in Paris of pictures, furniture, and other works of art, all of priceless value, for the decoration of his new palace in Fifth Avenue, and no diary of private expenditure was produced in court. Mrs Vanderdellen herself had said that after her husband's death, as all his affairs were in perfect order, she had destroyed his personal and private diaries.

"Thus, the counsel for the plaintiff was able to demolish the whole edifice of the defence bit by bit, for it rested on but very ephemeral foundations: a story related by a dead man.

"Judgment was entered for the plaintiff, although everyone's sympathy, including that of judge and of jury, was entirely for the defendant, who had so nobly determined to vindicate her husband's reputation.

"But Mrs Vanderdellen proved to the last that she was no ordinary everyday woman. She had kept one final sensation up her sleeve. Two days after she had legally been made to give up the Black Diamonds, she offered to purchase them back for £500,000. Her bid was accepted, and during last autumn, on the occasion of the last Royal visit to London and the consequent grand society functions, no one was more admired, more *fêted* and envied, than beautiful Mrs Vanderdellen as she entered a drawing-room exquisitely gowned, and adorned with the *parure*, of which an empress might have been proud."

The man in the corner had paused, and was idly tapping his fingers on the marble-topped table of the A.B.C. shop.

"It was a curious story, wasn't it?" said the funny creature after a while. "More like a romance than a reality."

"It is absolutely bewildering," I said.

"What is your theory?" he asked.

"What about?" I retorted.

"Well, there are so many points, aren't there, of which only one is quite clear, namely, that the *parure* of Black Diamonds disappeared from Eton Chase, Chislehurst, on 5th July 1902, and that the next time they were seen they were on the neck and head of Mrs Vanderdellen, the widow of one of the richest men of modern times, whilst the story of how her husband came by them was, to all intents and purposes, *legally* disbelieved."

"Then," I argued, "the only logical conclusion to arrive at in all this is that the Black Diamonds, owned by His Majesty the King of 'Bohemia', were not unique, and that Mr Vanderdellen bought some duplicate ones."

"If you knew anything about diamonds," he said irritably, "you would also know that your statement is an absurdity. There are no such things as 'duplicate' diamonds."

"Then what *is* the only logical conclusion to arrive at?" I retorted, for he had given up playing with the photos and was twisting and twining that bit of string as if his brain was contained inside it and he feared it might escape.

"Well, to me," he said, "the only logical conclusion of the affair is that the Black Diamonds which Mrs Vanderdellen wore were the only and original ones belonging to the Crown of 'Bohemia'."

"Then you think that a man in Mr Vanderdellen's position would have been fool enough to buy gems worth £500,000 at the very moment when there was a hue and cry for them all over Europe?"

"No, I don't," he replied quietly.

"But then—" I began.

"No?" he repeated once again, as his long fingers completed knot number one in that eternal piece of string. "The Black Diamonds which Mrs Vanderdellen wore were bought by her husband in all good faith from the mysterious vendor in Vienna in March 1902."

"Impossible!" I retorted. "Her Majesty the Queen of 'Bohemia' wore them regularly during the months of May and June, and they were stolen from Eton Chase on July the 5th."

"Her Majesty the Queen of 'Bohemia' wore a *parure* of Black Diamonds during those months, and those certainly were stolen on July the 5th," he said excitedly; "but what was there to prove that *those* were the genuine stones?"

"Why!—" I ejaculated.

"Point No. 2," he said, jumping about like a monkey on a stick; "although Mr Wilson was acknowledged to be innocent of the theft of the diamonds, isn't it strange that no one has ever been proved guilty of it?"

"But I don't understand—"

"Yet it is simple as daylight. I maintain that His Majesty the King of 'Bohemia' being short, very short, of money, decided to sell the celebrated Black Diamonds; to avoid all risks the stones were taken out of their settings, and a trusted and secret emissary is then deputed to find a possible purchaser; his choice falls on the multimillionaire Vanderdellen, who is travelling in Europe, is a noted collector of rare jewellery, and has a beautiful young wife—three attributes, you see, which make him a very likely purchaser.

"The emissary then seeks him out, and offers him the diamonds for sale. Mr Vanderdellen at first hesitates, wondering how such valuable gems had come in the vendor's possession, but the bargain suggested by the latter—the three months during which the gems are to be held on trust by the purchaser—seems so fair and above-board, that Mr Vanderdellen's objections fall to the ground; he accepts the bargain, and three months later completes the purchase."

"But I don't understand," I repeated again, more bewildered than before. "You say the King of 'Bohemia' sold the loose gems originally to Mr Vanderdellen; then, what about the *parure* worn by the queen and offered for sale to Mr and Mrs Wilson? What about the theft at Eton Chase?"

"Point No. 3," he shrieked excitedly, as another series of complicated knots went to join its fellows. "I told you that the King of 'Bohemia' was *very* short of money, everyone knows *that*. He sells the Black Diamonds to Mr Vanderdellen, but before he does it, he causes duplicates of them to be made, but this time in exquisite, beautiful, perfect Parisian imitation, and has these mounted into the original settings by some trusted man who, you may be sure, was well paid to hold his tongue. Then it is given out that the *parure* is for sale; a purchaser is found, and a few days later the false diamonds are stolen."

"By whom?"

"By the King of 'Bohemia's' valued and trusted friend, who has helped in the little piece of villainy throughout; it is he who drops a rope ladder through Her Majesty's bedroom window on to the terrace below, and then hands the imitation *parure* to his Royal master, who sees to its complete destruction and disappearance. Then there is a hue and cry for the *real* stones, and after a year or so they are found on the person of a lady, who is legally forced to give them up. And thus, His Majesty the King of 'Bohemia' got one solid million for the Black Diamonds, instead of half that sum, for if Mrs Vanderdellen had not purchased the jewels, someone else would have done so."

And he was gone, leaving me to gaze at the pictures of three lovely women, and wondering if indeed it was the Royal lady herself who could best solve the mystery of who stole the Black Diamonds.

The Murder of Miss Pebmarsh

1

"You must admit," said the man in the corner to me one day, as I folded up and put aside my *Daily Telegraph,* which I had been reading with great care, "that it would be difficult to find a more interesting plot, or more thrilling situations, than occurred during the case of Miss Pamela Pebmarsh. As for downright cold-blooded villainy, commend me to some of the actors in that real drama.

"The facts were simple enough: Miss Lucy Ann Pebmarsh was an old maid who lived with her young niece Pamela and an elderly servant in one of the small, newly built houses not far from the railway station at Boreham Wood. The fact that she kept a servant at all, and that the little house always looked very spick and span, was taken by the neighbours to mean that Miss Pebmarsh was a lady of means; but she kept very much to herself, seldom went to church, and never attended any of the mothers' meetings, parochial teas, and other social gatherings for which that popular neighbourhood has long been famous.

"Very little, therefore, was known of the Pebmarsh household, save that the old lady had seen better days, that she had taken her niece to live with her recently, and that the latter had had a somewhat chequered career before she had found her present haven of refuge; some more venturesome gossips went so far as to hint—but only just above a whisper—that Miss Pamela Pebmarsh had been on the stage.

"Certain it is that that young lady seemed to chafe very much under the restraint imposed upon her by her aunt, who seldom allowed her out of her sight, and evidently kept her very short of money, for, in spite of Miss Pamela's obvious love of fine clothes, she had latterly been constrained to wear the plainest of frocks and most unbecoming of hats.

"All very commonplace and uninteresting, you see, until that memorable Wednesday in October, after which the little house in Boreham Wood became a nine-days' wonder throughout newspaper-reading England.

"On that day Miss Pebmarsh's servant, Jemima Gadd, went over to Luton to see a sick sister; she was not expected back until the next morning. On that same afternoon Miss Pamela—strangely enough—seems also to have elected to go up to town, leaving her aunt all alone in the house and not returning home until the late train, which reaches Boreham Wood a few minutes before one.

"It was about five minutes past one that the neighbours in the quiet little street were roused from their slumbers by most frantic and agonized shrieks. The next moment Miss Pamela was seen to rush out of her aunt's house and then to hammer violently at the door of one of her neighbours, still uttering piercing shrieks. You may imagine what a commotion such a scene at midnight would cause in a place like Boreham Wood. Heads were thrust out of the windows; one or two neighbours in hastily donned miscellaneous attire came running out; and very soon the news spread round like wildfire that Miss Pamela on coming home had found her aunt lying dead in the sitting-room.

"Mr Miller, the local greengrocer, was the first to pluck up sufficient courage to effect an entrance into the house. Miss Pamela dared not follow him; she had become quite hysterical, and was shrieking at the top of her voice that her aunt had been murdered. The sight that greeted Mr Miller and those who had been venturesome enough to follow him, was certainly calculated to unhinge any young girl's mind.

"In the small bow-window of the sitting-room stood a writing-table, with drawers open and papers scattered all over and around it; in a chair in front of it, half-sitting and half-lying across the table, face downwards, and with arms outstretched, was the dead body of Miss Pebmarsh. There was sufficient indications to show to the most casual observer that, undoubtedly, the unfortunate lady had been murdered.

"One of the neighbours, who possessed a bicycle, had in the meantime had the good sense to ride over to the police station. Very soon two constables were on the spot; they quickly cleared the room of gossiping neighbours, and then endeavoured to obtain from Miss Pamela some lucid information as to the terrible event.

"At first, she seemed quite unable to answer coherently the many questions which were being put to her; however, with infinite patience and wonderful kindness, Sergeant Evans at last managed to obtain from her the following statement:

"'I had had an invitation to go to the theatre this evening; it was an old invitation, and my aunt had said long ago that I might accept it. When Jemima Gadd wanted to go to Luton, I didn't see why I should give up the theatre and offend my friend, just because of her. My aunt and I had some words about it, but I went . . . .I came back by the last train, and walked straight home from the station. I had taken the latchkey with me, and went straight into the sitting-room; the lamp was alight, and—and—'

"The rest was chaos in the poor girl's mind; she was only conscious of having seen something awful and terrible, and of having rushed out screaming for help. Sergeant Evans asked her no further questions then; a kind neighbour had offered to take charge of Pamela for the night, and took her away with her, the constable remaining in charge of the body and the house until the arrival of higher authorities."

2

"Although, as you may well suppose," continued the man in the corner, after a pause, "the excitement was intense at Boreham Wood, it had not as yet reached the general newspaper-reading public. As the tragic event had occurred at one o'clock in the morning, the papers the following day only contained a brief announcement that an old lady had been found murdered at Boreham Wood under somewhat mysterious circumstances. Later on, the evening editions added that the police were extremely reticent, but that it was generally understood that they held an important clue.

"The following day had been fixed for the inquest, and I went down myself in the morning, for somehow I felt that this case was going to be an interesting one. A murder which at first seems absolutely purposeless always, in my experience, reveals, sooner or later, an interesting trait in human nature.

"As soon as I arrived at Boreham Wood, I found that the murder of Miss Pebmarsh and the forthcoming inquest seemed to be the sole subjects of gossip and conversation. After I had been in the place half an hour the news began to spread like wildfire that the murderer had been arrested. Five minutes later the name of the murderer was on everybody's lips.

"It was that of the murdered woman's niece, Miss Pamela Pebmarsh.

"'Oh, oh!' I said to myself, 'my instincts have not deceived me: this case is indeed going to be interesting.'

"It was about two o'clock in the afternoon when I at last managed to find my way to the little police station, where the inquest was to be held. There was scarcely standing room, I can tell you, and I had some difficulty in getting a front place from which I could see the principal actors in this village drama.

"Pamela Pebmarsh was there in the custody of two constables— she, a young girl scarcely five-and-twenty, stood there accused of having murdered, in a peculiarly brutal way, an old lady of seventy, her relative who had befriended her and given her a home."

The man in the corner paused for a moment, and from the capacious pocket of his magnificent ulster he drew two or three small photos, which he placed before me.

"This is Miss Pamela Pebmarsh," he said, pointing to one of these; "tall and good-looking, in spite of the shabby bit of mourning with which she had contrived to deck herself. Of course, this photo does not give you an idea of what she looked like that day at the inquest. Her face then was almost ashen in colour; her large eyes were staring before her with a look of horror and of fear; and her hands were twitching incessantly, with spasmodic and painful nervousness.

"It was pretty clear that public feeling went dead against her from the very first. A murmur of disapproval greeted her appearance, to which she seemed to reply with a look of defiance. I could hear many uncharitable remarks spoken all round me; Boreham Wood found it evidently hard to forgive Miss Pamela her good looks and her unavowed past.

"The medical evidence was brief and simple. Miss Pebmarsh had been stabbed in the back with some sharp instrument, the blade of which had pierced the left lung. She had evidently been sitting in the chair in front of her writing-table when the murderer had caught her unawares. Death had ensued within the next few seconds.

"The medical officer was very closely questioned upon this point by the coroner; it was evident that the latter had something very serious in his mind, to which the doctor's replies would give confirmation.

"'In your opinion,' he asked, 'would it have been possible for Miss Pebmarsh to do anything after she was stabbed? Could she have moved, for instance?'

"'Slightly, perhaps,' replied the doctor; 'but she did not attempt to rise from her chair.'

"'No; but could she have tried to reach the handbell, for instance, which was on the table, or—the pen and ink—and written a word or two?'

"'Well, yes,' said the doctor thoughtfully; 'she might have done that, if pen and ink, or the handbell, were *very* close to her hand. I doubt, though, if she could have written anything very clearly, but still it is impossible to say quite definitely—anyhow, it could only have been a matter of a few seconds.'

"Delightfully vague, you see," continued the man in the corner, "as these learned gentlemen's evidence usually is.

"Sergeant Evans then repeated the story which Pamela Pebmarsh had originally told him, and from which she had never departed in any detail. She had gone to the theatre, leaving her aunt all alone in the house; she had arrived home at one o'clock by the late Wednesday-night train, and had gone straight into the sitting-room, where she had found her aunt dead before her writing-table.

"That she travelled up to London in the afternoon was easily proved; the station-master and the porters had seen her go. Unfortunately for her alibi, however, those late 'theatre' trains on that line are always very crowded; the night had been dark and foggy, and no one at or near the station could swear positively to having seen her arrive home again by the train she named.

"There was one thing more; although the importance of it had been firmly impressed upon Pamela Pebmarsh, she absolutely refused to name the friends with whom she had been to the theatre that night, and who, presumably, might have helped her to prove at what hour she left London for home.

"Whilst all this was going on, I was watching Pamela's face intently. That the girl was frightened—nay more, terrified—there could be no doubt; the twitching of her hands, her eyes dilated with terror, spoke of some awful secret which she dare not reveal, but which she felt was being gradually brought to light. Was that secret the secret of a crime—a crime so horrible, so gruesome, that surely so young a girl would be incapable of committing?

"So far, however, what struck everyone mostly during this inquest was the seeming purposelessness of this cruel murder. The old lady, as far as could be ascertained, had no money to leave, so why should Pamela Pebmarsh have deliberately murdered the aunt who provided her, at any rate, with the comforts of a home? But the police, assisted by one of the most able detectives on the staff, had not effected so sensational an arrest without due cause; they had a formidable array of witnesses to prove their case up to the hilt. One of these was Jemima Gadd, the late Miss Pebmarsh's servant.

"She came forward attired in deep black, and wearing a monumental crape bonnet crowned with a quantity of glistening black beads. With her face the colour of yellow wax, and her thin lips pinched tightly together, she stood as the very personification of Puritanism and uncharitableness.

"She did not look once towards Pamela, who gazed at her like some wretched bird caught in a net, which sees the meshes tightening round it more and more.

"Replying to the coroner, Jemima Gadd explained that on the Wednesday morning she had had a letter from her sister at Luton, asking her to come over and see her someday.

"'As there was plenty of cold meat in the 'ouse,' she said, 'I asked the mistress if she could spare me until the next day, and she said yes, she could. Miss Pamela and she could manage quite well.'

"'She said nothing about her niece going out, too, on the same day?' asked the coroner.

"'No,' replied Jemima acidly, 'she did not. And later on, at breakfast, Miss Pebmarsh said to Miss Pamela before me: "Pamela," she says, "Jemima is going to Luton, and won't be back until tomorrow. You and I will be alone, in the 'ouse until then."'

"'And what did the accused say?'

"'She says, "All right, Aunt."'

"'Nothing more?'

"'No, nothing more.'

"'There was no question, then, of the accused going out also, and leaving Miss Pebmarsh all alone in the house?'

"'None at all,' said Jemima emphatically. 'If there 'ad been I'd 'ave 'eard of it. I needn't 'ave gone that day. Any day would 'ave done for me.'

"She closed her thin lips with a snap, and darted a vicious look at Pamela. There was obviously some old animosity lurking beneath that gigantic crape monument on the top of Jemima's wax-coloured head.

"'You know nothing, then, about any disagreement between the deceased and the accused on the subject of her going to the theatre that day?' asked the coroner, after a while.

"'No, not about *that*,' said Jemima curtly, 'but there was plenty of disagreements between those two, I can tell you.'

"'Ah? what about?'

"'Money, mostly. Miss Pamela was over-fond of fine clothes, but Miss Pebmarsh, who was giving 'er a 'ome and 'er daily bread, 'adn't much money to spare for fallalery. Miss Pebmarsh 'ad a small pension from a lady of the haristocracy, but it wasn't much—a pound a week it was. Miss Pebmarsh might 'ave 'ad a lot more if she'd wanted to.'

"'Oh?' queried the coroner, 'how was that?'

"'Well, you see, that fine lady 'ad not always been as good as she ought to be. She'd been Miss Pamela's friend when they were both on the stage together, and pretty goings on, I can tell you, those two were up to, and —'

"'That'll do,' interrupted the coroner sternly. 'Confine yourself, please, to telling the jury about the pension Miss Pebmarsh had from a lady.'

"'I was speaking about that,' said Jemima, with another snap of her thin lips. 'Miss Pebmarsh knew a thing or two about this fine lady, and she 'ad some letters which she often told me that fine lady would not care for 'er 'usband or 'er fine friends to read. Miss Pamela got to know about these letters, and she worried 'er poor aunt to death, for she wanted to get those letters and sell them to the fine lady for 'undreds of pounds. I 'ave 'eard 'er ask for those letters times and again, but Miss Pebmarsh wouldn't give them to 'er, and they was locked up in the writing-table drawer, and Miss Pamela wanted those letters, for she wanted to get 'undreds of pounds from the fine lady, and my poor mistress was murdered for those letters—and she was murdered by that wicked girl 'oo eat 'er bread and 'oo would 'ave starved but for 'er. And so, I tell you, and I don't care 'oo 'ears me say it."

"No one had attempted to interrupt Jemima Gadd as she delivered herself of this extraordinary tale, which so suddenly threw an unexpected and lurid light upon the mystery of poor Miss Pebmarsh's death.

"That the tale was a true one, no one doubted for a single instant. One look at the face of the accused was sufficient to prove it beyond question. Pamela Pebmarsh had become absolutely livid; she tottered almost as if she would fall, and the constable had to support her until a chair was brought forward for her.

"As for Jemima Gadd, she remained absolutely impassive. Having given her evidence, she stepped aside automatically like a yellow waxen image, which had been wound up and had now run down. There was silence for a while. Pamela Pebmarsh, more dead than alive, was sipping a glass of brandy and water, which alone prevented her from falling in a dead faint.

"Detective Inspector Robinson now stepped forward. All the spectators there could read on his face the consciousness that his evidence would be of the most supreme import.

"'I was telegraphed for from the Yard,' he said, in reply to the coroner, 'and came down here by the first train on the Thursday morning. Beyond the short medical examination, the body had not been touched: as the constables know, we don't like things interfered with in cases of this kind. When I went up to look at deceased, the first thing I saw was a piece of paper just under her right hand. Sergeant Evans had seen it before, and pointed it out to me. Deceased had a pen in her hand, and the ink bottle was close by. This is the paper I found, sir.'

"And amidst a deadly silence, during which nothing could be heard but the scarcely perceptible rustle of the paper, the inspector handed a small note across to the coroner. The latter glanced at it for a moment, and his face became very grave and solemn as he turned towards the jury.

"'Gentlemen of the jury,' he said, 'these are the contents of the paper which the inspector found under the hand of the deceased.'

"He paused once more before he began to read, whilst we all in that crowded court held our breath to listen:

'I am dying. My murderess is my niece, Pam —'

"'That is all, gentlemen,' added the coroner, as he folded up the note. 'Death overtook the unfortunate woman in the very act of writing down the name of her murderess.'

"Then there was a wild and agonised shriek of horror. Pamela Pebmarsh, with hair dishevelled and eyes in which the light of madness had begun to gleam, threw up her hands, and without a word, and without a groan, fell down senseless upon the floor."

3

"Yes," said the man in the corner with a chuckle, "there was enough evidence there to hang twenty people, let alone that one fool of a girl who had run her neck so madly into a noose. I don't suppose that anyone left the court that day with the slightest doubt in their minds as to what the verdict would be; for the coroner had adjourned the inquest, much to the annoyance of the jury, who had fully made up their minds and had their verdict pat on the tips of their tongues: 'Wilful murder against Pamela Pebmarsh.'

"But this was a case which to the last kept up its reputation for surprises. By the next morning rumour had got about that 'the lady of the aristocracy' referred to by Jemima Gadd, and who was supposed to have paid a regular pension to Miss Pebmarsh, was none other than Lady de Chavasse.

"When the name was first mentioned, everyone—especially the fair sex—shrugged their shoulders, and said: 'Of course what else *could* one expect?'

"As a matter of fact, Lady de Chavasse, *née* Birdie Fay, was one of the most fashionable women in society; she was at the head of a dozen benevolent institutions, was a generous patron of hospitals, and her house was one of the most exclusive ones in London. True, she had been on the stage in her younger days, and when Sir Percival de Chavasse married her, his own relations looked somewhat askance at the showy, handsome girl who had so daringly entered the ancient county family.

"Sir Percival himself was an extraordinarily proud man—proud of his lineage, of his social status, of the honour of his name. His very pride had forced his relations, had forced society, to accept his beautiful young wife, and to Lady de Chavasse's credit be it said, not one breath of scandal as to her past life had ever become public gossip. No one could assert that they *knew* anything derogatory to Birdie Fay before she became the proud baronet's wife. As a matter of fact, all society asserted that Sir Percival would never have married her and introduced her to his own family circle if there had been any gossip about her.

"Now suddenly the name of Lady de Chavasse was on everybody's tongue. People at first spoke it under their breath, for everyone felt great sympathy with her. She was so rich, and entertained so lavishly. She was very charming, too; most fascinating in her ways; deferential to her austere mother-in-law; not a little afraid of her proud husband; very careful lest by word or look she betrayed her early connection with the stage before him.

"On the following day, however, we had further surprises in store for us. Pamela Pebmarsh, advised by a shrewd and clear-headed solicitor, had at last made up her mind to view her danger a little more coolly, and to speak rather more of the truth than she had done hitherto.

"Still looking very haggard, but perhaps a little less scared, she now made a statement which, when it was fully substantiated, as she stated it could be, would go far towards clearing her of the terrible imputation against her. Her story was this: on the memorable day in question, she did go up to town, intending to go to the theatre. At the station she purchased an evening paper, which she began to read. This paper in its fashionable columns contained an announcement which arrested her attention; this was that Sir Percival and Lady de Chavasse had returned to their flat in town at 51 Marsden Mansions, Belgravia, from 'The Chase', Melton Mowbray.

"'De Chavasse,' continued Pamela, was the name of the lady who paid my aunt the small pension on which she lived. I knew her years ago, when she was on the stage, and I suddenly thought I would like to go and see her, just to have a chat over old times. Instead of going to the theatre I went and had some dinner at Slater's, in Piccadilly, and then I thought I would take my chance, and go and see if Lady de Chavasse was at home. I got to 51 Marsden Mansions about eight o'clock, and was fortunate enough to see Lady de Chavasse at once. She kept me talking some considerable time; so much so, in fact, that I missed the 11 train from St Pancras. I only left Marsden Mansions at a quarter to eleven, and had to wait at St Pancras until twenty minutes past midnight.'

"This was all reasonable and clear enough, and, as her legal adviser had subpoenaed Lady de Chavasse as a witness, Pamela Pebmarsh seemed to have found an excellent way out of her terrible difficulties, the only question being whether Lady de Chavasse's testimony alone would, in view of her being Pamela's friend, be sufficient to weigh against the terribly overwhelming evidence of Miss Pebmarsh's dying accusation.

"But Lady de Chavasse settled this doubtful point in the way least expected by anyone. Exquisitely dressed, golden-haired, and brilliant-complexioned, she looked strangely out of place in this fusty little village court, amidst the local dames in their plain gowns and antiquated bonnets. She was, moreover, extremely self-possessed, and only cast a short, very haughty, look at the unfortunate girl whose life probably hung upon that fashionable woman's word.

"'Yes,' she said sweetly, in reply to the coroner, 'she was the wife of Sir Percival de Chavasse, and resided at 51 Marsden Mansions, Belgravia.'

"'The accused, I understand, has been known to you for some time?' continued the coroner.

"'Pardon me,' rejoined Lady de Chavasse, speaking in a beautifully modulated voice, 'I did know this young—hem—person, years ago, when I was on the stage, but, of course, I had not seen her for years.'

"'She called on you on Wednesday last at about nine o'clock?'

"'Yes, she did, for the purpose of levying blackmail upon me.'

"There was no mistaking the look of profound aversion and contempt which the fashionable lady now threw upon the poor girl before her.

"'She had some preposterous story about some letters which she alleged would be compromising to my reputation,' continued Lady de Chavasse quietly. 'These she had the kindness to offer me for sale for a few hundred pounds. At first her impudence staggered me, as, of course, I had no knowledge of any such letters. She threatened to take them to my husband, however, and I then—rather foolishly, perhaps—suggested that she should bring them to me first. I forget how the conversation went on, but she left me with the understanding that she would get the letters from her aunt, Miss Pebmarsh, who, by the way, had been my governess when I was a child, and to whom I paid a small pension in consideration of her having been left absolutely without means.'

"And Lady de Chavasse, conscious of her own disinterested benevolence, pressed a highly scented bit of cambric to her delicate nose.

"'Then the accused did spend the evening with you on that Wednesday?' asked the coroner, while a great sigh of relief seemed to come from poor Pamela's breast.

"'Pardon me,' said Lady de Chavasse, 'she spent a little time with me. She came about nine o'clock.'

"'Yes. And when did she leave?'

"'I really couldn't tell you—about ten o'clock, I think.'

"'You are not sure?' persisted the coroner. 'Think, Lady de Chavasse,' he added earnestly, 'try to think—the life of a fellow-creature may, perhaps, depend upon your memory.'

"'I am indeed sorry,' she replied in the same musical voice. 'I could not swear without being positive, could I? And I am not quite positive.'

"'But your servants?'

"'They were at the back of the flat—the girl let herself out.'

"'But your husband?'

"'Oh! when he saw me engaged with the girl, he went out to his club, and was not yet home when she left.'

"'Birdie! Birdie! won't you try and remember?' here came in an agonized cry from the unfortunate girl, who thus saw her last hope vanish before her eyes.

"But Lady de Chavasse only lifted a little higher a pair of very prettily arched eyebrows, and having finished her evidence she stepped on one side and presently left the court, leaving behind her a faint aroma of violet sachet powder, and taking away with her, perhaps, the last hope of an innocent fellow-creature."

4

"But Pamela Pebmarsh?" I asked after a while, for he had paused and was gazing attentively at the photograph of a very beautiful and exquisitely gowned woman.

"Ah yes, Pamela Pebmarsh," he said with a smile. "There was yet another act in that palpitating drama of her life—one act—the *dénouement* as unexpected as it was thrilling. Salvation came where it was least expected—from Jemima Gadd, who seemed to have made up her mind that Pamela had killed her aunt, and yet who was the first to prove her innocence.

"She had been shown the few words which the murdered woman was alleged to have written after she had been stabbed. Jemima, not a very good scholar, found it difficult to decipher the words herself.

"'Ah, well, poor dear,' she said after a while, with a deep sigh, ''er 'andwriting was always peculiar, seein' as 'ow she wrote always with 'er left 'and.'

"'*Her left hand!!!*' gasped the coroner, while public and jury alike, hardly liking to credit their ears, hung upon the woman's thin lips, amazed, aghast, puzzled.

"'Why, yes,' said Jemima placidly. 'Didn't you know she 'ad a bad accident to 'er right 'and when she was a child, and never could 'old anything in it? 'Er fingers were like paralysed; the inkpot was always on the left of 'er writing-table. Oh! she couldn't write with 'er right 'and at all.'

"Then a strange revulsion of feeling came over everyone there.

"Stabbed in the back, with her lung pierced through and through, how could she have done, dying, what she never did in life?

"Impossible!

"The murderer, whoever it was, had placed pen and paper to her hand, and had written on it the cruel words which were intended to delude justice and to send an innocent fellow-creature—a young girl not five-and-twenty—to an unjust and ignominious death. But, fortunately for that innocent girl, the cowardly miscreant had ignored the fact that Miss Pebmarsh's right hand had been paralysed for years.

"The inquest was adjourned for a week," continued the man in the corner, "which enabled Pamela's solicitor to obtain further evidence of her innocence. Fortunately for her, he was enabled to find two witnesses who had seen her in an omnibus going towards St Pancras at about 11.15 p.m., and a passenger on the 12.25 train, who had travelled down with her as far as Hendon. Thus, when the inquest was resumed, Pamela Pebmarsh left the court without a stain upon her character.

"But the murder of Miss Pebmarsh has remained a mystery to this day—as has also the secret history of the compromising letters. Did they exist or not? is a question the interested spectators at that memorable inquest have often asked themselves. Certain is it that failing Pamela Pebmarsh, who might have wanted them for purposes of blackmail, no one else could be interested in them except Lady de Chavasse."

"Lady de Chavasse!" I ejaculated in surprise. "Surely you are not going to pretend that that elegant lady went down to Boreham Wood in the middle of the night in order to murder Miss Pebmarsh, and then to lay the crime at another woman's door?"

"I only pretend what's logic," replied the man in the corner with inimitable conceit; "and in Pamela Pebmarsh's own statement, she was with Lady de Chavasse at 51 Marsden Mansions until eleven o'clock, and there is no train from St Pancras to Boreham Wood between eleven and twenty-five minutes past midnight. Pamela's alibi becomes that of Lady de Chavasse, and is quite conclusive. Besides, that elegant lady was not one to do that sort of work for herself."

"What do you mean?" I asked.

"Do you mean to say you never thought of the real solution of this mystery?" he retorted sarcastically.

"I confess—" I began a little irritably.

"Confess that I have not yet taught you to think logically, and to look at the beginning of things."

"What do you call the beginning of this case, then?"

"Why! the compromising letters, of course."

"But—" I argued.

"Wait a minute!" he shrieked excitedly, whilst with frantic haste he began fidgeting, fidgeting again at that eternal bit of string. "These did exist, otherwise why did Lady de Chavasse parley with Pamela Pebmarsh? Why did she not order her out of the house then and there, if she had nothing to fear from her?"

"I admit that," I said.

"Very well; then, as she was too fine, too delicate to commit the villainous murder of which she afterwards accused poor Miss Pamela, who was there sufficiently interested in those letters to try and gain possession of them for her?"

"Who, indeed?" I queried, still puzzled, still not understanding.

"Ay! who but her husband?" shrieked the funny creature, as with a sharp snap he broke his beloved string in two.

"Her husband!" I gasped.

"Why not? He had plenty of time, plenty of pluck. In a flat it is easy enough to overhear conversations that take place in the next room—he was in the house at the time, remember, for Lady de Chavasse said herself that he went out afterwards. No doubt he overheard everything—the compromising letters, and Pamela's attempt at levying blackmail. What the effect of such a discovery must have been upon the proud man I leave you to imagine—his wife's social position ruined, a stain upon his ancient name, his relations pointing the finger of scorn at his folly.

"Can't you picture him, hearing the two women's talk in the next room, and then resolving at all costs to possess himself of those compromising letters? He had just time to catch the 10 train to Boreham Wood.

"Mind you, I don't suppose that he went down there with any evil intent. Most likely he only meant to buy those letters from Miss Pebmarsh. What happened, however, nobody can say but the murderer himself.

"Who knows? But the deed done, imagine the horror of a refined, aristocratic man, face to face with such a crime as that.

"Was it this terror, or merely rage at the girl who had been the original cause of all this, that prompted him to commit the final villainy of writing out a false accusation and placing it under the dead woman's hand? Who can tell?

"Then, the deed done, and the *mise-en-scène* complete, he is able to catch the last train—11.23—back to town. A man travelling alone would pass practically unperceived.

"Pamela's innocence was proved, and the murder of Miss Pebmarsh has remained a mystery, but if you will reflect on my conclusions, you will admit that no one else—*no one else*—could have committed that murder, for no one else had a greater interest in the destruction of those letters."

The Lisson Grove Mystery

1

The man in the corner ordered another glass of milk, and timidly asked for a second cheesecake at the same time.

"I am going down to the Marylebone Police Court, to see those people brought up before the 'beak'," he remarked.

"What people?" I queried.

"What people!" he exclaimed, in the greatest excitement. "You don't mean to say that you have not studied the Lisson Grove Mystery?"

I had to confess that my knowledge on that subject was of the most superficial character.

"One of the most interesting cases that has cropped up in recent years," he said, with an indescribable look of reproach.

"Perhaps. I did not study it in the papers because I preferred to hear *you* tell me all about it," I said.

"Oh, if that's it," he replied, as he settled himself down in his corner like a great bird after the rain, "then you showed more sense than lady journalists usually possess. I can, of course, give you a far clearer account than the newspapers have done; as for the police—well! I never saw such a muddle as they are making of this case."

"I dare say it is a peculiarly difficult one," I retorted, for I am ever a champion of that hardworking department.

"H'm!" he said, "so, so—it is a tragedy in a prologue and three acts. I am going down this afternoon to see the curtain fall for the third time on what, if I mistake not, will prove a good burlesque; but it all began dramatically enough. It was last Saturday, 21st November, that two boys, playing in the little spinney just outside Wembley Park Station, came across three large parcels done up in American cloth.

"With the curiosity natural to their age, they at once proceeded to undo these parcels, and what they found so upset the little beggars that

292

they ran howling through the spinney and the polo ground, straight as a dart to Wembley Park Station. Half-frantic with excitement, they told their tale to one of the porters off duty, who walked back to the spinney with them. The three parcels, in point of fact, contained the remains of a dismembered human body. The porter sent one of the boys for the local police, and the remains were duly conveyed to the mortuary, where they were kept for identification.

"Three days later—that is to say, on Tuesday, 24th November— Miss Amelia Dyke, residing at Lisson Grove Crescent, returned from Edinburgh, where she had spent three or four days with a friend. She drove up from St Pancras in a cab, and carried her small box up herself to the door of the flat, at which she knocked loudly and re-peatedly—so loudly and so persistently, in fact, that the inhabitants of the neighbouring flats came out on to their respective landings to see what the noise was about.

"Miss Amelia Dyke was getting anxious. Her father, she said, must be seriously ill, or else why did he not come and open the door to her? Her anxiety, however, reached its culminating point when Mr and Mrs Pitt, who reside in the flat immediately beneath that occu-pied by the Dykes, came forward with the alarming statement that, as a matter of fact, they had themselves been wondering if anything were wrong with old Mr Dyke, as they had not heard any sound overhead for the last few days.

"Miss Amelia, now absolutely terrified, begged one of the neigh-bours to fetch either the police or a locksmith, or both. Mr Pitt ran out at once, both police and locksmith were brought upon the scene, the door was forcibly opened, and amidst indescribable excitement Constable Turner, followed by Miss Dyke, who was faint and trem-bling with apprehension, effected an entrance into the flat.

"Everything in it was tidy and neat to a degree, all the fires were laid, the beds made, the floors were clean and washed, the brasses pol-ished, only a slight, very slight layer of dust lay over everything, dust that could not have accumulated for more than a few days. The flat consisted of four rooms and a bathroom; in not one of them was there the faintest trace of old Mr Dyke.

"In order fully to comprehend the consternation which all the neighbours felt at this discovery," continued the man in the corner, "you must understand that old Mr Dyke was a helpless cripple; he had been a mining engineer in his young days, and a terrible blast-ing accident deprived him, at the age of forty, of both legs. They had been amputated just above the knee, and the unfortunate man—then a widower with one little girl—had spent the remainder of his life on crutches. He had a small—a very small—pension, which, as soon as his daughter Amelia was grown up, had enabled him to live in comparative comfort in the small flat in Lisson Grove Crescent.

"His misfortune, however, had left him terribly sensitive; he never could bear the looks of compassion thrown upon him, whenever he ventured out on his crutches, and even the kindliest sympathy was positive torture to him. Gradually, therefore, as he got on in life, he took to staying more and more at home, and after a while gave up going out altogether. By the time he was sixty-five years old and Miss Amelia a fine young woman of seven-and-twenty, old Dyke had not been outside the door of his flat for at least five years.

"And yet, when Constable Turner aided by the locksmith entered the flat on that memorable 24th November, there was not a trace anywhere of the old man.

"Miss Amelia was in the last stages of despair, and at first she seemed far too upset and hysterical to give the police any coherent and definite information. At last, however, from amid the chaos of tears and of ejaculations, Constable Turner gathered the following facts:

"Miss Amelia had some great friends in Edinburgh whom she had long wished to visit, her father's crippled condition making this extremely difficult. A fortnight ago, however, in response to a very urgent invitation, she at last decided to accept it, but in order to leave her father altogether comfortable, she advertised in the local paper for a respectable woman who would come to the flat every day and see to all the work, cook his dinner, make the bed, and so on.

"She had several applications in reply to this advertisement, and ultimately selected a very worthy looking elderly person, who, for seven shillings a week, undertook to come daily from seven in the morning until about six in the afternoon, to see to all Mr Dyke's comforts.

"Miss Amelia was very favourably impressed with this person's respectable and motherly appearance, and she left for Edinburgh by the 5.15 a.m. train on the morning of Thursday, 19th November, feeling confident that her father would be well looked after. She certainly had not heard from the old man while she was away, but she had not expected to hear unless, indeed, something had been wrong.

"Miss Amelia was quite sure that something dreadful had happened to her father, as he could not possibly have walked downstairs and out of the house alone; certainly, his crutches were nowhere to be found, but this only helped to deepen the mystery of the old man's disappearance.

"The constable, having got thus far with his notes, thought it best to refer the whole matter at this stage to higher authority. He got from Miss Amelia the name and address of the charwoman, and then went back to the station.

"There, the very first news that greeted him was that the medical officer of the district had just sent round to the various police stations his report on the human remains found in Wembley Park the previous Saturday. They had proved to be the dismembered body of an old man between sixty and seventy years of age, the immediate cause of whose death had undoubtedly been a violent blow on the back of the head with a heavy instrument, which had shattered the cranium. Expert examination further revealed the fact that deceased had had in early life both legs removed by a surgical operation just above the knee.

"That was the end of the prologue in the Lisson Grove tragedy," continued the man in the corner, after a slight and dramatic pause, "as far as the public was concerned. When the curtain was subsequently raised upon the first act, the situation had been considerably changed.

"The remains had been positively identified as those of old Mr Dyke, and a charge of wilful murder had been brought against Alfred Wyatt, of no occupation, residing in Warlock Road, Lisson Grove, and against Amelia Dyke for complicity in the crime. They are the two people whom I am going to see this afternoon brought before the 'beak' at the Marylebone Police Court."

2

"Two very important bits of evidence, I must tell you, had come to light, on the first day of the inquest and had decided the police to make this double arrest.

"In the first place, according to one or two of the neighbours, who happened to know something of the Dyke household, Miss Amelia had kept company for some time with a young man named Alfred Wyatt; he was an electrical engineer, resided in the neighbourhood, and was some years younger than Miss Dyke. As he was known not to be very steady, it was generally supposed that the old man did not altogether approve of his daughter's engagement.

"Mrs Pitt, residing in the flat immediately below the one occupied by the Dykes, had stated, moreover, that on Wednesday the 18th, at about midday, she heard very loud and angry voices proceeding from above, Miss Amelia's shrill tones being specially audible. Shortly afterwards she saw Wyatt go out of the house; but the quarrel continued for some little time without him, for the neighbours could still hear Miss Amelia's high-pitched voice, speaking very excitedly and volubly.

"'An hour later,' further explained Mrs Pitt, 'I met Miss Dyke on the stairs; she seemed very flushed and looked as if she had been crying. I suppose she saw that I noticed this, for she stopped and said to me:

"'"All this fuss, you know, Mrs Pitt, because Alfred asked me to go for a drive with him this afternoon, but I am going all the same."'

"'Later in the afternoon—it must have been quite half past four, for it was getting dark—young Wyatt drove up in a motorcar, and presently I heard Miss Dyke's voice on the stairs saying very pleasantly and cheerfully: "All right, Daddy, we shan't be long." Then Mr Dyke must have said something which I didn't hear, for she added, "Oh, that's all right; I am well wrapped up, and we have plenty of rugs."'

"Mrs Pitt then went to her window and saw Wyatt and Amelia Dyke start off in a motor. She concluded that the old man had been mollified, for both Amelia and Wyatt waved their hands affectionately up towards the window. They returned from their drive about six o'clock; Wyatt saw Amelia to the door, and then went off again. The next day Miss Dyke went to Scotland.

"As you see," continued the man in the corner, "Alfred Wyatt had become a very important personality in this case; he was Amelia's sweetheart, and it was strange—to say the least of it—that she had never as yet even mentioned his name. Therefore, when she was recalled in order to give further evidence, you may be sure that she was pretty sharply questioned on the subject of Alfred Wyatt.

"In her evidence before the coroner, she adhered fairly closely to her original statement:

"'I did not mention Mr Wyatt's name,' she explained, 'because I did not think it was of any importance; if he knew anything about my dear father's mysterious fate he would have come forward at once, of course, and helped me to find out who the cowardly murderer was who could attack a poor, crippled old man. Mr Wyatt was devoted to my father, and it is perfectly ridiculous to say that daddy objected to my engagement; on the contrary, he gave us his full consent, and we were going to be married directly after the New Year, and continue to live with father in the flat.'

"'But,' questioned the coroner, who had not by any means departed from his severity, 'what about this quarrel which the last witness

296

overheard on the subject of your going out driving with Mr Wyatt?'

"'Oh, that was nothing,' replied Miss Dyke very quietly. 'Daddy only objected because he thought that it was rather too late to start at four o'clock, and that I should be cold. When he saw that we had plenty of rugs he was quite pleased for me to go.'

"'Isn't it rather astonishing, then,' asked the coroner, 'seeing that Mr Wyatt was on such good terms with your father, that he did not go to see him while you were away?'

"'Not at all,' she replied unconcernedly; 'Alfred went down to Edinburgh on the Thursday evening. He couldn't travel with me in the morning, for he had some business to see to in town that day; but he joined me at my friends' house on the Friday morning, having travelled all night.'

"'Ah!' remarked the coroner dryly, 'then he had not seen your father since you left.'

"'Oh yes,' said Miss Amelia; 'he called round to see dad during the day, and found him looking well and cheerful.'

"Miss Amelia Dyke, as she gave this evidence, seemed absolutely unconscious of saying anything that might in any way incriminate her lover. She is a handsome, though somewhat coarse-looking, woman, nearer thirty I should say, than she would care to own. I was present at the inquest, mind you, for that case had too many mysteries about it from the first for it to have eluded my observation, and I watched her closely throughout. Her voice struck me as fine and rich, with—in this instance also—a shade of coarseness in it; certainly, it was very far from being high-pitched, as Mrs Pitt had described it.

"When she had finished her evidence she went back to her seat, looking neither flustered nor uncomfortable, although many looks of contempt and even of suspicion were darted at her from every corner of the crowded court.

"Nor did she lose her composure in the slightest degree when Mr Parlett, clerk to Messrs Snow and Patterson, solicitors, of Bedford Row, in his turn came forward and gave evidence; only while the little man spoke her full red lips curled and parted with a look of complete contempt.

"Mr Parlett's story was indeed a remarkable one, inasmuch as it suddenly seemed to tear asunder the veil of mystery which so far had surrounded the murder of old Dyke by supplying it with a motive—a strong motive, too: the eternal greed of gain.

"In June last, namely, it appears that Messrs Snow and Patterson received intimation from a firm of Melbourne solicitors that a man of the name of Dyke had died there recently, leaving a legacy of £4,000 to his only brother, James Arthur Dyke, a mining engineer, who in 1890 was residing at Lisson Grove Crescent. The Melbourne solicitors in their communication asked for Messrs Snow and Patterson's kind assistance in helping them to find the legatee.

"The search was easy enough, since James Arthur Dyke, mining engineer, had never ceased to reside at Lisson Grove Crescent. Armed, therefore, with full instructions from their Melbourne correspondent, Messrs Snow and Patterson communicated with Dyke, and after a little preliminary correspondence, the sum of £4,000 in Bank of Australia notes and various securities were handed over by Mr Parlett to the old cripple.

"The money and securities were—so Mr Parlett understood—subsequently deposited by Mr Dyke at the Portland Road Branch of the London and South-western Bank: as the old man apparently died intestate, the whole of the £4,000 would naturally devolve upon his only daughter and natural legatee.

"Mind you, all through the proceedings the public had instinctively felt that money was somewhere at the bottom of this gruesome and mysterious crime. There is not much object in murdering an old cripple except for purposes of gain, but now Mr Parlett's evidence had indeed furnished a damning motive for the appalling murder.

"What more likely than that Alfred Wyatt, wanting to finger that £4,000, had done away with the old man? And if Amelia Dyke did not turn away from him in horror, after such a cowardly crime, then she must have known of it and had perhaps connived in it.

"As for Nicholson, the charwoman, her evidence had certainly done more to puzzle everybody all round than any other detail in this strange and mysterious crime.

"She deposed that on Friday, 13th November, in answer to an advertisement in the *Marylebone Star,* she had called on Miss Dyke at Lisson Grove, when it was arranged that she should do a week's work at the flat, beginning Thursday, the 19th, from seven in the morning until six in the afternoon. She was to keep the place clean, get Mr Dyke—who, she understood, was an invalid—all his meals, and make herself generally useful to him.

"Accordingly, Nicholson turned up on the Thursday morning. She let herself into the flat, as Miss Dyke had entrusted the latchkey to her, and went on with the work. Mr Dyke was in bed, and she got him all his meals that day. She thought she was giving him satisfaction, and was very astonished when, at six o'clock, having cleared away his tea, he told her that he would not require her again. He gave her no explanation, asked her for the latchkey, and gave her her full week's money—seven shillings in full. Nicholson then put on her bonnet, and went away.

"Now," continued the man in the corner, leaning excitedly forward, and marking each sentence he uttered with an exquisitely complicated knot in his bit of string, "an hour later, another neighbour, Mrs Marsh, who lived on the same floor as the Dykes, on starting to go out, met Alfred Wyatt on the landing. He took off his hat to her, and then knocked at the door of the Dykes' flat.

"When she came home at eight o'clock, she again passed him on the stairs; he was then going out. She stopped to ask him how Mr Dyke was, and Wyatt replied: 'Oh, fairly well, but he misses his daughter, you know.'

"Mrs Marsh, now closely questioned, said that she thought Wyatt was carrying a large parcel under his arm, but she could not distinguish the shape of the parcel as the angle of the stairs, where she met him, was very dark. She stated, though, that he was running down the stairs very fast.

"It was on all that evidence that the police felt justified in arresting Alfred Wyatt for the murder of James Arthur Dyke, and Amelia Dyke for connivance in the crime. And now this very morning, those two young people have been brought before the magistrate, and at this moment evidence—circumstantial, mind you, but positively damning—is being heaped upon them by the prosecution. The police did their work quickly. The very evening after the first day of the inquest, the warrant was out for their arrest."

He looked at a huge silver watch which he always carried in his waistcoat pocket.

"I don't want to miss the defence," he said, "for I know that it will be sensational. But I did not want to hear the police and medical evidence all over again. You'll excuse me, won't you? I shall be back here for five o'clock tea. I know you will be glad to hear all about it."

3

When I returned to the A.B.C. shop for my tea at five minutes past five, there he sat in his accustomed corner, with a cup of tea before him, another placed opposite to him, presumably for me, and a long piece of string between his bony fingers.

"What will you have with your tea?" he asked politely, the moment I was seated.

"A roll and butter and the end of the story," I replied.

"Oh, the story has no end," he said with a chuckle; "at least, not for the public. As for me, why, I never met a more simple 'mystery'. Perhaps that is why the police were so completely at sea."

"Well, and what happened?" I queried, with some impatience.

"Why, the usual thing," he said, as he once more began to fidget nervously with his bit of string. "The prisoners had pleaded not guilty, and the evidence for the prosecution was gone into in full. Mr Parlett repeated his story of the £4,000 legacy, and all the neighbours had some story or other to tell about Alfred Wyatt, who, according to them, was altogether a most undesirable young man.

"I heard the fag end of Mrs Marsh's evidence. When I reached the court, she was repeating the story she had already told to the police.

"Someone else in the house had also heard Wyatt running helter-skelter downstairs at eight o'clock on the Thursday evening; this was a point, though a small one, in favour of the accused. A man cannot run downstairs when he is carrying the whole weight of a dead body, and the theory of the prosecution was that Wyatt had murdered old Dyke on that Thursday evening, got into his motorcar somewhere, scorched down to Wembley with the dismembered body of his victim, deposited it in the spinney where it was subsequently found, and finally had driven back to town, stabled his motor car, and reached King's Cross in time for the 11.30 night express to Edinburgh. He would have time for all that, remember, for he would have three hours and a half to do it in.

"Besides which the prosecution had unearthed one more witness, who was able to add another tiny link to the already damning chain of evidence built up against the accused.

"Wilfred Poad, namely, manager of a large cycle and motor-car depot in Euston Road, stated that on Thursday afternoon, 19th November, at about half past six o'clock, Alfred Wyatt, with whom he had had some business dealings before, had hired a small car from him, with the understanding that he need not bring it back until after 11 p.m. This was agreed to, Poad keeping the place open until just before eleven, when Wyatt drove up in the car, paid for the hire of it, and then walked away from the shop in the direction of the Great Northern terminus.

"That was pretty strong against the male prisoner, wasn't it? For, mind you, Wyatt had given no satisfactory account whatever of his time between 8 p.m., when Mrs Marsh had met him going out of Lisson Grove Crescent, and 11 p.m., when he brought back the car to the Euston Road shop. 'He had been driving about aimlessly,' so he said. Now, one doesn't go out motoring for hours on a cold, drizzly night in November for no purpose whatever.

"As for the female prisoner, the charge against her was merely one of complicity.

"This closed the case for the prosecution," continued the funny creature, with one of his inimitable chuckles, "leaving but one tiny point obscure, and that was, the murdered man's strange conduct in dismissing the woman Nicholson.

"Yes, the case was strong enough, and yet there stood both prisoners in the dock, with that sublime air of indifference and contempt which only complete innocence or hardened guilt could give.

"Then when the prosecution had had their say, Alfred Wyatt chose to enter the witness-box and make a statement in his own defence. Quietly, and as if he were making the most casual observation he said:

"'I am not guilty of the murder of Mr Dyke, and in proof of this I solemnly assert that on Thursday, 19th November, the day I am supposed to have committed the crime, the old man was still alive at half past ten o'clock in the evening.'

"He paused a moment, like a born actor, watching the effect he had produced. I tell you, it was astounding.

"'I have three separate and independent witnesses here,' continued Wyatt, with the same deliberate calm, 'who heard and saw Mr Dyke as late as half past ten that night. Now, I understand that the dismembered body of the old man was found close to Wembley Park. How could I, between half past ten and eleven o'clock, have killed Dyke, cut him up, cleaned and put the flat all tidy, carried the body to the car, driven on to Wembley, hidden the corpse in the spinney, and be back in Euston Road, all in the space of half an hour? I am absolutely innocent of this crime, and, fortunately, it is easy for me now to prove my innocence.'

"Alfred Wyatt had made no idle boast. Mrs Marsh had seen him running downstairs at 8 p.m. An hour after that, the Pitts in the flat beneath heard the old man moving about overhead.

"'Just as usual,' observed Mrs Pitt. 'He always went to bed about nine, and we could always hear him most distinctly.'

"John Pitt, the husband, corroborated this statement; the old man's movements were quite unmistakable because of his crutches.

"Henry Ogden, on the other hand, who lived in the house facing the block of flats, saw the light in Dyke's window that evening, and the old man's silhouette upon the blind from time to time. The light was put out at half past ten. This statement again was corroborated by Mrs Ogden, who also had noticed the silhouette and the light being extinguished at half past ten.

"But this was not all; both Mr and Mrs Ogden had seen old Dyke at his window, sitting in his accustomed armchair, between half past eight and nine o'clock. He was gesticulating, and apparently talking to someone else in the room whom they could not see.

"Alfred Wyatt, therefore, was quite right when he said that he would have no difficulty in proving his innocence. The man whom he was supposed to have murdered was, according to the testimony, alive at six o'clock; according to Mr and Mrs Ogden he was alive and sitting in his window until nine; again, he was heard to move about until ten o'clock by both the Pitts, and at half past ten only was the light put out in his flat. Obviously, therefore, as his dead body was found twelve miles away, Wyatt, who was out of the Crescent at eight, and in Euston Road at eleven, could not have done the deed.

"He was discharged, of course, the magistrate adding a very severe remark on the subject of 'carelessly collected evidence'. As for Miss Amelia she sailed out of the court like a queen after her coronation, for with Wyatt's discharge the case against her naturally collapsed. As for me, I walked out too, with an elated feeling at the thought that the intelligence of the British race had not yet sunk so low as our friends on the Continent would have us believe."

4

"But then, who murdered the old man?" I asked, for I confess the matter was puzzling me in an irritating kind of a way.

"Ah! who indeed?" he rejoined sarcastically, while an artistic knot went to join its fellows along that never-ending bit of string.

"I wish you'd tell me what's in your mind," I said, feeling peculiarly irritated with him just at that moment.

"What's in my mind?" he replied, with shrug of his thin shoulders. "Oh, only a certain degree of admiration!"

"Admiration at what?"

"At a pair of exceedingly clever criminals."

"Then you do think that Wyatt murdered Dyke?"

"I don't think—I am sure."

"But when did they do it?"

"Ah, that's more to the point. Personally, I should say between them on Wednesday morning, 18th November."

"The day they went for that motorcar ride?" I gasped.

"And carried away the old man's remains beneath a multiplicity of rugs," he added.

"But he was *alive* long after that!" I urged. "The woman Nicholson—"

"The woman Nicholson saw and spoke to a man in bed, whom she *supposed* was old Mr Dyke. Among the many questions put to her by those clever detectives, no one thought, of course, of asking her to describe the old man. But even if she had done so, Wyatt was far too great an artist in crime not to have contrived a make-up which, described by a witness who had never before seen Dyke, would easily pass as a description of the old man himself."

"Impossible!" I said, struck in spite of myself by the simplicity of his logic.

"Impossible, you say?" he shrieked excitedly.

"Why, I call that crime a masterpiece from beginning to end; a display of ingenuity which, fortunately, the criminal classes seldom possess, or where would society be? Here was a crime committed, where everything was most beautifully stage-managed, nothing left unforeseen. Shall I reconstruct it for you?"

"Do!" I said, handing across the table to him a brand-new, beautiful bit of string, on which his talon-like fingers fastened as upon a prey.

"Very well," he said, marking each point with a scientific knot. "Here, it is, scene by scene. There was Alfred Wyatt and Amelia Dyke— a pair of blackguards, eager to obtain that £4,000 which only the old man's death could secure for them. They decide upon killing him, and:

"*Scene 1*—Miss Amelia makes her arrangements. She advertises for a charwoman, and engages one, who is to be a very useful witness presently.

"*Scene 2*—The murder, brutal, horrible, on the person of an old cripple, whilst his own daughter stands by, and the dismembering of the body.

"*Scene 3*—The ride in the motorcar—after dark, remember, and with plenty of rugs, beneath which the gruesome burden is concealed. The scene is accompanied by the comedy of Miss Dyke speaking to her father, and waving her hand affectionately at him from below. I tell you, that woman must have had some nerve!

"Then, *Scene 4*—The arrival at Wembley, and the hiding of the remains.

"*Scene 5*—Amelia goes to Edinburgh by the 5.15 a.m. train, and thus secures her own alibi. After that, the comedy begins in earnest. The impersonation of the dead man by Wyatt during the whole of that memorable Thursday. Mind you, that was not very difficult; it only needed the brain to invent, and the nerve to carry it through. The charwoman had never seen old Dyke before; she only knew that he was an invalid. What more natural than that she should accept as her new master the man who lay in bed all day, and only spoke a few words to her? A very slight make-up of hair and beard would complete the illusion.

"Then, at six o'clock, the woman gone, Wyatt steals out of the house, bespeaks the motorcar, leaves it in the street in a convenient spot, and is back in time to be seen by Mrs Marsh at seven.

"The rest is simplicity itself. The silhouette at the window was easy enough to arrange; the sound of a man walking on crutches is easily imitated with a couple of umbrellas—the actual crutches were, no doubt, burned directly after the murder. Lastly, the putting out of the light at half past ten was the crowning stroke of genius.

"One little thing might have upset the whole wonderful plan, but that one thing only; and that was if the body had been found *before* the great comedy scene of Thursday had been fully played. But that spinney near Wembley was well chosen. People don't go wandering under trees and in woods on cold November days, and the remains were not found until the Saturday.

"Ah, it was cleverly stage-managed, and no mistake. I couldn't have done it better myself. Won't you have another cup of tea? No? Don't look so upset. The world does not contain many such clever criminals as Alfred Wyatt and Amelia Dyke."

The Tremarn Case

1

"Well, it certainly is most amazing!" I said that day, when I had finished reading about it all in *The Daily Telegraph*.

"Yet the most natural thing in the world," retorted the man in the corner, as soon as he had ordered his lunch. "Crime invariably begets crime. No sooner is a murder, theft, or fraud committed in a novel or striking way, than this method is aped—probably within the next few days—by some other less imaginative scoundrel.

"Take this case, for instance," he continued, as he slowly began sipping his glass of milk, "which seems to amaze you so much. It was less than a year ago, was it not? that in Paris a man was found dead in a cab, stabbed in a most peculiar way—right through the neck, from ear to ear—with, presumably, a long, sharp instrument of the type of an Italian stiletto.

"No one in England took much count of the crime, beyond a contemptuous shrug of the shoulders at the want of safety of the Paris streets, and the incapacity of the French detectives, who not only never discovered the murderer, who had managed to slip out of the cab unperceived, but who did not even succeed in establishing the identity of the victim.

"But this case," he added, pointing once more to my daily paper, "strikes nearer home. Less than a year has passed, and last week, in the very midst of our much-vaunted London streets, a crime of a similar nature has been committed. I do not know if your paper gives full details, but this is what happened: last Monday evening two gentlemen, both in evening dress and wearing opera hats, hailed a hansom in Shaftesbury Avenue. It was about a quarter past eleven, and the night, if you remember, was a typical November one—dark, drizzly, and foggy. The various theatres in the immediate neighbourhood were disgorging a continuous stream of people after the evening performance.

"The cabman did not take special notice of his fares. They jumped in very quickly, and one of them, through the little trap above, gave him an address in Cromwell Road. He drove there as quickly as the fog would permit him, and pulled up at the number given. One of the gentlemen then handed him up a very liberal fare—again through the little trap—and told him to drive his friend on to Westminster Chambers, Victoria Street.

"Cabby noticed that the 'swell', when he got out of the hansom, stopped for a moment to say a few words to his friend, who had remained inside; then he crossed over the road and walked quickly in the direction of the Natural History Museum.

"When the cabman pulled up at Westminster Chambers, he waited for the second fare to get out; the latter seemingly making no movement that way, cabby looked down at him through the trap.

"'I thought 'e was asleep,' he explained to the police later on. ''E was leaning back in 'is corner, and 'is 'ead was turned towards the window. I gets down and calls to 'im, but 'e don't move. Then I gets on to the step and give 'im a shake... There!—I'll say no more... We was near a lamppost, the mare took a step forward, and the light fell full on the gent's face. 'E was dead and no mistake. I saw the wound just underneath 'is ear, and "Murder!" I says to myself at once.'

"Cabby lost no time in whistling for the nearest point-policeman, then he called the night porter of the Westminster Chambers. The latter looked at the murdered man, and declared that he knew nothing of him; certainly, he was not a tenant of the Chambers.

"By the time a couple of policemen arrived upon the scene, quite a crowd had gathered around the cab, in spite of the lateness of the hour and the darkness of the night. The matter was such an important one that one of the constables thought it best at once to jump into the hansom beside the murdered man and to order the cabman to drive to the nearest police station.

"There the cause of death was soon ascertained; the victim of this daring outrage had been stabbed through the neck from ear to ear with a long, sharp, instrument, in shape like an antique stiletto, which, I may tell you, was subsequently found under the cushions of the hansom. The murderer must have watched his opportunity, when his victim's head was turned away from him, and then dealt the blow, just below the left ear, with amazing swiftness and precision.

"Of course, the papers were full of it the next day; this was such a lovely opportunity for driving home a moral lesson, of how one crime engenders another, and how—but for that murder in Paris a year ago—we should not now have to deplore a crime committed in the very centre of fashionable London, the detection of which seems likely to completely baffle the police.

"Plenty more in that strain, of course, from which the reading public quickly jumped to the conclusion that the police held absolutely no clue as to the identity of the daring and mysterious miscreant.

"A most usual and natural thing had happened; cabby could only give a very vague description of his other 'fare', of the 'swell' who had got out at Cromwell Road, and been lost to sight after having committed so dastardly and so daring a crime.

"This was scarcely to be wondered at, for the night had been very foggy, and the murderer had been careful to pull his opera hat well over his face, thus hiding the whole of his forehead and eyes; moreover, he had always taken the additional precaution of only communicating with the cabman through the little trapdoor.

"All cabby had seen of him was a clean-shaven chin. As to the murdered man, it was not until about noon, when the early editions of the evening papers came out with a fuller account of the crime and a description of the victim, that his identity was at last established.

"Then the news spread like wildfire, and the evening papers came out with some of the most sensational headlines it had ever been their good fortune to print. The man who had been so mysteriously murdered in the cab was none other than Mr Philip Le Cheminant, the nephew and heir-presumptive of the Earl of Tremarn."

2

"In order fully to realise the interest created by this extraordinary news, you must be acquainted with the various details of that remarkable case, popularly known as the 'Tremarn Peerage Case'," continued the man in the corner, as he placidly munched his cheesecake. "I do not know if you followed it in its earlier stages, when its many details—which read like a romance—were first made public."

I looked so interested and so eager that he did not wait for my reply.

"I must try and put it all clearly before you," he said; "I was interested in it all from the beginning, and from the numerous wild stories afloat I have sifted only what was undeniably true. Some points of the case are still in dispute, and will, perhaps, now for ever remain a mystery. But I must take you back some five-and-twenty years. The Hon.

Arthur Le Cheminant, second son of the late Earl of Tremarn, was then travelling round the world for health and pleasure.

"In the course of his wanderings he touched at Martinique, one of the French West Indian islands, which was devastated by volcanic eruptions about two years ago. There he met and fell in love with a beautiful half-caste girl named Lucie Legrand, who had French blood in her veins, and was a Christian, but who, otherwise, was only partially civilized, and not at all educated.

"How it all came about it is difficult to conjecture, but one thing is absolutely certain, and that is that the Hon. Arthur Le Cheminant, the son of one of our English peers, married this half-caste girl at the parish church of St Pierre, in Martinique, according to the forms prescribed by French laws, both parties being of the same religion.

"I suppose now no one will ever know whether that marriage was absolutely and undisputably a legal one—but, in view of subsequent events, we must presume that it was. The Hon. Arthur, however, in any case, behaved like a young scoundrel. He only spent a very little time with his wife, quickly tired of her, and within two years of his marriage callously abandoned her and his child, then a boy about a year old.

"He lodged a sum of £2,000 in the local bank in the name of Mme Le Cheminant, the interest of which was to be paid to her regularly for the maintenance of herself and child, then he calmly sailed for England, with the intention never to return. This intention fate itself helped him to carry out, for he died very shortly afterwards, taking the secret of his incongruous marriage with him to his grave.

"Mme Le Cheminant, as she was called out there, seems to have accepted her own fate with perfect equanimity. She had never known anything about her husband's social position in his own country, and he had left her what, in Martinique amongst the coloured population, was considered a very fair competence for herself and child.

"The grandson of an English earl was taught to read and write by the worthy *cure* of St Pierre, and during the whole of her life, Lucie never once tried to find out who her husband was, and what had become of him.

"But here the dramatic scene comes in this strange story," continued the man in the corner, with growing excitement; "two years ago St Pierre, if you remember, was completely destroyed by volcanic eruptions. Nearly the entire population perished, and every house and building was in ruins. Among those who fell a victim to the awful catastrophe was Mme Le Cheminant, otherwise the Hon. Mrs Arthur Le Cheminant, whilst amongst those who managed to escape and ultimately found refuge in the English colony of St Vincent, was her son, Philip.

"Well, you can easily guess what happened, can't you? In that English-speaking colony the name of Le Cheminant was, of course, well known, and Philip had not been in St Vincent many weeks, before he learned that his father was none other than a younger brother of the present Earl of Tremarn, and that he himself—seeing that the present peer was over fifty and still unmarried—was heir-presumptive to the title and estates.

"You know the rest. Within two or three months of the memorable St Pierre catastrophe Philip Le Cheminant had written to his uncle, Lord Tremarn, demanding his rights. Then he took passage on board a French liner and crossed over to Havre *en route* for Paris and London.

"He and his mother—both brought up as French subjects—had, mind you, all the respect which French people have for their papers of identification; and when the house in which they had lived for twenty years was tumbling about the young man's ears, when his mother had already perished in the flames, he made a final and successful effort to rescue the papers which proved him to be a French citizen, the son of Lucie Legrand by her lawful marriage with Arthur Le Cheminant at the church of the Immaculate Conception of St Pierre.

"What happened immediately afterwards it is difficult to conjecture. Certain it is, however, that over here the newspapers soon were full of vague allusions about the newly found heir to the Earldom of Tremarn, and within a few weeks the whole of the story of the secret marriage at St Pierre was in everybody's mouth.

"It created an immense sensation; the Hon. Arthur Le Cheminant had lived a few years in England after his return from abroad, and no one, not even his brother, seemed to have had the slightest inkling of his marriage.

"The late Lord Tremarn, you must remember, had three sons, the eldest of whom is the present peer, the second was the romantic Arthur, and the third, the Hon. Reginald, who also died some years ago, leaving four sons, the eldest of whom, Harold, was just twenty-three, and had always been styled heir-presumptive to the Earldom.

"Lord Tremarn had brought up these four nephews of his, who had lost both father and mother, just as if they had been his own children, and his affection for them, and notably for the eldest boy, was a very beautiful trait in his otherwise unattractive character.

"The news of the existence and claim of this unknown nephew must have come upon Lord Tremarn as a thunderbolt. His attitude, however, was one of uncompromising incredulity. He refused to believe the story of the marriage, called the whole tale a tissue of falsehoods, and denounced the claimant as a bare-faced and impudent impostor.

"Two or three months more went by; the public were eagerly awaiting the arrival of this semi-exotic claimant to an English peerage, and sensations, surpassing those of the Tichborne case, were looked forward to with palpitating interest.

"But in the romances of real life, it is always the unexpected that happens. The claimant did arrive in London about a year ago. He was alone, friendless, and moneyless, since the £2,000 lay buried somewhere beneath the ruins of the St Pierre bank. However, he called upon a well-known London solicitor, who advanced him some money and took charge of all the papers relating to his claim.

"Philip Le Cheminant then seems to have made up his mind to make a personal appeal to his uncle, trusting apparently in the old adage that 'blood is thicker than water'.

"As was only to be expected, Lord Tremarn flatly refused to see the claimant, whom he was still denouncing as an impostor. It was by stealth, and by bribing the servants at the Grosvenor Square mansion, that the young man at last obtained an interview with his uncle.

"Last New Year's Day he gave James Tovey, Lord Tremarn's butler, a five-pound note, to introduce him, surreptitiously, into his master's study. There uncle and nephew at last met face to face.

"What happened at that interview nobody knows; was the cry of blood and of justice so convincing that Lord Tremarn dare not resist it? Perhaps.

"Anyway, from that moment the new heir-presumptive was installed within his rights. After a single interview with Philip Le Cheminant's solicitor, Lord Tremarn openly acknowledged the claimant to be his brother Arthur's only son, and therefore his own nephew and heir.

"Nay, more, everyone noticed that the proud, bad tempered old man was as wax in the hands of this newly found nephew. He seemed even to have withdrawn his affection from the four other young nephews, whom hitherto he had brought up as his own children, and bestowed it all upon his brother Arthur's son—some people said in compensation for all the wrong that had been done to the boy in the past.

"But the scandal around his dead brother's name had wounded the old man's pride very deeply, and from this he never recovered. He shut himself away from all his friends, living alone with his newly found nephew in his gloomy house in Grosvenor Square. The other boys, the eldest of whom, Harold, was just twenty-three, decided very soon to leave a house where they were no longer welcome. They had a small private fortune of their own from their father and mother; the youngest boy was still at college, two others had made a start in their respective professions.

"Harold had been brought up as an idle young man about town, and on him the sudden change of fortune fell most heavily. He was undecided what to do in the future, but, in the meanwhile, partly from a spirit of independence, and partly from a desire to keep a home for his younger brothers, he took and furnished a small flat, which, it is interesting to note, is just off Exhibition Road, not far from the Natural History Museum in Kensington.

"This was less than a year ago. Ten months later the newly found heir to the peerage of Tremarn was found murdered in a hansom cab, and Harold Le Cheminant is once more the future earl."

3

"The papers, as you know, talked of nothing else but the mysterious murder in the hansom cab. Everyone's sympathy went out at once to Lord Tremarn, who, on hearing the terrible news, had completely broken down, and was now lying on a bed of sickness, from which they say he may never recover.

"From the first there had been many rumours of the terrible enmity which existed between Harold Le Cheminant and the man who had so easily captured Lord Tremarn's heart, as well as the foremost place in the Grosvenor Square household.

"The servants in the great and gloomy mansion told the detectives in charge of the case many stories of terrible rows which occurred at first between the cousins. And now everyone's eyes were already turned with suspicion on the one man who could most benefit by the death of Philip Le Cheminant.

"However careful and reticent the police may be, details in connection with so interesting a case have a wonderful way of leaking out. Already one other most important fact had found its way into the papers. It appears that in their endeavours to reconstruct the last day spent by the murdered man the detectives had come upon most important evidence.

"It was Thomas Sawyer, hall porter of the Junior Grosvenor Club, who first told the following interesting story. He stated that deceased was a member of the club, and had dined there on the evening preceding his death.

"'Mr Le Cheminant was just coming downstairs after his dinner,' explained Thomas Sawyer to the detectives, 'when a stranger comes into the hall of the club; Mr Le Cheminant saw him as soon as I did, and appeared very astonished. "What do you want?" he says rather sharply. "A word with you," replies the stranger. Mr Le Cheminant seemed to hesitate for a moment. He lights a cigar, whilst the stranger stands there glaring at him with a look in his eye I certainly didn't like.

"'Mind you,' added Thomas Sawyer, 'the stranger was a gentleman in evening dress, and all that. Presently Mr Le Cheminant says to him: "This way, then," and takes him along into one of the club rooms. Half an hour later the stranger comes out again. He looked flushed and excited. Soon after Mr Le Cheminant comes out too; but he was quite calm and smoking a cigar. He asks for a cab, and tells the driver to take him to the Lyric Theatre.'

"This was all that the hall porter had to say, but his evidence was corroborated by one of the waiters of the club who saw Mr Le Cheminant and the stranger subsequently enter the dining-room, which was quite deserted at the time.

"'They 'adn't been in the room a minute,' said the waiter, 'when I 'eard loud voices, as if they was quarrelling frightful. I couldn't 'ear what they said, though I tried, but they was shouting so, and drowning each other's voices. Presently there's a ring at my bell, and I goes into the room. Mr Le Cheminant was sitting beside one of the tables, quietly lighting a cigar. "Show this—er—gentleman out of the club," 'e says to me. The stranger looked as if 'e would strike 'im. "You'll pay for this," 'e says, then 'e picks up 'is 'at, and dashes out of the club helter-skelter. "One is always pestered by these beggars," says Mr Le Cheminant to me, as 'e stalks out of the room.'

"Later on, it was arranged that both Thomas Sawyer and the waiter should catch sight of Harold Le Cheminant, as he went out of his house in Exhibition Road. Neither of them had the slightest hesitation in recognising in him the stranger who had called at the club that night.

"Now that they held this definite clue, the detectives continued their work with a will. They made enquiries at the Lyric Theatre, but there they only obtained very vague testimony; one point, however, was of great value, the commissionaire outside one of the neighbouring theatres stated that, sometime after the performance had begun, he noticed a gentleman in evening dress walking rapidly past him.

"He seemed strangely excited, for as he went by, he muttered quite audibly to himself: 'I can stand it no longer, it must be he or I.' Then he disappeared in the fog, walking away towards Shaftesbury Avenue. Unfortunately, the commissionaire, just like the cabman, was not prepared to swear to the identity of this man, whom he had only seen momentarily through the fog.

"But add to all this testimony the very strong motive there was for the crime, and you will not wonder that, within twenty-four hours of the murder, the strongest suspicions had already fastened on Harold Le Cheminant, and it was generally understood that, even before the inquest, the police already had in readiness a warrant for his arrest on the capital charge."

4

"It would be difficult, I think, for anyone who was not present at that memorable inquest to have the least idea of the sensation which its varied and dramatic incidents caused among the crowd of spectators there.

"At first the proceedings were of the usual kind. The medical officer gave his testimony as to the cause of death; this was, of course, not in dispute. The stiletto was produced; it was of an antique and foreign pattern, probably of Eastern or else Spanish origin. In England, it could only have been purchased at some *bric-à-brac* shop.

"Then it was the turn of the servants at Grosvenor Square, of the cabman, and of the commissionaire. Lord Tremarn's evidence, which he had sworn to on his sickbed, was also read. It added nothing to the known facts of the case, for he had last seen his favourite nephew alive in the course of the afternoon preceding the latter's tragic end.

"After that the *employés* of the Junior Grosvenor Club retold their story, and they were the first to strike the note of sensation which was afterwards raised to its highest possible pitch.

"Both of them, namely, were asked each in their turn to look round the court and see if they could recognise the stranger who had called at the club that memorable evening. Without the slightest hesitation, both the hall porter and the waiter pointed to Harold Le Cheminant, who sat with his solicitor in the body of the court.

"But already an inkling of what was to come had gradually spread through that crowded court—instinctively everyone felt that behind the apparent simplicity of this tragic case there lurked another mystery, more strange even than that murder in the hansom cab.

"Evidence was being taken as to the previous history of the deceased, his first appearance in London, his relationship with his uncle, and subsequently his enmity with his cousin Harold. At this point a man was brought forward as a witness, who it was understood had communicated with the police at the very last moment, offering to make a statement which he thought would throw considerable light upon the mysterious affair.

"He was a man of about fifty years of age, who looked like a very seedy, superannuated clerk of some insurance office.

"He gave his name as Charles Collins, and said that he resided in Caxton Road, Clapham.

"In a perfectly level tone of voice, he then explained that some three years ago, his son William, who had always been idle and good for nothing, had suddenly disappeared from home.

"'We heard nothing of him for over two years,' continued Charles Collins, in that same cheerless and even voice which spoke of a monotonous existence of ceaseless, patient grind, 'but some few weeks ago my daughter went up to the West End to see about an engagement—she plays dance music at parties sometimes—when, in Regent Street, she came face to face with her brother William. He was no longer wretched, as we all are,' added the old man pathetically, 'he was dressed like a swell, and when his sister spoke to him, he pretended not to know her. But she's a sharp girl, and guessed at once that there was something strange there which William wished to hide. She followed him from a distance, and never lost sight of him that day, until she saw him about six o'clock in the evening go into one of the fine houses in Grosvenor Square. Then she came home and told her mother and me all about it.'

"I can assure you," continued the man in the corner, "that you might have heard a pin drop in that crowded court whilst the old man spoke. That he was stating the truth no one doubted for a moment. The very fact that he was brought forward as a witness showed that his story had been proved, at any rate, to the satisfaction of the police.

"The Collinses seem to have been very simple, good-natured people. It never struck any of them to interfere with William, who appeared, in their own words, to have 'bettered himself'. They concluded that he had obtained some sort of position in a rich family and was now ashamed of his poor relations at Clapham.

"Then one morning they read in the papers the story of the mysterious murder in the hansom cab, together with a description of the victim, who had not yet been identified. 'William,' they said with one accord. Michael Collins, one of the younger sons, went up to London to view the murdered man at the mortuary. There was no doubt whatever that it was William, and yet all the papers persisted in saying that the deceased was the heir to some grand peerage.

"'So, I wrote to the police,' concluded Charles Collins, 'and my wife and children were all allowed to view the body, and we are all prepared to swear that it is that of my son, William Collins, who was no more heir to a peerage than your worship.'

"And mopping his forehead with a large coloured handkerchief, the old man stepped down from the box.

"Well, you may imagine what this bombshell was in the midst of that coroner's court. Everyone looked at his neighbour, wondering if this was real life, or some romantic play being acted upon a stage. Amidst indescribable excitement, various other members of the Collins family corroborated the old man's testimony, as did also one or two friends from Clapham. All those who had been allowed to view the body of the murdered man pronounced it without hesitation to be that of William Collins, who had disappeared from home three years ago.

"You see, it was like a repetition of the Tichborne case, only with this strange difference: this claimant was dead, but all his papers were in perfect order, the certificate of marriage between Lucie Legrand and Arthur Le Cheminant at Martinique, as well as the birth and baptismal certificate of Philip Le Cheminant, their son. Yet there were all those simple, honest folk swearing that the deceased had been born in Clapham, and the mother, surely, could not have been mistaken.

"That is where the difference with the other noteworthy case came in, for in this instance, as far as the general public is concerned, the actual identity of the murdered man will always remain a matter of doubt—Philip Le Cheminant or William Collins took that part of his secret, at any rate, with him to his grave."

"But the murder?" I asked eagerly, for the man in the corner had paused, intent upon the manufacture of innumerable knots in a long piece of string.

"Ah, yes, the murder, of course," he replied, with a chuckle, "the second mystery in this extraordinary case. Well, of course, whatever the identity of the deceased really was, there was no doubt in the minds of the police that Harold Le Cheminant had murdered him. To him, at any rate, the Collins family were unknown; he only knew the man who had supplanted him in his uncle's affections, and snatched a rich inheritance away from him. The charge brought against him at the Westminster Court was also one of the greatest sensations of this truly remarkable case.

"It looked, indeed, as if the unfortunate young man had committed a crime which was as appalling as it was useless. Instead of murdering the impostor—if impostor he was—how much more simple it would have been to have tried to unmask him. But, strange to say, this he never seems to have done, at any rate, as far as the public knew.

"But here again mystery stepped in. When brought before the magistrate, Harold Le Cheminant was able to refute the terrible charge brought against him by the simple means of a complete alibi. After the stormy episode at the Junior Grosvenor Club, he had gone to his own club in Pall Mall, and fortunately for him, did not leave until twenty minutes past eleven, some few minutes *after* the two men in evening dress got into the hansom in Shaftesbury Avenue.

"But for this lucky fact, for which he had one or two witnesses, it might have fared ill with him, for feeling unduly excited, he walked all the way home afterwards; and had he left his club earlier, he might have found it difficult to account for his time. As it was, he was of course discharged.

"But one more strange fact came out during the course of the magisterial investigation, and that was that Harold Le Cheminant, on the very day preceding the murder, had booked a passage for St Vincent. He admitted in court that he meant to conduct certain investigations there, with regard to the identity of the supposed heir to the Tremarn peerage.

"And thus, the curtain came down on the last act of that extraordinary drama, leaving two great mysteries unsolved: the real identity of the murdered man, and that of the man who killed him. Some people still persist in thinking it was Harold Le Cheminant. Well, we may easily dismiss that supposition. Harold had decided to investigate the matter for himself; he was on his way to St Vincent.

"Surely common sense would assert that, having gone so far, he would assure himself first whether the man was an impostor or not, before he resorted to crime, in order to rid himself of him. Moreover, the witnesses who saw him leave his own club at twenty minutes past eleven were quite independent and very emphatic.

"Another theory is that the Collins gang tried to blackmail Philip Le Cheminant—or William Collins, whichever we like to call him— and that it was one of them who murdered him out of spite, when he refused to submit to the blackmailing process.

"Against that theory, however, there are two unanswerable arguments—firstly, the weapon used, which certainly was not one that would commend itself to the average British middle-class man on murder intent—a razor or knife would be more in his line; secondly, there is no doubt whatever that the murderer wore evening dress and an opera hat, a costume not likely to have been worn by any member of the Collins family, or their friends. We may, therefore, dismiss that theory also with equal certainty."

And he surveyed placidly the row of fine knots in his bit of string.

"But then, according to you, who was the man in evening dress, and who but Harold Le Cheminant had any interest in getting rid of the claimant?" I asked at last.

"Who, indeed?" he replied with a chuckle, "who but the man who was as wax in the hands of that impostor?"

"Whom do you mean?" I gasped.

"Let us take things from the beginning," he said with ever-growing excitement, "and take the one thing which is absolutely beyond dispute, and that is the authenticity of the *papers*—the marriage certificate of Lucie Legrand, etc.—as against the authenticity of the *man*. Let us admit that the real Philip Le Cheminant was a refugee at St Vincent, that he found out about his parentage, and determined to go to England. He writes to his uncle, then sails for Europe, lands at Havre, and arrives in Paris."

"Why Paris?" I asked.

"Because you, like the police and like the public, have persistently shut your eyes to an event which, to my mind, has bearing upon the whole of this mysterious case, and that is the original murder committed in Paris a year ago, also in a cab, also with a stiletto—which that time was not found—in fact, in the self-same manner as this murder a week ago.

"Well, that crime was never brought home to its perpetrator any more than this one will be. But my contention is, that the man who committed that murder a year ago, repeated this crime last week—that the man who was murdered in Paris was the real Philip Le Cheminant, whilst the man who was murdered in London was some friend to whom he had confided his story, and probably his papers, and who then hit upon the bold plan of assuming the personality of the Martinique *creole*, heir to an English peerage."

"But what in the world makes you imagine such a preposterous thing?" I gasped.

"One tiny unanswerable fact," he replied quietly. "William Collins, the impostor, when he came to London, called upon a solicitor, and deposited with him the valuable papers; *after that* he obtained his interview with Lord Tremarn. Then mark what happens. Without any question, immediately after that interview, and, therefore, without even having seen the papers of identification, Lord Tremarn accepts the claimant as his newly found nephew.

"And why?

"Only because that claimant has a tremendous hold over the earl, which makes the old man as wax in his hands, and it is only logical to conclude that that hold was none other than that Lord Tremarn had met his real nephew in Paris, and had killed him, sooner than to see him supplant his beloved heir, Harold.

"I followed up the subsequent history of that Paris crime, and found that the Paris police had never established the identity of the murdered man. Being a stranger, and moneyless, he had apparently lodged in one of those innumerable ill-famed little hotels that abound in Paris, the proprietors of which have very good cause to shun the police, and therefore would not even venture so far as to go and identify the body when it lay in the Morgue.

"But William Collins knew who the murdered man was; no doubt he lodged at the same hotel, and could lay his hands on the all-important papers. I imagine that the two young men originally met in St Vincent, or perhaps on-board ship. He assumed the personality of the deceased, crossed over to England, and confronted Lord Tremarn with the threat to bring the murder home to him if he ventured to dispute his claim.

"Think of it all, and you will see that I am right. When Lord Tremarn first heard from his brother Arthur's son, he went to Paris in order to assure himself of the validity of his claim. Seeing that there was no doubt of that, he assumed a friendly attitude towards the young man, and one evening took him out for a drive in a cab and murdered him on the way.

"Then came Nemesis in the shape of William Collins, whom he dared not denounce, lest his crime be brought home to him. How could he come forward and say: 'I know that this man is an impostor, as I happened to have murdered my nephew myself'?

"No; he preferred to temporize, and bide his time until, perhaps, chance would give him his opportunity. It took a year in coming. The yoke had become too heavy. 'It must be he or I!' he said to himself that very night. Apparently, he was on the best of terms with his tormentor, but in his heart of hearts he had always meant to be even with him at the last.

"Everything favoured him; the foggy night, even the dispute between Harold and the impostor at the club. Can you not picture him meeting William Collins outside the theatre, hearing from him the story of the quarrel, and then saying, 'Come with me to Harold's; I'll soon make the young jackanapes apologise to you'?

"Mind you, a year had passed by since the original crime. William Collins, no doubt, never thought he had anything to fear from the old man. He got into the cab with him, and thus this remarkable story has closed, and Harold Le Cheminant is once more heir to the Earldom of Tremarn.

"Think it all over, and bear in mind that Lord Tremarn *never* made the slightest attempt to prove the rights or wrongs of the impostor's claim. On this base your own conclusions, and then see if they do not inevitably lead you to admit mine as the only possible solution of this double mystery."

He was gone, leaving me bewildered and amazed staring at my *Daily Telegraph*, where, side by side with a long recapitulation of the mysterious claimant to the Earldom, there was the following brief announcement:

We regret to say that the condition of Lord Tremarn is decidedly worse today, and that but little hope is entertained of his recovery. Mr Harold Le Cheminant has been his uncle's constant and devoted companion during the noble earl's illness.

The Fate of the "Artemis"

1

"Well, I'm—!" was my inelegant mental comment upon the news in that morning's paper.

"So are most people," rejoined the man in the corner, with that eerie way he had of reading my thoughts. "The *Artemis* has come home, having safely delivered her dangerous cargo, and Captain Jutland's explanations only serve to deepen the mystery."

"Then you admit there is one in this case?" I said.

"Only to the public. Not to me. But I do admit that the puzzle is a hard one. Do you remember the earlier details of the case? It was towards the end of 1903. Negotiations between Russia and Japan were just reaching a point of uncomfortable tension, and the man in the street guessed that war in the Far East was imminent.

"Messrs Mills and Co. had just completed an order for a number of their celebrated quick-firing guns for the Russian Government, and these—according to the terms of the contract—were to be delivered at Port Arthur on or about 1st February 1904. Effectively, then, on 1st December last, the *Artemis*, under the command of Captain Jutland, sailed from Goole, with her valuable cargo on board, and with orders to proceed along as fast as possible, in view of the probable outbreak of hostilities.

"Less than two hours after she had started, Messrs Mills received intimation from the highest official quarters, that in all probability before the *Artemis* could reach Port Arthur, and in view of coming eventualities, the submarine mines would have been laid at the entrance to the harbour. A secret plan of the port was therefore sent to the firm for Captain Jutland's use, showing the only way through which he could possibly hope to navigate the *Artemis* safely into the harbour, and without which she would inevitably come in contact with one of those terrible engines of wholesale destruction, which have since worked such awful havoc in this war.

"But *there* was the trouble. This official intimation, together with the plan, reached Messrs Mills just two hours too late; it is a way peculiar to many official intimations. Fortunately, however, the *Artemis* was to touch at Portsmouth on private business of the firm's, and, therefore, it only meant finding a trustworthy messenger to meet Captain Jutland there, and to hand him over that all-important plan.

"Of course, there was no time to be lost, but, above all, someone of extreme trustworthiness must be found for so important a mission. You must remember that the great European Power in question is beset by many foes in the shape of her own disaffected children, who desire her downfall even more keenly than does her Asiatic opponent. Also, in times like these, when every method is fair which gives one adversary an advantage over the other, we must remember that our plucky little allies of the Far East are past masters in that art which is politely known as secret intelligence.

"All this, you see, made it an absolute necessity to keep the mission to Captain Jutland a profound secret. I need not impress upon you the fact, I think, that it is not expedient for the plans of an important harbour to fall under prying eyes.

"Finally, the choice fell on Captain Markham, R.N.R., lately of the mercantile marine, and at the time in the employ of our own Secret Intelligence Department, to which he has rendered frequent and valuable services. This choice was determined also mainly through the fact that Captain Markham's wife had relatives living in Portsmouth, and that, therefore, his journey thither could easily be supposed to have an unofficial and quite ordinary character—especially if he took his wife with him, which he did.

"Captain and Mrs Markham left Waterloo for Portsmouth at ten minutes past twelve on Wednesday, 2nd December, the secret plan lying safely concealed at the bottom of Mrs Markham's jewel case.

"As the *Artemis* would not touch at Portsmouth until the following morning, Captain Markham thought it best not to spend the night at an hotel, but to go into rooms; his choice fell on a place, highly recommended by his wife's relations, and which was situated in a quiet street on the Southsea side of the town. There he and his wife stayed the night, pending the arrival of the *Artemis*.

"But at twelve o'clock on the following morning the police were hastily called in by Mrs Bowden, the landlady of 49 Gastle Street, where the Markhams had been staying. Captain Markham had been found lying half-insensible, gagged and bound, on the floor of the sitting-room, his hands and feet tightly pinioned, and a woollen comforter wound closely round his mouth and neck; whilst Mrs Markham's jewel case, containing valuable jewellery and the secret plans of Port Arthur, had disappeared."

2

"Mind you," continued the man in the corner, after he had assured himself of my undivided attention, "all these details were unknown to the public at first. I have merely co-ordinated them, and told them to you in the actual sequence in which they occurred, so that you may be able to understand the subsequent events.

"At the time—that is to say, on 3rd December 1903—the evening papers only contained an account of what was then called 'the mysterious outrage at Gastle Street, Portsmouth'. A private gentleman was presumably assaulted and robbed in broad daylight, and inside a highly respectable house in a busy part of the city.

"Mrs Bowden, the landlady, was, as you may imagine, most excited and indignant. Her house and herself had been grossly insulted by this abominable outrage, and she did her level best to throw what light she could on this mysterious occurrence.

"The story she told the police was indeed extraordinary, and as she repeated it to all her friends, and subsequently to one or two journalists, it roused public excitement to its highest pitch.

"What she related at great length to the detective in charge of the case, was briefly this:

"Captain and Mrs Markham, it appears, arrived at 49 Gastle Street, on Wednesday afternoon, 2nd December, and Mrs Bowden accommodated them with a sitting-room and bedroom, both on the ground floor. In the evening Mrs Markham went out to dine with her brother, a Mr Paulton, who is a well-known Portsmouth resident, but Captain Markham stayed in and had dinner alone in his sitting-room.

"According to Mrs Bowden's version of the story, at about nine o'clock a stranger called to see Captain Markham. This stranger was obviously a foreigner, for he spoke broken English. Unfortunately, the hall at 49 Gastle Street was very dark, and, moreover, the foreigner was attired in a magnificent fur coat, the collar of which hid the lower part of his face. All Mrs Bowden could see of him was that he was very tall, and wore gold-rimmed spectacles.

"'He was so very peremptory in his manner,' continued Mrs

Bowden, 'that I had to show him in at once. The captain seemed surprised to see him—in fact he looked decidedly annoyed, I might say; but just as I was closing the door I heard the stranger laugh, and say quite pleasantly: "You gave me the slip, my friend, but you see I have found you out all right."

"Mrs Bowden, after the manner of her class, seems to have made vigorous efforts to hear what went on in the sitting-room after that," continued the man in the corner, "but she was not successful. Later on, however, the captain rang and ordered whiskies and sodas. Both gentlemen were then sitting by the fire, looking quite friendly.

"'I took a look round the room,' explained the worthy landlady, 'and took particular notice that the jewel case was on the table, with the lid open. Captain Markham, as soon as he saw me, closed it very quickly.'

"The stranger seems to have gone away again at about half past ten, and subsequently Mrs Markham came home, accompanied by her brother, Mr Paulton. The next morning, she went out at a quarter past eleven o'clock, and about half an hour later the mysterious stranger called again.

"This time he pushed his way straight into the sitting-room; but the very next moment he uttered a cry of intense horror and astonishment, and rushed back into the hall, gesticulating wildly, and shrieking: 'A robbery!—a murder!—I go for the police!' And before Mrs Bowden could stop him or even could realise what had occurred, he had dashed out of the house.

"'I called to Meggie,' continued Mrs Bowden, 'I was so frightened, I didn't dare go into the parlour alone. But she was more frightened than I was, and we stood trembling in the hall waiting for the police. At last, I began to have my suspicions, and I got Meggie to run out into the street and see if she could bring in a policeman.'

"When the police at last arrived upon the scene, they pushed open the sitting-room door, and there found Captain Markham in a most helpless condition, his hands tied behind his back and himself half-choked by the scarf over his mouth. As soon as he recovered his breath, he explained that he had no idea who his assailant was; he was standing with his back to the door, when he was suddenly dealt a blow on the head from behind, and he remembered nothing more.

"In the meantime, Mrs Markham had come home, and of course was horrified beyond measure at the outrage which had been committed. She declared that her jewel case was in the sitting-room when she went out in the morning—a fact confirmed by Captain Markham himself.

"But here, at once, the police were seriously puzzled. Mrs Bowden, of course, told her story of the foreigner—a story which was corroborated by her daughter, Meggie. Captain Markham, pressed by the police, and by his wife, admitted that a friend had visited him the evening before.

"'He is an old friend I met years ago abroad, who happened to be in Portsmouth yesterday, and quite accidentally caught sight of me as I drove up to this door, and naturally came in to see me,' was the captain's somewhat lame explanation.

"Nothing more was to be got out of him that day; he was still feeling very bewildered, he said, and certainly he looked very ill. Mrs Markham then put the whole matter in the hands of the police.

"Captain Markham had given a description of 'the old friend he had met years ago abroad'. This description vaguely coincided with that given by Mrs Bowden of the mysterious foreigner. But the captain's replies to the cross-questionings of the detectives in charge of the case were always singularly reticent and lame. 'I had lost sight of him for nearly twenty years,' he explained, 'and do not know what his present abode and occupation might be. When I knew him years ago, he was a man of independent means, without a fixed abode, and a great traveller. I believe that he is a German by nationality, but I don't think that I ever knew this as a fact. His name was Johann Schmidt.'

"I may as well tell you here, at once, that the mysterious foreigner managed to make good his escape. He was traced as far as the South-western Railway Station, where he was seen to rush through the barrier, just in time to catch the express up to town. At Waterloo he was lost sight of in the crowd.

"The police were keenly on the alert; no trace of the missing jewels had as yet been found. Then it was that, gradually, the story of the secret plan of Port Arthur reached the ears of the general public. Who first told it and to whom, it is difficult to conjecture, but you know what a way things of that sort have of leaking out.

"The secret of Captain Markham's mission had of necessity been known to several people, and a secret shared by many soon ceases to be one at all; anyway, within a week of the so-called 'Portsmouth outrage', it began to be loudly whispered that the robbery of Mrs Markham's jewels was only a mask that covered the deliberate theft of the plans of Port Arthur.

"And then the inevitable happened. Already Captain Markham's strange attitude had been severely commented upon, and now the public, backed by the crowd of amateur detectives who read penny novelettes and form conclusions of their own, had made up its mind that Captain Markham was a party to the theft—that he was either the tool or the accomplice of the mysterious foreigner, and that, in fact, he had been either bribed or terrorized into giving up the plan of Port Arthur to an enemy of the Russian Government. The crime was all the more heinous as by this act of treachery a British ship, manned by a British crew, had been sent to certain destruction.

"What rendered the whole case doubly mysterious was that Messrs Mills and Co. seemed to take the matter with complete indifference. They refused to be interviewed, or to give any information about the *Artemis* at all, and seemed callously willing to await events.

"The public was furious; the newspapers stormed; everyone felt that the *Artemis* should be stopped at any cost at her next port of call, and not allowed to continue her perilous journey.

"And yet the days went by; the public read with horror at Lloyd's that the *Artemis* had called at Malta, at Port Said, at Aden, and was now well on her way to the Far East. Feeling ran so high throughout England, that, if the mysterious stranger had been discovered by the police, no protection from them would have saved him from being lynched.

"As for Captain Markham, public opinion reserved its final judgment. A cloud hung over him, of that there was no doubt; many said openly that he had sold the secret plans of Port Arthur, either to the Japanese or to the Nihilists, either through fear or intimidation, if not through greed.

"Then the inevitable climax came: a certain Mr Carleton constituted himself the spokesman of the general public; he met Captain Markham one day at one of the clubs in London. There were hot words between them; Mr Carleton did not mince matters; he openly accused Captain Markham of that which public opinion had already whispered, and finally, completely losing his temper, he struck the captain in the face, calling him every opprobrious name he could think of.

"But for the timely interference of friends, there would have been murder committed then and there; as it was, Captain Markham was induced by his own friends to bring a criminal charge of slander and of assault against Mr Carleton, as the only means of making the whole story public, and possibly vindicating his character."

"A criminal action for slander and assault is always an interesting one," continued the man in the corner, after a while, "as it always argues an unusual amount of personal animosity on the part of the plaintiff.

"In this case, of course, public interest was roused to its highest pitch. Practically, though Captain Markham was the prosecutor, he would stand before his fellow-citizens after this action either as an innocent man, or as one of the most dastardly scoundrels this nation has ever known.

"The case for the captain was briefly stated by his counsel. For the defence Sir Arthur Inglewood, on behalf of Mr Carleton, pleaded justification. With wonderful eloquence Sir Arthur related the whole story of the secret plan of Port Arthur confided to the honour of Captain Markham, and which involved the safety of the British ship and the lives of a whole British crew.

"The first witnesses called for the defence were Mrs Bowden and her daughter, Meggie. Both related the story I have already told you. When they came to the point of having seen the jewel case open on the table during that interview between Captain Markham and the mysterious stranger, there was a regular murmur of indignation throughout the whole crowd, so much so, that the judge threatened to clear the court, for Sir Arthur argued this to be a proof that Captain Markham had been a willing accomplice in the theft of the secret plans, and had merely played the comedy of being assaulted, bound, and gagged.

"But there was more to come.

"It appears that on the morning of 2nd December—that is to say, before going to Portsmouth—Captain Markham, directly after breakfast, and while his wife was up in her own room, received a message, which seemed greatly to disturb him. It was Jane Mason, the parlourmaid at the Markhams' town house, who told the story.

"A letter bearing no stamp had been dropped into the letterbox; she had taken it to her master, who, on reading it, became greatly agitated; he tore up the letter, stuffed it into his pocket, and presently took up his hat and rushed out of the house.

"'When the master was gone,' continued Jane, 'I found a scrap of paper, which had fallen out of his pocket.'

"This scrap of paper Jane Mason had carefully put away. She was a shrewd girl, and scented some mystery. It was now produced in court, and the few fragmentary words were read out by Sir Arthur Inglewood, amidst boundless excitement:

. . . .if you lend a hand. . . . Port Arthur safely. . . .hold my tongue.

"And at the end there were four letters in large capitals, 'STOW'.

"In view of all the evidence taken, there was momentous significance to be attached to those few words, of which only the last four letters seemed mysterious, but these probably were part of the confederate's signature, who had—no one doubted it now—some hold upon Captain Markham, and had by a process of blackmail induced him to send the *Artemis* to her doom.

"After that, according to a statement made by the head clerk of Messrs Mills and Co., Captain Markham came round to the office, begging that someone else should be sent to meet Captain Jutland at Portsmouth. 'This,' explained the head clerk, who had been subpoenaed for the defence, 'was quite impossible at this eleventh hour, and in the absence of the heads of the firm, I had, on Mr Mills's behalf, to hold Captain Markham to his promise.'

"This closed the case for the defence, and, in view of the lateness of the hour, counsel's speeches were reserved for the following day. There was not a doubt in anybody's mind that Captain Markham was guilty, and but for the presence of a large body of police, I assure you he would have been torn to pieces by the crowd."

The man in the corner paused in his narrative and blinked at me over his bone-rimmed spectacles, like some lean and frowzy tom-cat eager for a fight.

"Well?" I said eagerly.

"Well, surely you remember what happened the following day?" he replied, with a dry chuckle. "Personally, I don't think that there ever was quite so much sensation in any English court of law.

"It was crowded, of course, when counsel for the plaintiff rose to speak. He made, however, only a short statement, briefly and to the point; but this statement caused everyone to look at his neighbour, wondering if he were awake or dreaming.

"Counsel began by saying that Messrs Mills and Co., in view of the obvious conspiracy that had existed against the *Artemis*, had decided, in conjunction with Captain Markham himself, to say nothing about the safety of the ship until she was in port; but now counsel had much pleasure in informing the court and public that the *Artemis* had safely arrived at Port Arthur, had landed her guns, and was on her way home again by now. A cablegram *via* St Petersburg had been received by Messrs Mills and Co. from Captain Jutland that very morning.

"That cablegram was read by counsel in court, and was received with loud and prolonged cheering which could not be suppressed.

"With heroic fortitude—explained counsel—Captain Markham had borne the gross suspicions against his integrity, only hoping that news of the safety of the *Artemis* would reach England in time to allow him to vindicate his character. But until Captain Jutland was safe in port, he had sworn to hold his tongue, and to bear insult and violence, sooner than once more jeopardise the safety of the British ship by openly avowing that she carried the plans of the important port with her.

"Well, you know the rest. The parties, at the suggestion of the judge, arranged the case amicably, and, Captain Markham being fully satisfied, Mr Carleton was nominally ordered to come up for trial when called upon.

"Captain Markham was the hero of the hour; but presently, after the first excitement had subsided, sensible people began to ponder. Everyone, of course, appreciated the fact that Messrs Mills and Co., prompted by the highest authorities, had insisted on not jeopardising the safety of the *Artemis* by shouting on the housetops that she was carrying the plans of Port Arthur on board. Hostilities in the Far East were on the point of breaking out, and I need not insist, I think, on the obvious fact that silence in such matters and at such a time was absolutely imperative.

"But what sensible people wanted to know was, what part had Captain Markham played in all this?

"In the evening of that memorable 2nd December, he was sitting amicably by the fire with the mysterious stranger, who was evidently blackmailing him, and with the jewel case, which contained the plans of Port Arthur, open between them. What, then, had caused Captain Markham to change his attitude? What dispelled the fear of the stranger? Was he really assaulted? Was the jewel case really stolen?

"Captain Jutland, of the *Artemis*, has explained that he was only on shore for one hour at Portsmouth on the memorable morning of 3rd December, namely, between 10.30 and 11.30 a.m. On landing at the Hard from his gig, he was met by a gentleman whom he did not know, and who, without a word of comment, handed him some papers, which proved to be plans of Port Arthur.

"Now, at that very hour Captain Markham was lying helpless in his bedroom, and the question now is, who abstracted the plans from the jewel case, and then mysteriously handed them to Captain Jutland? Why was it not done openly? Why?—why? and, above all, by whom?—"

4

"Indeed, why?" I retorted, for he had paused, and was peering at me through his bone-rimmed spectacles. "You must have a theory," I added, as I quietly handed him a beautiful bit of string across the table.

"Of course, I have a theory," he replied placidly; "nay, more, the only explanation of those mysterious events. But for this I must refer you to the scrap of paper found by Jane Mason, and containing the four fragmentary sentences which have puzzled everyone, and which Captain Markham always refused to explain.

"Do you remember," he went on, as he began feverishly to construct knot upon knot on that piece of string, "the wreck of the *Ridstow* some twenty years ago? She was a pleasure boat belonging to Mr Eyres, the great millionaire financier, and was supposed to have been wrecked in the South Seas, with nearly all hands. Five of her crew, however, were picked up by H.M.S. *Pomona*, on a bit of rocky island to which they had managed to swim.

"I looked up the files of the newspapers relating to the rescue of these five shipwrecked mariners, who told a most pitiable tale of the loss of the yacht and their subsequent escape to, and sufferings on, the island. Fire had broken out in the hull of the *Ridstow*, and all her crew were drowned, with the exception of three sailors, a Russian friend, or rather secretary, of Mr Eyres, and a young petty officer named Markham.

"You see, the letters 'STOW' had given me the clue. Clearly Markham, on receiving the message in the morning of 2nd December, was frightened, and when we analyse the fragments of that message and try to reconstruct the missing fragments, do we not get something like this:

"'*If you lend a hand* in allowing the *Artemis* to reach *Port Arthur safely*, and to land her cargo there, I will no longer *hold my tongue* about the events which occurred on board the *Rid*STOW.'

"Clearly the mysterious stranger had a great hold over Captain Markham, for every scrap of evidence, if you think it over, points to his having been *frightened*. Did he not beg the clerk to find someone else to meet Captain Jutland in Portsmouth? He did not wish *to lend a hand* in allowing the *Artemis* to reach *Port Arthur safely*.

"We must, therefore, take it that on board the *Ridstow* some such tragedy was enacted as, alas! is not of infrequent occurrence. The tragedy of a mutiny, a wholesale murder, the robbery of the rich financier, the burning of the yacht. Markham, then barely twenty, was no doubt an unwilling, perhaps passive, accomplice; one can trace the hand of a cunning, daring Russian in the whole of this mysterious tragedy.

"Since then, Markham, through twenty years' faithful service of his country, had tried to redeem the passive crime of his early years. But then came the crisis: the cunning leader of that bygone tragedy no doubt kept a strong hand over his weaker accomplices.

"What happened to the other three we do not know, but we have seen how terrified Markham is of him, how he dare not resist him, and when the mysterious Russian—some Nihilist, no doubt, at war with his own government—wishes to deal his country a terrible blow by possessing himself of the plan of her most important harbour, so that he might sell it to her enemies, Markham dare not say him nay.

"But mark what happens. Captain Markham terrorised, confronted with a past crime, threatened with exposure, is as wax in the hands of his unscrupulous tormentor. But beside him there is the saving presence of his wife."

"His wife?" I gasped.

"Yes, the woman! Did you think this was a crime without the inevitable woman? I sought her, and found her in Captain Markham's wife. To save her husband both from falling a victim to his implacable accomplice, and from committing another even more heinous crime, she suggests the comedy which was so cleverly enacted in the morning of 3rd December.

"When the landlady and her daughter saw the jewel case open on the table the evening before, Markham was playing the first act of the comedy invented by his wife. She had the plan safely in her own keeping by then. He pretended to agree to the Russian's demands, but showed him that he had not then the plan in his possession, promising, however, to deliver it up on the morrow.

"Then in the morning, Mrs Markham helps to gag and strap her husband down; he pretends to lie unconscious, and she goes out, carrying the jewel case. Her brother, Mr Paulton, of course, helps them both; without him it would have been more difficult; as it is, he takes charge of the jewel case, abstracts the plan and papers, and finally meets Captain Jutland at the Hard, and hands him over the plan of

Port Arthur.

"Thus, through the wits of a clever and devoted woman, not only are the *Artemis* and her British crew saved, but Captain Markham is effectually rid of the blackmailer, who otherwise would have poisoned his life, and probably out of revenge at being foiled, have ruined his victim altogether.

"To my mind, that was the neatest thing in the whole plan. The general public believed that Captain Markham (who obviously at the instigation of his wife had confided in Messrs Mills and Co.) held his tongue as to the safety of the *Artemis* merely out of heroism, in order not to run her into any further danger. Now, I maintain that this was the master-stroke of that clever woman's plan.

"By holding his tongue, by letting the public fear for the safety of the British crew and British ship, public feeling was stirred to such a pitch of excitement that the Russian now would never *dare* show himself. Not only—by denouncing Captain Markham now—would he never be even listened to for a moment, but, if he came forward at all, if he even showed himself, he would stand before the British public self-convicted as the man who had tried through the criminal process of blackmail to terrorise an Englishman into sending a British ship and thirty British sailors to certain annihilation.

"No; I think we may take it for granted that the Russian will not dare to show his face in England again."

And the funny creature was gone before I could say another word.

The Disappearance of Count Collini

1

He was very argumentative that morning; whatever I said he invariably contradicted flatly and at once, and we both had finally succeeded in losing our temper.

The man in the corner was riding one of his favourite hobby-horses.

"It is *impossible* for any person to completely disappear in a civilized country," he said emphatically, "provided that person has either friends or enemies of means and substance, who are interested in finding his or her whereabouts."

"Impossible is a sweeping word," I rejoined.

"None too big for the argument," he concluded, as he surveyed with evident pride and pleasure a gigantic and complicated knot, which his bony fingers had just fashioned.

"I think that, nevertheless, you should not use it," I said placidly. "It is not *impossible*, though it may be very difficult to disappear without leaving the slightest clue or trace behind you."

"Prove it," he said, with a snap of his thin lips.

"I can, quite easily."

"Now I know what is going on in your mind," said the uncanny creature; "you are thinking of that case last autumn."

"Well, I was," I admitted. "And you cannot deny that Count Collini has disappeared as effectually as if the sea had swallowed him up—many people think it did."

"Many idiots, you mean," he rejoined dryly. "Yes, I knew you would quote that case. It certainly was a curious one; all the more so, perhaps, as there was no inquest, no sensational police-court proceedings, nothing dramatic, in fact, save that strange and wonderful disappearance.

"I don't know if you call to mind the whole plot of that weird drama. There was Thomas Checkfield, a retired biscuit-baker of Reading, who died leaving a comfortable fortune, mostly invested in freehold property, and amounting to about £80,000, to his only child, Alice.

"At the time of her father's death Alice Checkfield was just eighteen, and at school in Switzerland, where she had spent most of her life. Old Checkfield had been a widower ever since the birth of his daughter, and seems to have led a very lonely and eccentric life, leaving the girl at school abroad for years, only going very occasionally to see her, and seemingly having but little affection for her.

"The girl herself had not been home in England since she was eight years old, and even when old Checkfield was dying he would not allow the girl to be apprised of his impending death, and to be brought home to a house of loneliness and mourning.

"'What's the good of upsetting a young girl, not eighteen,' he said to his friend, Mr Turnour, 'by letting her see all the sad paraphernalia of death? She hasn't seen much of her old father anyway, and will soon get over her loss, with young company round her, to help her bear up.'

"But though Thomas Checkfield cared little enough for his daughter, when he died, he left his entire fortune to her, amounting altogether to £80,000; and he appointed his friend, Reginald Turnour, to be her trustee and guardian until her marriage or until she should attain her majority.

"It was generally understood that the words 'until her marriage' were put in because it had all along been arranged that Alice should marry Hubert Turnour, Reginald's younger brother.

"Hubert was old Checkfield's godson, and if the old man had any affection for anybody, it certainly was for Hubert. The latter had been a great deal in his godfather's house, when he and Alice were both small children, and had called each other 'hubby' and 'wifey' in play, when they were still in the nursery. Later on, whenever old Checkfield went abroad to see his daughter, he always took Hubert with him, and a boy-and-girl flirtation sprang up between the two young people; a flirtation which had old Checkfield's complete approval, and no doubt he looked upon their marriage as a *fait accompli,* merely desiring the elder Mr Turnour to administer the girl's fortune until then.

"Hubert Turnour, at the time of the subsequent tragedy, was a good-looking young fellow, and by profession what is vaguely known as a 'commission agent'. He lived in London, where he had an office in a huge block of buildings close to Cannon Street Station.

"There is no doubt that at the time of old Checkfield's death,

Alice looked upon herself as the young man's *fiancée*. When the girl reached her nineteenth year, it was at last decided that she should leave school and come to England. The question as to what should be done with her until her majority, or until she married Hubert, was a great puzzle to Mr Turnour. He was a bachelor, who lived in comfortable furnished rooms in Reading, and he did not at all relish the idea of starting housekeeping for the sake of his young ward, whom he had not seen since she was out of the nursery, and whom he looked upon as an intolerable nuisance.

"Fortunately for him this vexed question was most satisfactorily and unexpectedly settled by Alice herself. She wrote to her guardian, from Geneva, that a Mrs Brackenbury, the mother of her dearest school-fellow, had asked her to come and live with them, at any rate for a time, as this would be a more becoming arrangement than that of a young girl sharing a bachelor's establishment.

"Mr Turnour seems to have hesitated for some time: he was a conscientious sort of man, who took his duties of guardianship very seriously. What ultimately decided him, however, was that his brother Hubert added the weight of his eloquent letters of appeal to those of Alice herself. Hubert naturally was delighted at the idea of having his rich *fiancée* under his eye in London, and after a good deal of correspondence, Mr Turnour finally gave his consent, and Alice Checkfield duly arrived from Switzerland in order to make a prolonged stay in Mrs Brackenbury's house."

2

"All seems to have gone on happily and smoothly for a time in Mrs Brackenbury's pretty house in Kensington," continued the man in the corner. "Hubert Turnour was a constant visitor there, and the two young people seem to have had all the freedom of an engaged couple.

"Alice Checkfield was in no sense of the word an attractive girl; she was not good-looking, and no effort on Mrs Brackenbury's part could succeed in making her look stylish. Still, Hubert Turnour seemed quite satisfied, and the girl herself ready enough at first to continue the boy-and-girl flirtation as of old.

"Soon, however, as time went on, things began to change. Now that Alice had become mistress of a comfortable fortune there were plenty of people ready to persuade her that a 'commission agent', with but vague business prospects, was not half-good enough for her, and that her £80,000 entitled her to more ambitious matrimonial hopes.

Needless to say, that in these counsels Mrs Brackenbury was very much to the fore.

"She lived in Kensington, and had social ambitions, foremost among which was to see her daughter's bosom friend married to, at least, a baronet, if not a peer.

"A young girl's head is quickly turned. Within six months of her stay in London, Alice was giving Hubert Turnour the cold shoulder, and the young man had soon realised that she was trying to get out of her engagement.

"Scarcely had Alice reached her twentieth birthday, than she gave her erstwhile *fiancée* his formal *congé*.

"At first Hubert seems to have taken his discomfiture very much to heart. £80,000 were not likely to come his way again in a hurry. According to Mrs Brackenbury's servants, there were one or two violent scenes between him and Alice, until finally Mrs Brackenbury herself was forced to ask the young man to discontinue his visits.

"It was soon after that that Alice Checkfield first met Count Collini at one of the brilliant subscription dances given by the Italian colony in London, the winter before last. Mrs Brackenbury was charmed with him, Alice Checkfield was enchanted! The count, having danced with Alice half the evening, was allowed to pay his respects at the house in Kensington.

"He seemed to be extremely well off, for he was staying at the Carlton, and, after one or two calls on Mrs Brackenbury, he began taking the ladies to theatres and concerts, always presenting them with the choicest and most expensive flowers, and paying them various other equally costly attentions.

"Mrs and Miss Brackenbury welcomed the count with open arms (figuratively speaking). Alice was shy, but apparently over head and ears in love at first sight.

"At first Mrs Brackenbury did her best to keep this new acquaintanceship a secret from Hubert Turnour. I suppose that the old matchmaker feared another unpleasant scene. But the inevitable soon happened. Hubert, contrite, perhaps still hopeful, called at the house one day, when the count was there, and, according to the story subsequently told by Miss Brackenbury herself, there was a violent scene between him and Alice. As soon as the fascinating foreigner had gone, Hubert reproached his *fiancée* for her fickleness in no measured language, and there was a good deal of evidence to prove that he then and there swore to be even with the man who had supplanted him in her affections. There was nothing to do then but for Mrs Brackenbury to 'burn her boats'. She peremptorily ordered Hubert out of her house, and admitted that Count Collini was a suitor, favoured by herself, for the hand of Alice Checkfield.

"You see, I am bound to give you all these details of the situation," continued the man in the corner, with his bland smile, "so that you may better form a judgment as to the subsequent fate of Count Collini. From the description which Mrs Brackenbury herself subsequently gave to the police, the count was then in the prime of life; of a dark olive complexion, dark eyes, extremely black hair and moustache. He had a very slight limp, owing to an accident he had had in early youth, which made his walk and general carriage unusual and distinctly noticeable. His was certainly not a personality that could pass unperceived in a crowd.

"Hubert Turnour, furious and heartsick, wrote letter after letter to his brother, to ask him to interfere on his behalf; this Mr Turnour did, to the best of his ability, but he had to deal with an ambitious matchmaker and with a girl in love, and it is small wonder that he signally failed. Alice Checkfield by now had become deeply enamoured of her count, his gallantries flattered her vanity, his title and the accounts he gave of his riches and his estates in Italy fascinated her, and she declared that she would marry him, either with or without her guardian's consent, either at once, or as soon as she had attained her majority, and was mistress of herself and of her fortune.

"Mr Turnour did all he could to prevent this absurd marriage. Being a sensible, middle-class Britisher, he had no respect for foreign titles, and little belief in foreign wealth. He wrote the most urgent letters to Alice, warning her against a man whom he firmly believed to be an impostor: finally, he flatly refused to give his consent to the marriage.

"Thus a few months went by. The count had been away in Italy all through the winter and spring, and returned to London for the season, apparently more enamoured with the Reading biscuit-baker's daughter than ever. Alice Checkfield was then within nine months of her twenty-first birthday, and determined to marry the count. She openly defied her guardian.

"'Nothing,' she wrote to him, 'would ever induce me to marry Hubert.'

"I suppose it was this which finally induced Mr Turnour to give up all opposition to the marriage. Seeing that his brother's chances were absolutely nil, and that Alice was within nine months of her majority he no doubt thought all further argument useless, and with great reluctance finally gave his consent.

"The marriage, owing to the difference of religion, was to be performed before a registrar, and was finally fixed to take place on 22nd October 1903, which was just a week after Alice's twenty-first birthday.

"Of course, the question of Alice's fortune immediately cropped up: she desired her money in cash, as her husband was taking her over to live in Italy where she desired to make all further investments. She, therefore, asked Mr Turnour to dispose of her freehold property for her. There again Mr Turnour hesitated, and argued, but once he had given his consent to the marriage, all opposition was useless, more especially as Mrs Brackenbury's solicitors had drawn up a very satisfactory marriage settlement, which the count himself had suggested, by which Alice was to retain sole use and control of her own private fortune.

"The marriage was then duly performed before a registrar on that 22nd of October, and Alice Checkfield could henceforth style herself Countess Collini. The young couple were to start for Italy almost directly but meant to spend a day or two at Dover quietly together. There were, however, one or two tiresome legal formalities to go through. Mr Turnour had, by Alice's desire, handed over the sum of £80,000 in notes to her solicitor, Mr R. W. Stanford. Mr Stanford had gone down to Reading two days before the marriage, had received the money from Mr Turnour, and then called upon the new countess, and formally handed her over her fortune in Bank of England notes.

"Then it was necessary, in view of immediate and future arrangements, to change the English money into foreign, which the count and his young wife did themselves that afternoon.

"At 5 o'clock p.m. they started for Dover, accompanied by Mrs Brackenbury, who desired to see the last of her young friend, prior to the latter's departure for abroad. The count had engaged a magnificent suite of rooms at the Lord Warden Hotel, and thither the party proceeded.

"So far, you see," added the man in the corner, "the story is of the utmost simplicity. You might even call it commonplace. A foreign count, an ambitious matchmaker, and a credulous girl; these form the ingredients of many a domestic drama that culminates at the police courts. But at this point this particular drama becomes more complicated, and, if you remember, ends in one of the strangest mysteries that has ever baffled the detective forces on both sides of the Channel."

The man in the corner paused in his narrative. I could see that he was coming to the palpitating part of the story, for his fingers fidgeted incessantly with that bit of string.

"Hubert Turnour, as you may imagine," he continued after a while, "did not take his final discomfiture very quietly. He was a very violent-tempered young man, and it was certainly enough to make anyone cross. According to Mrs Brackenbury's servants he used most threatening language in reference to Count Collini; and on one occasion was with difficulty prevented from personally assaulting the count in the hall of Mrs Brackenbury's pretty Kensington house.

"Count Collini finally had to threaten Hubert Turnour with the police court: this seemed to have calmed the young man's nerves somewhat, for he kept quite quiet after that, ceased to call on Mrs Brackenbury, and subsequently sent the future countess a wedding present.

"When the Count and Countess Collini, accompanied by Mrs Brackenbury, arrived at the Lord Warden, Alice found a letter awaiting her there. It was from Hubert Turnour. In it he begged her forgiveness for all the annoyance he had caused her, hoped that she would always look upon him as a friend, and finally expressed a strong desire to see her once more before her departure for abroad, saying that he would be in Dover either this same day or the next, and would give himself the pleasure of calling upon her and her husband.

"Effectively at about eight o'clock, when the wedding party was just sitting down to dinner, Hubert Turnour was announced. Everyone was most cordial to him, agreeing to let bygones be bygones: the count, especially, was most genial and pleasant towards his former rival, and insisted upon his staying and dining with them.

"Later on in the evening, Hubert Turnour took an affectionate leave of the ladies, Count Collini offering to walk back with him to the Grand Hotel, where he was staying. The two men went out together, and—well! you know the rest!—for that was the last the young Countess Collini ever saw of her husband. He disappeared as effectively, as completely, as if the sea had swallowed him up.

"'And so, it had,' say the public," continued the man in the corner, after a slight pause, "that delicious, short-sighted, irresponsible public is wondering, to this day, why Hubert Turnour was not hung for the murder of that Count Collini."

"Well! and why wasn't he?" I retorted.

"For the very simple reason," he replied, "that in this country you cannot hang a man for murder unless there is proof positive that a murder has been committed. Now, there was absolutely no proof that the count was murdered at all. What happened was this: the Countess Collini and Mrs Brackenbury became anxious as time went on and the count did not return. One o'clock, then two in the morning, and their anxiety became positive alarm. At last, as Alice was verging on hysterics, Mrs Brackenbury, in spite of the lateness of the hour, went round to the police station.

"It was, of course, too late to do anything in the middle of the night; the constable on duty tried to reassure the unfortunate lady, and promised to send word round to the Lord Warden at the earliest possible opportunity in the morning.

"Mrs Brackenbury went back with a heavy heart. No doubt Mr Turnour's sensible letters from Reading recurred to her mind. She had already ascertained from the distracted bride that the count had taken the strange precaution to keep in his own pocketbook the £80,000 now converted into French and Italian banknotes, and Mrs Brackenbury feared not so much that he had met with some accident, but that he had absconded with the whole of his girl-wife's fortune.

"The next morning brought but scanty news. No one answering to the count's description had met with an accident during the night, or been conveyed to a hospital, and no one answering his description had crossed over to Calais or Ostend by the night boats. Moreover, Hubert Turnour, who presumably had last been in Count Collini's company, had left Dover for town by the boat-train at 1.50 a.m.

"Then the search began in earnest after the missing man, and primarily Hubert Turnour was subjected to the closest and most searching cross-examination, by one of the most able men on our detective staff, Inspector Macpherson.

"Hubert Turnour's story was briefly this: He had strolled about on the parade with Count Collini for a while. It was a very blustery night, the wind blowing a regular gale, and the sea was rolling gigantic waves, which looked magnificent, as there was brilliant moonlight. 'Soon after ten o'clock,' he continued, 'the count and I went back to the Grand Hotel, and we had whiskies and sodas up in my room, and a bit of a chat until past eleven o'clock. Then he said goodnight and went off.'

"'You saw him down to the hall, of course?' asked the detective.

"'No, I did not,' replied Hubert Turnour. 'I had a few letters to write, and meant to catch the 1.50 a.m. back to town.'

"'How long were you in Dover altogether?' asked Macpherson carelessly.

"'Only a few hours. I came down in the afternoon.'

"'Strange, is it not, that you should have taken a room with a private sitting-room, at an expensive hotel, just for those few hours?'

"'Not at all. I originally meant to stay longer. And my expenses are nobody's business, I take it,' replied Hubert Turnour, with some show of temper. 'Anyway,' he added impatiently, after a while, 'if you choose to disbelieve me, you can make inquiries at the hotel, and ascertain if I have told the truth.'

"Undoubtedly, he had spoken the truth; at any rate, to that extent. Inquiries at the Grand Hotel went to prove that he had arrived there in the early part of the afternoon, had engaged a couple of rooms, and then gone out. Soon after ten o'clock in the evening he came in, accompanied by a gentleman, whose description, as given by three witnesses, *employés* of the hotel, who saw him, corresponded exactly with that of the count.

"Together the two gentlemen went up to Mr Hubert Turnour's rooms, and at half past ten they ordered whisky to be taken up to them. But at this point all trace of Count Collini had completely vanished. The passengers arriving by the 10.49 boat-train, and who had elected to spend the night in Dover, owing to the gale, had crowded up and filled the hall.

"No one saw Count Collini leave the Grand Hotel. But Mr Hubert Turnour came down into the hall at about half past eleven. He said he would be leaving by the 1.50 a.m. boat-train for town, but would walk round to the station as he only had a small bag with him. He paid his account, then waited in the coffee-room until it was time to go.

"And there the matter has remained. Mrs Brackenbury has spent half her own fortune in trying to trace the missing man. She has remained perfectly convinced that he slipped across the Channel, taking Alice Checkfield's money with him. But, as you know, at all ports of call on the South Coast, detectives are perpetually on the watch. The count was a man of peculiar appearance, and there is no doubt that no one answering to his description crossed over to France or Belgium that night. By the following morning the detectives on both sides of the Channel were on the alert. There is no disguise that would have held good. If the count had tried to cross over, he would have been spotted either on board or on landing; and we may take it as an absolute and positive certainty that he did not cross the Channel.

"He remained in England, but in that case, where is he? You would be the first to admit that, with the whole of our detective staff at his heels, it seems incredible that a man of the count's singular appearance could hide himself so completely as to baffle detection. Moreover, the question at once arises, that if he did not cross over to France or Belgium, what in the world did he do with the money? What was the use of disappearing and living the life of a hunted beast hiding for his life, with £80,000 worth of foreign money, which was practically useless to him?

"Now, I told you, from the first," concluded the man in the corner, with a dry chuckle, "that this strange episode contained no sensational incident, nor dramatic inquest or criminal procedure. Merely the complete, total disappearance, one may almost call it extinction, of a striking-looking man, in the midst of our vaunted civilization, and in spite of the untiring energy and constant watch of a whole staff of able men."

4

"Very well, then," I retorted in triumph, "that proves that Hubert Turnour murdered Count Collini out of revenge, not for greed of money, and probably threw the body of his victim, together with the foreign banknotes, into the sea."

"But where? When? How?" he asked, smiling good-humouredly at me over his great bone-rimmed spectacles.

"Ah! that I don't know."

"No, I thought not," he rejoined placidly. "You had, I think, forgotten one incident, namely, that Hubert Turnour, accompanied by the count, was in the former's room at the Grand Hotel drinking whisky at half past ten o'clock. You must admit that, even though the hall of the hotel was very crowded later on, a man would nevertheless find it somewhat difficult to convey the body of his murdered enemy through a whole concourse of people."

"He did not murder the count in the hotel," I argued. "The two men walked out again, when the hall was crowded, and they passed unnoticed. Hubert Turnour led the count to a lonely part of the cliffs, then threw him into the sea."

"The nearest point at which the cliffs might be called 'lonely' for purposes of a murder, is at least twenty minutes' walk from the Grand

Hotel," he said, with a smile, "always supposing that the count walked quickly and willingly to such a lonely spot at eleven o'clock at night, and with a man who had already, more than once, threatened his life. Mr Hubert Turnour, remember, was seen in the hall of the hotel at half past eleven, after which hour he only left the hotel to go to the station after 1 o'clock a.m.

"The hall was crowded by the passengers from the boat train a little after eleven. There was no time between that and half past to lead even a willing enemy to the slaughter, throw him into the sea, and come back again, all in the space of five-and-twenty minutes."

"Then what is your explanation of that extraordinary disappearance?" I retorted, beginning to feel very cross about it all.

"A simple one," he rejoined quietly, as he once more began to fidget with his bit of string. "A very simple one indeed; namely, that Count Collini, at the present moment, is living comfortably in England, calmly awaiting a favourable opportunity of changing his foreign money back into English notes."

"But you say yourself that that is impossible, as the most able detectives in England are on the watch for him."

"They are on the watch for a certain Count Collini," he said dryly, "who might disguise himself, perhaps, but whose hidden identity would sooner or later be discovered by one of these intelligent human bloodhounds."

"Yes? Well?" I asked.

"Well, that Count Collini never existed. It was *his* personality that was the disguise. Now it is thrown off. The count is not dead, he is not hiding, he has merely ceased to exist. There is no fear that he will ever come to life again. Mr Turnour senior will see to that."

"Mr Turnour!" I ejaculated.

"Why, yes," he rejoined excitedly; "do you mean to tell me you never saw through it all? The money lying in his hands; his brother about to wed the rich heiress; then Mrs Brackenbury's matrimonial ambitions, Alice Checkfield's coldness to Hubert Turnour, the golden prize slipping away right out of the family for ever. Then the scheme was evolved by those two scoundrels, who deserve to be called geniuses in their criminal way. It could not be managed, except by collaboration, but as it was, the scheme was perfect in conception, and easy of execution.

"Remember that disguise *previous* to a crime is always fairly safe from detection, for then it has no suspicion to contend against, it

342

merely deceives those who have no cause to be otherwise *but* deceived. Mrs Brackenbury lived in London, Reginald Turnour in Reading; they did not know each other personally, nor did they know each other's friends, of course; whilst Alice Checkfield had not seen her guardian since she was quite a child.

"Then the disguise was so perfect, I went down to Reading, some little time ago, and Reginald Turnour was pointed out to me: he is a Scotchman, with very light, sandy hair. That face clean-shaved, made swarthy, the hair, eyebrows, and lashes dyed a jet black, would render him absolutely unrecognisable. Add to this the fact that a foreign accent completely changes the voice, and that the slight limp was a master-stroke of genius to hide the general carriage.

"Then the winter came round; it was, perhaps, important that Mr Turnour should not be absent too long from Reading, for fear of exciting suspicion there; and the scoundrel played his part with marvellous skill. Can't you see him yourself leaving the Carlton Hotel, ostensibly going abroad, driving to Charing Cross, but only booking to Cannon Street?

"Then getting out at that crowded station and slipping round to his brother's office in one of those huge blocks of buildings where there is perpetual coming and going, and where any individual would easily pass unperceived?

"There, with the aid of a little soap and water, Mr Turnour resumed his Scotch appearance, went on to Reading, and spent winter and spring there, only returning to London to make a formal proposal, as Count Collini, for Alice Checkfield's hand. Hubert Turnour's office was undoubtedly the place where he changed his identity, from that of the British middle-class man, to the interesting personality of the Italian nobleman.

"He had, of course, to repeat the journey to Reading a day or two before his wedding, in order to hand over his ward's fortune to Mrs Brackenbury's solicitor. Then there were the supposed rows between Hubert Turnour and his rival; the letters of warning from the guardian, for which Hubert no doubt journeyed down to Reading, in order to post them there: all this was dust thrown into the eyes of two credulous ladies.

"After that came the wedding, the meeting with Hubert Turnour, who, you see, was obliged to take a room in one of the big hotels, wherein, with more soap and water, the Italian count could finally disappear. When the hall of the hotel was crowded, the sandy-haired

Scotchman slipped out of it quite quietly: he was not remarkable, and no one specially noticed him. Since then, the hue and cry has been after a dark Italian, who limps, and speaks broken English; and it has never struck anyone that such a person never existed.

"Mr Turnour is fairly safe by now; and we may take it for granted that he will not seek the acquaintanceship of the Brackenburys, whilst Alice Checkfield is no longer his ward. He will wait a year or two longer perhaps, then he and Hubert will begin quietly to reconvert their foreign money into English notes—they will take frequent little trips abroad, and gradually change the money at the various *bureaux de change* on the Continent.

"Think of it all, it is so simple—not even dramatic, only the work of a genius from first to last, worthy of a better cause, perhaps, but undoubtedly worthy of success."

He was gone, leaving me quite bewildered. Yet his disappearance had always puzzled me, and now I felt that that animated scarecrow had found the true explanation of it after all.

The Ayrsham Mystery

1

"I have never had a great opinion of our detective force here in England," said the man in the corner, in his funny, gentle, apologetic manner, "but the way that department mismanaged the affair at Ayrsham simply passes comprehension."

"Indeed?" I said, with all the quiet dignity I could command. "It is a pity they did not consult you in the matter, isn't it?"

"It is a pity," he retorted with aggravating meekness, "that they do not use a little common sense. The case resembles that of Columbus' egg, and is every bit as simple.

"It was one evening last October, wasn't it? that two labourers walking home from Ayrsham village turned down a lane, which, it appears, is a short cut to the block of cottages some distance off, where they lodged.

"The night was very dark, and there was a nasty drizzle in the air. In the picturesque vernacular of the two labourers, 'You couldn't see your 'and before your eyes.' Suddenly they stumbled over the body of a man lying right across the path.

"'At first we thought 'e was drunk,' explained one of them subsequently, 'but when we took a look at 'im, we soon saw there was something very wrong. Me and my mate turned 'im over, and "foul play" we both says at once. Then we see that it was Old Man Newton. Poor chap, 'e was dead, and no mistake.'

"Old Man Newton, as he was universally called by his large circle of acquaintances, was very well known throughout the entire neighbourhood, most particularly at every inn and public bar for some miles round.

"He also kept a local sweet-stuff shop at Ayrsham. No wonder that the men were horrified at finding him in such a terrible condition; even in their uneducated minds there could be no doubt that the old man had been murdered, for his skull had been literally shattered by a fearful blow, dealt him from behind by some powerful assailant.

"Whilst the labourers were cogitating as to what they had better do next, they heard footsteps also turning into the lane, and the next moment Samuel Holder, a well-known inhabitant of Ayrsham, arrived upon the scene.

"'Hello! is that you, Mat Newton?' shouted Samuel, as he came near.

"'Ay! 'tis Old Man Newton, right enough,' replied one of the labourers, 'but 'e won't answer you no more.'

"Samuel Holder seemed absolutely horrified when he saw the body of Old Man Newton; he uttered various ejaculations, which the two labourers, however, did not take special notice of at the time.

"Then the three men held a brief consultation together, with the result that one of them ran back to Ayrsham village to fetch the local police, whilst the two others remained in the lane to guard the body.

"The mystery—for it seemed one from the first—created a great deal of sensation in Ayrsham and all round the neighbourhood, and much sympathy was felt for, and shown to, Mary Newton, the murdered man's only child, a young girl about two- or three-and-twenty, who, moreover, was in ill health.

"True, Old Man Newton was not a satisfactory protector for a young girl. He was very much addicted to drink; he neglected the little bit of local business he had; and, moreover, had recently shamefully ill-treated his daughter, the neighbours testifying to the many and loud quarrels that occurred in the small back parlour behind the sweet-stuff shop.

"A case of murder—the moment an element of mystery hovers around it—immediately excites the attention of the newspaper-reading public, who is always seeking for new sensations.

"Very soon the history of Old Man Newton and of his daughter found its way into the London and provincial dailies, and the Ayrsham murder became a topic of all-absorbing interest.

"It appears that Old Man Newton was at one time a highly respectable local tradesman, always in a very small way, as there is not much business doing at Ayrsham. It is a poor and straggling village, although its railway station is an important junction on the Midland system.

"There is some very good shooting in the neighbourhood, and about four or five years ago some of it, together with The Limes, a pretty house just outside the village, was rented for the autumn by Mr Ledbury and his brother.

"You know the firm of Ledbury and Co., do you not—the great small-arms manufacturers? The elder Mr Ledbury was the recipient of birthday honours last year, and is the present Lord Walterton. His younger brother, Mervin, was in those days, and is still, a handsome young fellow in the Hussars.

"At the time—I mean about five years ago—Mary Newton was the local beauty of Ayrsham; she did a little dressmaking in her odd moments, but it appears that she spent most of her time in flirting. She was nominally engaged to be married to Samuel Holder, a young carpenter, but there was a good deal of scandal talked about her, for she was thought to be very fast; village gossip coupled her name with that of several young men in the neighbourhood, who were known to have paid the village beauty marked attention, and among these ad-mirers of Mary Newton during the autumn of which I am speaking, young Mr Mervin Ledbury figured conspicuously.

"Be that as it may, certain it is that Mary Newton had a very bad reputation among the scandalmongers of Ayrsham, and though eve-rybody was shocked, no one was astonished when one fine day in the winter following, she suddenly left her father and her home, and went no one knew whither. She left, it appears, a very pathetic letter be-hind, begging for her father's forgiveness, and that of Samuel Holder, whom she was jilting, but she was going to marry a gentleman above them all in station, and was going to be a real lady; then only would she return home.

"A very usual village tragedy, as you see. Four years went by, and Mary Newton did not return home. As time went by and with it no news of his daughter, Old Man Newton took her disappearance very much to heart. He began to neglect his business, and then his house, which became dirty and ill-kept by an occasional charwoman who would do a bit of promiscuous tidying for him from time to time. He was ill-tempered, sullen, and morose, and very soon became hopelessly addicted to drink.

"Then suddenly, as unexpectedly as she had gone, Mary Newton returned to her home one fine day, after an absence of four years. What had become of her in the interim no one in the village ever knew; she was generally supposed to have earned a living by dress-making, until her failing health had driven her well-nigh to starvation, and then back to the home and her father she had so heedlessly left.

"Needless to say, that all talk of her 'marriage with a gentleman above her in station' was entirely at an end. As for Old Man Newton, he seems, after his daughter's return, to have become more sullen and morose than ever, and the neighbours now busied themselves with talk of the fearful rows which frequently occurred in the back parlour of the little sweet-stuff shop.

"Father and daughter seemed to be leading a veritable cat-and-dog life together. Old Man Newton was hardly ever sober, and at the village inns he threw out weird and strange hints about 'breach of promise actions with £5,000 damages, which his daughter should get, if only he knew where to lay hands upon the scoundrel'.

"He also made vague and wholly useless enquiries about young Mervin Ledbury, but in a sleepy, out-of-the-way village like Ayrsham, no one knows anything about what goes on beyond a narrow five-mile radius at most. The Limes and the shooting were let to different tenants year after year, and neither Lord Walterton nor Mr Mervin Ledbury had ever rented them again."

2

"That was the past history of old Newton," continued the man in the corner, after a brief pause; "that is to say, of the man who on a dark night last October was found murdered in a lonely lane, not far from Ayrsham. The public, as you may well imagine, took a very keen interest in the case from the outset; the story of Mark Newton, of the threatened breach of promise, of the £5,000 damages, roused masses of conjecture to which no one as yet dared to give definite shape.

"One name, however, had already been whispered significantly, that of Mr Mervin Ledbury, the young Hussar, one of Mary Newton's admirers at the very time she left home in order, as she said, to be married to someone above her in station.

"Many thinking people, too, wanted to know what Samuel Holder, Mary's jilted *fiancée*, was doing close to the scene of the murder that night, and how he came to make the remark: 'Hello! is that you, Mat Newton?' when the old man lived nearly half a mile away, and really had no cause for being in that particular lane, at that hour of the night in the drizzling rain.

"The inquest, which, for want of other accommodation, was held at the local police station, was, as you imagine, very largely attended.

"I had read a brief statement of the case in the London papers, and had hurried down to Ayrsham Junction as I scented a mystery, and knew I should enjoy myself.

"When I got there, the room was already packed, and the medical evidence was being gone through.

"Old Man Newton, it appears, had been knocked on the head by a heavily leaded cane, which was found in the ditch close to the murdered man's body.

"The cane was produced in court; it was as stout as an old-fashioned club, and of terrific weight. The man who wielded it must have been very powerful, for he had only dealt one blow, but that blow had cracked the old man's skull. The cane was undoubtedly of foreign make, for it had a solid silver ferrule at one end, which was not English hallmarked.

"In the opinion of the medical expert, death was the result of the blow, and must have been almost instantaneous.

"The labourers who first came across the body of the murdered man then repeated their story; they had nothing new to add, and their evidence was of no importance. But after that there was some stir in the court. Samuel Holder had been called and sworn to tell the whole truth, and nothing but the truth.

"He was a youngish, heavily built man of about five-and-thirty, with a nervous, not altogether prepossessing, expression of face. Pressed by the coroner, he gave us a few details of Old Man Newton's earlier history, such as I have already told you.

"'Old Mat,' he explained, with some hesitation, 'was for ever wanting to find out who the gentleman was who had promised marriage to Mary four years ago. But Mary was that obstinate, and wouldn't tell him, and this exasperated the old man terribly, so that they had many rows on the subject.'

"'I suppose,' said the coroner tentatively, 'that you never knew who that gentleman was?'

"Samuel Holder seemed to hesitate for a moment. His manner became even more nervous than before; he shifted his position from one foot to the other; finally, he said:

"'I don't know as I ought to say, but —'

"'I am quite sure that you must tell us everything you know which might throw light upon this extraordinary and terrible murder,' retorted the coroner sternly.

"'Well,' replied Samuel Holder, whilst great beads of perspiration stood out upon his forehead, 'Mary never would give up the letters she had had from him, and she would not hear anything about a breach of promise case and £5,000 damages; but old Mat 'e often says to me, says 'e, "It's young Mr Ledbury," 'e says, "she's told me that once. I got it out of 'er, and if I only knew where to find 'im—"'

"'You are quite sure of this?' asked the coroner, for Holder had paused, and seemed quite horrified at the enormity of what he had said.

"'Yes—yes—your worship—your honour—' stammered Holder. "'E's told me 'twas young Mr Ledbury times out of count, and—'

"But Samuel Holder here completely broke down; he seemed unable to speak, his lips twitched convulsively, and the coroner, fearing that the man would faint, had him conveyed into the next room to recover himself, whilst another witness was brought forward.

"This was Michael Pitkin, landlord of the Fernhead Arms, at Ayrsham, who had been on very intimate terms with old Newton during the four years which elapsed after Mary's disappearance. He had a very curious story to tell, which aroused public excitement to its highest pitch.

"It appears that to him also the old man had often confided the fact that it was Mr Ledbury who had promised to marry Mary, and then had shamefully left her stranded and moneyless in London.

"'But of course,' added the jovial and pleasant-looking landlord of the Fernhead Arms, 'the likes of us down here didn't know what became of Mr Ledbury after he left The Limes, until one day I reads in the local paper that Sir John Fernhead's daughter is going to be married to Captain Mervin Ledbury. Of course, your honour and me, and all of us know Sir John, our squire, down at Fernhead Towers, and I says to old Mat: "It strikes me," I says, "that you've got your man." Sure enough it was the same Mr Ledbury who rented The Limes years ago, who was engaged to the young lady up at The Towers, and last week there was grand doings there—lords and ladies and lots of quality staying there, and also the captain.'

"'Well?' asked the coroner eagerly, whilst everyone held their breath, wondering what was to come.

"'Well,' continued Michael Pitkin, 'Old Man Newton went down to The Towers one day. 'E was determined to see young Mr Ledbury, and went. What 'appened I don't know, for old Mat wouldn't tell me, but 'e came back mighty furious from 'is visit, and swore 'e would ruin the young man and make no end of a scandal, and he would bring the law agin' 'im and get £5,000 damages.'

"This story, embellished, of course, by many details, was the gist of what the worthy landlord of the Fernhead Arms had to say, but you may imagine how everyone's excitement and curiosity was aroused; in the meanwhile, Samuel Holder was getting over his nervousness, and was more ready to give a clear account of what happened on the fatal night itself.

"'It was about nine o'clock,' he explained, in answer to the coroner, 'and I was hurrying back to Ayrsham, through the fields; it was dark and raining, and I was about to strike across the hedge into the lane when I heard voices—a woman's, then a man's. Of course, I could see nothing, and the man spoke in a whisper, but I had recognised Mary's voice quite plainly. She kept on saying: "'Tisn't my fault!" she says, "it's father's, 'e 'as made up 'is mind. I held out as long as I could, but 'e worried me, and now 'e's got your letters, and it's too late."'

"Samuel Holder again paused a moment, then continued:

"They talked together for a long time: Mary seemed very upset and the man very angry. Presently 'e says to 'er: "Well, tell your father to come out here and speak to me for a moment. I'll see what I can do." Mary seemed to 'esitate for a time, then she went away, and the man waited there in the drizzling rain, with me the other side of the 'edge watchin' 'im. I waited for a long time, for I wanted to know what was goin' to 'appen; then time went on. I thought perhaps that old Mat was at the Fernhead Arms, and that Mary couldn't find 'im, so I went back to Ayrsham by the fields, 'oping to find the old man. The stranger didn't budge. 'E seemed inclined to wait—so I left 'im there—and—and—that's all. I went to the Fernhead Arms, saw old Mat wasn't there—then I went back to the lane—and—Old Man Newton was dead, and the stranger was gone.'

"There was a moment or two of dead silence in the court when Samuel Holder had given his evidence, then the coroner asked quietly:

"'You do not know who the stranger was?'

"'Well, I couldn't be sure, your honour,' replied Samuel nervously, 'it was pitch-dark. I wouldn't like to swear a fellow-creature's life and character away.'

"'No, no, quite so,' rejoined the coroner; 'but do you happen to know what time it was when all this occurred?'

"'Oh yes, your honour,' said Samuel decisively, 'as I walked away from the Fernhead Arms I 'eard Ayrsham church clock strike ten o'clock.'

"'Ah that's always something,' said the coroner, with a sigh of satisfaction. 'Call Mary Newton, please.'"

"You may imagine," continued the man in the corner, after a slight pause, "with what palpitating interest we all watched the pathetic little figure, clad in deep black, who now stepped forward to give evidence.

"It was difficult to imagine that Mary Newton could ever have been pretty; trouble had obviously wrought havoc with her good looks. She was now a wizened little thing, with dark rings under her eyes, and a pale, anaemic complexion. She stood perfectly listlessly before the coroner, waiting to be questioned, but otherwise not seeming to take the slightest interest in the proceedings. In an even, toneless voice she told her name, age, and status, then waited for further questions.

"'Your father went out a little before ten o'clock on Tuesday night last, did he not?' asked the coroner very kindly.

"'Yes, sir, he did,' replied Mary quietly.

"'You had brought him a message from a gentleman whom you had met in the lane, and who wished to speak with your father?'

"'No, sir,' replied Mary, in the same even and toneless voice; 'I brought no message to father, and he went out on his own.'

"'But the gentleman you met in the lane?' insisted the coroner with some impatience.

"'I didn't meet anyone in the lane, sir. I never went out of the house that Tuesday night, it rained so.'

"'But the last witness, Samuel Holder, heard you talking in the lane at nine o'clock.'

"'Samuel Holder was mistaken,' she replied imperturbably; 'I wasn't out of the house the whole of that night.'

"It would be useless for me," continued the man in the corner, "to attempt to convey to you the intense feeling of excitement which pervaded that crowded court, as that wizened little figure stood there for over half an hour, quietly and obstinately parrying the most rigid cross-examination.

"That she was lying—lying to shield the very man who perhaps had murdered her father—no one doubted for a single instant. Yet there she stood, sullen, apathetic, and defiant, flatly denying Samuel Holder's story from end to end, strictly adhering and swearing to her first statement, that her father went out 'on his own', that she did not know where he was going to, and that she herself had never left the house that fatal Tuesday night.

"It did not seem to occur to her that by these statements she was hopelessly incriminating Samuel Holder, whom she was thus openly accusing of deliberate lies; on the contrary, many noticed a distinct touch of bitter animosity in the young girl against her former sweetheart, which was singularly emphasised when the coroner asked her whether she approved of the idea of a breach of promise action being brought against Mr Ledbury.

"'No,' she said; 'all that talk about damages and breach of promise was between father and Sam Holder, because Sam had told father that he wouldn't mind marrying me if I had £5,000 of my own.'

"It would be impossible to render the tone of hatred and contempt with which the young girl uttered these words. One seemed to live through the whole tragedy of the past few months—the girl, pestered by the greed of her father, yet refusing obstinately to aid in causing a scandal, perhaps disgrace, to the man whom she had once loved and trusted.

"As nothing more could be got out of her, and as circumstances now seemed to demand it, the coroner adjourned the inquest. The police, as you may well imagine, wanted to make certain enquiries. Mind you, Mary Newton flatly refused to mention Mr Ledbury's name; she was questioned and cross-questioned, yet her answer uniformly was:

"'I don't know what you're talking about. The person I was going to marry four years ago has gone out of my life—I have never seen him since. I saw no one on that Tuesday night.'

"Against that, when she was asked to swear that it was *not* Mr— now Captain—Ledbury who had promised her marriage she flatly refused to do so.

"Of course, there was not a soul there who had not made up his or her mind that Captain Ledbury *had* met Mary Newton in the lane, and had heard from her that all his love-letters to her were now in her father's hands, and that the old man meant to use these in order to extort money from him.

"Fearing the exposure and disgrace of so sensational a breach of promise action, and not having the money with which to meet Mat Newton's preposterous demands, he probably lost control over himself, and in a moment of impulse and mad rage had silenced the old man forever.

"I assure you that at the adjourned inquest everybody expected to see Captain Ledbury in the custody of two constables. The police in the interim had been extremely reticent, and no fresh details of the extraordinary case had found its way into the papers, but fresh details of a sensational character were fully expected, and I can assure you the public were not disappointed.

"It is no use my telling you all the proceedings of that second most memorable day; I will try and confine myself to the most important points of this interesting mystery.

"I must tell you that the story told by the landlord of the Fernhead Arms was fully corroborated by several witnesses, all of whom testified to the fact that the old man came back from his visit to Fernhead Towers in a terrible fury, swearing to bring disgrace upon the scoundrel who had ruined his daughter.

"What occurred during that visit was explained by Edward Sanders, the butler at The Towers. According to the testimony of this witness, there was a large house-party staying with Sir John Fernhead to celebrate the engagement of his daughter; the party naturally included Captain Mervin Ledbury, his brother, Lord Walterton, with the latter's newly married young wife, also many neighbours and friends.

"At about six o'clock on Monday evening, it appears, a disreputable-looking old man, who Edward Sanders did not know, but who gave the name of Newton, rang at the front door bell of The Towers and demanded to see Mr Ledbury. Sanders naturally refused to admit him, but the old man was so persistent, and used such strange language, that the butler, after much hesitation, decided to apprise Captain Ledbury of his extraordinary visitor.

"Captain Ledbury, on hearing that Old Man Newton wished to speak to him, much to Sanders' astonishment, came downstairs and elected to interview his extraordinary visitor in the dining-room, which was then deserted. Sanders showed the old man in, and waited in the hall. Very soon, however, he heard loud and angry voices, and the next moment Captain Ledbury threw open the dining-room door, and said:

"'This man is mad or drunk; show him out, Sanders.'

"And without another word the captain walked upstairs, leaving Sanders the pleasant task of 'showing the old man out'. That this was done very speedily and pretty roughly we may infer from Old Man Newton's subsequent fury, and the threats he uttered even while he was being 'shown out'.

"Now you see, do you not?" continued the man in the corner, "that this evidence seemed to add another link to the chain which was incriminating young Mr Ledbury in this terrible charge of murdering Old Man Newton.

"The young man himself was now with his regiment stationed at

York. It appears that the house-party at Fernhead Towers was breaking up on the very day of Old Man Newton's strange visit thither. Lord and Lady Walterton left for town on the Tuesday morning, and Captain Ledbury went up to York on that very same fatal night.

"You must know that the small local station of Fernhead is quite close to The Towers. Captain Ledbury took the late local train there for Ayrsham Junction after dinner that night, arriving at the latter place at 9.15, with the intention of picking up the Midland express to the North at 10.15 p.m. later on.

"The police had ascertained that Captain Ledbury had got out of the local train at Ayrsham Junction at 9.15, and aimlessly strolled out of the station. Against that, it was definitely proved by several witnesses that the young man did catch the Midland express at 10.15 p.m., and travelled up north by it.

"Now, there was the hitch, do you see?" added the funny creature excitedly. "Samuel Holder overheard a conversation in the fatal lane between Mary Newton and the stranger, whom everybody by now believed to be Captain Ledbury. Good! That was between 9 p.m. and 10 p.m., and, as it happened, the young man does seem to have unaccountably strolled about in the neighbourhood whilst waiting for his train; but remember that when Sam Holder left the stranger waiting in the lane, and went back towards Ayrsham in order to try and find Old Man Newton, he distinctly heard Ayrsham church clock striking ten.

"Now, the lane where the murder occurred is two and a half miles from Ayrsham Junction station, therefore it could not have been Captain Ledbury who was there lying in wait for the old man, as he could not possibly have had his interview with old Mat, quarrelled with him and murdered him, and then caught his train two and a half miles further on, all in the space of fifteen minutes.

"Thus, even before the final verdict of 'wilful murder against some person or persons unknown', the case against Captain Mervin Ledbury had completely fallen to the ground. He must also have succeeded in convincing Sir John Fernhead of his innocence, as I see by the papers that Miss Fernhead has since become Mrs Ledbury.

"But the result has been that the Ayrsham tragedy has remained an impenetrable mystery.

"'Who killed Old Man Newton? and why?' is a question which many people, including our clever criminal investigation department, have asked themselves many a time.

"It was not a case of vulgar assault and robbery, as the old man was not worth robbing, and the few coppers he possessed were found intact in his waistcoat pocket.

"Many people assert that Samuel Holder quarrelled with the old man and murdered him, but there are three reasons why that theory is bound to fall to the ground. Firstly, the total absence of any motive. Samuel Holder could have no possible object in killing the old man, but still, we'll waive that; people do quarrel—especially if they are confederates, as these two undoubtedly were—and quarrels do sometimes end fatally. Secondly, the weapon which caused the old man's death—a heavily leaded cane of foreign make, with solid silver ferrule.

"Now, I ask you, where in the world could a village carpenter pick up an instrument of that sort? Moreover no one ever saw such a thing in Sam Holder's hands or in his house. When he walked to the Fernhead Arms in order to try and find the old man, he had nothing of the sort in his hand, and in spite of the most strenuous efforts on the part of the police, the history of that cane was never traced.

"Then, there is a third reason why obviously Sam Holder was not guilty of the murder, though that reason is a moral one; I am referring to Mary Newton's attitude at the inquest. She lied, of that there could not be a shadow of doubt; she was determined to shield her former lover, and incriminated Sam Holder only because she wished to save another man.

"Obviously, old Newton went out on that dark, wet night in order to meet someone in the lane; that someone could not have been Sam Holder, whom he met anywhere and everywhere, and every day in his own house.

"There! you see that Sam Holder was obviously innocent, that Captain Ledbury could not have committed the murder, that surely Mary Newton did not kill her own father, and that in such a case, common sense should have come to the rescue, and not have left this case, what it now is, a tragic and impenetrable mystery."

4

"But," I said at last, for indeed I was deeply mystified, "what does common sense argue?—the case seems to me absolutely hopeless."

He surveyed his beloved bit of string for a moment, and his mild blue eyes blinked at me over his bone-rimmed spectacles.

"Common sense," he said at last, with his most apologetic manner, "tells me that Ayrsham village is a remote little place, where a daily paper is unknown, and where no one reads the fashionable intelligence or knows anything about birthday honours."

"What *do* you mean?" I gasped in amazement.

"Simply this, that no one at Ayrsham village, certainly not Mary Newton herself, had realised that one of the Mr Ledburys, whom all had known at The Limes four years ago, had since become Lord Walterton."

"Lord Walterton!" I ejaculated, wholly incredulously.

"Why, yes!" he replied quietly. "Do you mean to say you never thought of that? that it never occurred to you that Mary Newton may have admitted to her father that Mr Ledbury had been the man who had so wickedly wronged her, but that she, in her remote little village, had also no idea that the Mr Ledbury she meant was recently made, and is now styled, Lord Walterton?

"Old Man Newton, who knew of the gossip which had coupled his daughter's name, years ago, with the younger Mr Ledbury, naturally took it for granted that she was referring to him. Moreover, we may take it from the girl's subsequent attitude that she did all she could to shield the man whom she had once loved; women, you know, have that sort of little way with them.

"Old Newton, fully convinced that young Ledbury was the man he wanted, went up to The Towers and had the stormy interview, which no doubt greatly puzzled the young Hussar. He undoubtedly spoke of it to his brother, Lord Walterton, who, newly married and of high social position, would necessarily dread a scandal as much as anybody.

"Lord Walterton went up to town with his young wife the following morning. Ayrsham is only forty minutes from London. He came down in the evening, met Mary in the lane, asked to see her father, and killed him in a moment of passion, when he found that the old man's demands were preposterously unreasonable. Moreover, Englishmen in all grades of society have an innate horror of being bullied or blackmailed; the murder probably was not premeditated, but the outcome of rage at being browbeaten by the old man.

"You see, the police did not use their common sense over so simple a matter. They naturally made no enquiries as to Lord Walterton's movements, who seemingly had absolutely nothing to do with the case. If they had, I feel convinced that they would have found that his lordship would have had some difficulty in satisfying everybody as to his whereabouts on that particular Tuesday night.

"Think of it, it is so simple—the only possible solution of that strange and unaccountable mystery."

The Affair at the Novelty Theatre

1

"Talking of mysteries," said the man in the corner, rather irrelevantly, for he had not opened his mouth since he sat down and ordered his lunch, "talking of mysteries, it is always a puzzle to me how few thefts are committed in the dressing-rooms of fashionable actresses during a performance."

"There have been one or two," I suggested, "but nothing of any value was stolen."

"Yet you remember that affair at the Novelty Theatre a year or two ago, don't you?" he added. "It created a great deal of sensation at the time. You see, Miss Phyllis Morgan was, and still is, a very fashionable and popular actress, and her pearls are quite amongst the wonders of the world. She herself valued them at £10,000, and several experts who remember the pearls quite concur with that valuation.

"During the period of her short tenancy of the Novelty Theatre last season, she entrusted those beautiful pearls to Mr Kidd, the well-known Bond Street jeweller, to be restrung. There were seven rows of perfectly matched pearls, held together by a small diamond clasp of 'art-nouveau' design.

"Kidd and Co. are, as you know, a very eminent and old-established firm of jewellers. Mr Thomas Kidd, its present sole representative, was sometime president of the London Chamber of Commerce and a man whose integrity has always been held to be above suspicion. His clerks, salesmen, and bookkeeper had all been in his employ for years, and most of the work was executed on the premises.

"In the case of Miss Phyllis Morgan's valuable pearls, they were restrung and reset in the back shop by Mr Kidd's most valued and most trusted workman, a man named James Rumford, who is justly considered to be one of the cleverest craftsmen here in England.

"When the pearls were ready, Mr Kidd himself took them down to the theatre, and delivered them into Miss Morgan's own hands.

"It appears that the worthy jeweller was extremely fond of the theatre; but, like so many persons in affluent circumstances, he was also very fond of getting a free seat when he could.

"All along he had made up his mind to take the pearls down to the Novelty Theatre one night, and to see Miss Morgan for a moment before the performance; she would then, he hoped, place a stall at his disposal.

"His previsions were correct. Miss Morgan received the pearls, and Mr Kidd was on that celebrated night accommodated with a seat in the stalls.

"I don't know if you remember all the circumstances connected with that case, but to make my point clear, I must remind you of one or two of the most salient details.

"In the drama in which Miss Phyllis Morgan was acting at the time, there is a brilliant masked ball scene which is the crux of the whole play; it occurs in the second act, and Miss Phyllis Morgan, as the hapless heroine dressed in the shabbiest of clothes, appears in the midst of a gay and giddy throng; she apostrophises all and sundry there, including the villain, and has a magnificent scene which always brings down the house, and nightly adds to her histrionic laurels.

"For this scene a large number of supers are engaged, and in order to further swell the crowd, practically all the available stage hands have to 'walk on' dressed in various coloured *dominoes*, and all wearing masks.

"You have, of course, heard the name of Mr Howard Dennis in connection with this extraordinary mystery. He is what is usually called 'a young man about town', and was one of Miss Phyllis Morgan's most favoured admirers. As a matter of fact, he was generally understood to be the popular actress's *fiancée*, and as such, had of course the *entrée* of the Novelty Theatre.

"Like many another idle young man about town, Mr Howard Dennis was stage-mad, and one of his greatest delights was to don nightly a mask and a blue *domino*, and to 'walk on' in the second act, not so much in order to gratify his love for the stage, as to watch Miss Phyllis Morgan in her great scene and to be present, close by her, when she received her usual salvo of enthusiastic applause from a delighted public.

"On this eventful night—it was on 20th July last—the second act was in full swing; the supers, the stage hands, and all the principals were on the scene, the back of the stage was practically deserted. The beautiful pearls, fresh from the hands of Mr Kidd, were in Miss Morgan's dressing-room, as she meant to wear them in the last act.

"Of course, since that memorable affair, many people have talked of the foolhardiness of leaving such valuable jewellery in the sole charge of a young girl—Miss Morgan's dresser—who acted with unpardonable folly and carelessness, but you must remember that this part of the theatre is only accessible through the stage door, where sits enthroned that incorruptible dragon, the stage doorkeeper.

"No one can get at it from the front, and the dressing-rooms for the supers and lesser members of the company are on the opposite side of the stage to that reserved for Miss Morgan and one or two of the principals.

"It was just a quarter to ten, and the curtain was about to be rung down, when George Finch, the stage doorkeeper, rushed excitedly into the wings; he was terribly upset, and was wildly clutching his coat, beneath which he evidently held something concealed.

"In response to the rapidly whispered queries of the one or two stage hands that stood about, Finch only shook his head excitedly. He seemed scarcely able to control his impatience, during the close of the act, and the subsequent prolonged applause.

"When at last Miss Morgan, flushed with her triumph, came off the stage, Finch made a sudden rush for her.

"'Oh, madam!' he gasped excitedly, 'it might have been such an awful misfortune! The rascal! I nearly got him, though! but he escaped—fortunately it is safe—I have got it—!'

"It was some time before Miss Morgan understood what in the world the otherwise sober stage doorkeeper was driving at. Everyone who heard him certainly thought that he had been drinking. But the next moment from under his coat he pulled out, with another ejaculation of excitement, the magnificent pearl necklace which Miss Morgan had thought safely put away in her dressing-room.

"'What in the world does all this mean?' asked Mr Howard Dennis, who, as usual, was escorting his *fiancée*. 'Finch, what are you doing with madam's necklace?'

"Miss Phyllis Morgan herself was too bewildered to question Finch; she gazed at him, then at her necklace, in speechless astonishment.

"'Well, you see, madam, it was this way,' Finch managed to explain at last, as with awestruck reverence he finally deposited the precious necklace in the actress' hands. 'As you know, madam, it is a very hot night. I had seen everyone into the theatre and counted in the supers; there was nothing much for me to do, and I got rather tired and very thirsty. I seed a man loafing close to the door, and I ask him to fetch me a pint of beer from round the corner, and I give him some coppers; I had noticed him loafing round before, and it was so hot I didn't think I was doin' no harm.'

"'No, no,' said Miss Morgan impatiently. 'Well!'

"'Well,' continued Finch, 'the man, he brought me the beer, and I had some of it—and—and—afterwards, I don't quite know how it happened—it was the heat, perhaps—but—I was sitting in my box, and I suppose I must have dropped asleep. I just remember hearing the ring-up for the second act, and the call-boy calling you, madam, then there's a sort of a blank in my mind. All of a sudden, I seemed to wake with the feeling that there was something wrong somehow. In a moment I jumped up, and I tell you I was wide awake then, and I saw a man sneaking down the passage, past my box, towards the door.

"'I challenged him, and he tried to dart past me, but I was too quick for him, and got him by the tails of his coat, for I saw at once that he was carrying something, and I had recognised the loafer who brought me the beer. I shouted for help, but there's never anybody about in this back street, and the loafer, he struggled like old Harry, and sure enough he managed to get free from me and away before I could stop him, but in his fright the rascal dropped his booty, for which Heaven be praised! and it was your pearls, madam. Oh, my! but I did have a tussle,' concluded the worthy doorkeeper, mopping his forehead, 'and I do hope, madam, the scoundrel didn't take nothing else.'

"That was the story," continued the man in the corner, "which George Finch had to tell, and which he subsequently repeated without the slightest deviation. Miss Phyllis Morgan, with the light-heartedness peculiar to ladies of her profession, took the matter very quietly; all she said at the time was that she had nothing else of value in her dressing-room, but that Miss Knight—the dresser—deserved a scolding for leaving the room unprotected.

"'All's well that ends well,' she said gaily, as she finally went into her dressing-room, carrying the pearls in her hand.

"It appears that the moment she opened the door, she found Miss Knight sitting in the room, in a deluge of tears. The girl had overheard George Finch telling his story, and was terribly upset at her own carelessness.

"In answer to Miss Morgan's questions, she admitted that she had gone into the wings, and lingered there to watch the great actress' beautiful performance. She thought no one could possibly get to the dressing-room, as nearly all hands were on the stage at the time, and of course George Finch was guarding the door.

"However, as there really had been no harm done, beyond a wholesome fright to everybody concerned, Miss Morgan readily forgave the girl and proceeded with her change of attire for the next act. Incidentally she noticed a bunch of roses, which were placed on her dressing-table, and asked Knight who had put them there.

"'Mr Dennis brought them,' replied the girl.

"Miss Morgan looked pleased, blushed, and dismissing the whole matter from her mind, she proceeded with her *toilette* for the next act, in which, the hapless heroine having come into her own again, she was able to wear her beautiful pearls around her neck.

"George Finch, however, took some time to recover himself; his indignation was only equalled by his volubility. When his excitement had somewhat subsided, he took the precaution of saving the few drops of beer which had remained at the bottom of the mug, brought to him by the loafer. This was subsequently shown to a chemist in the neighbourhood, who, without a moment's hesitation, pronounced the beer to contain an appreciable quantity of chloral."

2

"The whole matter, as you may imagine, did not affect Miss Morgan's spirits that night," continued the man in the corner, after a slight pause.

"'All's well that ends well,' she had said gaily, since almost by a miracle, her pearls were once more safely round her neck.

"But the next day brought the rude awakening. Something had indeed happened which made the affair at the Novelty Theatre, what it has ever since remained, a curious and unexplainable mystery.

"The following morning Miss Phyllis Morgan decided that it was foolhardy to leave valuable property about in her dressing-room, when, for stage purposes, imitation jewellery did just as well. She therefore determined to place her pearls in the bank until the termination of her London season.

"The moment, however, that, in broad daylight, she once more handled the necklace, she instinctively felt that there was something wrong with it. She examined it eagerly and closely, and, hardly daring to face her sudden terrible suspicions, she rushed round to the nearest jeweller, and begged him to examine the pearls.

"The examination did not take many moments: the jeweller at once pronounced the pearls to be false. There could be no doubt about it; the necklace was a perfect imitation of the original, even the clasp was an exact copy. Half-hysterical with rage and anxiety, Miss Morgan at once drove to Bond Street, and asked to see Mr Kidd.

"Well, you may easily imagine the stormy interview that took place. Miss Phyllis Morgan, in no measured language, boldly accused Mr Thomas Kidd, late president of the London Chamber of Commerce, of having substituted false pearls for her own priceless ones.

"The worthy jeweller, at first completely taken by surprise, examined the necklace, and was horrified to see that Miss Morgan's statements were, alas! too true. Mr Kidd was indeed in a terribly awkward position.

"The evening before, after business hours, he had taken the necklace home with him. Before starting for the theatre, he had examined it to see that it was quite in order. He had then, with his own hands, and in the presence of his wife, placed it in its case, and driven straight to the Novelty, where he finally gave it over to Miss Morgan herself.

"To all this he swore most positively; moreover, all his *employés* and workmen could swear that they had last seen the necklace just after closing time at the shop, when Mr Kidd walked off towards Piccadilly, with the precious article in the inner pocket of his coat.

"One point certainly was curious, and undoubtedly helped to deepen the mystery which to this day clings to the affair at the Novelty Theatre.

"When Mr Kidd handed the packet containing the necklace to Miss Morgan, she was too busy to open it at once. She only spoke to Mr Kidd through her dressing-room door, and never opened the packet till nearly an hour later, after she was dressed ready for the second act; the packet at that time had been untouched, and was wrapped up just as she had had it from Mr Kidd's own hands. She undid the packet, and handled the pearls; certainly, by the artificial light she could see nothing wrong with the necklace.

"Poor Mr Kidd was nearly distracted with the horror of his position. Thirty years of an honest reputation suddenly tarnished with this awful suspicion—for he realised at once that Miss Morgan refused to believe his statements; in fact, she openly said that she would—unless immediate compensation was made to her—place the matter at once in the hands of the police.

"From the stormy interview in Bond Street, the irate actress drove at once to Scotland Yard; but the old-established firm of Kidd and Co. was not destined to remain under any cloud that threatened its integrity.

"Mr Kidd at once called upon his solicitor, with the result that an offer was made to Miss Morgan, whereby the jeweller would deposit the full value of the original necklace, *i.e.*, £10,000, in the hands of Messrs Bentley and Co., bankers, that sum to be held by them for a whole year, at the end of which time, if the perpetrator of the fraud had not been discovered, the money was to be handed over to Miss Morgan in its entirety.

"Nothing could have been more fair, more equitable, or more just, but at the same time nothing could have been more mysterious.

"As Mr Kidd swore that he had placed the real pearls in Miss Morgan's hands, and was ready to back his oath by the sum of £10,000, no more suspicion could possibly attach to him. When the announcement of his generous offer appeared in the papers, the entire public approved and exonerated him, and then turned to wonder who the perpetrator of the daring fraud had been.

"How came a valueless necklace in exact imitation of the original one to be in Miss Morgan's dressing-room? Where were the real pearls? Clearly the loafer who had drugged the stage doorkeeper, and sneaked into the theatre to steal a necklace, was not aware that he was risking several years' hard labour for the sake of a worthless trifle. He had been one of the many dupes of this extraordinary adventure.

"Macpherson, one of the most able men on the detective staff, had, indeed, his work cut out. The police were extremely reticent, but, in spite of this, one or two facts gradually found their way into the papers, and aroused public interest and curiosity to its highest pitch.

"What had transpired was this:

"Clara Knight, the dresser, had been very rigorously cross-questioned, and, from her many statements, the following seemed quite positive.

"After the curtain had rung up for the second act, and Miss Morgan had left her dressing-room, Knight had waited about for some time, and had even, it appears, handled and admired the necklace. Then, unfortunately, she was seized with the burning desire of seeing the famous scene from the wings. She thought that the place was quite safe, and that George Finch was as usual at his post.

"'I was going along the short passage that leads to the wings,' she exclaimed to the detectives, 'when I became aware of someone moving some distance behind me. I turned and saw a blue *domino* about to enter Miss Morgan's dressing-room.

"'I thought nothing of that,' continued the girl, 'as we all know that Mr Dennis is engaged to Miss Morgan. He is very fond of "walking on" in the ballroom scene, and he always wears a blue *domino* when he does; so I was not at all alarmed. He had his mask on as usual, and he was carrying a bunch of roses. When he saw me at the other end of the passage, he waved his hand to me and pointed to the flowers. I nodded to him, and then he went into the room.'

"These statements, as you may imagine, created a great deal of sensation; so much so, in fact, that Mr Kidd, with his £10,000 and his reputation in mind, moved heaven and earth to bring about the prosecution of Mr Dennis for theft and fraud.

"The papers were full of it, for Mr Howard Dennis was well known in fashionable London society. His answer to these curious statements was looked forward to eagerly; when it came it satisfied no one and puzzled everybody.

"'Miss Knight was mistaken,' he said most emphatically, 'I did not bring any roses for Miss Morgan that night. It was not I that she saw in a blue *domino* by the door, as I was on the stage before the curtain was rung up for the second act, and never left it until the close.'

"This part of Howard Dennis' statement was a little difficult to substantiate. No one on the stage could swear positively whether he was 'on' early in the act or not, although, mind you, Macpherson had ascertained that in the whole crowd of supers on the stage, he was the only one who wore a blue *domino*.

"Mr Kidd was very active in the matter, but Miss Morgan flatly refused to believe in her *fiancée's* guilt. The worthy jeweller maintained that Mr Howard Dennis was the only person who knew the celebrated pearls and their quaint clasp well enough to have a facsimile made of them, and that when Miss Knight saw him enter the dressing-room, he actually substituted the false necklace for the real one; while the loafer who drugged George Finch's beer was—as everyone supposed—only a dupe.

"Things had reached a very acute and painful stage, when one more detail found its way into the papers, which, whilst entirely clearing Mr Howard Dennis' character, has helped to make the whole affair a hopeless mystery.

"Whilst questioning George Finch, Macpherson had ascertained that the stage door-keeper had seen Mr Dennis enter the theatre some time before the beginning of the celebrated second act. He stopped to speak to George Finch for a moment or two, and the latter could swear positively that Mr Dennis was not carrying any roses then.

"On the other hand, a flower-girl, who was selling roses in the neighbourhood of the Novelty Theatre late that memorable night, remembers selling some roses to a shabbily dressed man, who looked like a labourer out of work. When Mr Dennis was pointed out to her, she swore positively that it was not he.

"'The man looked like a labourer,' she explained. 'I took particular note of him, as I remember thinking that he didn't look much as if he could afford to buy roses.'

"Now you see," concluded the man in the corner excitedly, "where the hitch lies. There is absolutely no doubt, judging from the evidence of George Finch and of the flower-girl, that the loafer had provided himself with the roses, and had somehow or other managed to get hold of a blue *domino*, for the purpose of committing the theft. His giving drugged beer to Finch, moreover, proved his guilt beyond a doubt.

"But here the mystery becomes hopeless," he added with a chuckle, "for the loafer dropped the booty which he had stolen—that booty was the false necklace, and it has remained an impenetrable mystery to this day as to who made the substitution and when.

"A whole year has elapsed since then, but the real necklace has never been traced or found; so, Mr Kidd has paid, with absolute quixotic chivalry, the sum of £10,000 to Miss Morgan, and thus he has completely cleared the firm of Kidd and Co. of any suspicion as to its integrity."

3

"But then, what in the world is the explanation of it all?" I asked bewildered, as the funny creature paused in his narrative and seemed absorbed in the contemplation of a beautiful knot he had just completed in his bit of string.

"The explanation is so simple," he replied, "for it is obvious, is it not? that only four people could possibly have committed the fraud."

"Who are they?" I asked.

"Well," he said, whilst his bony fingers began to fidget with that eternal piece of string, "there is, of course, old Mr Kidd; but as the worthy jeweller has paid £10,000 to prove that he did not steal the real necklace and substitute a false one in its stead, we must assume that he was guiltless. Then, secondly, there is Mr Howard Dennis."

"Well, yes," I said, "what about him?"

"There were several points in his favour," he rejoined, marking each point with a fresh and most complicated knot; "it was not he who bought the roses, therefore it was not he who, clad in a blue *domino*, entered Miss Morgan's dressing-room directly after Knight left it.

"And mark the force of this point," he added excitedly.

"Just before the curtain rang up for the second act, Miss Morgan had been in her room, and had then undone the packet, which, in her own words, was just as she had received it from Mr Kidd's hands.

"After that Miss Knight remained in charge, and a mere ten seconds after she left the room, she saw the blue *domino* carrying the roses at the door.

"The flower-girl's story and that of George Finch have proved that the blue *domino* could not have been Mr Dennis, but it was the loafer who eventually stole the false necklace.

"If you bear all this in mind you will realise that there was no time in those ten seconds for Mr Dennis to have made the substitution *before* the theft was committed. It stands to reason that he could not have done it afterwards.

"Then, again, many people suspected Miss Knight, the dresser; but this supposition we may easily dismiss. An uneducated, stupid girl, not three-and-twenty, could not possibly have planned so clever a substitution. An imitation necklace of that particular calibre and made to order would cost far more money than a poor theatrical dresser could ever afford; let alone the risks of ordering such an ornament to be made.

"No," said the funny creature, with comic emphasis, "there is but one theory possible, which is my own."

"And that is?" I asked eagerly.

"The workman, Rumford, of course," he responded triumphantly. "Why! it jumps to the eyes, as our French friends would tell us. Who other than he, could have the opportunity of making an exact copy of the necklace which had been entrusted to his firm?

"Being in the trade he could easily obtain the false stones without exciting any undue suspicion; being a skilled craftsman, he could easily make the clasp, and string the pearls in exact imitation of the original; he could do this secretly in his own home and without the slightest risk.

"Then the plan, though extremely simple, was very cleverly thought out. Disguised as the loafer—"

"The loafer!" I exclaimed.

"Why, yes! the loafer," he replied quietly; "disguised as the loafer, he hung round the stage door of the Novelty after business hours, until he had collected the bits of gossip and information he wanted; thus, he learnt that Mr Howard Dennis was Miss Morgan's accredited *fiancée*; that he, like everybody else who was available, 'walked on' in the second act; and that during that time the back of the stage was practically deserted.

"No doubt he knew all along that Mr Kidd meant to take the pearls down to the theatre himself that night, and it was quite easy to ascertain that Miss Morgan—as the hapless heroine—wore no jewellery in the second act, and that Mr Howard Dennis invariably wore a blue *domino*.

"Some people might incline to the belief that Miss Knight was a paid accomplice, that she left the dressing-room unprotected on purpose, and that her story of the blue *domino* and the roses was pre-arranged between herself and Rumford, but that is not my opinion.

"I think that the scoundrel was far too clever to need any accomplice, and too shrewd to put himself thereby at the mercy of a girl like Knight.

"Rumford, I find, is a married man: this to me explains the blue *domino*, which the police were never able to trace to any business place, where it might have been bought or hired. Like the necklace itself, it was 'home-made'.

"Having got his properties and his plans ready, Rumford then set to work. You must remember that a stage doorkeeper is never above accepting a glass of beer from a friendly acquaintance; and, no doubt, if George Finch had not asked the loafer to bring him a glass, the latter would have offered him one. To drug the beer was simple enough; then Rumford went to buy the roses, and, I should say, met his wife somewhere round the corner, who handed him the blue *domino* and the mask; all this was done in order to completely puzzle the police subsequently, and also in order to throw suspicion, if possible, upon young Dennis.

"As soon as the drug took effect upon George Finch, Rumford slipped into the theatre. To slip a mask and *domino* on and off is, as you know, a matter of a few seconds. Probably his intention had been—if he found Knight in the room—to knock her down if she attempted to raise an alarm; but here fortune favoured him. Knight saw him from a distance, and mistook him easily for Mr Dennis.

"After the theft of the real necklace, Rumford sneaked out of the theatre. And here you see how clever was the scoundrel's plan: if he had merely substituted one necklace for another there would have been no doubt whatever that the loafer—whoever he was—was the culprit—the drugged beer would have been quite sufficient proof for that. The hue and cry would have been after the loafer, and, who knows? there might have been someone or something which might have identified that loafer with himself.

"He must have bought the shabby clothes somewhere; he certainly bought the roses from a flower-girl; anyhow, there were a hundred and one little risks and contingencies which might have brought the theft home to him.

"But mark what happens: he steals the real necklace, and keeps the false one in his hand, intending to drop it sooner or later, and thus sent the police entirely on the wrong scent. As the loafer, he was supposed to have stolen the false necklace, then dropped it whilst struggling with George Finch. The result is that no one has troubled about the loafer; no one thought that he had anything to do with the substitution, which was the main point at issue, and no very great effort has ever been made to find that mysterious loafer.

"It never occurred to anyone that the fraud and the theft were committed by one and the same person, and that that person could be none other than James Rumford."

The Tragedy of Barnsdale Manor

1

"We have heard so much about the evils of Bridge," said the man in the corner that afternoon, "but I doubt whether that fashionable game has ever been responsible for a more terrible tragedy than the one at Barnsdale Manor."

"You think, then," I asked, for I saw he was waiting to be drawn out, "you think that the high play at Bridge did have something to do with that awful murder?"

"Most people think that much, I fancy," he replied, "although no one has arrived any nearer to the solution of the mystery which surrounds the tragic death of Mme Quesnard at Barnsdale Manor on the 23rd September last.

"On that fateful occasion, you must remember that the house party at the manor included a number of sporting and fashionable friends of Lord and Lady Barnsdale, among whom Sir Gilbert Culworth was the only one whose name was actually mentioned during the hearing of this extraordinary case.

"It seems to have been a very gay house party indeed. In the daytime Lord Barnsdale took some of his guests to shoot and fish, whilst a few devotees remained at home in order to indulge their passion for the modern craze of Bridge. It was generally understood that Lord Barnsdale did not altogether approve of quite so much gambling. He was not by any means well off; and although he was very much in love with his beautiful wife, he could ill afford to pay her losses at cards.

"This was the reason, no doubt, that Bridge at Barnsdale Manor was only indulged in whilst the host himself was out shooting or fishing; in the evenings there was music or billiards, but never any cards.

"One of the most interesting personalities in the Barnsdale *ménage* was undoubtedly Madame Nathalie Quesnard, a sister of Lord Barnsdale's mother, who, if you remember, was a Mademoiselle de la Trémouille. This Mme Quesnard was extremely wealthy, the widow of a French West Indian planter, who had made millions in Martinique.

"She was very fond of her nephew, to whom, as she had no children or other relatives of her own, she intended to leave the bulk of her vast fortune. Pending her death, which was not likely to occur for some time, as she was not more than fifty, she took up her abode at Barnsdale Manor, together with her companion and amanuensis, a poor girl named Alice Holt.

"Mme Quesnard was seemingly an amiable old lady, the only unpleasant trait in her character being her intense dislike of her nephew's beautiful and fashionable young wife. The old Frenchwoman, who, with all her wealth, had the unbounded and innate thriftiness peculiar to her nation, looked with perfect horror on Lady Barnsdale's extravagances, and above all on her fondness for gambling; and subsequently several of the servants at the manor testified to the amount of mischief the old lady strove to make between her nephew and his young wife.

"Mme Quesnard's dislike for Lady Barnsdale seems, moreover, to have been shared by her dependent and companion, the girl Alice Holt. Between them, these two ladies seem to have cordially hated the brilliant and much-admired mistress of Barnsdale Manor.

"Such were the chief inmates of the manor last September, at the time the tragedy occurred. On that memorable night Alice Holt, who occupied a bedroom immediately above that of Mme Quesnard, was awakened in the middle of the night by a persistent noise, which undoubtedly came from her mistress' room. The walls and floorings at the old manor are very thick, and the sound was a very confused one, although the girl was quite sure that she could hear Mme Quesnard's shrill voice raised as if in anger.

"She tried to listen for a time, and presently she heard a sound as if some piece of furniture had been knocked over, then nothing more. Somehow the sudden silence seemed to have frightened the girl more than the noise had done. Trembling with nervousness she waited for some few minutes, then, unable to bear the suspense any longer, she got out of bed, slipped on her shoes and dressing-gown, and determined to run downstairs to see if anything were amiss.

"To her horror she found on trying her door that it had been locked on the outside. Quite convinced now that something must indeed be very wrong, she started screaming and banging against the door, determined to arouse the household, which she, of course, quickly succeeded in doing.

"The first to emerge from his room was Lord Barnsdale. He at once realised that the shrieks proceeded from Alice Holt's room. He ran upstairs helter-skelter, and as the key had been left in the door, he soon released the unfortunate girl, who by now was quite hysterical with anxiety for her mistress.

"Altogether, I take it, some six or seven minutes must have elapsed from the time when Alice Holt was first alarmed by the sudden silence following the noise in Mme Quesnard's room until she was released by Lord Barnsdale.

"As quickly and as coherently as she could, she blurted forth all her fears about her mistress. I can imagine how picturesque the old Manor House must have looked then, with everybody, ladies and gentlemen, and servants, crowding into the hall, arrayed in various *négligé* attire, asking hurried questions, getting in each other's way, and all only dimly to be seen by the light of candles, carried by some of the more sensible ones in this motley crowd.

"However, in the meanwhile, Lord Barnsdale had managed to understand Alice Holt. He ran downstairs again and knocked at his aunt's door; he received no reply—he tried the handle, but the door was locked from the inside.

"Genuinely frightened now, he forced open the door, and then recoiled in horror.

"The window was wide open, and a brilliant moonlight streamed into the room, weirdly illumining Mme Quesnard's inanimate body, which lay full length upon the ground. Hastily begging the ladies not to follow him, Lord Barnsdale quickly went forward and bent over his aunt's body.

"There was no doubt that she was dead. An ugly wound at the back of her head, some red marks round her throat, all testified to the fact that the poor old lady had been assaulted and murdered. Lord Barnsdale at once sent for the nearest doctor, whilst he and Miss Holt lifted the unfortunate lady back to bed.

"The messenger who had gone for the doctor was at the same time instructed to deliver a note, hastily scribbled by Lord Barnsdale, at the local police station.

"That a hideous crime had been committed, with burglary for its object, no one could be in doubt for a moment. Lord Barnsdale and two or three of his guests had already thrown a glance into the next room, a little *boudoir*, which Mme Quesnard used as a sitting-room. There the heavy oak bureau bore silent testimony to the motive of this dastardly outrage.

"Mme Quesnard, with the unfortunate and foolhardy habit peculiar to all French people, kept a very large quantity of loose and ready money by her. That habit, mind you, is the chief reason why burglary is so rife and so profitable all over France.

"In this case the old lady's national characteristic was evidently the chief cause of her tragic fate; the drawer of the bureau had been forced open, and no one could doubt for a moment that a large sum of money had been abstracted from it.

"The burglar had then obviously made good his escape through the window, which he could do quite easily, as Mme Quesnard's apartments were on the ground floor. She suffered from shortness of breath, it appears, and had a horror of stairs; she was, moreover, not the least bit nervous, and her windows were usually barred and shuttered.

"One very curious fact, however, at once struck all those present, even before the arrival of the detectives, and that was, that the old lady was partially dressed when she was found lying on the ground. She had slipped on an elaborate dressing-gown, had smoothed her hair, and put on her slippers. In fact, it was evident that she had in some measure prepared herself for the reception of the burglar.

"Throughout these hasty and amateurish observations conducted by Lord Barnsdale and two of his male guests, Alice Holt had remained seated beside her late employer's bedside sobbing bitterly. In spite of Lord Barnsdale's entreaties she refused to move; and wildly waved aside any attempt at consolation offered to her by one or two of the older female servants who were present.

"It was only when everybody at last made up their minds to return to their rooms, that someone mentioned Lady Barnsdale's name. She had been taken ill and faint the evening before, and had not been well all night. Jane Barlow, her maid, expressed the hope that her ladyship was none the worse for this awful commotion, and must be wondering what it all meant.

"At this, suddenly, Alice Holt jumped up, like a madwoman.

"'What it all means?' she shrieked, whilst everyone looked at her in speechless horror. 'It means that that woman has murdered my mistress, and robbed her. I know it—I know it—I know it!'

"And once more sinking beside the bed, she covered her dead mistress' hand with kisses, and sobbed and wailed as if her heart would break."

"You may well imagine the awful commotion the girl's wild outburst had created in the old Manor House. Lady Barnsdale had been taken ill the previous evening, and, of course, no one had breathed a word of it to her, but equally, of course, it was freely talked about at Barnsdale Manor, in the neighbourhood, and even so far as in the London clubs. Lord and Lady Barnsdale were very well known in London society, and Lord Barnsdale's adoration for his beautiful wife was quite notorious.

"Alice Holt, after her frantic outburst, had not breathed another word. Silent and sullen she went up to her room, packed her things, and left the house, where, of course, it became impossible that she should stay another day. She refused Lord Barnsdale's generous offer of money and help, and only stayed long enough to see the detectives and reply to the questions they thought fit to put to her.

"The whole neighbourhood was in a fever of excitement; many gossips would have it that the evidence against Lady Barnsdale was conclusive, and that a warrant for her arrest had already been applied for.

"What had transpired was this:

"It appears that the day preceding the tragedy, Bridge was, as usual, being played for, I believe, guinea-points. Lord Barnsdale was out shooting all day, and though the guests at the manor were very loyal to their hostess, and refused to make any positive statements, there seems to be no doubt that Lady Barnsdale lost a very large sum of money to Sir Gilbert Culworth.

"Be that as it may, nothing further could be gleaned by enterprising reporters fresh from town; the police were more than usually reticent, and everyone eagerly awaited the opening of the inquest, when sensational developments were expected in this mysterious case.

"It was held on September the 25th, in the servants' hall of Barnsdale Manor, and you may be sure that the large room was crowded to its utmost capacity. Lord Barnsdale was, of course, present, so was Sir Gilbert Culworth, but it was understood that Lady Barnsdale was still suffering from nervous prostration, and was unable to be present.

"When I arrived there, and gradually made my way to the front rank, the doctor who had been originally summoned to the murdered lady's bedside was giving his evidence.

"He gave it as his opinion that the fractured skull from which Mme Quesnard died was caused through her hitting the back of her head against the corner of the marble-topped washstand, in the immediate proximity of which she lay outstretched, when Lord Barnsdale first forced open the door. The stains on the marble had confirmed him in that opinion. Mme Quesnard, he thought, must have fallen, owing to an onslaught made upon her by the burglar; the marks round the old lady's throat testified to this, although these were not the cause of death.

"After this there was a good deal of police evidence with regard to the subsequent movements of the unknown miscreant. He had undoubtedly broken open the drawer of the bureau in the adjoining *boudoir*, the door of communication between this and Mme Quesnard's bedroom being always kept open, and it was presumed that he had made a considerable haul both in gold and notes. He had then locked the bedroom door on the inside and made good his escape through the window.

"Immediately beneath this window, the flower-bed, muddy with the recent rain, bore the imprint of having been hastily trampled upon; but all actual footmarks had been carefully obliterated. Beyond this, all round the house the garden paths are asphalted, and the burglar had evidently taken the precaution to keep to these asphalted paths, or else to cross the garden by the lawns.

"You must understand," continued the man in the corner, after a slight pause, "that throughout all this preliminary evidence, everything went to prove that the crime had been committed by an inmate of the house or at any rate by someone well acquainted with its usages and its *ménage*. Alice Holt, whose room was immediately above that of Mme. Quesnard, and who was, therefore, most likely to hear the noise of the conflict and to run to her mistress's assistance, had been first of all locked up in her room. It had, therefore, become quite evident that the miscreant had commenced operations from inside the house, and had entered Mme Quesnard's room by the door, and not by the window, as had been at first supposed.

"But," added the funny creature excitedly, "as the old lady had, according to evidence, locked her door that night, it became more and more clear, as the case progressed, that she must of her own accord have admitted the person who subsequently caused her tragic death. This was, of course, confirmed by the fact that she was partially dressed when she was subsequently found dead.

"Strangely enough, with the exception of Alice Holt, no one else had heard any noise during the night. But, as I remarked before, the walls of these old houses are very thick, and no one else slept on the ground floor.

"Another fact which in the early part of the inquest went to prove that the outrage was committed by someone familiar with the house, was that Ben, the watchdog, had not raised any alarm. His kennel was quite close to Mme Quesnard's windows, and he had not even barked.

"I doubt if the law would take official cognizance of the dumb testimony of a dog; nevertheless, Ben's evidence was in this case quite worthy of consideration.

"You may imagine how gradually, as these facts were unfolded, excitement grew to fever pitch, and when at last Alice Holt was called, everyone literally held their breath, eagerly waiting to hear what was coming.

"She is a tall, handsome-looking girl, with fine eyes and a rich voice. Dressed in deep black she certainly looked an imposing figure as she stood there, repeating the story of how she was awakened in the night by the sound of her mistress's angry voice, of the noise and sudden silence, and also of her terror, when she found that she had been locked up in her room.

"But obviously the girl had more to tell, and was only waiting for the coroner's direct question.

"'Will you tell the jury the reason why you made such an extraordinary and unwarrantable accusation against Lady Barnsdale?' he asked her at last, amid breathless silence in the crowded room.

"Everyone instinctively looked across the room to where Lord Barnsdale sat between his friend Sir Gilbert Culworth and his lawyer, Sir Arthur Inglewood, who had evidently come down from London in order to watch the case on his client's behalf. Alice Holt, too, looked across at Lord Barnsdale for a moment. He seemed attentive and interested, but otherwise quite calm and impassive.

"I, who watched the girl, saw a look of pity cross her face as she gazed at him, and I think, when we bear in mind that the distinguished English gentleman and the poor paid companion had known each other years ago, when they were girl and boy together in old Mme Quesnard's French home, we may make a pretty shrewd guess why Alice Holt hated the beautiful Lady Barnsdale.

"'It was about six o'clock in the afternoon,' she began at last, in the same quiet tone of voice. 'I was sitting sewing in *madame's boudoir*, when Lady Barnsdale came into the bedroom. She did not see me, I know, for she began at once talking volubly to *madame* about a serious loss she had just sustained at Bridge; several hundred pounds, she said.'

"'Well?' queried the coroner, for the girl had paused, almost as if she regretted what she had already said. She certainly threw an appealing look at Lord Barnsdale, who, however, seemed to take no notice of her.

"'Well,' she continued with sudden resolution, '*madame* was very angry at this; she declared that Lady Barnsdale deserved a severe lesson; her extravagances were a positive scandal. "Not a penny will I give you to pay your gambling debts," said *madame*; "and, moreover, I shall make it my business to inform my nephew of your goings-on whilst he is absent."

"'Lady Barnsdale was in a wild state of excitement. She begged and implored *madame* to say nothing to Lord Barnsdale about it, and did her very best to try to induce her to help her out of her difficulties, just this once more. But *madame* was obdurate. Thereupon Lady Barnsdale turned on her like a fury, called her every opprobrious name under the sun, and finally flounced out of the room, banging the door behind her.

"'*Madame* was very much upset after this,' continued Alice Holt, 'and I was not a bit astonished when directly after dinner she rang for me, and asked to be put to bed. It was then nine o'clock.

"'That is the last I saw of poor *madame* alive.

"'She was very excited then, and told me that she was quite frightened of Lady Barnsdale—a gambler, she said, was as likely as not to become a thief, if opportunity arose. I offered to sleep on the sofa in the next room, for the old lady seemed quite nervous, a thing I have never known her to be. But she was too proud to own to nervousness, and she dismissed me finally, saying that she would lock her door, for once, a thing she scarcely ever did.'

"It was a curious story, to say the least of it, which Alice Holt thus told to an excited public. Cross-examined by the coroner, she never departed from a single point of it, her calm and presence of mind being only equalled throughout this trying ordeal by that of Lord Barnsdale, who sat seemingly unmoved whilst these terrible insinuations were made against his wife.

"But there was more to come. Sir Gilbert Culworth had been called; in the interests of justice, and in accordance with his duty as a citizen, he was forced to stand up and, all unwillingly, to add another tiny link to the chain of evidence that implicated his friend's wife in this most terrible crime.

"Right loyally he tried to shield her in every possible way, but cross-questioned by the coroner, harassed nearly out of his senses, he was forced to admit two facts—namely, that Lady Barnsdale had lost nearly £800 at Bridge the day before the murder, and that she had paid her debt to himself in full, on the following morning, in gold and notes.

"He had been forced, much against his will, to show the notes to the police; unfortunately for the justice of the case, however, the numbers of these could not be directly traceable as having been in Mme Quesnard's possession at the time of her death. No diaries or books of accounts of any kind were found. Like most French people, she arranged all her money affairs herself, receiving her vast dividends in foreign money, and converting this into English notes and gold, as occasion demanded, at the nearest moneychanger's that happened to be handy.

"She had, like a great many foreigners, a holy horror of banks. She would have mistrusted the Bank of England itself; as for solicitors, she held them in perfect abhorrence. She only went once to one in her life, and that was in order to make a will leaving everything she possessed unconditionally to her beloved nephew, Lord Barnsdale.

"But in spite of this difficulty about the notes, you see for yourself, do you not? how terribly strong was the circumstantial evidence against Lady Barnsdale. Her losses at cards, her appeal to Mme Quesnard, the latter's refusal to help her, and finally the payment in full of the debt to Sir Gilbert Culworth on the following morning.

"There was only one thing that spoke for her, and that was the very horror of the crime itself. It was practically impossible to conceive that a woman of Lady Barnsdale's refinement and education should have sprung upon an elderly woman, like some navvy's wife by the docks, and then that she should have had the presence of mind to jump out of the window, to obliterate her footmarks in the flower-bed, and, in fact, to have given the crime the look of a clever burglary.

"Still, we all know that money difficulties will debase the noblest of us, that greed will madden the sanest and most refined. When the inquest was adjourned, I can assure you that no one had any doubt whatever that within twenty-four hours Lady Barnsdale would be arrested on the capital charge."

3

"But the detectives in charge of the case had reckoned without Sir Arthur Inglewood, the great lawyer, who was watching the proceedings on behalf of his aristocratic clients," said the man in the corner, when he had assured himself of my undivided attention.

"The adjourned inquest brought with it, I assure you, its full quota of sensation. Again, Lord Barnsdale was present, calm, haughty, and impassive, whilst Lady Barnsdale was still too ill to attend. But she had made a statement upon oath, in which, whilst flatly denying that her interview with the deceased at 6 p.m., had been of an acrimonious character as alleged by Alice Holt, she swore most positively that all through the night she had been ill, and had not left her room after 11.30 p.m.

"The first witness called after this affidavit had been read was Jane Barlow, Lady Barnsdale's maid.

"The girl deposed that on that memorable evening preceding the murder, she went up to her mistress' room at about 11.30 in order to get everything ready for the night. As a rule, of course, there was nobody about in the bedroom at that hour, but on this occasion when Jane Barlow entered the room, which she did without knocking, she saw her mistress sitting by her desk.

"'Her ladyship looked up when I came in,' continued Jane Barlow, 'and seemed very cross with me for not knocking at the door. I apologised, then began to get the room tidy; as I did so I could see that my lady was busy counting a lot of money. There were lots of sovereigns and banknotes. My lady put some together in an envelope and addressed it, then she got up from her desk and went to lock up the remainder of the money in her jewel safe.'

"'And this was at what time?' asked the coroner.

"'At about half past eleven, I think, sir,' repeated the girl.

"'Well,' said the coroner, 'did you notice anything else?'

"'Yes,' replied Jane, 'whilst my lady was at her safe, I saw the envelope in which she had put the money lying on the desk. I couldn't help looking at it, for I knew it was ever so full of banknotes, and I saw that my lady had addressed it to Sir Gilbert Culworth.'

"At this point Sir Arthur Inglewood jumped to his feet and handed something over to the coroner; it was evidently an envelope which had been torn open. The coroner looked at it very intently, then suddenly asked Jane Barlow if she had happened to notice anything about the envelope which was lying on her ladyship's desk that evening.

"'Oh yes, sir!' she replied unhesitatingly, 'I noticed my lady had made a splotch, right on top of the "C" in Sir Gilbert Culworth's name.'

"'This, then, is the envelope,' was the coroner's quiet comment, as he handed the paper across to the girl.

"'Yes, there's the splotch,' she replied. 'I'd know it anywhere.'

"So, you see," continued the man in the corner, with a chuckle, "that the chain of circumstantial evidence against Lady Barnsdale was getting somewhat entangled. It was indeed fortunate for her that Sir Gilbert Culworth had not destroyed the envelope in which she had handed him over the money on the following day.

"Alice Holt, as you know, heard the conflict and raised the alarm much later in the night, when everybody was already in bed, whilst long before that Lady Barnsdale was apparently in possession of the money with which she could pay back her debt.

"Thus, the motive for the crime, so far as she was concerned, was entirely done away with. Directly after the episode witnessed by Jane Barlow, Lady Barnsdale had a sort of nervous collapse, and went to bed feeling very ill. Lord Barnsdale was terribly concerned about her; he and the maid remained alternately by her bedside for an hour or two; finally, Lord Barnsdale went to sleep in his dressing-room, whilst Jane also finally retired to rest.

"Ill as Lady Barnsdale undoubtedly was then, it was absolutely preposterous to conceive that she could after that have planned and carried out so monstrous a crime, without any motive whatever. To have locked Alice Holt's door, then gone downstairs, forced her way into the old lady's room, struggled with her, to have jumped out of the window, and run back into the house by the garden, might have been the work of a determined woman, driven mad by the desire for money, but became absolutely out of the question in the case of a woman suffering from nervous collapse, and having apparently no motive for the crime.

"Of course, Sir Arthur Inglewood made the most of the fact that no mud was found on any shoes or dress belonging to Lady Barnsdale. The flowerbed was very soft with the heavy rain of the day before, and Lady Barnsdale could not possibly have jumped even from a ground-floor window and trampled on the flowerbed, without staining her skirts.

"Then there was another point which the clever lawyer brought to the coroner's notice. As Alice Holt had stated in her sworn evidence that Mme Quesnard had owned to being frightened of Lady Barnsdale that night, was it likely that she would *of her own accord* have opened the door to her in the middle of the night, without at least calling for assistance?

"Thus, the matter has remained a strange and unaccountable puzzle. It has always been called the 'Barnsdale Mystery' for that very reason. Everyone, somehow, has always felt that Lady Barnsdale did have something to do with that terrible tragedy. Her husband has taken her abroad, and they have let Barnsdale Manor; it almost seems as if the ghost of the old Frenchwoman had driven them forth from their own country.

"As for Alice Holt, she maintains to this day that Lady Barnsdale was the culprit, and I understand that she has not yet given up all hope of collecting a sufficiency of evidence to have the beautiful and fashionable woman of society arraigned for this hideous murder."

4

"Will she succeed, do you think?" I asked at last.

"Succeed? Of course, she won't," he retorted excitedly. "Lady Barnsdale never committed that murder; no woman, except, perhaps, an East-end factory hand, could have done it at all."

"But then—" I urged.

"Why, then," he replied, with a chuckle, "the only logical conclusion is that the robbery and the murder were not committed by the same person, nor at the same hour of the night; moreover, I contend that there was no premeditated murder, but that the old lady died from the result of a pure accident."

"But how?" I gasped.

"This is my version of the story," he said excitedly, as his long bony fingers started fidgeting, fidgeting with that eternal bit of string. "Lady Barnsdale, pressed for money, made an appeal to Mme Quesnard, which the latter refused, as we know. Then there was an acrimonious dispute between the two ladies, after which came the dinner hour, then madame, feeling ill and upset, went up to bed at nine o'clock.

"Now my contention is that undoubtedly the robbery had been committed before that, between the dispute and madame's bedtime."

"By whom?"

"By Lady Barnsdale, of course, who, as the mistress of the house, could come and go from room to room without exciting any comment; who, moreover, at 6 p.m. was hard pressed for money, and who but a few hours later was handling a mass of gold and banknotes.

"But the strain of committing even an ordinary theft is very great upon a refined woman's organisation. Lady Barnsdale has a nervous breakdown. Well! what is the most likely thing to happen? Why! that she should confess everything to her husband, who worships her, and no doubt express her repentance at what she had done.

"Then imagine Lord Barnsdale's horror! The old lady had not discovered the theft before going to bed. That was only natural, since she was feeling unwell, and was not likely to sit up at night counting her money; the lock of the bureau drawer having been tampered with would perhaps not attract her attention at night.

"But in the morning, the very first thing, she would discover everything, at once suspect the worst, and who knows? make a scandal, talk of it before Alice Holt, Lady Barnsdale's archenemy, and all before restitution could be made.

"No, no, that restitution must be made at once; not a minute must be lost, since any moment might bring forth discovery, and perhaps an awful catastrophe.

"I take it that Mme Quesnard and her nephew were on very intimate terms. He hoped to arouse no one by going to his aunt's room, but in order to make quite sure that Alice Holt, hearing a noise in her mistress' room, should not surreptitiously come down, and perhaps play eavesdropper at the momentous interview, he turned the key of the girl's door as he went past, and locked her in.

"Then he knocked at his aunt's door (gently, of course, for old people are light sleepers), and called her by name. Mme Quesnard, recognising her nephew's voice, slipped on her dressing-gown, smoothed her hair, and let him in.

"Exactly what took place at the interview it is, of course, impossible for any human being to say. Here even I can but conjecture," he added, with inimitable conceit, "but we can easily imagine that, having heard Lord Barnsdale's confession of his wife's folly, the old lady, who as a Frenchwoman was of quick temper and unbridled tongue, would indulge in not very elegant rhetoric on the subject of the woman she had always disliked.

"Lord Barnsdale would, of course, defend his wife, and the old lady, with feminine obstinacy, would continue the attack. Then some insulting epithet, a word only, perhaps, roused the devoted husband's towering indignation—the meekest man on earth becomes a mad bull when he really loves, and the woman he loves is insulted.

"I maintain that the old lady's death was really due to a pure accident; that Lord Barnsdale gripped her by the throat, in a moment of mad anger, at some hideous insult hurled at his wife; of that I am as convinced as if I had witnessed the whole scene. Then the old lady fell, hit her head against the marble, and Lord Barnsdale realised that he was alone at night in his aunt's room, and that he had killed her.

"What would anyone do under the circumstances?" he added excitedly. "Why, of course, collect his senses and try to save himself from what might prove to be consequences of the most awful kind. This Lord Barnsdale thought he could best do by giving the accident, which looked so like murder, the appearance of a burglary.

"The lock of the desk in the next room had already been forced open; he now locked the door on the inside, threw open the shutter and the window, jumped out as any burglar would have done; and, being careful to obliterate his own footmarks, he crept back into the house, and thence into his own room, without alarming the watch-dog, who naturally knew his own master. He was, of course, just in time before Alice Holt succeeded in rousing the household with her screams.

"And thus, you see," he added, "there are no such things as mysteries. The police call them so, so do the public, but every crime has its perpetrator, and every puzzle its solution. My experience is that the simplest solution is invariably the right one."

LEONAUR

ALSO FROM LEONAUR

AVAILABLE IN SOFTCOVER OR HARDCOVER WITH DUST JACKET

MR MUKERJI'S GHOSTS *by S. Mukerji*—Supernatural tales from the British Raj period by India's Ghost story collector.

KIPLINGS GHOSTS *by Rudyard Kipling*—Twelve stories of Ghosts, Hauntings, Curses, Werewolves & Magic.

THE COLLECTED SUPERNATURAL AND WEIRD FICTION OF WASHINGTON IRVING: VOLUME 1 *by Washington Irving*—Including one novel 'A History of New York', and nine short stories of the Strange and Unusual.

THE COLLECTED SUPERNATURAL AND WEIRD FICTION OF WASHINGTON IRVING: VOLUME 2 *by Washington Irving*—Including three novelettes 'The Legend of the Sleepy Hollow', 'Dolph Heyliger', 'The Adventure of the Black Fisherman' and thirty-two short stories of the Strange and Unusual.

THE COLLECTED SUPERNATURAL AND WEIRD FICTION OF JOHN KENDRICK BANGS: VOLUME 1 *by John Kendrick Bangs*—Including one novel 'Toppleton's Client or A Spirit in Exile', and ten short stories of the Strange and Unusual.

THE COLLECTED SUPERNATURAL AND WEIRD FICTION OF JOHN KENDRICK BANGS: VOLUME 2 *by John Kendrick Bangs*—Including four novellas 'A House-Boat on the Styx', 'The Pursuit of the House-Boat', 'The Enchanted Typewriter' and 'Mr. Munchausen' of the Strange and Unusual.

THE COLLECTED SUPERNATURAL AND WEIRD FICTION OF JOHN KENDRICK BANGS: VOLUME 3 *by John Kendrick Bangs*—Including twor novellas 'Olympian Nights', 'Roger Camerden: A Strange Story', and ten short stories of the Strange and Unusual.

THE COLLECTED SUPERNATURAL AND WEIRD FICTION OF MARY SHELLEY: VOLUME 1 *by Mary Shelley*—Including one novel 'Frankenstein or the Modern Prometheus', and fourteen short stories of the Strange and Unusual.

THE COLLECTED SUPERNATURAL AND WEIRD FICTION OF MARY SHELLEY: VOLUME 2 *by Mary Shelley*—Including one novel 'The Last Man', and three short stories of the Strange and Unusual.

THE COLLECTED SUPERNATURAL AND WEIRD FICTION OF AMELIA B. EDWARDS *by Amelia B. Edwards*—Contains two novelettes 'Monsieur Maurice', and 'The Discovery of the Treasure Isles', one ballad 'A Legend of Boisguilbert' and seventeen short stories to cill the blood.

LEONAUR

ALSO FROM LEONAUR
AVAILABLE IN SOFTCOVER OR HARDCOVER WITH DUST JACKET

THE COMPLETE FOUR JUST MEN: VOLUME 2 *by Edgar Wallace*—*The Law of the Four Just Men* & *The Three Just Men*—disillusioned with a world where the wicked and the abusers of power perpetually go unpunished, the Just Men set about to rectify matters according to their own standards, and retribution is dispensed on swift and deadly wings.

THE COMPLETE RAFFLES: 1 *by E. W. Hornung*—*The Amateur Cracksman* & *The Black Mask*—By turns urbane gentleman about town and accomplished cricketer, life is just too ordinary for Raffles and that sets him on a series of adventures that have long been treasured as a real antidote to the 'white knights' who are the usual heroes of the crime fiction of this period.

THE COMPLETE RAFFLES: 2 *by E. W. Hornung*—*A Thief in the Night* & *Mr Justice Raffles*—By turns urbane gentleman about town and accomplished cricketer, life is just too ordinary for Raffles and that sets him on a series of adventures that have long been treasured as a real antidote to the 'white knights' who are the usual heroes of the crime fiction of this period.

THE COLLECTED SUPERNATURAL AND WEIRD FICTION OF WILKIE COLLINS: VOLUME 1 *by Wilkie Collins*—Contains one novel 'The Haunted Hotel', one novella 'Mad Monkton', three novelettes 'Mr Percy and the Prophet', 'The Biter Bit' and 'The Dead Alive' and eight short stories to chill the blood.

THE COLLECTED SUPERNATURAL AND WEIRD FICTION OF WILKIE COLLINS: VOLUME 2 *by Wilkie Collins*—Contains one novel 'The Two Destinies', three novellas 'The Frozen deep', 'Sister Rose' and 'The Yellow Mask' and two short stories to chill the blood.

THE COLLECTED SUPERNATURAL AND WEIRD FICTION OF WILKIE COLLINS: VOLUME 3 *by Wilkie Collins*—Contains one novel 'Dead Secret,' two novelettes 'Mrs Zant and the Ghost' and 'The Nun's Story of Gabriel's Marriage' and five short stories to chill the blood.

FUNNY BONES *selected by Dorothy Scarborough*—An Anthology of Humorous Ghost Stories.

MONTEZUMA'S CASTLE AND OTHER WEIRD TALES *by Charles B. Cory*—Cory has written a superb collection of eighteen ghostly and weird stories to chill and thrill the avid enthusiast of supernatural fiction.

SUPERNATURAL BUCHAN *by John Buchan*—Stories of Ancient Spirits, Uncanny Places & Strange Creatures.

LEONAUR

ALSO FROM LEONAUR
AVAILABLE IN SOFTCOVER OR HARDCOVER WITH DUST JACKET

THE COLLECTED SCIENCE FICTION AND FANTASY OF STANLEY G. WEINBAUM 1—INTERPLANETARY ODYSSEYS *by Stanley G. Weinbaum*—Classic Tales of Interplanetary Adventure Including: A Martian Odyssey, its Sequel Valley of Dreams, the Complete 'Ham' Hammond Stories and Others.

THE COLLECTED SCIENCE FICTION AND FANTASY OF STANLEY G. WEINBAUM 2—OTHER EARTHS *by Stanley G. Weinbaum*—Classic Futuristic Tales Including: *Dawn of Flame* & its Sequel The Black Flame, plus The Revolution of 1960 & Others.

THE COLLECTED SCIENCE FICTION AND FANTASY OF STANLEY G. WEINBAUM 3—STRANGE GENIUS *by Stanley G. Weinbaum*—Classic Tales of the Human Mind at Work Including the Complete Novel The New Adam, the 'van Manderpootz' Stories and Others.

THE COLLECTED SCIENCE FICTION AND FANTASY OF STANLEY G. WEINBAUM 4—THE BLACK HEART *by Stanley G. Weinbaum*—Classic Strange Tales Including: the Complete Novel The Dark Other, Plus Proteus Island and Others.

THE COLLECTED SCIENCE FICTION & FANTASY OF JACK LONDON 1—BEFORE ADAM & OTHER STORIES *by Jack London*—included in this Volume Before Adam The Scarlet Plague A Relic of the Pliocene When the World Was Young The Red One Planchette A Thousand Deaths Goliah A Curious Fragment The Rejuvenation of Major Rathbone.

THE COLLECTED SCIENCE FICTION & FANTASY OF JACK LONDON 2—THE IRON HEEL & OTHER STORIES *by Jack London*—included in this Volume The Iron Heel The Enemy of All the World The Shadow and the Flash The Strength of the Strong The Unparalleled Invasion The Dream of Debs.

THE COLLECTED SCIENCE FICTION & FANTASY OF JACK LONDON 3—THE STAR ROVER & OTHER STORIES *by Jack London*—included in this Volume The Star Rover The Minions of Midas The Eternity of Forms The Man With the Gash.